DRUMBEAT
NO LIE!

a novel of murder, intrigue and romance

Martha Crikelair
Wohlford

Serenity
Press

To Connor / You're here! Enjoy!

Marty Wohlford
Horned Guy
3/25/11

Serenity
Press

Copyright © 2000 by Martha Wohlford

Published by Serenity Press.

For information regarding permissions, email marty@mwpr.com.

ISBN 13: 978-0-9787981-1-6
ISBN 10: 0-9787981-1-2

Printed in the U.S.A.
Printed October 2008

DRUMBEAT
NO LIE!

a novel of murder, intrigue and romance

Martha Crikelair
Wohlford

About the Book

This fictional caper involves drug smugglers operating on a laid-back, pristine little island somewhere in the Bahamas. Where pirates and rumrunners once plied the waters under sail, the drug cartels now use speedboats and helicopters – and the cargo is not plundered gold and booze but pot and cocaine. The opening chapter develops the tone of resentment against the new breed invading this idyllic locale.

Woody Cameron, the principal bad guy, sets up operations at an abandoned island resort that he has purchased, recruiting help among the riffraff eager to make a big score and the free spirits hoping to bankroll an island-hopping cruise, courtesy of the drug trade. Pete Mathews, proprietor of the Sandy Cay Club on a neighboring island, keeps a watchful and disgusted eye on Cameron and the comings and goings of his henchmen.

This is a story of intrigue, drug busts, murder, and romance, with its share of humorous, rock-happy characters. Anyone who has visited the Bahamas or dreamed of visiting the Caribbean will be caught up in the story.

***

"I think you have something really terrific with "Drumbeat"... The way you move your characters in such a nice even flow entices the reader right along. Very good writing, very snappy and crisp. I find it not only inviting but compelling and really like all the visual pictures you paint along the way. You're especially good at creating tactile characters. They're so real, as if the reader can touch them, feel them, embrace them, They are certainly easy to relate to."

Harry Hilson
Fine Art, Inc.
art@negia.net

In memory of
Dr. Robert Saunders, Captain Lou Kenedy, Harold Hartman,
Steve and Rita Thomas, Lucille Nelson, Art Mueller, Karl Hess,
and
Captain Bob Chamberlain,
and for all those still enjoying a shared dream
in a very special place.

A special thanks to Carl Zettelmeyer and Edee Greene for their
editorial help.

PART ONE

Chapter 1

Arrival — Sandy Cay

The water was gin-clear as he snorkeled to the sleek red-hulled ocean racer tied to the dock.

He glanced upward, water blurring the bottom half of his mask and looked around. No one was on the next boat and no one aboard the racer could see him. He took a breath and followed the chine of the boat to the exhaust pipe, feeling the new, smooth paint on the hull. Just forward were the engines. He carefully attached the plastic explosive with underwater adhesive, then slowly, without making a ripple, came up for air.

Through water droplets clinging to the mask, he could still see that no one was paying attention to him. The owners, with their flashy gold jewelry and dark tanned bodies, were still boasting about their last deal, getting ready to move on toward the States.

He quietly snorkeled back to the swimming ladder on the dock, mingling with others enjoying the underwater panorama, chasing the tiny tropical fish that clustered around the grass-clad pilings. Nice work, he thought, climbing the dock ladder.

The engines started, disrupting the usual quiet of the island, the lines cast off. The boat eased away from the dock, then rocketed toward the cut and to open water. Black smoke poured out of the exhaust pipes from fuel feeding the hungry engines.

As the vessel cleared the opening between the islands, he saw it turn north. And then, as planned, it violently exploded, sending a black plume of smoke billowing on the prevailing breeze. The illegal cargo was burning as were human beings who made their living destroying others. It was quick, clean and only he saw what happened.

Pete Mathews smiled as he put the cap back on the vessel's gas tank. Wouldn't it be nice, he thought, relishing his disgust with the crew, if it could really happen, if I could get away with it, if it would only stop, if the island could return to Paradise....

Instead, the sleek gas-guzzler loaded below the water line

started its engines, roared off through the cut and went on its way. Again. Like the boat before it. And the planes. And the mother ships. Like the pirates of yesteryear but with faster boats, faster women and faster highs.

Welcome to de Islands, thought Pete, as he coiled the fuel hose on the dock, then walked back toward the club.

He shook his head, trying to rid his mind of the plots and schemes that could easily become reality if he were to give in. He knew all about underwater demolition and explosives. It was his MOS in the marines, blowing bridges and unfriendly vessels.

Ever since Woody Cameron had bought Smugglers Cay things had changed.

Pete sat down on the front porch of the club, stroking his graying beard, watching the natives clean fish and crack open conch shells, and the yachtsmen working endlessly on their prized vessels. Woody had arrived on a laid-back day. Pete closed his eyes and reminisced as if it were yesterday instead of almost six months ago.

He was sitting in an old barrel chair at the Sandy Cay Club sipping his coffee, only half-listening to the low-key banter of yachtsmen already at the bar. Some boats had been fueled and watered and were on their way.

It was a typical June day, slow paced, even tempered, with the humidity intensifying the brilliant sunlight that was already reflecting a myriad of blues in the harbor. A few boats swung lazily at anchor on the incoming tide, and the cruising crowd, slowly multiplying at the straw-wrapped bar, sipped pineapple juice laced with rum.

Jackson, the native dockmaster, sat next to him, glancing at an old newspaper. Seagulls loitered on the dock pilings.

As usual, he and Jackson were dressed almost identically — navy club T-shirt over worn jeans, Pete with leather boat shoes, Jackson in canvas sneakers. There the similarity ended, he thought, smiling. Pete's rugged white complexion was weathered by the sun, while Jackson's smooth black skin revealed a comfortable adaptation to his native land.

Twenty years in the tropics had drained much of the early ambition from his body, whereas Jackson, a youthful thirty, had keen senses and remarkable drive.

They had both been working since seven that morning, fueling boats, checking the generators, watermakers and the bar inventory that never coincided with the receipts.

Both heard the drone of a small plane as it approached the island.

"You 'spectin' anyone?" Jackson asked Pete, in the lilting island dialect. "De club plane not due till tomorrow."

Pete had gotten up, pushing open the screened door. "No, but then who knows? Probably some tourist to join this alert crew." He cocked his head toward the bar, brightly decorated with yacht burgees and marine articles that had been donated by boats passing through. They hung from the rafters and were posted to every available space. Odds and ends which washed up on the beach — shells and driftwood, glass balls and sea fans, lined the ledges of the open screened walls.

The plane came closer, and within seconds, buzzed the club. "I'll go," he had said. "Keep an eye on the cash box."

He walked toward the aging vehicle, twenty years ago called a Jeep, lovingly renamed *Cyclops* when it lost a headlight years ago. Pete chuckled to himself as he checked the gas in the cork-stoppered bottle. He climbed onto the rusting seat, turned the key and listened to the gears groan as he swung the wheel forward. The metal and wood hulk seemed to leap onto the path that wove through the tiny native village to the airstrip.

Pete mused as to who was on the plane. More new faces. A lot of new people had been coming lately. He remembered when few people knew of the island, when a visitor a week was an event. Times were changing. Since the airstrip had been built, people just came...to drink rum punch, to look for excitement and happy times in the tropics.

He turned toward the airstrip. Three people and a pile of luggage were already spilling out of a small single engine plane. Pete stared at the man who stood grinning and sweating.

I'll be damned, thought Pete, recognizing the familiar face. The loudmouth from Sand Dollar Island. Pete forced a smile, his clear blue eyes piercing through the fat little man with the short leg and booming voice who limped toward him.

"Heya, Pete! How ya doin', mon? Remember me? Woody Cameron here. Met you last year when we swung by these parts. Going to be regulars now. Neighbors." He grinned a bloated smile and turned to his quiet companion, a woman of slight frame Pete also recalled meeting.

"Grab that bag, Laura," boomed Woody. "That one. Yeah, Pete, we're here to stay. You ever meet the wife?" He motioned toward Laura and kept on talking. "We bought Smugglers Cay, old man. Going to make it come alive. Big bucks. Paid big bucks for it. More will come. Hurry it up, Laura. There they are." He grabbed a stack of papers and waved them in front of Pete. "Mine island," he grinned.

The pilot brought over the last carton from the plane and Woody off-handedly introduced him as Jock.

While Woody talked, the pilot lethargically loaded *Cyclops*. Pete began grinning, a slow-to-begin grin that defied what he really thought of the pompous little ass spouting off good neighborly sentiments. Pete hadn't liked Woody the first time he met him and the feeling was reinforced the more he talked.

Laura, a shy, quiet woman, just stood, watching as Jock loaded *Cyclops* and Woody talked. Pete wondered how she put up with him.

Jock nodded sheepishly as the last box was loaded, then he locked up the plane. He was tall, slightly overweight and slovenly. What a contrast to the club's pilot, thought Pete. Jock wore a faded yellow shirt, khaki shorts and dirty sneakers without socks. Charlie would arrive tomorrow in a crisp white shirt, shoulders properly decorated. Pete turned to Laura as she carefully climbed aboard the makeshift wood box bolted to *Cyclops*.

"Think you'll be happy anchored to a rock with this guy?" he asked. There was no disguising his sarcasm.

"Ah just go where mah Woody takes me," she smiled, a thick Southern accent reflecting genteel upbringing. "It looks like a lovely place."

Pete smiled pathetically at the pale-skinned woman, remembering the day his wife, Helen, had committed herself to the island way of life. She, too, was a gentle, shy woman who

6

had naively adapted to the rugged lifestyle the island demanded.

Jock gave Woody a hand as he climbed aboard *Cyclops*, struggling with his bad leg. He sat on a suitcase, then boomed to Pete as the engine started.

"Just take us to the club, Pete. Gotta get a boat to Smugglers. Figured you'd have one. By damn, these parts are going to see changes, old man. Big times coming. Smell the air, Laura. Pure air."

And what you are emitting is pure bullshit, thought Pete, smiling to himself and wondering why Woody would want an island. How different he was from most resort owners, who were mellow and laid-back. Woody was a Big Mouthed American used to doing things his way. Well, thought Pete, let him spend his bucks. Maybe all the talk about somebody buying Smugglers was true. But Woody Cameron would have a hard lesson to learn.

He glanced back at his passengers. Woody was overweight and puffy around the eyes, balding, about five-feet-six on his good leg, wearing a white golf shirt over a pot belly and brown plaid Bermuda shorts. Like Jock, Woody looked washed and worn. In contrast, Laura looked yachty crisp in a white short-sleeved shirt worn loosely over a navy halter, white shorts and boat shoes. She caught Pete's eye and smiled, quietly accepting her husband's boorish behavior.

Woody insisted on shouting over the racket of *Cyclops*, pointing to the colorful homes tucked into a ridge on the east end of the island. The red-roofed church, used as a navigational aid by sailors approaching the island, was the focal point of the village. The road turned to follow the coastline, past Conch Inn and Marina, more tiny homes, the community picnic beach, miniature school and clinic, and finally, the Sandy Cay Club.

"Nice place, huh?" Woody shouted to Jock. "Told you the strip was okay. We can bring in heavier birds, don't you think? Perfect place. Look at it."

Pete sensed there was more to Woody's island purchase than the need for a hideaway. A frown creased his forehead, then he dismissed what he feared. He glanced back as Jock nodded agreement with Woody and again felt uneasy.

7

The island had remained unchanged for a long time. Pete began to take in the scenery as if seeing it for the first time.

From the air, it looked like many of the surrounding cays, only with crude roadways carved into the coral rock. On the ground, it took on a different flavor. The pungent smell of jasmine, the dwarfed trees that struggled annually for the slight rainfall and hungered for good soil, colorful pink hibiscus and purple bougainvillea, shrunken corn stalks climbing toward the hot sun out of deep potholes, pink and blue and yellow houses.

He automatically waved to the women plaiting palm tops under the ancient almond tree in the center of the village. The long green plaited strips would eventually become dried straw hats and bags decorated with colorful shells and straw ribbon for the tourists. Children waved from the white sand picnic beach, their tiny dark bodies glistening in the transparent water.

A native woman, lowering a pail for water at the village well, nodded and smiled as they drove by.

Ahead, the road became a narrow path, with the tiny cottages of the club poking through casuarina trees along the water. Pete pulled *Cyclops* over to the side and eased off his seat as Jackson came to see who had arrived. He glanced at the visitors, then at Pete. He, too, had met this man before.

"You stayin' at de club?" he asked, a wide smile masking his thoughts.

"No way, buddy. Jackson, right? Hey, mon, we got our own place now. None of this high rent business. We need you to take us to our own island. You remember me, don't you? Woody Cameron. That's Laura. That's our pilot, Jock." He pointed as he talked.

"I 'member you," laughed Jackson, his eyes dancing as he tilted his cap back to scratch his head. "What island you gets?"

"Smugglers," boomed Woody with a challenging grin.

"Dat true?" Jackson asked, turning to Pete, who just shrugged his shoulders.

"The man says he bought Smugglers, so who are we to doubt his word?" he said, tugging at his pants that needed a belt. "Better take all this stuff to the dock so he can be on his way. Don't suppose you all want a little welcome drink, huh, Woody?

I remember that was a big part of your stay here the last time."

"By God, you're right, Pete. I'll take you up on it. Come on, Laura, Jock. Put that crap down. A drink's a great idea. Have to see who's around. Gotta let everyone know what's happening. They don't have to hang out here. We'll give 'em a new place."

Pete and Jackson listened to Woody ramble, knowing he was too fast-paced to do anything but make a verbal impression today. Pete opened the screened door and took his place behind the bar, but Woody's words were getting to him. The Sandy Cay Club was a tradition unchallenged in the island chain. He glanced around as conversation died and the regulars eyed Woody and his crew.

"Gimme a Pauli Girl, Pete. A cold one. How's the ice machine doing? Hey, Laura, you want a beer? Make it two, Pete. We gotta relax. Give Jock a Coke. He's gotta fly."

Woody leaned over the bar and eased himself onto a stool as Laura and Jock sat down in a couple of barrel chairs. Beads of perspiration lined Jock's forehead, but Laura seemed comfortable despite the heat. Pete opened the cooler and put down two beers.

"Four bucks," he said, lighting a cigarette and eyeing Woody across the bar.

"Now, what really brings you back, Woody?" he asked pointedly. "Heard you left these parts when the boys took over Sand Dollar Island. What's really up?" He tugged at his pants and winked at an old-timer hunched over the bar.

Woody was one of a breed who resurfaced year after year with a new gig every time. Always going to get rich. He was a typical marcher in the parade of life's escapees that island life seemed to attract. Pete had seen them all, ever since he'd left the streets of Chicago to run a charter sailboat twenty-four years ago. He didn't doubt Woody had bought Smugglers, but as a resort it was a dying project. Still...the uneasiness wouldn't leave him.

With the mention of Sand Dollar Island, conversation died at the bar. Six months ago, Sand Dollar had been bought by a Colombian big-wig who had improved the airstrip for night landings and had closed the island to cruising yachtsmen and

9

visiting pilots. It was now barricaded to the outside world complete with machine-gun carrying guards and sophisticated surveillance. Rumor had it that a government official had been bought so the island could be used as an import base for illegal drugs. No one knew the full story, but everyone had the sense to stay away.

"Got out of that mess just in time," said Woody, a little louder than necessary, wriggling on the hard stool. "Don't know what's gonna happen there."

He squirmed a bit more, obviously uneasy, then regained his confidence.

"Like I told you, I'm here to revive Smugglers Cay. There'll be some big changes, now that I've got it. Bought out Miller. That crazy Limey doesn't know shit about running a place. Watch and see. There'll be boats and planes full of people coming to these parts."

He was talking much louder than necessary, chugging his beer between sentences.

"Is that so?" challenged Pete, looking directly at Woody with penetrating blue eyes as he stroked his beard. "Last time we talked you didn't have much. Your old lady die or something?" A chuckle went along the bar and Pete had his audience. He tugged at his pants with his thumbs, and laugh lines creased his face.

"You get the bucks on that big land rip-off at Sand Dollar? I hear the developer's under indictment and crying poor. But you wouldn't be part of that now, would you?"

Pete smiled quizzically at Woody, who chose to ignore him. Pete had him and Woody knew it, so Pete continued. "What are you going to do with those two ramshackle rentals, a bar that has a tough time producing even a warm beer, and a dining room that seats less than a dozen guests?" he probed.

"Smugglers isn't a gold mine, you know. Look at this place. The club brought the island into the twentieth century, but it's taken years. No one came here before it opened. You think you can do better? You're too old, Woody. This is a game for a young man with an impossible dream. I know. I once had it. Take a better look at Smugglers. Those docks need work.

Miller's been buying fuel from us for months, and there's no fresh water. You got guts, old man, to say nothing about dreams."

Pete shook his head, serious about what he was saying, as he blended another batch of rum punches for the still rather silent crowd at the bar. As he filled their glasses, Pete marked on tabs how much each owed. Ticks for drinks were easier to handle than cash since everyone was on the honor system anyway when no one was formally tending bar.

"Another dreamer in Paradise, eh?" Pete looked around the bar, gaining confidence as heads nodded in agreement.

Still, he somehow felt threatened. Talk began again, this time about Smugglers, how it was a pretty little island with a lot of potential if the back harbor could be dredged for larger yachts.

Talk drifted to all the possibilities, about the money and time it would take and the work involved.

Woody seemed to gloat at all the attention his project was getting. He listened as they told how the island had been neglected, how people didn't visit like they did years ago. Ever since Miller started locking visitors in the shop or store for no reason and had gone into tantrums over the slightest provocation, people steered clear of Smugglers. Most figured Miller went "rock happy," that he'd been on the island too long.

Now, the docks needed repair, the kitchen, the club, the grounds, the rental units, everything needed redoing. Work was not a favorite word in the tropics. If it didn't just "happen" it was tough to get anything fixed The natives enjoyed a slow pace, and building took months, even for a small structure. Repairs went on forever.

Woody, somewhat deflated over his cool reception at the Sandy Cay Club, tossed a hundred dollar bill on the bar and slid off the stool, leaning on the shorter of his two legs.

"Probably can't change that, but you can put it toward a boat rental. Oh yeah," he said, "toss in a cooler of ice and a couple of bottles of Jamaican rum. Don't want to die of thirst. Drink up, Laura. Jock, come on. Anybody available to take us off this rock? It's crowded. Need our own space, you know, our own place."

Pete sensed Woody's agitation, unlocked the cash box, picked up the hundred and counted out a mixture of U.S. and local bills and coins. Could he change it? He smirked. Hundreds were like ones when you didn't take plastic.

"You wanna run a tab like all the regulars or aren't you staying too long?" he asked Woody with a touch of irony. "You'll need gas and diesel and fresh water. The generator running? Shit, you'll be down here by nightfall begging for a cottage!"

A chuckle went around the bar and Woody realized that no one was taking his new venture seriously. He'd show them. After all, three hundred grand was a lot of bucks. They'd see. Just wait, he thought, you bastards will eat your doubting words. Just wait.

Woody grabbed his change and the duffel beside him which held his papers and limped out the squeaking door, motioning for Laura and Jock to follow. Pete laughed and turned to the customers at the bar.

The bright sun almost blinded Woody as he reached for his sunglasses. Jackson was working on the dock.

"Hey, mon," called Woody. "You gonna take us to Smugglers? Good tip in it. Good tip. Remember what I tell you, Jackson. Those dummies in there don't believe me, but you natives have faith. I'll help you out. Wait and see. You gonna take us?"

His loud mouth was back in full swing and Woody was in control. Jackson sensed his urgency, but continued to coil the fuel hose at his own pace. He nodded toward an outboard skiff.

"Put your gears in dere," he said. "I be back after I sees Pete." He walked to the club and Laura, Woody and Jock looked at the little boat. Woody took Jock aside, gave him some money from a generous wad of bills, and talked in a low voice. Jock nodded, gave the thumbs-up signal and walked away as Jackson came toward them. Boxes, a couple of duffels, the cooler, a smaller canvas bag and some grocery sacks were lowered down a ladder to the little boat.

Jackson followed Woody and Laura, untied the boat and

made his way to the outboard engine. The pale Americans were already beginning to burn. Woody especially looked wrung out from the little bit of heat as he helped himself to a can of beer. Laura shook her head when he offered one to her. She had not said anything since the airstrip, and her fixed smile obscured her thoughts on the island setting. Jackson started the engine, and as the boat backed down, he pulled up the stern anchor that kept it off the dock when the tide changed.

"Let's go," he said, deciding to make the most of the short trip. "I'll get you dere so you can fix a big dinner, eh?"

He smiled. He loved to tease Americans. They never knew how to take him. Few supplies had been loaded into the little boat and he knew that even fewer stores remained at Smugglers. What Miller had left behind the natives took in justification of back wages.

No, they'd probably be back to the Sandy Cay Club tomorrow, thought Jackson, if not to eat, then to call the pilot to come get them. It was more peaceful when this type didn't come around.

Jackson kept his thoughts and feelings hidden, which was typical of the natives. Intuition ran deep in his quiet, hardworking breed, and the outsider rarely had a glimpse of the person inside. Smiles and "yessirs" always got a native further than gut honesty, and this was learned early in life. It was the way of the islands, and Woody Cameron would not know what Jackson was thinking.

It was only about two miles to Smugglers Cay, and Jackson took the inside route, following the chain of islands. Navigating was easy if you knew how to read the water, and Jackson was a pro. He had grown up at Rocky Point and had shipped aboard as a helper to his uncle, a captain on a big powerboat owned by an American politician. His father and grandfather had been fishermen.

Jackson could dock a 60-footer and navigate anywhere in the island chain before he was ten years old. He knew the various hues of blue, even when the sun wasn't directly overhead, and could tell if he had five inches or eight feet of water under him. He knew how to read the little sand spits that jutted out from random corners of coral islands, depending on the currents and tide. He could probably have taken Woody to Smugglers blindfolded.

When they were out of sight of the Sandy Cay Club, Woody shouted to Jackson above the whine of the outboard.

"You're pretty quiet, Jackson," he boomed, shifting his weight to a seat closer to the stern, where Jackson sat. "What do you think of me buying Smugglers? We'll probably need your help along the way, especially since you know all the natives."

Jackson laughed, a lilting, quiet chuckle.

"I gots a job, mon. Been dere since I was a kid. What do I want wit' more work? I put in fifteen hours a day now and only gits half o' Sunday off. When I fine time for you? Same people might come back dat were dere before. No problem, mon."

"I've heard that 'no problem, mon' before, and it usually means I GOT a problem," boomed Woody over the engine noise.

He eyed Jackson's strong, slim frame, big eyes set in a solid black face, neatly trimmed hair. Jackson was legendary at the Sandy Cay Club. It would be hard to lure him to Smugglers, if not impossible.

Better to stay on his good side right from the beginning, thought Woody. A respected native was an asset.

The motor kept up a steady whine as Jackson navigated the channel between the islands, and Woody, finally quiet, began taking in the scenery. Low, scrubby islands were fringed with the whitest of sand, offset by stark, jagged outcroppings of coral. Laura seemed pleasantly happy, and he hoped she would stay contented in her new life.

In fifteen minutes, they pulled into the dock at Smugglers Cay. When all their gear was loaded onto the sagging pier, Jackson declined an offer to come ashore and started the motor to head back. He looked behind as he pulled away, eyeing the Camerons on Smugglers Cay. He couldn't help but smile.

Another island tale was about to begin.

Jock, the pilot, walked back along the dock toward the Sandy Cay Club after watching Woody and Laura head toward Smugglers with Jackson and he began assessing the club operation.

Four small cottages lined a placid sea and sandy beach. A fire alarm system was lashed to a casuarina tree and a workshop in the back hummed with generators churning out electricity. Fuel tanks high on a ridge above the club gravity-fed the docks and power plant. An aluminum swimming pool connected to a roof catchment system served as a cistern. Cables and pipes were only partially buried in the hard limestone bedrock of the island.

He followed the only path toward the village, passing a small building labeled "clinic." It was freshly painted but the door was bolted.

Heaven help anyone needing it, thought Jock.

On top of the ridge, a small schoolhouse looked down on more hut-like homes and a basketball hoop that had long since lost its net. Past the well and picnic beach the village took more shape, with paths cut between the little one- and two-room cottage homes. Clean laundry hung from propped-up lines, washtubs alongside homes. Native children played in sandy yards, some enjoying the fresh air with only underwear covering their dark little frames in the heat. Most stared as he walked past, while mothers warned "hush" from behind walls.

Tucked among the houses were a miniature post office the size of a walk-in closet, two grocery stores aptly named the Yellow Store and the Pink Store, and a tiny gift shop with French perfume bottles and a small collection of straw hats, bags and mats.

A small Baptist church brought memories back to Jock, now thousands of miles from his native Kansas where his father was a preacher. He mused on how he had learned to fly when he was sixteen, and how he later joined the crop dusting circuit. As he followed the fields, he eventually came to Florida, where the daily pressure of low altitude flying had forced him to turn to other kinds of flying.

Even though he only held a private rating, he had no trouble finding people like Woody who were willing to pay him for his services, and he made a modest living as a "bootleg" pilot.

Dusting had given him a devil-may-care attitude and when he met Woody and his friends, Jock knew he could handle their flying needs whatever they were. He didn't question motives or orders.

When he was told the chemicals he was flying could kill him, he rarely took all the standard precautions. Life was that way. You never did it all the way right or life would be unbearably dull.

That's the way it had been growing up, he thought, gazing at the little church. He had abandoned his family years ago. Still single and in his late thirties, he was content with a life driven by the excitement of the unknown.

He took his eyes off the church and glanced around him, embarrassed that an old woman plaiting straw had been watching him. He smiled sheepishly, then walked past a sign announcing "Conch Inn and Marina." Next to it, on a worm-eaten piece of driftwood, was hand-lettered "Maxwell Hynes — Mechanic — Outboards and Engine Repair." Max the mechanic. Woody had wanted Jock to meet him before he left the island.

Jock turned and walked past another tiny hut that housed the island's only telephone to the outside world and entered the courtyard of Conch Inn.

To the right was a pile of greasy tools, miscellaneous parts and torn down engines which marked Maxwell's shop. A man of medium build was hunched over an engine, glasses down on his nose, shaggy hair hiding his features. Jock guessed him to be about his own age. He wore faded jeans and a shirt that had seen many washings without the aid of bleach. Jock sized up the makeshift shop and disorganized work area. This had to be Max.

Jock had heard from Woody that first day they met in a smoke-filled Key West bar about the monopoly the misplaced Australian enjoyed, being the only mechanic with a work permit in the area. Woody told him that Max was the man to know on the island, the one who'd be his contact.

16

The man turned slightly to let the light fall on his work, and noticed Jock staring at him. He pushed his glasses up on his nose with his arm and picked up a rag to wipe his hands.

"Hello. What can I do for you?" His Aussie accent confirmed Jock's assumption.

"Jock Maynard. You must be Max," he said, extending his hand, then withdrawing it as Maxwell offered a greasy one in return. The two forced a smile and the introduction was complete.

"Understand you know Howard," said Jock, nonchalantly examining Maxwell's current project. "Woody says we'd make good friends."

"Been waiting for you," said Maxwell, with no expression. He reached for a wrench. "He's got his schooner on the dock here. Ever meet him?"

Jock shook his head.

"No. Just know him from what Woody has said. Understand you met him and Woody in Florida not too long ago."

Maxwell nodded. "Hold the lower end there, would you? Woody's a bloody nut, but don't underestimate him. They've got a good plan. Our part will be here, on the island, but we have to stay clear of the Sandy Cay Club people. They'd bugger things up for sure, the bloody hypocrites." His normally expressionless face began to scowl.

"Pretty straight?" asked Jock. Maxwell nodded. "What's that Pete character really like?"

Maxwell stiffened up and wiped his hands on an oil-stained rag, the blood vessels in his neck pulsing as a strange look crept into his face.

"He's a son of a bitch," he said, his voice now low and raspy. "If it takes a lifetime, I'm gonna get him. It's no secret I hate him and we keep our distance. But I'm going to get even with that bastard."

Instinctively, Jock stepped back as Maxwell clenched his fists. Whatever had happened to cause his rage was serious. He decided then and there not to upset him. The stakes would be too high. He would never want this wiry guy to turn on him in vengeance. As quickly as he had become angered, though,

Maxwell composed himself.

"Sorry to dump that on you but he's a bloody thorn in my side," he said, returning to his normal voice. "Even his name makes me want to get the son of a bitch. Give me a hand, will you? Then I'll show you around. If you stay, Howard's got a couple of birds on board that don't look too bad." He spoke matter-of-factly, with little enthusiasm, his diction more from the street than from the halls of a university.

Jock helped Maxwell, then the two walked toward the marina. A schooner about 50 feet long was tied to the long face dock. Two bikini-clad girls in their twenties were sunning on deck. Pickings had been slim since he'd gotten tied up with Woody, and Jock looked forward to a possible score.

"They easy?" he asked Max.

"They come over to get laid. You might as well do it as anyone," said Maxwell, his voice still dry. "Take it when you can over here. Nothing worse than being on this bloody rock without a woman for weeks on end."

No one knew better than Maxwell the inconvenience of having no white women available for long periods of time. When he did enjoy an occasional tussle in the past, it had been with someone else's wife or girlfriend bored with her personal situation. Women who had stayed with him on the island only did so for short periods of time — until Pat. She arrived at the island disenchanted with her yacht-bum boyfriend, had taken to Maxwell and married him.

For the first time in his life, Maxwell felt secure with a woman. Pat did his laundry, cooking and cleaning, and in general, took care of him. She was perfect in his eyes, with a slight but full figure, long brown hair bleached by the sun. She had a friendly personality. Everyone reminded him how lucky he was.

"What's Howard like?" asked Jock, breaking into Maxwell's thoughts as they walked past a little sailboat sporting blue sail covers.

"Hard man to describe," said Maxwell in a clipped monotone still reminiscent of his Australian upbringing. "Cruises quite a bit from island to island. Think it's his business,

18

not pleasure that keeps him moving. Has a young wife. Takes aboard girls looking for a little excitement during college vacations. Usually they're daughters of well-meaning, but ignorant friends."

As they approached the schooner, Jock noticed the name *Michelle* carved on a wooden plate at the bow. He smiled sheepishly at the girls sunning on deck, then noticed a couple sitting in the cockpit.

"Come aboard, Max. Who's with you?" asked a tall, lean, bronze-tanned man wearing a French cut swimsuit and heavy gold necklace.

"Hello, Howard, Marjorie," said Maxwell, pushing his glasses back onto the bridge of his nose. "This is Jock, the pilot."

"Been waiting for you," said Howard in a deep, masculine voice. "Come aboard. Did you meet the girls?"

Jock shook his head and Howard shouted to the sun worshippers.

"Nel, Sharon, meet Jock." The girls looked up, waved and went back to sunning. "This is Marjorie," he said, motioning to his wife.

Jock nodded, fidgeting slightly. He hadn't seen three such exquisite bodies in a long time.

Marjorie disappeared below decks for a pitcher of rum punch and Howard engaged in small talk about the boat. As he stood up to check a fitting on the boom, Jock noticed his imposingly tall frame. Howard stood almost six-and-a-half feet and defied his age. He was in his fifties, but didn't look it, especially with a wife in her twenties. He knew he had an overwhelming stance and often toyed with the idea of piercing an ear, but Marjorie wouldn't have it. "Don't want to be married to a pirate," she said, so he kept the innocent fantasy to himself.

As Marjorie came back on deck, Jock eyed her beauty. She had long, dark hair tied at the neck with a pink ribbon and wore a black bikini trimmed with pink along the edges, outlining a full bosom and emphasizing a small waist and flat stomach. Pink nail polish on fingers and toes made her look impeccably groomed, even though she was almost naked. Howard noticed Jock surveying his wife.

"I suggest you get friendly with Nel," he said pointedly. "Sharon leaves tomorrow."

Hearing her name, Nel sat up and waved. Her strawberry blonde hair was piled on top of her head. Like Marjorie, she left little to the imagination in a brief yellow bikini. As she stood up, Jock felt a strange nervousness enveloping him — a feeling that often confronted him in situations with women. As she walked over, he stood up and extended his hand, clammy, even in the heat. She took it, smiled, and said, "Aren't you the pilot who flew in a while ago? I saw you in that old Jeep. It must be great to fly, so free."

"I'll take you up sometime," he said, acting like a young schoolboy confronted with his first romance.

"That sounds inviting," she said, making a mental note to remind him when she wanted to go home to the States. He wasn't her type, but she was always looking for a ride back and forth so she could spend as much time as possible in the islands. His handshake hadn't been very firm and she wondered why he seemed so flustered. Most older men she had met were cocky or at least had some confidence in front of her.

"Well," said Howard, standing. "It's time to talk. Come below, Jock, Maxwell. Girls, enjoy yourselves. We've got business."

The men took their rum punches below and the gals went back to sunning, enjoying the lazy afternoon.

* * *

At the Sandy Cay Club, Jackson returned from Smugglers and, after a few words with Pete, went into the village.

Pete was left to tend the bar and docks. A big motor yacht was maneuvering to come in and he walked to the end of the face dock to handle the lines. As the yacht was secured, Pete happened to glance across the shallow bay toward Conch Inn. He straightened up and squinted. He could barely see the three figures standing on the dock next to the schooner that had been tied up for two weeks. There was no mistaking the owner of the boat. Howard's frame stood out like a human mast. Maxwell he knew instinctively. He was Pete's cross to bear, a poisonous sea urchin that had driven its spines into his side.

But the third figure puzzled him. He looked like Woody's disheveled pilot. How did he know Maxwell, and why were they talking to the owner of *Michelle*? Howard had made fun of the crazy Aussie mechanic as he sat at the Sandy Cay bar a couple nights before. Why the association?

Again, Pete had an uneasy feeling. He shook his head, trying to dismiss what he had seen and walked back to the club.

It was late afternoon and one of the native girls would soon come to tend bar. A few years ago, no one was needed to serve guests. They just wrote down what they took and paid before they left the island. But lately there had been an increase in liquor consumption and a drop in revenue on the honor system, so Pete had hired someone for the evenings.

He and Jackson did what they could during the day, but times had changed. No longer were visitors sleepy cruising types on slow sailboats. The breed arriving now had fast speed boats, fancy sport fishing rigs and paid crews. The average yacht-bum had a tough time with fuel prices and boat costs rising. Cruising was no longer a pleasure for the average person. Today's yachtsman had to have a few bucks to spend.

Behind the bar, Pete counted the cash, pocketed a wad of bills and waited. He listened to the yachtsmen's banter, little changed from a few hours earlier. He was happy to see Wanda arrive. At eighteen, she already had two children and could handle the late night hours at the club. She was pretty, her dark native hair drawn back tightly in a bun and only a hint of eye and lip makeup on her face. Revenues had risen since she had been hired and she seemed to be the answer to Pete's problem. For now, anyway.

He talked with her briefly, then walked toward the screened door. He glanced down the docks and climbed into *Cyclops* and drove to his home, set on a high ridge overlooking the harbor. Sunsets were spectacular from the front porch and, in the distance, Pete had a good view of the club docks.

Abigail, their dog, gave a quiet yip and wagged her tail,

21

welcoming him home. He patted her head. She was only seven years old, but heartworm and a series of other illnesses plagued the terrier so that she seemed much older. Only the native "potcake" breed had adapted to island living.

Pete walked into the house, empty with Helen and Johnny in the village. Until now, there had been no need for locks anywhere on the island. A native home had been robbed recently, causing a stir on the island, where everyone respected the belongings of another.

That's another change, thought Pete. The last year really had been different from the others. Ever since Maxwell had been let go as mechanic, things seemed to change.

Pete kicked off his shoes, went to the kitchen and poured himself a glass of orange juice. He shook his head at the thought of Maxwell, reflecting on how the mechanic had made a public statement that he would ruin Pete and all that he stood for. Pete chuckled. Maxwell was doing a fairly good job of making his life miserable. Although it was common knowledge there was no love between them, Pete couldn't for the life of him understand why Maxwell had to keep stirring up trouble.

Maxwell and his letters.

At the slightest provocation, he'd get out his ancient typewriter with rusted keys and pound out complaints to the various ministers of government functions. He never cared about what he wrote, how much truth was involved or what the consequences would be. He knew only one thing — stir up trouble and make it difficult for the club to exist. Customs, immigration, the aviation board — everyone heard from Maxwell at one time or another.

It wasn't a situation Pete could ignore. Every day there was a reminder, if only in the fact that he was without a mechanic.

Ever since Pete let him go, there had been problems. He reflected on how Maxwell had arrived at the island, out of money, and left behind by a sailboat on which he had been crewing. Story was he left his native Australia after his girlfriend ditched him, hitching from yacht to yacht until he ended up at Sandy Cay. Pete had taken pity on the slim, beaten-down sailor who seemed to have nowhere to go and hired him as mechanic, not even knowing his level of competence. They agreed on a percentage basis for work done, a simple, gentlemen's agreement. Max would have the shop and use of all the tools and equipment that Pete had accumulated over the years. Pete would send Max the business, and Max, in turn, would give a percentage back for use of the shop and the opportunity to work.

Simple, thought Pete. Then he chuckled to himself. If he hadn't stopped drinking, he might never have realized that Maxwell had been ripping him off for years. Once Pete had realized the deceit, dishonesty and greed in Maxwell, he had let him go.

If he had been a good mechanic, Pete thought, something could have been worked out.

But Max had cost the club money — a lot of money, in righting the mistakes he had made — serious mistakes. The final straw had been the work on an expensive yacht owned by one of the club's wealthier members. Maxwell had done a complete generator over-haul. The yacht had left the dock, and two days later reports came back that it had burned to the waterline with the owner and his wife barely escaping. The fire was traced to generator problems. There had been no use talking it over with Maxwell because communication had stopped long before. Pete kept Maxwell on until the off-season, then let him go when the club was closed down.

After Pete and his family left for vacation in the States, Maxwell emptied the shop of tools, and convinced Manny, the native owner of Conch Inn, that he needed a mechanic. Maxwell set up shop and to everyone's knowledge, had not paid a nickel's worth of rent since. As long as he kept Conch Inn's aging generator going, things went smoothly for him. When it broke down, the natives hassled him for the few volts which they needed to run lights and a few appliances.

Pete finished his juice and headed for the bedroom. He lay down and stared at the ceiling, thankful he had air-conditioned the house and added fans.

Why do I always have to think about Maxwell, he wondered? The bastard has a hold on me and I allow him to get to me.

Pete mused on how he did his best to ignore the situation, to stay away from Maxwell and to give as few digs as possible when Maxwell's name came up in conversation. But it was difficult, for by nature, Pete knew he was sarcastic. He knew he often said the right thing to the wrong person and that it found its way back to Maxwell, fueling his growing insanity. It had become a game, but not a fun one. The whole village was suffering from the cancerous hate emitted by Maxwell, yet everyone tolerated his presence. His yearly work permit was renewed simply because there was no one else to keep the village generators and engines running. The young natives who had gone to the States for training had opted to stay there. Life in the city's fast lane was much more exciting than the hermit crab's pace on the island. The villagers felt trapped.

Me too, thought Pete. And now there's Woody to contend with. The fact is, I'm committed to this island, to the club I built and I'll stay no matter what happens.

Out loud, he turned to Abigail and said, "We'll ride this one out like any other storm, old girl." His convictions renewed, Pete drifted off to sleep with Abigail thumping her tail at the bottom of the bed. The swish-swish of the ceiling fan soothed his mind and body.

* * *

While Pete napped, happy hour went into full swing at the club. Guests enjoyed drinks at half-price and talk centered on Smugglers Cay. Each had his own idea of what to do to make the place successful, with every suggestion costing a great deal of money.

"You wouldn't have to dredge that back harbor if you just got a big old powerboat in there and blew out the sand at low tide," said Captain Ned Kilpatrick, one of the most respected regulars at the club, in his naturally gruff voice.

"Good idea, but who'd risk getting all that sand and crap in the props to make that little SOB happy?" pointed out another rather surly sailboat owner. "God, that guy's obnoxious.

24

Neighborhood'll go to hell with him around, just like it did at Sand Dollar."

"He can't be any worse than old mad Miller," said someone else, slurring his words.

"Bullshit!" boomed Captain Kilpatrick, his prickly beard bristling. "Just plain bullshit, that man. No good."

He set an empty can on the bar, pointed to the cooler and winked at Wanda as she pulled out another Pauli Girl. She opened the bottle and gave it to the aging captain, knowing that his wife Lucy would probably be in soon to harass him on his drinking. He was the type that didn't say much, but when he did, his word was respected. If he thought Woody Cameron was full of bullshit, chances were pretty good he was.

Wanda watched the old man assert himself and smiled. He grinned back, a twinkle in his eye giving sparkle to a worn face. Bushy gray eyebrows matched his thinning hair, and, hunched over the bar, he minimized his six-foot frame.

There were many stories on the captain's past, how he'd been through the rum running days of Prohibition and been a merchant seaman. It was published fact that his schooner had been torpedoed at the beginning of World War II and that he and his crew had spent days in a lifeboat looking for land. Captain Kilpatrick, now in his seventies, was a dying breed. He and Lucy had raised three daughters aboard their various sailing vessels and he was considered as salty as the sea itself. He didn't move quite as fast as he used to, and everyone had a babysitting attitude toward him, particularly after a few beers. He resented needing or getting help from anyone — "can run my own life, thank you." But his voice always hid a real tenderness, a trait he kept from most people. In reality, he was a typical grandpa with his daughters' children and secretly delighted in the simple things of life.

The squeaky screen door opened and a well-endowed woman in her late twenties joined the group. She was used to the stares when she went braless and inwardly got a kick out of people meeting her for the first time.

"Hi, gang," she chirped. "Oh, does that look good. Gimme a rum punch too, Wanda. What's up?" she asked, as always, waiting for anyone to answer. Bonnie was crew on a big charter sailboat that frequented the island. As usual, she was thirsty after a long day and enjoyed the company of the yacht club.

"Did anyone see those people with Jackson this afternoon?" she continued, asking no one in particular. "I asked him when he came back and all he'd do is laugh, shake his head and say 'Oh, mon!' Who are they and why did they go to Smugglers? No one's there."

"They are now," said the sailboat owner. "Claims he's the new owner, that he's gonna fix the place up and give the Sandy Cay Club a run for its money. We've been talking about all the work he's got ahead of him. Don't envy him at all."

"Jesus," she said, shaking her head. "We walked the dog there the other day. Even HE turned up his nose at the place. After he'd done his job, of course," she giggled and lit a cigarette. "What's some more bullshit, huh? This whole place is crazy. You think you have it figured out and it turns inside out again. Shit, you wouldn't believe the group on board right now. We've got an old man who's so blind, we're afraid he'll fall overboard. He tends to walk in his sleep and has no balance. And the old lady with him doesn't eat fish. Can you imagine shipping on board a charter boat and not liking fish? You can't win. When's Charlie due in, anyway? We're gonna ship the old man back to the States."

"He bringin' cottage guests tomorrow," said Wanda, filling a glass with ice.

Bonnie's complaints turned the conversation from Smugglers to the pitfalls of chartering. How the crew was at the beck and call of those paying for their week in Paradise; how it was really a thankless, endless job of getting ready for guests, working during their stay, cleaning up after for the next group, and trying to maintain the boat and some sanity in between.

"I've been waiting for the good charters to outweigh the bad ones," said Bonnie, sipping her rum punch, brown hair tied with a red ribbon at the back of her neck. "Hey, does anyone want my job? Pay's great, you know. Get to sleep with the captain."

A chuckle went around the bar and someone pointed out that the captain "wasn't such a bad sort."

26

"Oh, I know," she said, smiling. "I think he's great, but sometimes...." Her voice trailed off and she wiped the condensation from her glass. "Wanda, how about another one?"

She lifted her shirt and pulled a couple of soggy native bills out of her cutoff jeans, unfolding them as she laid them on the bar. Two years ago, it was more the boat than the captain that had captured her love. The 65-foot custom trimaran was loaded with all the goodies that made cruising fun — inflatable boats, scuba tanks, sailboards, and a collection of mismatched masks, snorkels and fins. It easily held eight guests and a crew of three.

Bonnie put out her cigarette and rested her head on her hand, only half-listening to the talk around the bar.

This was the only place where she could unleash her feelings. When charter parties were aboard it was impossible to have time to herself. At the club, she could escape in the late afternoon, knowing the cruising crowd would give her some sympathy. She had shipped aboard as first mate, with plenty of dreams and hopes for adventure the job promised.

Now, two years later, she was in the same spot, financially, as the day she took the job. Mentally, the flow of new guests each week had drained her. Physically, she was in great shape, with a deep tan and a limber, but strong, muscular frame. A few rum punches a day soothed over the problems, and yes, the captain had been good to her. But she knew her enlistment was coming to an end. Time was running out if she was to have the home and kids she'd always dreamed of having. She knew her present situation was a dead end. She sipped her rum punch, looked at the ship's clock in back of the bar, and said, "I'd better be going. Time to start dinner. I'll take this one with me, Wanda — one for the dinghy ride, eh?"

The bar began clearing out as the dinner hour approached, and the cruising crowd was replaced by the cottage guests emerging from naps after a day of sun, sand and snorkeling. Sandy Cay was perfect for anyone who enjoyed the water. Guests could go exploring in little runabouts and could do their own thing, whether skinny dipping on a deserted island beach or enjoying the undersea panorama with a mask. Nothing was fancy and no one cared who anyone was. Shorts were acceptable attire for dinner. Celebrities could be anonymously comfortable with common, ordinary folks. The club's reputation was worldwide for quaintness and solitude, yet it remained a word-of-mouth hideaway.

No big advertising campaign lured tourists to the island, but visitors usually returned. It was the Sandy Cay Club that had fueled the dreams of a procession of owners at nearby Smugglers, but so far, all it had become was a financial disaster. Tourists and yachtsmen preferred Sandy Cay.

* * *

Pete thought of Woody as he awoke from his nap. He sat on the edge of the bed, rubbed his eyes, and thought about what Woody's reaction would be at Smugglers.

He began to chuckle, seeing the humor in the situation. Abigail raised her head and thumped her tail. By now, he thought, Woody would have been hit with the full force of the chaotic, hurricane-force mess. He chuckled some more.

Time to tend to your own business, he told himself. In due time you'll hear all about Woody's woes. He chuckled again, got up, stretched and headed for the shower. Time would tell the story.

Chapter 2

Arrival — Smugglers Cay

As Woody and Laura watched the wake of Jackson's runabout, they realized that they were on their own island at last. Although they could see some planks missing from the dock and the grounds overgrown with thistle weeds, neither was prepared for what was ahead. The initial shock set Woody fuming and Laura into silent panic.

The main building was a shambles.

"Goddamnit, Laura," said Woody, surveying the clubroom with its broken tables and chairs, clutter, torn curtains and graffitied walls. "You tell me. What the hell gives the damn bastards the right to do this? Look at the place. Shit. We're no goddamn cleaning crew. What the hell do you think happened to this goddamn rock?" He raged, limping and stomping from the main club room into the kitchen. The refrigerator was full of maggots and roaches. Rice was spilled in the pantry and the rats had had a feast. A mangy dog left on the island hung its head and slowly wagged its tail, indicative of the condition of the club. The bar was depleted of anything consumable and the place was covered with fine sand and sticky salt from the sea breeze blowing through broken windows.

Everywhere Woody looked, in the rooms, in the shop area, there was total chaos.

Laura was stunned.

Her first reaction was to cry, but she knew it would only infuriate Woody. She felt like Scarlet O'Hara returned to Tara, a dream disintegrated before her eyes. She had never been subjected to such degrading work before. But there was no help left on Smugglers Cay. She brushed off a chair with a tissue from her bag and sat down, shocked and disappointed.

Angered, Woody grabbed a dusty glass from the bar, stomped outside, took a bottle of rum and some melting ice from the cooler and fixed a drink, swirling it with his fingers as he came back inside.

Tears were now rolling down Laura's face.

"Cut the crap, Laura. For Christ sake, don't pull this shit on me," boomed Woody, unnerved. "We've got to get off our butts and get this place in shape. You think for one minute one of those black bastards is going to come back and help us get the place in order? It's just you and me, and right now, everyone is sitting on their fat ass at the Sandy Cay Club having a good laugh over us and this goddamn mess. You gonna stand for it? Huh? Shit! Wipe your goddamn tears and look for a broom, for Christ sake. No way am I gonna give the goddamn bastards the satisfaction of going back for help. Jesus," he said, looking around. "Where do we start?"

He sounded as pathetic as Laura felt, and this gave her strength. She looked around, seriously taking stock of the situation. It was definitely not Paradise. It was a deplorable mess. She wished now that Woody had come ahead, with her following later, like the original plan. She hated to see him enraged, but when things didn't go exactly as he planned, this was standard behavior. Laura was used to being his victim. She dried her eyes and stood up.

"Ah'll start the refrigerator so we can at least put the food away," she sighed. She stepped over empty boxes, a broken ketchup bottle and squashed egg carton. "Do we have electricity?"

Woody stopped picking up trash and looked at her, almost in disbelief that she thought of it. She was right. Get the generator going. Nightfall would come soon enough.

"Good thinking, Bunchy," he said. "That's my gal. I guess I better get that bad news, too. I'll be making love to the generator if you want me."

Laura smiled. Now the old Woody was returning. She watched him fix another drink from the cooler, then limp around the corner of the club room and out of sight.

Woody followed the conch shell-lined walkway to the generator shed.

What a blasted hot day to come to an island, he thought, wiping the sweat from his already burning forehead.

He had been given a quick course in the operation of the

generator the day Maxwell had shown him the island. But that was three months ago, when Miller was still around. Now, as Woody opened the door to the generator shed, he realized it might take some doing to get the rusting keg of bolts humming again.

He swung open a wooden shutter to let in some light and checked the day tank for fuel. Half full. He leaned over the generator and found the oil dip stick. Low. Needed oil. Now where the hell is it he asked himself. There. He picked up a rusty screwdriver, drove two holes in the can and began pouring.

"Christ, this'll take all day," he muttered to himself, patience not being his strong point. When the engine was full of oil, he leaned on his short leg and looked at the motor skeptically.

"Now, what say we get down to some serious business," he said to himself. "You better start, you little bastard. Now, where's the crank? Should be right here," he said, looking at the empty slot. "Shit!" he wailed, frantically looking around. "Goddamnit," he yelled, stomping his short leg. "Who stole the goddamn crank for this friggin' thing? Laura!" he yelled, limping out of the shed to the main building. "Laura!" She came running, thinking surely he had hurt himself.

"Laura, I can't possibly get the goddamn thing to run," he whined. "The fucking crank is missing and there ain't no way I'm gonna stick my arm into the goddamn hole and crank that son of a bitch over. Shit!" He stomped. "Who would take a crank?"

"Well," said Laura slowly, wiping her hands on a dirty towel. "It must be here somewhere. Maybe you could ask someone?"

"Ask someone?" he bellowed. "Did you say ASK someone? Who, goddamnit? You tell me who. And then tell me how. It's our island, our problem. We're stuck, plain and simple. Up a creek without a paddle and all that bullshit."

"Well, you can at least take a look around...." Her voice trailed after him. Woody was already out the door, heading back toward the generator. She returned to the refrigerator, wiping it out with a dirty rag found on a pile of dish towels that needed laundering. If nothing else, the refrigerator would be a clean place to store what little food they had brought. The racks inside were rusted and the ice trays were missing. The door was speckled with rust, the seal was cracked, but it would have to do. She looked past the sink and counter, both full of dishes caked with the remains of food and roach leavings. A good sweeping would probably be the next thing to do.

Woody came back, a little less agitated, but still mad, the rum slowly taming his frustration.

"I can't find the damn thing," he said, slumping into a chair. "I guess the next thing for me to do is get some communication going. We can't be stranded here. Besides, I told Chubby I'd try to reach him tonight. Give me a hand. We'll just have to make do."

Laura was used to his changing moods and was glad he had calmed down so quickly. She knew he had to get things done. He had a time schedule to meet and getting upset wouldn't help anything. She watched him fix another rum, then he went through the supplies they had brought.

"Ah put the single sideband under the canned goods in that box, if that's what you're looking for," she said, pointing to a pile of boxes on the dock where Jackson had dropped them earlier. "The VHF and aircraft radios are in my duffel."

Woody picked up the box of groceries and carried it into the club, setting it down on one of the tables in the dining area. Laura brought in her duffel and felt around for the small hand-held VHF radio.

"The antenna for this is in the box," she said, nodding. "What do you have to do to hook it up?"

"I'm not as concerned about the VHF and aircraft radios as I am the sideband," he said, taking out cans of food to get to the brown box beneath.

"Once we make our contact, then we'll talk to the boats. Gotta get something going so if we have to we can at least get outta here. Nice place to be stuck, huh? What does the brochure promise? Fine dining, comfortable rooms overlooking a placid sea of blue. Paradise found?" He mocked reality and looked around. "All this lovely Paradise is ours. Now what the hell should we do with it?"

Laura giggled, grateful the rum was having a pleasant effect on Woody. Sometimes it made him unbearable.

"Ah think the first thing to do with it, sir, is to get the sideband working," she exaggerated, mimicking his earlier words. No one ever called Woody "sir" and it sounded totally ridiculous to both of them. "You brought a battery pack, Ah hope?" she said, more seriously.

"In my duffel. I'll get it."

As Woody walked outside, he noticed the breeze had dropped to nothing. Within seconds, the no-see-ums descended, taking miniature bites while dodging the quick slaps Woody laid on himself.

Nothing was worse in the tropics than the little bastard sand flies, he thought, slapping another one. You couldn't see them until their jaws did a number on you. And he knew of nothing that would stop them except a breeze. Or a fan, he thought. No generator. So no fan.

He picked up his duffel and another bag and lugged them inside.

"Visitors," he announced. "We got real nice visitors. Remember how the no-see-ums ate you alive in Florida last summer? Well, they found out you're here and came to welcome you. And me. And this whole fucking island. Laura, would you help me here?" he pleaded, suddenly changing his disposition. "I'm pissed and upset and angry but we gotta get this place organized. You know that, don't you? I can't screw up the plan."

She knew it, and also knew Woody needed her silent support now more than ever. Whenever he felt inadequate, he reverted to a childish manner. He almost looked pathetic, she thought, balancing on his shorter leg and looking at her pleadingly.

"It's all right, Sweety," she said, comfortingly. "We'll get the place cleaned up and looking like we want it. Never mind the bugs and all. Let's just do what we can."

She walked over to him, put her arms around him and kissed his sweaty face. Almost instantly, he snapped back to the old Woody.

"This must be true love, huh? Kissing a soppy wet face and hugging a clammy body?" He smiled as he hugged her back.

"Kinda nice, just the two of us, huh? Even with this mess." He gave her a quick kiss and squeeze. "More later, okay? Promise?"

"Promise," she said, smiling.

* * *

Two hours later, Woody wrung his hands, stood back and gloated over the various connections he had made with the radio.

"Well, this is it," he said. "We're hooked up. Now let's see if the goddamn thing works."

Laura hoped so.

She had listened to a constant tirade from Woody as he read the directions that were outlined for him. Electronics wasn't his long suit and she secretly hoped everything would work. She was tiring fast of cleaning, listening to Woody, keeping him supplied with rum, and wondering how they could possibly spend the night in what she felt must be the equivalent of a ghetto "flea bag."

Woody flipped the on switch and Laura crossed her fingers as he adjusted the squelch of the multi-channel radio. They could hear others on the frequency and Woody seemed pleased that he had hooked it up right.

"I told Chubby to listen up around 8:30 tonight," he said, trying to distinguish a transmission. "Supposedly, we're all pre-tuned so we won't sound like Donald Duck. Hope he remembers to make contact. He's been a little fuzzy-headed lately."

"Especially with that beard he's trying to grow," she said. Chubby was a pain to her, ill-mannered with a know-it-all arrogance. She never knew if he was kidding or telling the truth, and she doubted if he even knew the difference sometimes. Life was a game to Chubby. A game where you played cops and robbers without letting anyone know which one you were. He rode the highway patrol at night for kicks and monitored radio frequencies for Woody's friends off-hours, putting together "deals." He didn't make sense to Laura.

"Eight-twenty," said Woody, unable to sit still. "Think he'll be on? Let's give it a try. *Naughty Lady, Naughty Lady,* Woodpecker calling *Naughty Lady.*" He repeated himself several times, listening each time for an answer.

"Where the hell is he?" he asked, knowing Laura wouldn't answer. He began pacing, stepping over cartons of sorted debris and piles of swept up sand and dirt. He came back, sat next to the radio and looked at it determinedly. "Once more, then I'm working on the VHF. *Naughty Lady, Naughty Lady*, come in *Naughty Lady*."

"*Naughty Lady*, here. Read you loud and clear, Woodpecker. Any traffic?" Chubby's voice boomed nonchalantly, although it sounded miles away. The radio was working!

"*Naughty Lady*, good evening. Just checking equipment. No traffic, but stand by at 0700 tomorrow. Copy?"

"Roger, Woodpecker. 0700 Tomorrow. *Naughty Lady* clear."

"Whooee!" yelled Woody, grabbing Laura. "We're in business, kid. We're in business. I don't care what a pigsty this place is right now. We're in business. Big business!"

The VHF system was easy. He connected a few wires, hooked up to the battery pack and hoped it would work. By the time Laura fixed both of them another drink he was ready to try it. Laura was glad something was going as planned. Woody would at least be bearable, and if she kept the drinks down for the rest of the night, he wouldn't swing too far in either direction.

"Cross your fingers," he said, chugging the rum. He turned to Channel 16 and called "Conch Inn, Woodpecker here. You copy?"

A few seconds lapsed, then a clipped voice came back.

"Conch Inn. Go to 6-8."

Woody changed channels, then said, "Hey, there, this is Woodpecker. That you, Maxwell?"

"Roger, old man. How do you like that place?" His twangy Aussie accent and sardonic humor crackled across the air waves as Woody detected his sarcasm.

"Don't be funny. You know d..darn well what I found here. You wouldn't happen to know where the crank is for the generator, would you? Can't start the friggin' thing without it." Woody had to watch his language on the radio. He couldn't risk another violation. A minute seemed to elapse.

"Maxwell, you still there?"

"Roger. Listen, old chap. Sorry about the generator. Never thought till you mentioned it. I borrowed the crank the other day. I'll bring it there tonight, soon as I track it down. Jock'll come with me. He stuck around."

"Well...I'm not going to kick your you-know-what over the radio because I'm trying to mind my manners, but I sure would appreciate a fan to blow the bugs away tonight. I'll expect you. Going back to 16."

"Roger. 16."

"So. That mystery is solved," said Woody. "But why would any sane person take the crank off a generator to another location?" He looked at Laura, who was leaning on a broom.

"I have this horrible feeling that everything we've ever heard about Maxwell as a mechanic is probably true," he said, shaking his head and finishing his rum. "But, at least we might have power tonight. How's the rum doing? Better have Maxwell bring some more." He keyed the transmitter and told Max to bring a couple of bottles of rum and some ice. When he was through talking, he turned to Laura.

"Looks like party time coming up. Let's give this dump one more bulldozing."

He tore off the corner of a box, then bent over for Laura to sweep the last bit of dirt off the kitchen floor. The counters were fairly clean and the dishes were soaking in the sink filled with salt water. The sun had long since disappeared, and the two worked in the glow of a kerosene lamp which Woody had brought in earlier from the work room. Mosquitoes and a variety of other bugs swarmed near the light.

"On second thought, let's have a couple of rums before those looneys arrive and say to hell with it. We haven't stopped since Jackson dumped us on this rock," he said.

It was true. Laura had paused just long enough to make sandwiches, washed down with rum and water. She wished they had some fresh limes to make it taste better, but she had not thought to bring any.

"Ah hear you get used to just plain rum after a while in the tropics," she mused, swirling the melting cubes with her finger. "Ah've already compromised on the lime."

"Get used to it," said Woody. "Remember, it's a hell of a lot easier to get a bottle of rum than a bottle of fresh water down here. So, any way you drink it is okay." He leaned back in his chair, folded his arms across his stomach, glass in hand, and looked at Laura. Her brown hair had kinked up with the humidity and her bare feet were unbelievably black. Her white shorts and shirt were streaked with dirt.

"Bunchy, you're looking pretty good in spite of all the shit," he said, gazing upon her as a prized possession. "Hard work becomes you and you never knew it. Don't look at me like that. I'm serious. Screwing up your face spoils this new look. You even got a little tan today. Come here."

Obediently, she pulled her chair next to his. He leaned over and stretched out her navy halter top.

"Yeah, you got sun all right…mmm…tomorrow you should go to the beach and get the sun all over, huh?" She tapped his cheek with her hand and covered herself once again.

"Same old Woody," she sighed. "Fifteen years and you're still a letch."

"I like your boobs and your butt," he said, "especially your butt." He reached over to grab her and she stood up just beyond his reach and took his glass. She knew he was getting drunk but didn't care. He usually treated her better after a few drinks, but lately, the booze sometimes backfired. She was grateful he was in a friendly mood, especially with no electricity.

"You want another drink? Ah do, especially with those characters coming. Shouldn't we put a lantern out on the dock?" she asked.

"You're right. They probably can't even see by now."

Woody grabbed the lantern and Laura followed with the drinks. It was pleasantly cool and the no-see-ums had disappeared. "This is what I love about the tropics," he said. "Hot days and cool nights." Ripples on the water reflected a starry sky, the rainbow of hues now gone. The moon sat like a sliver of eggshell overhead. On rare impulse, Woody put his arms around Laura. They stood there, enjoying the complete quiet until the silence was broken by the distant hum of a boat. It got louder as it approached Smugglers Cay.

"Boys are making good time," said Woody.

"They're always making time," said Laura, sarcastically.

The small runabout approached, slowed down, and as it neared the dock, they could distinguish Max, Jock, Max's wife, Pat, and another girl.

"Jock doesn't waste time, does he?" said Laura. Woody shrugged his shoulders. Jock was always looking, usually found, but never kept. Women were always impressed with him as a pilot, until they found out he only flew the small planes. When the flying novelty wore off, Jock was left hanging. So Woody viewed the extra visitor as just that.

"So, you're the asshole who stole the crank," he shouted to Maxwell. "It's a damn good thing I didn't know earlier or you'd probably be dead."

Maxwell looked up, shoved his glasses on his nose and didn't smile. Brash American talk irritated him, particularly when it was directed at him personally.

"I'll give you a hand with it to make up for it," he said dryly. "Here's the rum you ordered."

"Great! Laura, fix a round for all of us. Thought you were leaving, Jock. What happened? Those hot pants get to you?" He chided Jock as he stepped onto the dock and reached a hand to the slender blonde.

"Meet Nel," said Jock. "This is Woody, a real gentleman."

"Hi, Woody. Jock tells me you bought this island. Far out! Your own island. Wow!" She extended her hand, and Woody couldn't help but notice her tanned body, even by dim kerosene lamp light. A white cotton shirt was tied around her midriff, unbuttoned above low cut hip hugger shorts.

"Come on, everyone," he said, reluctantly taking his eyes off Nel. "Sit down. Laura will be back in a second with the drinks. You wouldn't have believed this place. Been working since we arrived. What a mess. Pigs would have thought it the Ritz. What happened to the natives, Max? You must have heard something."

"They packed up, got in the smack boats and went back to Rocky Point," he said matter-of-factly, as if it was normal for the help to just pack up and leave. "Now that you're here, they might come back looking for work. But don't bother to ask them what happened, old chap. All they'll say is 'Don't know nuttin', mon, don't know nuttin,' and it'll just get you more upset. Even if they come back, you won't know what you've got. Miller left them here by themselves with no pay. You can't leave a place to the natives. Their family moves in and you don't stand a chance. Then when you come back they all mysteriously disappear with all your supplies and only your crew is left saying, 'Don't know nuttin', mon. Don't know nuttin'.'"

Everyone laughed at Maxwell's rare attempt at humor, but Woody made a mental note to make sure one of his people was always on the island.

Laura poured the drinks, scooping the last of the original melting ice and opened the new cooler just brought from Conch Inn.

"Ya'll have to pardon our style tonight," she said, her drawl contrasting with Maxwell's clipped accent. "In the States, Ah wouldn't think of inviting ya'll under such primitive conditions, but Ah'll make up for it later. Ah've got some great ideas for the place. You must be Pat," she said, looking at the woman with Maxwell. "And who's your friend, Jock?"

Introductions were made and everyone started talking about the possibilities to make Smugglers Cay the best resort in the area, better than the Sandy Cay Club. The women tossed around decorating ideas as the men headed for the generator shed.

"You ought to go along the oceanside and look for old fish nets," said Pat, refreshing in a one-piece strapless yellow terry jumpsuit, hair clasped high on her head. "I found a perfect one the other day, just ratty enough to have character and good enough to hold glass balls I've collected. Glass ones are hard to find now. Fishermen are replacing them with styrofoam and metal balls."

"Ah've seen the glass ones," said Laura. "Don't they drift across the ocean?"

"Uh-huh," said Pat, sipping her rum. "They hold up the fishing nets in Portugal or some place over there."

"You could find some nice shells, too," said Nel. "I'd love

to work on a place like this. It would be neat to work with a real place rather than just study interior design ideas like I'm doing now."

In front of the generator shed, Woody puffed, "This little mother better work," illuminating the machine with a flashlight. "I can't tell you how pissed I was this afternoon, Max. It's a good thing rum calms me down."

"Understandable, old chap. Sort of like the domino theory. One disappeared in the village, so I came and got yours. But I don't know where you would have gone to find one. The next island over is locked up right now, and the caretaker at Mossy Cay won't let anyone on the island without an invitation from the owner. You'd have been out of luck," he said, dryly. "We'll get it running. Did you check the oil?"

"Of course," said Woody, indignantly. "It should turn over with a couple of turns."

Max fit the crank into the front of the generator, pushed his glasses back on his nose and gave it a full turn. The generator sputtered, then stopped. He cranked again. And again.

"Groans like it wants to run," said Woody, anxiously. "Try her again, this time like you mean it."

Max put more muscle into it and within seconds, the generator was running on its own. Woody was elated. He limped out of the generator building and yelled up the path.

"Hey, Laura!," he boomed. "Turn on some lights!"

Laura groped toward the door, remembering a switch she had seen earlier. She flipped it and the lights miraculously came on.

"Eeeeeeeiiii!" screamed Nel, holding one hand over her mouth and pointing to the far corner of the room. A rat, as big as a tomcat, stared back. "Oooooogh!" she shuddered, frozen to the floor as the rat casually ambled off. Pat had seen it too. It WAS big. Laura felt weak all over, a clammy feeling raising the hair on her arms. The men came running.

"What was THAT all about?" demanded Woody as he tripped over the small lip at the entrance to the door. "What's the matter?"

"There was a huge rat when we turned on the light," said

Laura, as frightened as her companions but keeping her voice in check. "Ah swear, Woody, that generator better run all night. Ah'm not sleepin' in this dreadful place without a light on."

Then she remembered. In the back cupboard, behind the cake pans, she had seen some traps.

"Woody, Ah've got an idea. If ya'll can figure out what to put in them, there's traps in the kitchen. Ah won't stay here if there's rats. Ya'll decide, me or them."

Woody knew she was serious and more frightened than she was letting on.

"I think there's some poison in the storeroom, if I remember rightly," volunteered Maxwell. "Give me the lantern, old man. Get the traps, but I think the poison is a better idea. You won't have to clean them up." He headed for the storeroom, Jock following. The girls stood in place, transfixed.

Woody rummaged in the kitchen, then found the traps and looked for something to use as bait.

"Peanut butter. Heard somewhere the little bastards like peanut butter. Where'd you put it, Laura?"

"In the box with the rest of the canned goods," she said. "Ah should've put it all away earlier."

He found the peanut butter under the soups and canned stews.

"Crunchy. This should do it," said Woody. "Whatever happened to the old cheese theory?"

"We can afford to part with the peanut butter, but cheese is too hard to get when you're away from civilization," said Laura. "Besides, Ah think we forgot the cheese, Woody. Ah don't remember seeing any when Ah put the perishables in the 'frigerator."

Max and Jock returned, carrying a sack of dry rat poison.

"We'll put it around the outside and in the kitchen corners where you don't have food," said Maxwell, taking charge as if he had confronted the situation before.

"Don't worry about the food," said Laura, almost wistfully. "Ah remember now. We left two bags in the trunk of the car back in the States. Most of the food was left behind." The tone of her voice echoed dismay. "Ya'll want another drink? It seems to be the only thing we have."

She was getting tired of the long day, the constant upsets, the hard work and now a group of strangers. She had hoped for a nice, quiet romantic night with Woody, on their own island, enjoying the sunset and all the dreams of Paradise. But that wasn't reality. Dirt, and rats, broken down tables, and too much rum. That's what she had. Laura poured another drink, following suit as the others freely filled their glasses. She looked around. Woody always seemed to attract the boozers and freeloaders. Why should this night be any different, she asked herself? Jock was beginning to fall over Nel and they were playing a game of peek-a-boo with her open shirt. He was getting overbearing and Laura sensed uneasiness in Nel as she caught her eye.

"Hey, Laura, have you ever been to this island before or did Woody just surprise you?" She got up and avoided Jock's hands reaching out to her. He followed her like a puppy dog, then headed for the bottle of rum and fixed another drink, hardly taking his eyes off Nel. Nel looked at Jock, then at Laura and rolled her eyes to the ceiling.

"He's not exactly what I thought a knight in shining armor would be," she confided to Laura in a low voice. "He's rather creepy, wouldn't you say?"

"Ah personally can't stand him, but that's mah feeling," said Laura. "Lots of women can't stand Woody and Ah think he's fine." She shrugged her shoulders and went to be with him, avoiding involvement in Nel's affair. Woody was shuffling through a box of old cassette tapes, promising to liven the place up with some island music.

"Christ!" he shouted, slamming down a broken tape. "Doesn't ANYTHING work on this goddamn rock? Hey Jock, you know electronics. Help me with this fucking machine."

Jock reluctantly took his eyes off Nel and walked over to Woody, who had a tape unraveled to his knees.

"We don't need it tonight, Woody. Let's wait till morning. I can't see straight," said Jock, looking back at Nel.

"You're having trouble walking, too," said Woody. "Fix yourself another one. Fix her one, too. Maybe your luck will change."

Maxwell and Pat were off on their own in the kitchen, helping themselves to peanut butter and crackers. Woody gave up on the stereo, took a drink and glanced at his watch. 11:30. He staggered a bit as he walked over to Laura, who was sitting quietly at a table, looking over the club with the same distant gaze she had earlier in the day. As he came close to her chair, he tripped, sending the rum into her face.

"Ah thank ya'll for that," she said, keeping her composure and casually wiping herself off. "When ya goin' to call it quits? Ah'm tired, Woody."

"Me too," he said, hiccuping. "Everybody's tired, right?" he shouted, carelessly sweeping the room with his hand. "You're all invited for the night. No sense navigating those dark, shark-infested waters, right?"

Laura was stunned. Overnight guests meant linens and clean rooms, and she hadn't even found where she and Woody would sleep the night.

"Good idea," said Maxwell, emerging from the kitchen, Pat right behind him. "Dibs on the pool table."

"The pool table?" asked Laura, bewildered.

"Good sleeping," he said. "Beats one of those cottages, right, Pat?" She nodded, snuggling up next to him.

Nel was fast losing the battle with Jock, who was trying to figure out where to bed her down.

"That corner over there," he nodded, pointing to an area out of the beam of light. "You got any blankets or anything Woody?"

Laura had seen some linens in the storeroom earlier.

"Woody, bring the lantern. Ah'm so tired Ah could die. Let's find some blankets." He led the way, and in a few minutes, they returned with an armload of sheets and pillows and blankets, musty from the storeroom. No one paid any attention.

"Well, here they are...." her voice trailed off, realizing that their first guests were warmed from within, and that no one would freeze in the tropical air.

Woody shrugged his shoulders, looked at Laura and smiled.

"You made a promise earlier. Let's find a bed in this joint. We'll take the lantern so nothing can scare you, okay, Bunchy?"

"Okay," she smiled. Woody had a way, she thought.

They walked past Jock and Nel, intertwined in a rattan easy chair in the far corner, oblivious to all but themselves. The owner's quarters for the resort were upstairs in a little room overlooking the harbor. Cobwebs and dirt glared back at the lantern light, but Laura was too tired to care. She'd clean tomorrow. All she wanted was a place to lie down, make love if Woody had it in him and go to sleep. The bed didn't look too bad and there was a ceiling fan overhead. Woody flipped the switch, found the light was working and turned off the lantern. Aside from a slight womp-womp of the fan as it turned, all was quiet. Laura tossed a sheet on the bed.

"Not exactly Tara in its prime," she said. Woody shrugged and yawned.

"All I need now…" he came over, put his arms around Laura and eased her onto the bed. His voice trailed off and their night began, the moon still hanging like an eggshell out the small window hazy with dirt in the reflected light. They could hear the water lapping on the shore, just barely, their own bodies joined in the gentle rhythm of the sea. "Tomorrow would be a new beginning," thought Laura. In a few minutes, Woody was snoring.

Chapter 3

Sunday

Every other day of the week the bar usually opened by 8:00 a.m. with someone asking for a Bloody Mary or a cold beer.

But on Sundays, the first thing Pete did was put an old wine bottle on the corner of the bar with a sign "Bar is Closed."

It didn't matter. Some went about the self-serve concept, ignoring the sign, and some obviously needed a drink to calm nerves of the night before. Pete tried to keep things in line, because he'd promised the village he'd close on Sundays, at least until the late afternoon when happy hour began. It wasn't always easy, but even Jackson frowned at anyone drinking on the Lord's Day. The Sabbath was strictly kept on Sandy Cay, and visitors to the island were always welcomed at the tiny Baptist church.

During the tourist season, the church overflowed, with natives and visitors joining in song. For that hour of the morning, the island adopted a different attitude. Whatever happened, the good Lord would take care of it.

Pete watched Jackson pump gas on the dock, then tab up the bill for a 60-foot trawler. As he walked toward the club he couldn't help but smile to himself. Jackson, now in his early thirties, had come to the island from Rocky Point as a boy of fourteen, looking for work. Pete had taken him in, taught him how to read, how to tabulate bills and run the business. He was an amazing, hard-working native with one of the most constructive attitudes toward life Pete had ever seen.

Jackson's willingness and natural aptitude defied the classical description of the lazy tropical native. He got things done on time and walked with a quick step. Jackson had come a long way. The only thing that kept him in the same category as the other natives was his speech. There was no way an American could teach him to say "th." It always came out "t" or "d." But his speech camouflaged a keen mind and deep inner thoughts.

Jackson went behind the bar, checked his figures on the

calculator and said to the captain who had followed him, "Dat's $437.80, Cap. You comin' back soon?" He carefully counted a mixture of traveler's checks and local currency as he half listened to the captain's lengthy itinerary.

"You gonna make all dose islands, eh? Bet you be back next week. All you lookin' for is right here, mon," Jackson tipped his hat back and looked the captain straight in the eye with a smile toward Pete. It was true. What the yachting crowd was constantly seeking was usually found right at Sandy Cay, and around-the-world voyagers often dropped anchor for many months before cruising on or back to where they had started.

When the captain walked out the door, Jackson turned to Pete.

"All right iffen I leabe now? Be back 'bout dinner time if anyone lookin' fo' me."

"Take it easy, Jackson. The place'll still be here."

Pete knew Jackson would head for home and change his entire image. Jeans and T-shirt would give way to a full suit, complete to dress shoes and tie. Jackson would then go to church and play the electric guitar and organ for the choir. He was completely self-taught in everything, and had gained the respect of his own people.

The church bell rang. Ten o'clock. It always rang exactly one hour before services began, although the natives didn't need a reminder. The choir would begin warming up in a few minutes, their voices carrying on the morning breeze over the entire island. The kitchen help had hurried Sunday breakfast for the couple of guests, and had returned to the village to get ready for church.

Pete sat, enjoying the quiet, reading an old boating magazine. He chuckled over an article about cruising the Caribbean. It never was what anyone expected it to be. But people usually returned, if for no other reason than to confirm what they saw the first time. He glanced beyond the harbor. Two boats were on the horizon, a big sailboat and a cruiser. He'd wait until they got closer to see if they were coming to his dock or Conch Inn. If they needed a good supply of fresh water, diesel or gas and ice, they would come to his dock. If they were pretty self-sufficient and didn't mind running their own generator for power, they might tie up at Conch Inn. Pete went back to reading.

"Sandy Cay Club. *Dolphin Hunter*. Come in."

Pete set the magazine aside, went inside and took the mike for the VHF off a makeshift hook.

"*Dolphin Hunter* go ahead. Yacht club here."

"Just checking dockage availability for two boats, Pete. We're 65. *Sea Lady* is a 45 and a blowboat. Can you handle us?"

"Roger. Let the sailboat take the inside dock to the south. You lie on the outside face dock. Glad to see you back. Need anything?"

"No, we're here for a few days. Jackson still there?"

"No, he's gone to church. Day off, you know."

"Yeah, we know. He doesn't get many. See you in a bit. *Dolphin Hunter* clear."

Two boats were coming in, plus guests for two cottages would arrive about noon with Charlie. Business might be picking up, he thought. The club had suffered from a recent slump in the American economy, and new tax laws no longer allowed corporations to write off their large yachts. Many of them had ceased to operate and it had hurt business because corporate yachts carried big spenders. They liked their fresh water showers and air-conditioned staterooms. On a per-gallon rate for water and metered electric charge for big yachts, the club did quite well. The whole island felt the drop in revenue from the big-time regulars. It affected everyone, because sixty percent of the employable natives worked at the club. The rest did laundry for yachtsmen, baked bread or did odd jobs. When the big yachts were in port the fishing guides were busy and there was always activity. The visitors loved their fun and didn't mind paying for it.

Pete watched a couple get off their boat and walk down the dock, the woman wearing a dress instead of her usual bikini.

How different people looked when they were off to church, thought Pete. How different. The couple waved as they walked by. Pete went back to his magazine.

Better check the radios, he thought. Charlie was due in about noon. Pete stepped into the radio room, filled with cartons of cigarettes, cases of liquor and beer and miscellaneous parts, and supply catalogs. He turned the squelch on the unicom aircraft radio and checked to see if there was traffic on the sideband radio. He had talked earlier to the office to confirm departure of the plane and number of incoming guests, and Charlie was on schedule. Dependable Charlie. He would come and go on the island, never staying more than a few days. Pete chuckled at how Charlie always said he couldn't stay too long or he'd go rock-happy like the rest of them, that SOMEONE had to hold a little sanity in the midst of the carnival.

Pete mused how Charlie viewed the operation like a juggler. As long as all the balls were kept in the air and they could be caught at the right time, things went smoothly. When one of the balls fell, everyone knew it. It could be a mechanical delay on the airplane, a "lost" passenger who didn't know the right day of the week for the flight waiting for him, a generator or engine part that was brought over that wasn't right.

Charlie was Pete's link to the outside world, his grasp on reality. He had set up an office stateside with radio communication to the club, allowing some privacy beyond the one telephone on the island that periodically bled to the VHF frequencies, so everyone for miles could hear what people said. Now, instead of waiting weeks for parts, it was only a matter of days and sometimes only hours.

"Tings" were different now, as the natives would say.

Pete smiled to himself, then looked out to see the two vessels approaching the dock. He squinted at the water reflecting the morning sun as he went to help with the lines. Halfway down the dock he stopped, peering beyond the boats at anchor. In the distance, he could see Max's runabout approaching from the direction of Smugglers. As it got closer, he could see Pat and Woody's pilot and another girl. That's odd for a Sunday morning, thought Pete, scratching his head. He walked to the end of the face dock as the powerboat pulled up.

"Hey there, Captain, welcome back. Wanna throw me a line and we'll get you secured?" Pete liked Captain and Mrs. Edmond. They were easygoing people who knew the islands.

"Hi there, Pete. Good to be back. At least we can be assured of water and ice here. You wouldn't believe how primitive it's been. Other islands are out of everything. Here, catch."

He tossed a spring line and Pete wrapped it around a piling. The sailboat had come around the inside dock and a crew member was securing lines. It was good when people knew what they were doing. So many people rented boats, he never knew if they were going to take the dock with them or land safely. This group knew the currents and tides.

"We know it's Sunday, so don't worry about us," said Edmond. "We've got guests aboard this time. Any chance of feeding eight people tonight?"

"No problem," said Pete. "Maria's fixing conch chowder, fritters and grouper. Sound okay?"

"Sounds great. Put us down. We'll wash the decks and then get some playtime in. I'm having to entertain a bit this trip as our guests are here for the first time. You go on with what you were doing."

Mrs. Edmond came out of the main salon, smiled and waved. She looked a little more tired than usual. Pete waved back. It was a pleasure when people like the Edmonds came, he thought, not like the demanding captains who wanted everything NOW at a special price just because they were obnoxious.

Pete chuckled as he walked back to the club, listening to the church bells announcing the beginning of services.

He wasn't much of a churchgoer, but Helen and Johnny would be there, singing the hymns with old Matthew leading the choir and listening to Reverend Johnston's sermon. The minister's style was pleasant, especially when he welcomed all that "come from de sky or come from de sea to dis island Paradise." Jackson would play the organ, Maria's voice would be heard in the soprano section and for an hour, life on Sandy Cay would be devoted to the Lord.

Pete went back to reading his magazine, wondering if all was going well with Charlie. He was bringing some parts for *Cyclops* and a few fittings for the brackish water system.

Always something, he thought. If it wasn't the generators it was the water. If they weren't out of fuel they were out of T-shirts. It was impossible to keep everything going one hundred percent of the time.

The guests off the *Dolphin Hunter* came in while the Edmonds worked on their boat.

"The bar isn't really closed, is it? I mean, we can at least get a beer, can't we?" The man was dressed in bleached white shorts and a navy and white striped shirt, while his wife wore a lime green linen shorts outfit. They didn't look like the type the Edmonds would have on board as friends. Probably business, thought Pete.

"Sorry, but the Reverend doesn't like us serving alcohol of any kind on Sunday mornings. You see the sign on the bar?"

"Yeah, but we just got in. If we can't get it here we'll have to go back aboard. I KNOW we can get it there. Thought this was supposed to be a hospitable place, honey, but the man won't serve us," he said, turning to his wife.

"Rules are rules, Edgar." She smiled at Pete apologetically. "He always takes things personally and can't understand rules that don't suit him."

"Marge, cut the talk, would you? Make me look like a fool. If I want a beer on Sunday morning, goddamnit, I'll have a beer. It's my vacation."

With that, the two walked out of the bar, down the dock, and stepped aboard the Edmond's yacht. Pete was content standing ground.

There was a time a few years ago when he would have opened the bar, stashed the wine bottle and its sign and said to hell with the Reverend. But things were going too well. Reverend Johnston had publicly commended his closing the bar on Sundays and Pete had gained more respect from Maria, who headed the kitchen staff, and from Jackson. Now, it felt good to close the bar on Sunday. If people wanted a drink, they could get it somewhere else. Better to keep the island people happy than to make a couple of bucks. It paid off in the end.

The drone of engines could be heard in the distance. 11:45. Charlie was right on schedule. Pete went into the radio storeroom and called, "Whiskey Yankee, that you?"

"Whisky Yankee. It's me, all right. Got four for you. Be at

the strip in fifteen minutes. Whiskey Yankee clear."

"Sandy Cay clear."

It was always good when Charlie came in. He brought the mail, any phone messages, and occasionally a mutual friend just wanting a ride to come fish for a few days. Normally, he'd fly right over the club and buzz everyone, but not on Sunday. Reverend Johnston had long ago put an end to disruption of church services with airplanes flying too low over the village. Charlie didn't always remember when it was Sunday, but had a pretty good average in keeping the Reverend happy.

Pete locked the padlock on the front screen door and climbed into his Jeep. Best investment he'd ever made, he thought. Five hundred bucks plus the shipping and duty and it was as good as a new Mercedes on the island. He backed up, then headed for the village, turning just past the school and driving the back road so as not to disturb church services.

Within minutes, he was nearing the ramp area of the runway. The wind sock showed a dead crosswind. Didn't matter. Charlie was so used to crosswind landings he claimed he always screwed up when the wind was on the nose.

Good pilot, that Charlie, thought Pete. One of the best.

He watched as the twin-engine bird steadily descended to the beginning of the runway, just beyond a tidal pool that had gained the nickname "Plane Wash Area." At least two or three planes landed there each year, either getting caught in a downdraft before landing, or in misjudging the crosswind and length of the strip.

Pete was good at pulling planes out. He'd developed a sophisticated salvage system. He could float just about anything, with old inner tubes, air compressors and tanks. And he did. Boats, planes, it made no difference.

Wheels on the ground. Brakes applied. Charlie coasted past the tie down area, then turned the plane around near Pete's single-engine plane, chocked with a couple of rocks on the front tire. Charlie smiled and waved as he shut down. In a few seconds, the rear door opened and Charlie, dressed in a white shirt with the club monogram and light blue jeans, was the first down the steps. He was tall, had thick sandy hair, square jaw,

51

blue eyes, was clean-cut and had a quick smile. He reached his hand to Pete.

"Hi, Pete. Back again. Whew! It's a hot one today." He turned back toward the plane in time to give a hand to an older woman. "Look who we have here. Mrs. Cross hasn't been back for at least a couple of years that I remember. She brought some friends." Charlie winked at Pete as three more elderly ladies with floppy straw hats, cotton dresses and big handbags, were helped down the steps.

Pete just sat there smiling, his cigarette dangling out the side of his mouth. Old Lady Cross.

Better put on some extra help, he thought.

She liked her toddies and as a result became tipsy. The others would probably be the same type. Birds of a feather and all that, he thought. Even old birds. He sighed, knowing what was ahead. Most elderly visitors were delightful guests, but Mrs. Cross had earned her reputation over the years. She was a real character, and each year required more attention strictly for her safety.

"Hi, ladies. Welcome to our island Paradise," he smiled, getting out of the Jeep to help unload baggage. "Too bad you didn't arrive yesterday. Bar's closed and I can't offer you your welcome drink until later on. That okay?" he asked, directing his gaze, with a twinkle in his eye, to Mrs. Cross.

"Oh, Pete, don't worry about THAT!" she giggled. "I always carry my own personal supply." With that, all the ladies giggled with her. They'd been nipping already, thought Pete. Oh well, at least he didn't have to worry about the club runabouts with this crew. They never took a boat by themselves. Bonus there. If the boats weren't used, they couldn't get broken.

Mrs. Cross began pointing out all the sights to her friends, as they rode in from the airstrip, starting with the straw market. Then she asked about the girls in the kitchen and about Jackson.

"Can't hear you too good, Mrs. Cross. Wait until we get to the club," said Pete, tactfully, chuckling to Charlie. It was always embarrassing when people asked questions about everyone as they drove near the village homes. You never knew who was listening to what and it didn't make sense to conduct small talk over the Jeep's groan.

As they neared the club, Pete was stopped in the middle of the road by Bonnie, the girl off the charter boat.

"Charlie!" she shouted. "Charlie! You've got to help us. We can't sail with this guy."

A man in a bright Hawaiian shirt and baggy Bermuda shorts who appeared to be in his eighties stood there smiling, not looking at anyone or anything in particular. Bonnie's face was a bit frantic, and as she talked, she pointed to her eyes and twirled her finger around her head. Crazy blind man, thought Pete. Great.

"Why not turn around and we'll talk inside the club," said Charlie, giving her the A-OK sign. "We'll take care of everything for you. If this man wants to jump ship, I can't really blame him, knowing your crew." He winked, and Bonnie's face relaxed into a grin.

"Thanks, Charlie. C'mon Harry. Take my hand and we'll go sit on the front porch of the club for a little while. Charlie will take you back to the States and help you get a jet home." Harry tried pushing her away, his knobby knees slightly bowed above white socks and leather shoes.

"I can walk there myself, hussy. Don't act like I'm helpless. Sailed around the world, I have. Sailed around the world," he blinked several times, trying to see who was in the Jeep.

"Yeah, but in what century and on what square-rigger?" she said. "I'm tired of being nice, Harry. You're being a pain in the butt and we can't sail with you on board. We've been over it before. If you can't see where you're going and if you don't have any balance, we can't possibly be responsible for you. With our luck we'd put a lifeline on you and you'd hang yourself. Come on."

Bonnie had lost patience after three days of terror with the old man aboard and the other passengers wanting to move on to another island. And his lady companion! She didn't like fish, but she was adamant about staying aboard. "Last big fling," she kept saying, and fling she would. Bonnie told her as long as she could see what she was doing she didn't mind her picking around the food, but the old man had to go. The old lady had waved goodbye as Harry was put into the dinghy, and had gone back to sunbathing her wrinkles on the foredeck.

Charlie followed Pete into the club and fixed a Coke. Bonnie came in and sat at the bar.

"I don't care what it costs, Charlie. I'd give a week's pay, which I don't get anyway," she giggled. "Anyway, this is serious stuff. The old bat is dangerous. Here's his wife's name." She gave him a torn-off piece of paper. "Can you believe? He came down with another woman! Man's incredible. At mid-eighties he's still trying to make it. Gotta give him credit, I guess, but he's still gotta get off the goddamn boat. Anyway, give her a call. I called her ship-to-shore yesterday and told her to expect a call from you telling her when he's arriving. Can you handle it for me?" This time she was really pleading. "I've got his bags all packed and he's ready to go."

"Yeah, I guess I can go back today. He's my only passenger, so we'll get the old codger where he's gotta go. Just give me a little time here to catch up on business with Pete and we'll be on our way."

"Gee, thanks. I owe you, okay? Don't forget! I'm gonna head on out so we can pull up anchor and head south. I'll leave him here."

As she walked out the door, Harry was sitting with the four ladies and their bottle of hooch as if he'd known them for years, patting their knees and having a gay old time. The ladies doted on him, fussing with his shirt and asking him questions. They'd poured a toddy for him into a paper cup from a stack sticking out of one of their satchels, never minding ice, taking complete charge of him. It didn't matter that he could hardly see. He knew what the ladies had.

Bonnie shook her head and said, "Bye, Harry. Take it easy there," and headed for her dinghy. The big boat sure looked good.

* * *

Inside, Pete motioned for Charlie to follow. They headed to the far table of the dining area, so no one could hear them. They referred to the area as their "conference room."

"Hey, man, good to see you. What's happening?" Pete opened a pack of cigarettes.

"Nothing unusual. Couple of calls for reservations and dockage, but nothing in particular. What's going on here?"

"Don't really know right now, but something's cooking. Remember Woody Cameron, that short little guy with the limp and big mouth from Sand Dollar who dropped in here a few months ago?"

Charlie thought, then said, "Obnoxious, right?"

"You got it. Anyway, he arrived yesterday. Claims he paid big bucks for Smugglers Cay. Can't really figure it out, but I'm a bit concerned on his motives. Can't trust the guy, you know? People at Sand Dollar threw him off. Those guys had to have a reason. And the last I heard he was broke. Now he shows up with a wad."

The two looked at each other, eyebrows slightly raised, both hesitating to say what was on their minds.

"What do you think?" he asked Charlie.

A few seconds passed as Charlie flicked the ashes off his cigarette several times.

"We've been pretty safe here for a long time with the dopers going everywhere else. We might have us some, but let's wait and see. Watch the operation and see what goes on, but keep your ideas to yourself and treat him like anyone else. Shit. We can sure do without scammers around here. Always thought this island was too special for them to bother with, but that might be their perfect opportunity. Warn Jackson not to get too friendly."

"I don't think I have to worry there. He can't stand the bastard," said Pete with a chuckle. "You should have seen the place yesterday when he arrived. Guess all we can do is wait and see. Well, you better get that old man off this island or he'll have a harem by nightfall. I'll let you know any new happenings here, but I don't like what I suspect."

"Doesn't sound good, but it was bound to happen. Corruption everywhere. People don't understand that some of us just want to make an honest living and continue on. I was offered fifty grand last week for one run. Had to stop and think, and that made me mad. No thinking's necessary. Don't need that shit, you know. Well, I better get going. Call the office, if you can, and give them an ETA on me. I'll be in touch and will check out more on the other situation."

He walked out of the club, clapped his hands together, and turned to the old man. "Ready, Harry? We're gonna go now. Kiss the ladies good-bye and we'll be on our way." He took the old man's arm and picked up his duffel, but, after a closer look at Harry, knew he wasn't going to go without a bit of argument. The five of them were well on their way.

"Nah, nah, I don't want to go home," said Harry, working his jaw as if false teeth were bothering him. "I've been invited to stay. All proper, you know. My lady friends, here, said they'd take care of me."

"Harry," laughed Charlie, "I'm sure these ladies would take better care of you than you deserve. But I won't be in for a few days and I promised Bonnie I'd take you back."

"A man of his age should be able to make his own decisions," said Mrs. Cross, a bit defiantly.

"A man his age SHOULDN'T make his own decisions," countered Charlie. "What are you ladies going to do with a drooling old blind man? This is too much. Come on, Harry. Girls, why don't you give him your address, or at least get his, and maybe you can call each other back in the States. Harry, your wife wouldn't mind, would she?"

"Hell, she ain't minded for years. Glad to get rid of me. Can't keep up with all my energy," he winked at one of the old ladies who let out a giggle. "Still works, you know. Still works." The girls were trying not to show their enjoyment of the old coot, putting their hands across their mouths to conceal their smiles. It was nice to meet a man of their vintage who still liked being a man and who still liked skirts. But Harry knew he didn't stand a chance and finally gave in, after exchanging names, addresses, and phone numbers with his golden-age girlies.

Pete stood in the background, taking in the whole scene with a chuckle. What a delightful relief they were after talking about Woody. Bad vibes. That's what Woody gives me, he thought. Bad vibes.

The three climbed into the Jeep and no one talked on the way to the airstrip.

"There's Woody's pilot," said Pete in a low voice to Charlie, nodding to Jock. "Came in yesterday. He was with Maxwell and that whole bunch, then I think they went to Smugglers last night. Nice picture, huh? Well, I'll leave you so I can be back for lunch. Be in touch, okay? And let me know if you hear anything."

Charlie helped Harry out of the Jeep and began preflighting the plane. As he was checking the fuel sumps, Jock strode over. Pete left, not wanting to get in the middle of the conversation.

"Hi," said Jock sheepishly. "You Charlie?"

"That's right," he said. "Anything I can do for you?"

"No, not now. Name's Jock," he said, extending, then withdrawing his hand. "I'll be flying in and out and just wanted to meet you. Maybe I can help you out sometime. You know, with extra passengers or whatever."

Charlie straightened up and looked Jock in the eye, bypassing his wrinkled clothes and unshaven face. "Do you have a license to carry passengers for hire? Because if you don't, there isn't any way you can help me out. I earn my living flying and hold all the certificates. What do you have?"

Jock shuffled his feet, a challenging grin on his face.

"I got a private license. Don't need anymore. People don't know the difference," he smiled, his expression phony.

"Well, Jock, let me tell you. I don't want to see you taking any of my passengers or soliciting business unless you have the ratings and certificates. I've gotta get going." He turned away from Jock, who was standing in dirty sneakers with no laces and wearing a shirt that looked slept in.

"Hey, Harry, step up here so we can be on our way." Charlie helped him in, then followed the old man into the plane. Before closing the door he turned around and emphasized what he had just said with a look to Jock. Bootlegger, he thought. A goddamn bootlegger.

57

* * *

Back at the club, Pete found some of the regulars sitting on the front porch drinking beer and talking. If he didn't sell it he couldn't control it, so what the hell. I've done my Sunday bit, he thought.

"Hi, Pete. Heard any more from that Woody guy? Man, he was mad when he found out his generator crank was missing." Captain Kilpatrick gave a gruff chuckle.

"Oh, yeah? That's one I haven't heard," said Pete. "What happened?"

"We were in Conch Inn last night when he called on the VHF and Maxwell went to Smugglers with the crank and his tail between his legs. Boy, that must have been some night. Saw them come back this morning. Heard the place is a real mess, but he's got all kinds of radios hooked up already. Looks like he's going into business."

"Question is what kind of business," said Pete sarcastically. "The crank was missing and Max had it, eh? Too much."

He chuckled, tugging on his beard. Max was always borrowing from one thing to fix another and it was common for him to get caught in his own merry-go-round chasing parts and tools around the islands. He hadn't changed. That's the same sort of thing that drove me up the wall, thought Pete. Now it's someone else's turn.

"Heard them on the radio at seven this morning, a bit hung over, but they switched to a channel we don't have," said Captain Kilpatrick. "That's kinda odd. Thought I had all the working channels, but I couldn't find them. Didn't really want to, though."

Pete shook his head and went into the club, still chuckling to himself over Max and Woody and the generator. Typical. Absolutely typical. Mrs. Cross and her party had settled into their cottage and were enjoying the sun. What a perfect day to go diving and fishing, thought Pete, trying to remember the last time he had taken the day off with his family. Summer was slipping by. To hell with it, he thought, picking up his key.

"You can sit here, but I've got other plans," said Pete. He

58

locked the screen door, scribbled a sign on the dinner menu blackboard outside the club and stood back to look at it. "Gone fishing. Back at 4." He smiled to himself, waved at the captain and walked to his Jeep, letting out a low whistle. Yep, a good fishing day, he thought.

As he headed for home, his son, now almost eleven, came racing over the hill on his bike.

"Hey, Johnny. Go tell your Mom we're going fishing. All of us. I closed the place up."

Johnny let out a yelp and did a wheely on his bike, turning around and beating his father up the steep hill to their home. It was a game to them. Whenever Johnny saw his Dad coming, he'd cut in front and race up the hill. He always won, of course.

"Mom! Mom!" he yelled, rushing through the front door. "Dad's taking us fishing! Let's go!"

Helen, a tall, pretty woman with short, curly dark hair, came out of the kitchen, wiping her hands on a towel, as Pete walked in the door. She was still in her church clothes.

"Is it true? Are you really taking us fishing? What about the club?"

"Screw it," said Pete, smiling, his blue eyes lighting up. "I haven't taken any time off, it's slow today and I'm entitled to a couple of hours. Let's get our suits and gear together, and get going. I'll ready the boat. Pack some sandwiches, and don't forget some lemonade or something. Can you handle that?"

"Sure. It just takes me by surprise. You need it, Honey. We all need it and I'm really glad. I'll be down in ten minutes, as soon as I get organized." Her oval face broke into a smile and she winked, dimples showing off hazel eyes.

Pete headed for the boat, realizing how lucky he was. Helen was an angel, as far as he was concerned. What woman would have put up with all the crap he'd dished out over the years? He thanked the good Lord every day that she'd stuck with him. In the early days, they had literally been isolated from the outside world. Only in the last couple of years, when Pete had learned to fly and Charlie started coming to the island, did they have contact with the States. Things were more tolerable now, knowing they could get a change of pace. Helen deserved a good fishing day. We all do, he thought.

* * *

The sea was calm and the boat made a wake that trailed to the horizon as Pete sped toward a favorite reef. It was good to take some time. Helen smiled and Johnny — tall, tan and skinny with a head of tousled blonde hair — was busy rigging the sling-type spears and fishing lines.

Soon Pete slowed down and began peering into the clear water. On the surface, it looked like a mirror reflecting the cloudless sky, but when he looked through a glass-bottom bucket, the underwater world came alive. Deep staghorn corals jutted toward the surface, surrounded by brown basket sponges and purple sea fans. A grouper lurked in a crevice, ready to disappear in the many-roomed mansion of the reef.

"Here we are. Pretty good, huh? Came right to it. Get the anchor, Johnny. Let's try our luck."

Johnny tossed the anchor overboard and followed it with his eye as it sank twenty feet to the bottom. He loved coming here with his Dad. He always got some fish.

"Here, Mom. You can use my pole. I'm going diving today, right, Dad? I've been practicing with the older kids."

"Let's both go diving today. You brought my mask and fins, right?"

"Over there, under the towels," said Johnny, adjusting his face mask and snorkel. "I'm going in first." He picked up his sling and jumped in. The water was just cool enough to take his breath for the first few seconds and warm enough to let him stay in for quite a while without getting chilled.

Pete followed, and the two swam along the surface, looking for fish and becoming part of the undersea world. Tiny blue and black blueheads swam past their faces, seemingly unaware of the human intrusion. A diver in the water became one with the reef. Another breed of fish in a sea of life, Pete thought. Despite the vastness of the sea, each coral reef, or head, was an entity of its own, totally interdependent upon all the life within it. Reefs were like individual cities on a great plain.

60

Johnny pointed to a yellowtail snapper and cocked his spear. As he let go, the fish scooted into the reef and poked its head out another hole only a foot away, turning to see what creature was after him. Johnny took a breath, felt his snorkel fill with water and dived down to retrieve his spear. Surfacing, he cleared his snorkel, face still in the water, and rigged the spear for another try. As he looked around, his Dad was swimming to the boat, a large grouper on his spear. Below, a starfish lay in the sandy bottom on the edge of a mound of coral, while a school of grunts darted in and out of coral passages, playing follow the leader. A stingray lay buried in the sand, only the eyes and tail visible, its giant wings outlined by sand ripples. Colorful parrotfish nibbled at the minute algae as Johnny looked for a larger fish.

Pete motioned to Johnny to follow him. It was time his son became a skilled hunter of the reef, to know the difference between the kill for food, and the importance of not disturbing nature's delicate systems. He had seen careless, greedy divers poison reefs for a few lobsters, with no thought of how the living things of the reef would survive.

He pointed to another big grouper and held Johnny back as he cocked his spear. Raising a finger, he motioned for him to take his time and concentrate. Johnny swam over the fish, lined up his spear and pulled the sling back as far as he could, his thin arm quivering. He held his breath as the fish swam further out of the hole, then he let the spear fly. He had him! He was so excited, he didn't even realize that water had seeped into his mask.

He took a breath, dove down, grabbed the spear, and surfaced with his prize. Pete was elated. The boy had terrific form. He'd be a good diver, a good fisherman.

The two swam back to the boat, content with their catch. On board, Helen was dangling a pole over the side. She really didn't care if she caught anything.

"What a beautiful fish, Johnny. Wow! Aren't you proud!" Even excited, she was soft-spoken.

Johnny dropped the sling and fish inside the boat, then climbed aboard ahead of his Dad.

"I think it's a good time to eat," said Helen. "You want a

sandwich? Here, have a soft drink, Johnny. You're beat after that dive. Did the fish fight?"

"No. Just lined him right up and let go. Got him on the first try," Johnny grinned, happy to show his Dad he could finally bring home dinner too. He wrapped himself in a towel, his wet hair matted together.

"That was a good shot. You took your time. That's what's important. You can't go at them like you're out to get them," said Pete, drying himself. "Sneak up and pretend you're another fish. You did great. Good lunch, Honey, especially with such short notice." He winked at Helen, who smiled back.

"I can move pretty fast when we're going to do something together. We should do this more often," she said.

After lunch, they sat, enjoying the sun and occasionally diving off the boat to cool off. This was the way to enjoy the tropics, thought Pete. Soak up the rays, dive to the underworld and catch a few fish for dinner.

"It's odd," said Pete, reminiscing. "This is what I came here for years ago. Funny how you get caught up in everything else. Time I did more of this. But as Charlie says, 'it's difficult to think your original purpose was to drain the swamp when you're ass deep in alligators,' he chuckled, and Johnny giggled. Even Helen could see the truth and humor.

The gentle rocking of the boat in the sun almost made them drowsy as the three relaxed. After a while, Pete looked at his watch.

"Well, it's almost 3:30," he said. "We should probably head back. Don't want to do too much of a good thing or we'll all get spoiled. Think you can get up the anchor, Johnny? It might be hooked on a rock on the reef."

Pete started the engine and Johnny worked the line, and eventually the anchor gave way. He pulled it aboard and within seconds, they were skimming over the water toward the club.

As they came closer, Pete slowed down. What the hell, he thought, eyeing the dock. Whose boat was that? He stared ahead, peering at a sleek ocean racer painted red with white stripes. It had been a while since one of those had come in. They guzzled too much fuel to be of much use in the islands, and people weren't usually in that big a hurry nor wanted the amount of punishment it gave its riders.

Pete eased the boat to the dinghy dock so that Helen and Johnny could climb up the ladder. At low tide, there was a difference of almost three feet.

"Who's that?" asked Helen, a little frown line showing on her forehead, as she looked at the sleek boat.

"I don't know, but I'm going to find out. Let me go ahead. Johnny, you put the anchor out, tie up and help your Mom. I better see to business."

"Okay, Dad."

Pete climbed the ladder and walked down the dock to where the speed boat had tied up. There were sophisticated radio antennae and the cockpit was almost completely enclosed to protect it from the salt spray. Two men, both deeply tanned with dark hair and muscular builds, were securing lines on a piling.

"What can we do for you today?" asked Pete. They were tough-looking men, both of them.

"Need some gas. Got any?" A gold medallion hung on a heavy chain around his neck, showing off a hairy chest.

"Sorry, pal, we're closed on Sunday. Be glad to help you tomorrow morning, but this is the dockmaster's day off and everyone sort of gears his schedule around it. Conch Inn might have some. Try there."

"Toss the line back, would you? Closed on Sunday. Who the hell out here even knows it's Sunday? Do you sell with prior arrangement?"

"Not on Sunday," smiled Pete, delighted to turn them down. "On Monday, fine. But not on Sunday."

As soon as the lines were aboard, they fired the boat up. The second man hadn't said one word and was rather aloof. The boat made a deafening roar as it sped to Conch Inn.

As Pete walked back toward the club, Helen and Johnny were walking past the front porch. They waved, and he fumbled for the keys in his pocket, unlocking the club door.

"See you later. Are we eating at the club tonight or at home?" she asked. "Maybe Maria would like this fish."

"No, Mom. That's just for us," said Johnny. He'd caught it

and he wanted to eat it.

"Okay. Let's have dinner at home, Pete, all right? We can come down later to talk with the guests. I'll fix Johnny's grouper."

"Sounds good. Oh, I almost forgot to tell you. When you hear who arrived today for the cottages, you'll be glad we're eating at home. Old Lady Cross and three of her ancient drinking buddies. Nice of Charlie to warn us, huh?"

"Oh, no. Remember the last time? She almost fell off the railing of her cottage into the drink!" Helen could remember the "Cross Watches" as the help called them. "You never know around here, do you?" she laughed softly. "Well, if you see her tell her hello for me. We better get going and clean these fish, Johnny."

As they walked past the cottages, she could see the four old girls sitting around a table, playing cards. Imagine, she thought, coming all this way to sit inside and play cards.

As soon as everyone realized that Pete was back, people began drifting into the club.

"You gonna open the bar now, or you gonna keep us doing this Sunday penance?" Captain Kilpatrick had followed Pete into the club, his gruff voice booming.

"Well, Captain Ned, the best to you on this lovely day. If you've properly talked to the Lord today, I guess we can crack open a can of beer for you," said Pete, knowing that the old man had probably not made it to church earlier in the day.

He picked up the wine bottle with its sign on the corner of the bar and put it on a shelf next to a painting of a schooner.

"Beer okay, or do you want something stronger? Where's Lucy? Haven't seen her around."

"On the mainland with the girls, thank God," a little smirk on his face to go with a twinkle in his eye. "You think I'd have the courage to come in here on a Sunday if she were on the island? Boy, she's been after me lately. An old man doesn't have any peace. Right?" He turned to a couple who had walked in behind him. They shrugged their shoulders, looking at each other as if trying to figure out why he was talking to them.

"Guess so, if you say so, Cap. Hey, Pete. You probably

don't remember us. Came through here a couple of years ago on the *Sea 'n' Be*," the young man said, perching on a stool.

"I remember you," said Pete smiling, eyeing the man's straight, blonde-streaked hair, clean-shaven face and greenish-gray eyes. "Had some engine trouble and we flew in some parts for you. Maxwell did the work, right?"

"Botched it up, you mean. When we got back the whole job had to be done again, but at least we could limp home. Terry's the name. This is Juney. We got married two months ago."

A slender girl with dark, wavy hair smiled back. She was wearing a one-piece black swimsuit cut away at the hips and down the front, below the waist. Pete took a little breath as he quickly eyed her. Looks like she hasn't taken off her honeymoon suit, he thought.

"I remember. Hi, Juney," he said, a little more composed. "You were part of the crew then, right?" She nodded.

"Yeah," said Terry. "Owner didn't want the boat anymore, I came into a little inheritance and bought the old girl. Nice boat. Real nice. Handles the sea like a tanker. Comfortable, too. Got a deep freeze, loran, a single sideband, washer and dryer, microwave ... all the goodies. We call her home now."

"Well, glad to have you aboard and congratulations on getting married. Stay as long as you like. This area's nice for cruising. Lot of nice folks up and down the island chain," said Pete.

"Thanks. We'll probably head south for awhile, but we'll be in and out."

The screen door opened and more people came in, ordering up drinks for happy hour. Wanda would be in any minute and then Pete could split. He didn't feel like getting caught up in the bar talk tonight. He could choke on some of the bullshit dished out, and he wanted to be with his family.

"Smugglers calling Sandy Cay Club. You there, Pete?"

He walked to the radio. Just what I need to hear, thought Pete.

"Yeah, Woody. I'm here. What can we do for you?"

"What's all this about no gas on Sunday? My friends weren't too happy. I told them to charge it. Said you wouldn't

65

pump anything today. Guess I better come talk to you."

"Everyone knows we don't pump gas on Sunday. It's no good to talk about it. What's the big hurry?"

"You wouldn't understand. Well, I'll be in to talk to you anyway, probably tomorrow. Smugglers clear."

"Yacht club clear." Pete shook his head as he came out of the tiny room. He didn't say anything, but inside he was boiling mad. He had heard about the type that comes in and tries to run your business, how they make it desirable for you to do things their way. But he wasn't going to be bought or bribed. Woody could whistle. Not this guy. No way. Not worth it, thought Pete.

Wanda walked in looking like she'd just stepped out of a cool shower, with her hair tied back and a pink hibiscus flower behind her ear. Pete commented on how nice she looked and gave her the keys to the cash box.

"Bye, everyone. See you later," he said with a wave, abruptly walking out the door and down the path to his Jeep. No way. Woody had better keep his shit on his own island, thought Pete. No way was he going to let an obnoxious little fat man with a limp push him around.

* * *

As Pete came to the top of the road that led to his house he could see the red speed boat flying in high gear toward Smugglers, leaving only a small wake as the bow reared up and engines churned like eggbeaters gone crazy.

He stopped before going into the house, watching the wake broaden out until it encompassed almost the entire harbor, gently rocking sailboats at anchor, ripples heading toward shore. He thought about all the history books he had read on the island realm, and flashed back to tales of the Spanish Main and its array of famous pirates. Today's breed wasn't much different, he thought. Only the design and speed of the boat. Time would tell, he thought, time would tell.

Chapter 4

The Legacy

The next day, Pete went about business as usual, checking the generators, making sure the ice machine was working, and listening to the banter around the bar. After some assurance that everything was running as it should, he took his favorite seat on the front porch, lit a cigarette, and propped his feet on the wood railing that had recently been treated for termites. He smiled to himself. Termites. Charlie always said if they ever stopped holding hands the place would fall down.

Behind him, the little storeroom hummed with the chatter of boats over the various radios.

Pete put his head back and reminisced how the radio room had begun as a little shack-like structure. When he had arrived at the island in his early twenties, he was like many of the adventurers who had visited over the years. His boat, an old schooner he had sunk his life savings into when he left the streets of Chicago, was in dire need of repair. Pete chuckled. He had arrived at the broken down dock needing fuel that was pumped from 55-gallon drums that arrived once a month via an inter-island freight boat from the main province.

Pete had fallen in love with the friendly people and when a job was offered to run the fuel stop, he figured why not? Months became years, visitors kept arriving and eventually, he accumulated enough in back pay to buy the little ramshackle beginnings of the club. It was rough going in those early years, with Pete living aboard his schooner, hauling fuel himself when the freighter broke down, and serving as chief Mr. Fixit of everything mechanical within miles.

Those early years were rough from another standpoint, he thought, and on this one he was in full sympathy with Maxwell. Only occasionally did a pretty single woman come to the island. The day Helen arrived on a friend's schooner was a day he would never forget. He fell in love instantly, and the boat stayed anchored for a few weeks as they got to know each other. Helen had gone back to the States, but after many weeks and letters, she returned, ready for island life on a permanent basis as his wife.

They were married in the island church, with friends and family arriving via freight boat to join the natives in celebrating the unusual ceremony. Pete shook his head a little, recalling Helen's difficult transition from city girl to "belonger" on the harsh island. It was a totally new beginning.

As the only white woman, Helen had become midwife and teacher, helper and counselor. She took on a number of roles simply because they needed filling. Johnny's arrival a few years later had made life complete for both of them, thought Pete.

They lived aboard their schooner in the early years as the club took shape. Gradually, a tiny structure was built, with the rough lean-to expanding to a kitchen, bar and small eating area. Pete thought how he rarely made any money the first few years but always made sure the help was paid. He smiled to himself.

With his own lack of formal education and his background as a truck driver, he was a curiosity to the natives, who didn't understand how he got to Sandy Cay or why he stayed. I wonder, too, sometimes, he smiled. Over the years, word spread of his little club and people found their way on yachts or the freight boat. Eventually, Pete built some tiny one-room, thatched roof frame cottages overlooking the water. He expanded as the need arose, but maintained the original character of the club. Over the years, nothing had changed but an occasional refurbishing of drapes, linens and furnishings. People still showered with brackish water and air-conditioning didn't exist. The club was like a magnet to cruising yachtsmen, and it became customary for those visiting to leave something behind. Over the years, the main clubroom was filled with memorabilia from all over the world — burgees, personal emblems, family crests, unusual pieces of driftwood, sketches of happenings, remembrances of good times. Royalty and escapees could sit at the bar together, sharing life tales in a manner not usual in most parts of the world.

"Hi, anyone home?" Helen tapped his head and Pete grabbed her hand.

"Hey, Honey, I was just recalling the good ol' days of this place. I think we're a little crazy," said Pete, shaking his head and lighting a cigarette.

"But you wouldn't have it any other way," she said, her soft voice complementing warm eyes and smile. "I'm going for my walk. I think Maria wants you for something in the kitchen. She was mumbling about being out of supplies."

"So what's new?" Pete asked, standing and tugging at his pants. Better tell Charlie to bring a belt, he thought. He pushed his cap back on his head and scratched behind his ear. "Always out of something," he said, waving to Helen as she left on her walk.

As Helen rounded the club complex and headed up the rocky, narrow road, she almost stumbled on Jackson who was lying across the path tinkering with the undersides of *Cyclops*.

"Hello, Jackson. This thing really doesn't like to run, does it?" she asked, peering at a puddle of water and the broken hose he was holding. "What's new, right?" She smiled.

"I tell you what's new," he said, sitting up. "Lots o' tings goin' on dat we wonder 'bout."

"Like what?" asked Helen, prodding quietly.

"Different tingums."

Helen laughed softly.

"Tons o' tingums goin' on I tink. Crazy Americans come and mon, I can't figure dem out. You fine out an' let me know, okay? Den we all be confused." He laughed and shook his head as he walked toward the club for a new hose.

Then he stopped and looked up. A small plane was coming in low, buzzing the club. He recognized it as the same plane that had brought Woody. Minutes later, Maxwell came tearing along the road in his open Jeep, swerving around *Cyclops*, ignoring Helen and Jackson, looking straight ahead. Helen shook her head. Crazy Maxwell. Bless the day of the famous upset, she sighed. Such a shame. Then they both heard the roar of a speedboat.

"What's THAT?" she asked Jackson, who was still standing on the path holding the hose, a little perplexed at the sudden flurry of activity. "Is that part of the different tingums,

Jackson?"

"Yes, mum," he said, not smiling. "Caused trouble on de dock yesterday cause we no sell dem gas. New man who bought Smugglers got mad. Wants ta change tings, he does, but dis island already seen too many changes. Maybe de boat has to do wid de plane, no? I be watchin' what go on. We all watch what go on. I tell yo' I had bad dream 'bout dese new people dat come. I wonder how to take dem, you know?"

He scratched his head, then rubbed his face with his hand as if massaging away pending trouble.

Helen didn't like Jackson's fear. It meant it would spread to the entire island. It could mean trouble for the easygoing natives. Like children, they would readily grab a lollipop put in their hands. She began to understand Jackson's tingum theory. The pulse was quickening on the island. Instead of the sleek and beautiful sailboat pace of six or seven knots, a speed the islanders could live with, the red boat signified speed. It would be good to talk with Pete about what had taken place.

She shook her head as if to get rid of her thoughts and spoke reassuringly to Jackson.

"We'll all have to watch what goes on," she said. "This is too pretty an island to have it spoiled by people who don't appreciate it."

"Yes, mum," he said, scratching his head again. "I better be back to me job wid dis hunk o' junk." The twinkle was back in his eye as he motioned to *Cyclops*. He headed toward the club and Helen picked her way along the road toward the ocean ridge.

* * *

Later that night, after guests had been served dinner and the Cross party made a big to-do about having the right kind of wine, Pete and Helen sat at the far corner table of the dining room, drinking coffee, recounting the events of the past two days.

"I don't want to jump to any conclusions right now," said Pete, cautiously, "but I think we should keep an eye on the situation. Don't let anyone know we're watching or that could

70

mean trouble too. Don't try to second guess them. Our best defense, if something IS going on, is to play dumb and stupid. In the meantime, I'll try to do some checking around on who the game players are — not that I'll be able to find out anything, but you never know."

Helen nodded, silently wondering what would happen. Pete sat quietly also, drawing on his cigarette, tapping the half-empty pack on the table. Then he looked around the club and stood up.

"Well, we might as well join the crowd for a while. We might be reading something into a situation that doesn't exist, too. I saw them loading some supplies and boxes aboard the speed boat before it headed to Smugglers, but I didn't see Woody aboard. Jock came back. You see him? What a contrast to Charlie," he chuckled. "Anyway, they're not on this island tonight so let's not worry about it."

As he followed Helen toward the bar, he figured it would be okay to spend some time and chat with the guests. She'd leave with him when she knew he'd had enough or when the crowd got boisterous. There were some new faces at the bar along with the regulars. The newlyweds were there and the old ladies had two games of checkers going in a corner of the barroom. They were dressed in cotton print frocks, and their gray heads bobbed back and forth as they leaned to make their moves.

Pete noticed that Mrs. Cross had been on better behavior, compared to previous visits, but it was only her second day on the island. Her friends seemed to be a little more refined in both their actions and drinking habits. Gin rummy and checkers were Mrs. Cross's favorites, and she liked to lure more youthful opponents to her games. There would be some good action at the tables over the next few days, he thought.

Pete went and sat in his usual chair next to the radio room within an arm's length of the bar and struck up a conversation with Terry, now in a comfortable tan shirt and brown Levis. His bride had a little more covering her body, but the strapless dress with the slit up the side was still suggestive.

"That's really great you were able to buy the *Sea 'n' Be*," said Pete. "Most young people today can't begin to afford to own, much less to cruise and maintain, a boat like that."

71

"Well, I sort of look at it as a business, too," Terry chuckled. "Long as it's paid for, I don't have to do too much."

"You thinking of chartering her, or what?" asked Pete.

"We thought about that. Woody Cameron — you know, the guy who bought Smugglers? Well, he told us to come here and he'd find plenty for us to do with the boat. I don't know how long we'll stick around or what he has in mind. We're just hanging loose, you know. Just hanging loose, right, Sweetie?"

He leaned over and nipped Juney's ear. Large gold hoops dangled from small lobes, contrasting her dark hair. She was deeply tanned, and as Terry talked, she snuggled up and gave him a hug.

Woody again, thought Pete. Why was everything Woody-oriented? The guy lands and two days later he's the great white hero.

Pete smiled at the two of them, gave Terry a pat on the back, and wished him luck.

The crew on the big motor yacht and sailboat were around the bar and a few others from some of the boats anchored out. The decibel level had been steadily rising with people enjoying themselves, and Wanda tuned in a native radio station for some tropical music.

It was nice, thought Pete. Here, those cruising on a tight budget could tell tales alongside those who cruised with no thought of expense. The contrast is what made the yacht club comfortable for anyone on a boat, big or little, sail or power. It didn't matter. This was a common watering hole, the oasis at the end of a long stretch of unpopulated islands and multi-blue sea.

The Woodies of the world could never penetrate the underlying importance of such a congenial place, thought Pete. Pick at it, yes, but penetrate, no.

* * *

While the yacht club catered to its clientele, Manny Smith was serving up drinks behind the bar at Conch Inn on the other end of the island.

He was a tall, good looking native with skin as dark as a

72

moonless night and eyes as bright as shooting stars. He was strong and muscular, and wore a white T-shirt with Conch Inn's shell logo across the front. His hair was short and he was always clean shaven. As proprietor and part owner, Manny had watched the inn and marina grow from mere barroom talk to a reality eight years ago.

Now, like the yacht club, it attracted yachtsmen and adventurers from all over the world. It was not uncommon for guests to start at one establishment and end up at the other, or to drift back and forth between them during the course of an evening.

But Manny had his regulars who generally stayed with him all evening just as the yacht club had its standard customers. Tonight, the crowd was solid regular. Howard and his girls, a couple who lived aboard their thirty-foot sloop, Maxwell and Pat and Jock, considered a newcomer, sat on one of the bar stools Manny had ordered especially for the inn, with large conch shell designs on padded vinyl seats.

Aside from this bit of decor, the place was fairly utilitarian — a square room with dining table on one side, photographs of some government officials sprinkled among snapshots of various partygoers and regulars of the inn and a few pieces of fishnet and driftwood art work. There was a small stage for the occasional band that arrived to play on the island when officials were visiting, or for holiday occasions, and a U-shaped bar that jutted out into the main room. The dining area was separated by a divider along half the room. The restroom was not up to high standards but no one seemed to care.

Nor did they care when Manny ran out of ice or water. One dry season for several weeks he couldn't offer a guest a glass of fresh water. But people made do. It gave them more to talk about when they returned home.

Manny went to the corner of the room where the little stage seemed scrunched under the low ceiling and switched on the stereo, dancing to the tropical beat as he went back behind the bar. He opened another beer for himself and smiled at Sharon, who was vying for a little attention from Howard.

Marjorie caught Manny's eye, raised her eyebrows

indicating "Well, there goes Howard again" and gave Manny a weak smile.

Howard was all show with his following, and she knew it. But the rest of the world would have interpreted his actions differently.

Manny leaned over the bar toward Marjorie, noticing a faint smell of perfume in her long, freshly washed hair. She had beautiful blue eyes, framed with green eye shadow and only a hint of liner and mascara. A snug red body shirt revealed all the right curves and indentations above white shorts.

"You want one on de house?" he asked, out of Howard's earshot, reaching into the cooler and still looking at her. "No ice, but we gots electric tonight. Cold beer?"

She nodded.

"Might as well, Manny. Everyone's off to a good start, wouldn't you say? Can I have a glass this time? Howard always forgets and I'm usually too thirsty to bother on the first one." He reached for a glass, gave it to her and watched as she poured the golden bubbles. He leaned over, elbows and arms on the bar.

"Slow tonight, ya know. Better when we have a band." Manny liked to rely on his smile more than his conversation, but that suited most people. Marjorie smiled back, tapping her fingers to the rhythmic beat of the music. It was loud.

"Wanna dance?" he asked.

"Sure," she said, still smiling as she slid off the stool, moving her whole body to the music.

Manny came from behind the bar and took her in his arms, smiling into her soft eyes and gently hugging her waist. He pushed her away, then brought her closer, as they moved to the music. Manny never made any bones about it. He loved dancing with white women and took advantage of the situation whenever possible. As he held her a little closer, he could see Howard and Sharon moving toward the dance area.

He glanced down as Marjorie's breasts pressed against his chest, and he moved his hand lower on her hips, gently squeezing her as the beat seemed to get louder. Some woman, this Marjorie. One of the best, he thought. Her hair brushed his cheek and she raised her arm, sliding it around the back of his neck with encouraging fingers.

"Here comes Howard," she whispered. "We better switch partners." With a gentle push, she swung around to face Howard, then gently nudged Sharon out as his partner. Sharon, wearing a loose shift tied at the shoulders, shrugged and turned just as Manny caught her waist, no one missing a beat in the partner exchange.

"Hey, Manny, you do some quick steppin', mon. Dis de wife, you know," Howard mimicked the native talk, a medallion glistening on his light green V-neck.

Manny kept smiling, moving Sharon a few steps away. He'd tangled with Howard a couple times before over Marjorie, and he didn't want him to think there was anything going on. But he kept glancing at her, catching the quick muscular movement of her thighs in the tight white shorts. She never wore anything on her feet but thin leather strap sandals, which gave the impression she was barefoot. She looks even better than usual tonight, thought Manny. Sweet Mama, oh sweet Mama she was.

The music stopped and Manny quickly ducked under the opening of the bar to serve more guests. It was hard to get help these days. With generator problems, not many room guests, a water shortage and his wife on the mainland visiting relatives, the revenue hadn't been pouring in lately, or at least it didn't seem to like in years past. Always something breaking or running out — beer, electricity or tourists — the result was the same. But the bar usually did well. And so did Manny, right along with them. He liked to party and everyone knew it. He opened a couple more beers and put them on the bar.

"How do you expect to make a profit by giving those away?" asked Maxwell dryly, sitting on a stool near the door. "I keep telling you and you don't listen. You don't give anything away free. Nothing. You give anything free and you'll be a poor man before you know it. You don't see me giving anything away free, do you? That's why I got money in the bank. Right, Pat?"

"Right!" she said, rather loudly, swaying slightly on her stool, a loose tan blouse tied at the waist over khaki shorts giving the impression she had nothing on, top and bottom blending with her tanned body and light brown hair. "Whatever you say, Max."

"Ooowee. Are we off to de races," said Manny. Pat's eyes were dilated and she had had more than just a few beers. Maxwell gave her a stern look and Pat took another sip.

"Let's dance," he said, taking her arm and guiding her off the stool. As they moved out of earshot, Maxwell growled at her.

"What the hell are you doing? What do you think you're doing?" he repeated, wanting to shake her.

Pat just laughed and leaned back.

"Having a GREAT TIME, Max, a GREAT TIME. How about you?"

He grabbed her and held her close.

"Calm down, would you? Ride it out slow and easy or Max might not take care of you. Got the picture, my little bird?" His grip was tight on her arm.

"Got it," she said, jerkily moving to the music and giving Max a big smile. "Got it, mon," she said mockingly, twirling around. Max caught her as she went off balance.

"Sit down," he said, angrily realizing she wasn't listening. "You want some chips?"

"No. Need another beer, though. I'll be good. Promise," she smiled, sitting down. "I'll be good to Maxwell."

He went behind the bar and got a bag of chips. Probably stale, he thought, but Pat wouldn't know the difference. He reached in the cooler, held up the beer to show Manny, and walked back to the table where Pat was sitting, head in her hand, propped up by a swaying elbow, watching people gyrate to the pulsing beat.

Howard and Marjorie were still together and Jock was sitting by himself, taking in the action.

Nel was hustling some yacht captain at the pool table and hadn't said much to Jock all night. Even though Jock had left, and come back to the island, he didn't look much different from the first day anyone had seen him. Pat focused her eyes, moving her head to the music. She noticed that Jock had put laces in his shoes.

The music stopped, and everyone drifted back to the bar for refills. Howard glanced at Maxwell and tipped his head in the direction of the door, then caught Jock's eye and made the same motion. The music began again and the three walked out, telling the women they'd be back.

Secret conference again, thought Pat, and she walked over to Marjorie.

"Those guys sure do have a lot to talk about lately. What's going on?"

"You know Howard. Wouldn't tell you if he knew lightning would strike you dead at a given moment. Must be business of some sort. Said earlier he was glad that Jock's a pilot. He also met that Woody character. You know Howard. If there's money anywhere he smells it and starts his deals. The best one, though, just took place. I can't say anything about it, but I'm really excited. He'll probably tell everyone tomorrow."

"Oh, come on. You can tell me," said Pat with a whine, holding onto the edge of the bar.

"Like the last time I gave you a tidbit, huh? No, really, Pat, I can't say anything about it now. Trust, okay? As soon as I can, I'll tell you."

"Tell you what?" asked Sharon, barely catching the conversation.

"Nothing," said Marjorie, acting as if Pat's state of mind was what it was all about. "Nothing. Just passing time while those dummies out there are planning their strategy or whatever. Want another beer, Sharon?" She looked over to the other end of the bar, raising her arm slightly. "Hey, Manny, how about a couple more for your favorite girls?"

He caught her eye, gave a big smile and pulled three beers out of the cooler, then walked slowly over to the other side of the bar, swaying to a slower melody.

"Pat doesn't need another," said Marjorie, pushing one back. "Save it," she said, lighting up a cigarette and giving him a long stare with a steady smile. "I might need another before too long."

More boat people walked in and Manny figured it was time to make a rum punch. He had a special blend of light and dark Jamaican rums, pineapple juice, coconut rum and a variety of fruit juices that always went over great. If the blender worked he was in business. One of the natives ducked under the bar.

"Hey, Manny. Help you fo' a couple o' drinks?"

"Sure, mon. Okay."

It often worked that way. Play the music loud and the people came from all over. Those already bedded down on a gently rocking boat often threw on some clothes to join the crowd, many holding out until the late hours before coming in for a nightcap with the crowd. No one had work schedules to make and morning was always in the distant future.

The beat's so sweet, thought Manny, snapping his fingers. Beat's so sweet. The blender whirled and he smiled, moving his feet to the rhythm. Beat's so sweet.

* * *

About an hour later, with the bar still going strong, Marjorie, Pat and Sharon were ready to go. The men hadn't returned, so Marjorie talked the girls into coming aboard the *Michelle* for a nightcap and a little peace and quiet.

A few native teenagers were standing around smoking and trying to be part of the bar crowd, but on the whole, things were pretty quiet outside.

Pat had simmered down, but the effect of an earlier high had made her quieter than usual. Sharon, too, wasn't saying much. She'd danced with a few of the natives and boaters, but had begun to get bored. She was happy to leave. Nel had latched on to the captain.

"What time is it, anyway?" asked Marjorie.

"About 11:30 the last I looked," said Sharon. "The guys left about ten as I recall. Boy, is it dark. Don't go so fast."

"I forget you haven't been here as long as we have," said Marjorie. "I've navigated this walk in the weirdest conditions. It's like second nature now."

"Just don't walk straight and you're safe," said Pat, weaving naturally. "Manny always said he was going to cut a path from the bar to the dock but he never got around to it."

They had walked out of the bar, turned toward the little church, then back down another path that led behind the bar toward the docks. Manny had two buildings with a few modest hotel rooms, and the entrance to the dock led right between them.

With a shortage of tourists on the island and generator problems, no one was staying in the rooms. The place was pitch black, with the tree branches rustling in the slight breeze. Only a few lights aboard boats tied to the dock gave an indication of where everything was, reflections dancing on the water and outlining the docks and pilings.

As the girls walked between the buildings, they could see a group of men in a small boat tied alongside the *Michelle*.

"Jeez," said Marjorie. "You see what I see? It's that fast little red boat that's been running between Smugglers and Conch Inn. I hope Howard doesn't mind us coming out, but he can't expect us to sit in that place all night. Come on. Let's join the party."

"I don't know, they sure look pretty serious," said Pat cautiously. Maxwell never liked her interfering in what he did. His attitude was one of "you take care of me, and I'll take care of you but don't ask me any questions."

As the women neared the boat, the men noticed them coming and broke up their conversation.

"Hi, Marjorie," said Howard. "Just finishing up here. What's going on at the bar? Anything?"

"No, just the usual BS," she said. "Looks like we've got company."

"Woody's friends just wanted to come and talk about some of his plans for the island. He's got some good ideas," he said. "Hey, how about everyone coming aboard the *Michelle* for a drink?" He turned to include the men in the red boat.

"Thanks, but we'll get going," said the husky dark-haired man. His companion was already revving up the engines as Max and Jock stepped off.

"You feeling any better?" Max asked Pat, almost as a challenge.

"Yeah, I'm all right. Just tired," she said. "What's going on?"

"Don't ask any questions, okay? We don't need any silly

79

broad screwing us up. Not that you're a silly broad." He attempted a smile, but only his lips moved.

"Okay, Max. I didn't mean for you to go into detail. Let's go home, huh? I'm really tired. Overdid a little bit earlier tonight."

"I know. You embarrassed me. I'm not going to get any more for you if you can't handle it. Too small an island. I don't want people talking about my woman."

"Okay," she said, a bit meekly.

"Come on," said Max. "Howard, I'll get with you in the morning. Jock — where you staying?" He pointed to the *Michelle*. "Okay. See you. Good night."

The path disappeared into the bush as Max and Pat left the dock, the moonless night enveloping the world in black.

"Let me get a light from Howard. This is ridiculous," said Max. "Stay put. I'll be right back." Max went back to the boat and Pat stood as if cemented to the path. She held her hand in front of her and couldn't see it. It was an eerie feeling, the gentle breeze rustling the bush, punctuating an imagined fear. In a minute, Max was back, swinging a flashlight as he walked, revealing the small path framed with conch shells.

As they walked past Conch Inn, Max waved good night.

"Manny's off and running," he said in a rather low voice. "He's been getting pissed a lot lately. Should mind that place better."

"Oh hell," said Pat. "He's just having his fun. He's gotta keep up his traditions, as he says. He's doing what he's always done."

"Yeah, but the place is going downhill. No one in the rooms, him giving away beers, but he's beginning to listen to me. I'll show him how to make a buck. Squeeze it out of the tourists. If they get this far they should have money. If they don't, they can wire for it. The tourists and yachtsmen should pay."

"Old Max the Miser, right?" she said in humor, but Max took offense.

"Look. It's okay if my customers call me that but not my wife."

Deep down, Pat had mixed feelings about Max, but he was a good provider. She liked the island way of life and felt that things would get better as time went on. Max had been a long time without a steady girl and marriage to her was what everyone said he needed. Pat was over qualified on the marriage game, a product of a father and four stepfathers. Her mother had told her to go ahead — nothing was forever. She had agreed to marry Max, truly believing that she loved him, never having experienced the type of love a solid family created.

The flashlight bounced off the path and a hermit crab scooted off into the bushes, lugging its awkward top shell. A rustle in the bushes gave away a lizard or a mouse. Max and Pat's footsteps ground loose sand into the pitted road surface. Normally, Max drove the rusting Jeep, but tonight they had walked into the village. It was only about a half-mile and if a breeze was blowing, the heat wasn't too oppressive. By nightfall, it had gotten cooler and now at almost midnight, Pat felt the bumps rise on her skin, although it was still oppressively humid. She shuddered a little, then yawned.

In a few minutes they were past the Sandy Cay Club and heading up the rocky path to the little bungalow overlooking the water.

In the blackness, Max went ahead of her and lit the kerosene lamp. In minutes, Pat was stripped and in bed. Max took a drink from the fresh water jug and followed. He liked when she shed her clothes and climbed into bed and he did the same. Beyond the screened porch and past the wild bush growth, he could hear the water lapping the shore. Pat was almost asleep when he reached to touch her, and she responded willingly and completely.

* * *

About midnight, Pete and Helen were sitting on their front porch talking, sipping coffee and enjoying the blackness in front of them. Usually, the stars formed a halo in the sky and the moon lit the endless ripples on the sea. But tonight was unusual, and they enjoyed it for what it was. Suddenly, they were jarred from their solitude by the roar of engines.

"Christ! What's this place coming to?" said Pete, trying to

peer into the darkness. "You hear that, Helen? It's that goddamn red boat. I can't see it, but I'm sure that's what it is. Sounds like it's coming from Conch Inn. Doesn't even have its running lights on. Pretty expensive taxi."

Helen sat quietly, listening to the engines pierce the stillness of the night as it sped toward Smugglers.

"Maybe you ought to go there tomorrow, don't you think?" she asked.

"Me? Go THERE? You gotta be kidding. No way, Helen, not this boy. They come to me I'll talk with them but I'll be damned to go after them and find out what's going on. They'll tell me, in no uncertain terms, that it's none of my business and you know something? They're right. One hundred percent. None of my business. And that's the way I want it. Come on, kid. Let's go to bed and forget all this nonsense. You know, I really resent that boat intruding into my silence. Aggravating. Come on. Let's go inside."

The two went in, Pete locking the door behind them. The air-conditioning was on and the little house was pleasantly cool. It had been comfortable outside, but a little muggy. The air-conditioning took away the clamminess.

Long after Helen was asleep, Pete was still thinking about the events of the past few days. He usually fell asleep as his head hit the pillow, but not tonight. An hour passed before he drifted off, his dreams mixed with the confusion intruding into his life.

Chapter 5

Ospreys and Other Birds

The next morning, after Jock and Sharon took off for the mainland, an airplane arrived with a pouch of documents for Howard. It was now official. He had bought the ridge house, aptly named Osprey Nest, and all the papers were in order.

Howard had been waiting for this day for three months.

It represented a missing link and he was anxious to get settled, to make his new position on the island known. As a landowner, his status changed from cruising yachtsman to belonger. Marjorie was thrilled. She'd been aboard long enough and was now longing for a bed that didn't rock with the changing tides, a kitchen instead of a galley and a bathroom instead of a head.

"When can we move up there?" she asked Howard excitedly as she glanced over the plans. They had poked around the house and had looked inside and knew it would be a fun place to live. Now she wanted to turn the key, walk in and settle down — at least for a while.

"I'd say we can start today, if you like. We'll get Max's wheels and Manny's Jeep and get some of the native kids to help with all our shit. You know what this house means, Honey? It's money in our pockets. And the view! Just what I need to see what's going on."

"I was thinking more of scenery for the sake of lovely scenery," she said. "You know — beaches and salt ponds and the chain of islands stretching in both directions, the boats at anchor and the little winding roads all over the island. I can't wait. I'm going to wake up every morning and enjoy that 360 degree view. It's gotta be beautiful."

She began gathering some things, mentally noting what she'd need from the mainland. Only the bare essentials were on the *Michelle*, even though they had been aboard for long periods of time. The *Michelle* was still a moving vessel, not completely home to Marjorie, and she longed to get her feet on solid floors, with windows instead of portholes and doors instead of hatches. As she tossed some boxes on deck, she looked up and saw Manny peering down into the boat.

"Hey, mon, we hear de good news. Want me ta load up dem tings and help gits you started? You be like residents now, not boat bums, eh?" he laughed as he picked up a couple of boxes and a duffel Marjorie had hurriedly stuffed with linens and towels.

"No matter what, Manny, a woman always appreciates a good house. I'll be sleeping there tonight, you can be sure." She went on packing, Howard having gone to the communications center to make a phone call.

Funny, she thought. He usually used the radio, not relying on the local system. Oh well. Better to be bothered with what to take on the first load. A house, she thought. An honest-to-goodness house with walls and floors, not bulkheads and overheads. A real house with a fantastic view.

"Come on, Lady. You takes all de day? We pick up Howard as we goes by."

Within minutes Manny was driving Howard and Marjorie to Osprey Nest.

They took the shortest way, past the church, toward the airstrip, down the runway and across the other side. Then, Manny put the Jeep into four-wheel drive for the steep climb to the top of the ridge. Marjorie hung on. She'd walked this many times, her calves aching each time from straining the muscles down the back of her legs. It wasn't much easier in the Jeep as she struggled to maintain an upright position on the incline. Once on the ridge, Manny again shifted into higher gear, and it was then only a short ride to the house. Altogether, it was little less than a mile from either the yacht club or Conch Inn, depending on the road taken. As Manny rounded the last little turn on the dirt path skirting the top of the ridge, he pulled up in front of the house. Marjorie had seen pictures of osprey nests and the place was well named.

It was octagonal, with picture windows and glass doors giving it the appearance of a gigantic beast's home atop the highest point on the island. The rough-sawn cedar gave it a rustic look, and Marjorie began losing patience as Howard fumbled with the key.

As they walked inside, a little bathroom was off to the left of the entrance, the kitchen to the right. Wherever she stood, with the exception of the bathroom, she could see for miles in all directions. Salt spray had dimmed the windows, but a little cleanup would take care of that, she thought.

The living room took advantage of the view with a center seating arrangement that fanned out, with convertible sofas for guests. A railed porch circled the building on six sides, with the roof overhang providing protection from rain. To one side of the small living area, steps led to the upper level.

Marjorie stood in the middle of the room, looking in every direction. It was incredible. There wasn't a closet in the house, but the view made up for it.

A real bachelor pad, she thought. But, what could they expect? It was built by a bachelor for only one thing. Well, she smiled to herself, you needn't be a bachelor to enjoy this place.

"Hey, Howard," she called down. "You see this room up here? Guy who built it knew what he was doing. It REALLY turns you on."

Howard climbed the steep steps, ducking his head at the top where the roofline didn't expect anyone so tall.

"Fantastic," he said, looking all around. "I'm going to put a telescope right here," he indicated, pacing to the center of the room.

He could see the entire airstrip, the length of beach on the deep ocean side of the island, the tops of islands beyond Sandy Cay. Once the scope was in place he'd even be able to see Smugglers. Perfect, he thought. Worth every cent.

"Just don't spoil this room with a whole bunch of crap," said Marjorie. "I like the uncluttered lines. A telescope's okay, though. Think we can spy on the houses on the other end of the island? Anyway, thanks, Honey. I'm happy with it. I really need to get on dry land for a while."

She walked over, put her arms around Howard, and he held her close for a few seconds before kissing her on the forehead. He was shirtless, wearing only shorts, and with the humid heat, left a damp impression on Marjorie's white knit shirt.

"Hey, mon. What's goin' on up dere? You kiss de lady and I maybe not sees you fo' awhile. You come down, mon. Lots o' work to gets your tings over dat ridge. Come on," said Manny. "I gots udder tings to do. Run de place, you know. Nuttin' much, but I don't hab de time to watch you hanky panky all de day."

"You're right, Manny. Look out below. We're coming down. Boy, this is steep. Watch yourself, Marge old girl, or you'll come tumbling down on top of me. Don't want that kind of scene at the bottom of the stairs."

"You don't mind anywhere else," she said slyly, out of Manny's hearing range. Howard smiled and pointed a finger.

"Later," he said, patting her butt after she was down the ladder. He turned toward the door.

"Okay, Manny. Let's go."

Soon they were careening down the ridge, straining in four-wheel drive, off to the *Michelle* for another load of gear.

"Hot day," shouted Howard. "When's it going to start cooling off? By ten in the morning you're fried."

"Oh, couple o' mont's more and it should cools off a bit," said Manny, knowing that it was more like four months before the northers would begin and the island would get relief.

They were back at Conch Inn in no time, and Marjorie disappeared below decks to gather more clothing and odds and ends. She made sure to put in a pitcher, a jug of fresh water, and a packet of lemonade for the next trip over.

* * *

At the yacht club that morning, Pete saw the red boat heading toward the dock with Woody at the controls. He ignored him, walked into the radio room to turn on the communication network and went about his routine. A little later as he was reaching into the cooler for a pineapple juice, Woody walked in. Pete mustered up a big, toothy smile and looked at him, now tanned, but with skin peeling on his shoulders, nose and the top of his head.

"Hey, mon, looks like you're doing better than any of us

expected. Got the place in shape yet?" Pete still smiled, pulling on his jeans with his thumbs.

"No problem. No problem. Just gotta get in there and do all that shit. We'll have an opening celebration in no time," Woody bragged. "You got any coffee this morning? Could sure go for some. It's on the grocery list on the way back to the mainland now."

"Sure. How you like it? Black? Me too. Hold on a sec and I'll be right back."

Pete went to the kitchen. The coffee was ready and Maria and the girls were fixing breakfast for the guests, singing to the gospel music on the radio and hardly noticing Pete. Wonder what he wants from me, thought Pete on his way back to the bar area, two mugs spilling a bit as he walked.

"Thanks," said Woody, in a more normal voice than the loud pitch he had been using.

"Pete," he said, seriously, looking intently at his graying beard, thinning hair and piercing blue eyes. "This thing on Sunday really ticked me off, you know. I understand you got your policies and all, but it wouldn't hurt to give a little. I'm willing to pay double on Sunday if we need fuel. It can be quiet and no one has to know about it. Can we make a deal?"

Pete lit a cigarette, pulled on his beard and took his time answering. A crease came to his forehead and when he finally spoke, it was in a confidential tone of voice.

"I'd really like to help you out, even at the regular price, but you haven't been down here long. Ever hear the saying about the drums beating? Well, let me tell you. Nothing happens on this island without the natives knowing about it. Don't ask me how or why, but I think all their superstitions about these little haunted urchins are true. Nothing goes on without them knowing. But they'll never tell you they know. It's just assumed that you know they know, so there are really no secrets.

"We close on Sunday for them, not for us. You think I LIKE losing money? Hell no. But the reason we're here as long as we are is because we respect their traditions. And one of them is no work on Sunday. No way, Woody. I can't do it at any price. I'd be selling my soul for sure."

"Why does Manny sell on Sunday? He especially shouldn't, then, being a native," said Woody accusingly.

Pete took his time answering, pulling on his beard, the forehead crease deepening. He didn't want to say too much to this little loudmouth, but felt he should at least give him some friendly advice gleaned over the years.

"I can't answer for him," he said, avoiding the issue. "If Manny wants to sell on Sunday, that's his business. He has to live with his people. But remember, he's one of them." He drew on the cigarette and tapped the ashes into a used plastic glass, the ashes hissing as they hit the stale liquid from the night before. "You know, Woody, it's all well and good to spread the bucks down here, but one thing is basic. You're white, mon. Understand? Don't ever forget it and you'll get along fine. It's their island, their country, their ways. Twenty some years hasn't made a bit of difference, except in my feelings. I used to fight it, but now know it's the only way for their system to work. The less I rock their boat, the better it is for everyone. That's why I won't sell gas on Sunday. I would destroy the trust."

"Man, you sure are a sensitive old bastard. You supply their livelihood and then let them walk all over you. Where'd they be without this place? I wouldn't let them get away with it myself. No way," he said, the loud voice beginning its characteristic tone. "Guess I'll have to talk with Manny and make some sort of arrangement with him. Just thought you'd want the business."

"I do, don't get me wrong," said Pete, still talking quietly. "Any other day of the week. Why not come in late Saturday or early Monday? What's the big deal on Sunday?"

"Sunday's when we're going to need it," said Woody, emphatically. "Can't explain. But we're gonna need fuel on Sunday. Well, thanks for the coffee, old man. Don't get upset with me. Still want to live with you down here and all that shit."

"No problem," said Pete, reaching out his hand. Woody took it, gave a short shake and left, limping down the dock to the red boat.

He started the engine and headed to Conch Inn.

Pete sat thinking, then noticed the Cross party coming from their cottages. The ladies had on Bermuda shorts, floppy hats and cotton blouses. A tinge of pink showed on their legs and they wore white tennis shoes. Pete chuckled, then walked out to greet them.

"Good morning, ladies. My, you sure look sporty today." They giggled, Mrs. Cross hiding behind sunglasses soothing two red eyes from the night before.

"We were wondering, Pete. Do you think you could find time to take us fishing today? We can't possibly go ourselves, and we told everyone back home we were going to fish," explained Mrs. Cross, slightly bent over by the weight of her handbag and what appeared to be a heavy head. "Not long. Maybe an hour or so."

Pete thought. He had to fly to the main province for supplies and wanted to make a few phone calls back to the mainland while there.

"If you hurry, right after breakfast, we can go. I have some yellowtails all staked out for you, okay? But it can't be for long. I'm due on the main province by noon."

"We'll hurry. I'm sure Maria's got breakfast ready for us."

With that, the four walked rather slowly into the dining room. Pete headed back to his house for the list he had made the night before. Taking the ladies fishing wouldn't interrupt his plans. An hour in the sun and they'd be baked for the day. As he was about to turn into his drive, Jackson flagged him down on *Cyclops*. Pete stopped and waited for him. He was dressed in the usual navy T-shirt and jeans. Jackson looked serious.

"Heard de news 'bout de ridge house?" he asked, leaning on the Jeep. Pete shook his head, no. "Papers just delibered to Howard. Word is he boughts it. What you tink?" His eyes were questioning, and the happy smile was gone from Jackson's face. Instead, his forehead was creased, his usual quick steps deliberate.

"You're sure?" Pete asked. "You know how rumors get going."

"I'm sure, mon. Dey already gettin' dere tings togeder and Manny's loading de Jeep. Dey wastin' no time, mon. Movin' right in. Oh well. You goin' flyin' today?"

Pete nodded. "After I take the old ladies fishing. That

shouldn't take long. I'll just throw some warm beer in the cooler and forget the ice. We'll be back in ten minutes." He chuckled, knowing he'd never get away with it. Mrs. Cross always made sure of her supply.

"Some boats comin' in today. Called on de radio late yesterday from couple islands away. We could use a busy day, eh?" Jackson smiled now, more his old self.

"Woody was in this morning complaining about Sunday, but I stood my ground," said Pete. "I don't want anyone pushing me around. Been in this business too long to compromise. Be sure to check the generator. It was pulsating a few minutes ago. Also, the watermaker may need another filter."

"Okay. I check it all outs. Neber you mind."

Jackson climbed back aboard *Cyclops* and eased the groaning engine into gear. Pete headed up the steep incline to his home. He had a tight schedule today, but nothing he couldn't handle.

Helen had gone on her usual morning stroll to the ocean side of the island and Johnny was in the village playing with friends.

The ridge house, pondered Pete, walking into his living room. Interesting. He wondered why Howard would want it. The house was completely isolated, hard to walk to, difficult to supply and away from other homes on the island. It had been Barney's dream home. His little escape. The pinch on finances must have been greater than anyone thought. What a shame. Barney'd miss the place, thought Pete, even though he'd only lived in it a few months. Sold his airplane and now his house. And to Howard.

Didn't make sense, he thought, although it wouldn't make sense for anyone to buy it. Except someone like Barney. And Howard sure wasn't a Barney. For all outward appearances of the house, Barney was quiet, soft-spoken, didn't drink or smoke and was totally unpretentious. Which is why he probably left the island, mused Pete. Barney had looked at the balance sheet and quietly left, but no one thought it would be forever. He'd spent fifteen years on the island and would return. It was just a question of when. But now, with the house sold.... Pete shook his head, then picked up his list, shelving thoughts about

Howard and the ridge house. Better get going and get old lady Cross and her cronies fishing.

They were ready to go when he arrived at the club, sitting with poles, a cooler and a bucket of conch for bait.

"Okay, ladies. Let's go. Got everything?"

They followed him to his boat, carefully watching each step on the dock. The tide was out, but with less effort than he anticipated, the old girls were aboard, cold beers passed around, and they were off. Pete made a mental note to come in soon. Their skin was too pink to chance bad burns. That's all he would need. He sped out to a reef within sight of the club and dropped the anchor. Mrs. Cross was in her glory.

"Now, Mary, see this? You cut a hunk of meat off, then throw the foot away," she said, carefully cutting up a conch to bait their hooks. Pete just sat, letting her entertain him. Mrs. Cross liked to direct the fishing expedition and usually managed to bring in enough catch for their lunch. It wasn't difficult, really. The fish were plentiful and if there was even a suggestion of bait overboard, they'd usually bite. Pete grabbed his glass bottom bucket and peered overboard.

"Lots of fish down there ladies...grouper, yellowtail, margate, barracuda...."

"Barracuda! How big?" asked Mary, hesitantly.

"Oh, don't mind them," said Mrs. Cross. "Never bothered my fishing before." With that, she cast her line out and began reeling in. As she turned to take a sip from her beer, she had a strike. It caught her off balance, and before anyone realized what was happening, she was overboard, hanging on to her pole for dear life, beer sinking to the bottom, and her screaming for all she was worth.

"Help!" she yelled, coming up for air, straw hat floating away, gray hair matted to her head, glasses hanging onto one ear and both hands on the pole.

"Let go of the pole and swim, for God's sake," yelled Pete, stripping off his shirt and jumping in after her.

"I don't want to lose one that big," she yelled back, gulping water and still bobbing. Her cotton blouse floated to the surface filled with air bubbles revealing a worn bra and white skin. She was treading water, arms flopping, and refused to let go of the pole, the fish still tugging out line. Her glasses had fallen off and she was squinting with the bright sun and water.

"Let go, you crazy fool," yelled Pete, struggling to pull her back to the boat, her friends shouting orders and squealing exclamations.

"Get the ladder and hook it over the side," Pete ordered. Old lady Cross finally let go of the pole, but was thrashing about to stay afloat, dunking Pete several times in the process. In what seemed like an eternity, Mary produced the ladder.

"Now, carefully fit it into those two holes in the brackets right above us. Okay. That's good. Now, Mrs. Cross, PLEASE, Mrs. Cross. You want to drown me? Here, hold onto the ladder and we'll get you back up. Ladies!" He shouted, sinking with the weight of Mrs. Cross, trying to get her foot on the first rung of the ladder. "For Christ sake, get to the other side of the boat or you'll flip the whole fucking thing over!"

"Oh dearie me," said one of them as she stepped to the other side. "Oh dearie me." She took a slug of beer and watched, as Mrs. Cross flopped over the side, totally drenched, complaining about her glasses, clothes clinging to her sagging figure. Pete rested a few minutes holding onto the ladder, then asked for his mask and fins to retrieve the fishing pole and glasses. He dived down and brought up the pole. The line was slack and whatever had been at the end was long gone. He held it up for the ladies to grab and began looking for the glasses.

After a few dives, he found them, partially buried in the sand next to a basket sponge. He picked them up and climbed aboard, the ladies cheering his find.

"I like your style, old girl," he said dryly to Mrs. Cross, now shivering and without a towel. "You pull that stunt often?" She was rather pathetic, and Pete realized what a shock the incident must have been. He began to smile and within seconds, all five were giggling, including Mrs. Cross.

"It would have been better to catch it," she said, emphatically. "Now, who's going to believe me? My hat! Where's my hat?" She grabbed her head. They scanned the water, but it was nowhere to be seen.

"Well, you can kiss the hat good-bye. As to the fish, well, you're not supposed to drink and fish. Didn't you hear? Against native law," Pete chuckled. "Now, you want me to help you or can you do it?"

She reached for another hook, some conch, and baited the line. The hot sun calmed her shivers and she began to dry. The rest of the fishing trip was uneventful. Pete watched the ladies catch a couple of grouper and some snapper and when they had enough for their lunch, said, "Time to go. Haul in your lines, ladies." He started the motor, pulled up the anchor, and within a few minutes, they were back at the club, the ladies recounting their adventure about the big one that got away and the big one that went into the drink.

Made their day, thought Pete. Mine too, he chuckled. Jackson was laughing so hard he had tears in his eyes as they talked. Mrs. Cross in the water. Too much.

"Hey, Jackson, I'm on my way. Have to change clothes first. Didn't expect to go swimming, you know. I'll be back about four." As he walked toward the door, he remembered to grab his list from behind the bar.

"Okay, mon. Maybe we hab more news for you when you return, eh? All we needs is more news dese days, huh?" He was still laughing over Mrs. Cross.

* * *

Pete was dressed and at his airplane in twenty minutes. As he was preflighting, checking the controls, fuel and oil, he noticed a man walking down the runway carrying a container. As he got closer, he could see a gasoline can. No one else was at the strip, so Pete waved and walked over to him, a bit curious.

"Can I help you?" he asked, as they neared each other.

"Need some gas, some av fuel. Got any?" He was stone-faced, dressed in wrinkled Levis and a plain light blue shirt. He reminded Pete of a grown-up hippy, with disheveled hair, a new growth of beard and dark penetrating eyes.

"There's no gas here," said Pete. "Didn't you look on the chart? There's never been gas here. You'll have to fly to the

93

main province or another island to the east. What are you flying?"

The man ignored his question and pointed to the tie-down area.

"What about those? Can I get some fuel from one of them?"

"Friend," smiled Pete, a bit agitated. "I wouldn't advise it unless you check with the owners. You might find one of them in the village who would lend you some, but since there's no fuel available here, most pilots tend to keep what they carry. But you can check. How low are you?"

The guy shook his head as if he didn't want to be bothered with questions, then turned back toward his plane.

Well, thought Pete, there goes another one. It was the style of amateur scammers to misjudge the distance from South America. Pete was in too much of a hurry himself to pursue the pilot's predicament. He finished preflighting his single-engine and climbed into the cockpit. He used the plane in the islands like one would use a car on the mainland. Hop in and go to the grocery store. Or the dentist. Or church. Whatever. It got him where he needed to go.

As he taxied to the end of the runway, he could see the plane that was low on fuel. The pilot was walking rather quickly toward it, and as Pete neared the end of the runway, he could see bales packed into the light twin, hardly concealed, stashed in burlap bags. Another man sat under the wing, out of the hot sun.

Pete pretended not to look too closely, did his run-up and began rolling. No sense wasting any time. He loved the feeling of takeoff, when suddenly he was free of the earth's bindings, when gravity was defied. Every time he took off, it was like soloing all over again. He loved it. Below, the island faded away, the salt pond reflecting like a beacon as the sun caught its surface. Osprey Nest shrank to a pinhead as Pete gained altitude. In seconds, he was over Smugglers.

"What the HELL?" he asked himself out loud. Below him, in the tiny harbor of Smugglers, lay a huge seaplane. He got on the radio.

"Hey, Lucky, that you down there? Come in Lucky."

"Hiya Pete, Lucky Daye here all right. You see my new toy

94

from up there?"

"Sure do. Heard about it. What did you do with the little seaplane?"

"Use it as a go-cart now. You gotta see this one, Pete. When you coming back? I'll buzz in to see you."

"What you doing at Smugglers? Thought you traveled in higher circles — you know — in the clouds," chided Pete.

"Yeah," he chuckled. "Heard there was someone new at Smugglers. Just a neighborly visit, that's all. Just saying hi to the folks."

"I'm getting out of range, Lucky," said Pete. "Talk to you again. That's some bird you got. We'll clear with you."

"Lucky clear."

As he continued flying, Pete wondered about the coincidence of Lucky at Smugglers. Lucky was a legend in his lifetime, even if only half of what was said about him was true. Lucky was known throughout the Caribbean as a happy-go-lucky daredevil who didn't have one particular occupation, and who did everything with a flare that surpassed anything the ordinary man would think of doing. He didn't just fly an airplane. He flew a seaplane. He didn't just flit from island to island. He bought or leased the most lavish homes he could find, complete with servants and exotic furnishings. And his women.

Ohh, his women, thought Pete. Always plural and always beautiful. French stewardesses. Models. Actresses. Lucky was a living James Bond and the women fell for him, tall, with curly light brown hair and a big smile. Always and wherever. Pete chuckled. Yep. He'd probably fly into Sandy Cay to visit in that thing. Pete hoped he would. He had heard stories of how Lucky had a king-size waterbed in the main cabin and a dinghy for going ashore.

What a character, thought Pete, tuning in the tower frequency. He could already see the main province. Lucky Daye. The guy was aptly named. Everyone wondered if it was his real name and no one had ever been able to find out.

Typical of Lucky, thought Pete. Now get down to business, he told himself. Land this bird and get on with the chores. Lucky would fly to Sandy Cay some time. He always did.

Pete got clearance to enter the traffic pattern and was cleared to land. Fuel pump on. Flaps. Prop forward. He turned base and came in on the numbers. Good landing, he thought.

* * *

At four o'clock, Pete was back at his plane, taking care of the fueling, and filing his flight plan to return to Sandy Cay. As he checked his fuel, he noticed Jock getting out of his single on the parking ramp.

"Hey," shouted Pete, walking over to him, a bit curious. "You're really getting around. Weren't you at Sandy Cay this morning?"

Jock shuffled his feet and gave Pete a toothy grin.

"Yeah. Woody wanted me to stop here for some supplies and things. You know where the generator place is? Need some spare parts. Woody doesn't trust that old bucket. Wants to be on the safe side," he said, looking around as if expecting someone.

"On Reef Road, about five miles from here. The guy in the shop should be able to help you out. Think that's where old Miller bought the thing a few years ago. Well, I gotta get back. You flying back today?"

Jock nodded yes.

"Fly low and slow, eh?" Pete said jokingly. Jock gave a faint smile, mumbled something about crop dusting, and continued to look around.

Weird guy, thought Pete. Strange dude.

Pete had loaded the groceries, odds and ends of pipe fittings, a tire for *Cyclops* and a cooler of ice cream — a real treat. He didn't want to waste any time getting it into the freezer on the island.

In minutes, the engine was running and he was talking to the tower. Traffic was slow and he was cleared to the active runway for takeoff. Everything went on schedule, the weather and visibility good. Pete feared late afternoon thunderstorms, but today everything was fine.

He took in the sights as he flew over island after island, nestled in blues that would challenge an artist's pallet. White water on sand, pale turquoise in a few feet, deeper and deeper to a cerulean hue, then finally, the dark blue of the ocean trough. He knew the islands and coves by name, and could almost spot a crawfish on mottled brown reefs. In a short time, he was nearing Smugglers. Lucky's seaplane was no longer in the harbor.

When overhead, he could see two boats, the red speed boat and another, similar type in a dark color, and a few people near the dock.

The place was showing improvement even after only a few days.

Pete passed over the island, rocked his wings to say hi, and continued to Sandy Cay. He buzzed the club and saw Jackson wave from the dock.

Pete noticed a couple more boats. Good. Business was picking up.

He entered the pattern, checked for traffic and came in to land. Crosswind as usual. Crab it in. Good landing. He turned into the parking ramp, noticing that the plane low on fuel earlier was gone. Pete hoped no one was ripped off. As he began unloading the supplies, Jackson arrived with *Cyclops*. Good timing, thought Pete. Just like clockwork. As they were putting the cooler on *Cyclops*, Pete heard another plane come in, but paid little attention as he recounted the day to Jackson. As the plane stopped on the far side of the ramp, Pete and Jackson looked at each other. It was Jock, and right behind was Woody racing from Conch Inn in Max's Jeep.

What goes now? thought Pete.

* * *

Jock, surprised to see Pete at the main province airport that morning, had watched him take off for Sandy Cay and recognized the plane coming in behind him for a landing. Good. He glanced at his watch. 4:15. Chubby was right on time. He watched him taxi and waved as Chubby turned the plane next to the others in the line. As Chubby got out, he motioned to the line boy that he wouldn't need fuel, and walked over to Jock.

"Here it is," he said, smiling as he gave a briefcase to Jock. "Guard it good or your ass is you-know-what. How's Woody doing? Sounds pretty good on the radio. Howard got that house, too. Real good."

Chubby fit his nickname. A rather tall man, he was always on a diet, but the scales kept tipping up rather than down. He'd stop smoking and consume candy. He'd go back to smoking, stop eating candy and get on an ice cream kick. Everyone was always teasing him. Today, in a white golf shirt, the rolls were quite evident, and Jock accused him of flying the airplane over gross.

"Hey, watch what you say, there," said Chubby, light brown eyes taking the joke good naturedly. His hair was beginning to thin, but he was far from bald, and he had just shaved off a month's growth of beard, his cheeks pale below his tanned forehead .

Jock began talking about Woody and Smugglers, and Chubby motioned he didn't really need to hear.

"I gotta get back. Have radio contact at eight tonight and things to do. Be sure Woody gets that briefcase as soon as possible. He needs to go over some papers and count what's in there before we talk tonight. Give 'em all my best, okay? Tell Woody I might drop in next week, so he doesn't feel marooned on that rock."

"He's gotten off a couple of times," said Jock. "Laura's the one who may need a little R and R. Been working her butt off."

"And she's not used to it," said Chubby. "Well, you go your way and I'll go mine. Have a good one."

With that, he climbed back into the plane and started the engines. Jock walked over to his plane, tossed the case onto the copilot's seat and started the engine.

"No need to preflight," he thought. Engine's barely cooled off. He taxied behind Chubby and one, then the other was given the go for takeoff, Chubby heading toward the States, Jock down islands.

In what seemed like only minutes but was actually much longer, Jock was over Smugglers. He circled, buzzed, and headed toward Sandy Cay. Woody waved and Jock saw him jump in the red boat. He'll probably be there when I land, he thought. As Jock taxied to the parking ramp, he could see Pete and Jackson loading *Cyclops*, and Woody coming down the road in Max's deteriorating wheels. As Jock stepped out of the plane, Woody was there.

"Nice going, Jocko. How's Chubby? Ornery as ever? Hey, gimme that little piece," he said, reaching for the briefcase. "All right. You coming to the island with us or staying in town tonight? You're welcome, you know. Maybe a good idea if you come with me tonight. I can clue you in on a few things. Besides, I may need some info on the flying business. Bring your charts."

Woody talked nonstop as Jock climbed back into the plane, then waved to Pete and Jackson. He decided to be friendly and limped over to *Cyclops*, now loaded and ready to go.

"Hey, old man. You gotta come see what we've done to the place," he shouted, a confident grin on his round, sunburned face.

"Love to," said Pete. "Did Jock find that generator place?"

"The what?" asked Woody, the grin disappearing.

"Yeah. He asked me where the generator place was for some spare parts. Guess you don't need them after all, huh?"

"Shit, Jock don't know what he's doing half the time. Send him for one thing he brings another. Typical of the island pilots, eh? Just like the rest of them." Woody was talking abnormally fast and loud. He knew it and Pete knew it. Woody turned to Jock.

"Hey, mon," he shouted, slapping him on the back. "Next time remember the generator shit, okay? Can't get reliable help these days." He winked at Jock and Jock smiled, getting the message. "Good ol' Woody," thought Jock. Sharp old coot. Get you out of a pinch any time.

Pete climbed aboard and Jackson started *Cyclops*. Jock and Woody followed the ancient vehicle to where it turned to take the back road to the yacht club, the Jeep heading toward Conch Inn. As Jackson and Pete reached the club, they could see Woody, Jock and Max speeding toward Smugglers in the red boat. Jackson and Pete looked at each other, shrugged, and didn't say anything. But they were both thinking. Best to leave it that way.

Chapter 6

Operation Seagull

Laura was surprised to see Woody arrive with Max and Jock. As they stepped ashore, she sensed something had happened. Jock wasn't due back for a couple of days and Woody only invited Max when he needed him for something. She grabbed the line that Woody tossed to her, and he patted her butt as he stepped on the dock. She was wearing a peach-colored terry cloth dress, and her hair was already taking highlights from the sun.

"Okay, Laura, we got some stuff to go over. Listen on the SSB, okay? Chubby's going to call when he gets back to the States. Let me know when you hear him, but don't answer, okay?"

"Sure thing," she said, rather wistfully. "Ah see ya'll made contact. Nice timing, Jock, but Ah thought you were leaving again," she smiled. Jock shuffled his feet and smiled back.

"Yeah," he said. "Change of plans. No problem."

"What do you mean, no problem?" shouted Woody. "You done fucked up talking about that generator shit with Pete. Didn't make you look too good and made me look worse. Put your thinking cap on, man. Those people aren't stupid, you know. Next time, I won't be so easy on you. Come on."

Jock looked at Max, shrugged the incident off as insignificant and followed them into a back storeroom. Large plastic barrels marked gasoline had been stacked to one side of the room.

"Where'd you get all that?" asked Jock, surprised.

"Don't ask so many questions, Jocko. Could be bad for your health. Let's just say I solved our fuel problems, okay? Now, let's get down to business."

With that, he unlocked the briefcase, using a special combination to release a hidden locking pin. As he opened it, all three smiled. There it was. Fifty big ones and all the paperwork they'd been expecting. Woody opened an envelope with his name on it and quickly read a scribbled note. "Code 5-6." Okay, he thought, reaching for an old address book in his back pocket. "5-6." Got the frequency.

"Okay, guys, I'll be right back. Double count the green stuff. I don't want anyone coming back to me later saying I ripped 'em off. I'll make the contact and see how it's going."

With that, he headed for the radio room in the far corner of the clubhouse. Laura was already there, reading a magazine. He had separated the area from the rest of the club with a makeshift partition. He'd have a little privacy should anyone come in while he was talking. He tuned in the frequency to coincide with the code numbers and listened. Reception was a little fuzzy, with static on the air.

"Woodpecker calling *Seagull II*. Come in *Seagull II*. Do you copy?" Seconds passed, and there was more static. Come in, he thought. Come in, damn it. Laura was quiet.

"Woodpecker to *Seagull II*. Come in." He began drumming his fingers on the counter, beads of sweat forming on his head in the closed-in area.

"*Seagull II* to Woodpecker. Good copy. Been waiting. Got problems. We're dead in the water for twelve hours and been waiting for your call."

"Where are you? You got a fix on your location?"

"We've been drifting. Batteries are down and we're going easy on the power. We think we're about ten miles from you, but we're not sure."

Woody thought, still tapping his fingers.

"Listen. I'll send an airplane out to spot you and a boat with a mechanic. The pilot'll be there in no time. Flash a red light four times in sequence every minute when you spot the plane. We'll see what we can do. In the meantime, keep in contact on this frequency. I'll also be in contact with the plane."

"Will do. *Seagull II* standing by."

Woody raced out of the club and over to the storeroom, glancing at his watch and ignoring his limp. 6:15. Not much daylight left. They'd have to hurry. He opened the storeroom and there they sat, Max and Jock on a giggly high feeling the dollar bills.

"Okay, guys, everything's turned to shit. Listen up and don't get one detail wrong. Jock, you head back to Sandy Cay, clue Howard in that *Seagull's* broke down, and fly southeast till you see the boat, a shrimp-type vessel. They'll be flashing a red light four times every minute to let you know it's them. Max, you take the black boat, grab any tools you can find around here, and start heading out. Jock'll kinda lead the way. Take the portable VHF with you. You take one in the plane, too, Jock, so we don't have a screw-up. Tell Howard to get his ass up to Osprey Nest, Jock, 'cause I think there's going to be a change in plans. This deal wasn't supposed to come together until Sunday and I don't know what the fuck's up now. Anyway, get in the air, Jocko, and Max, see if you can get those engines turning. If you can't, we'll figure something out. Too much is riding on this one. Come on. Get your butts going."

They were already out the door and heading to the boats. Max went around the point of land that would take him the fastest way to the sea, and Jock took off along the backside of the island to Sandy Cay, putting the boat in high gear. He was alongside the *Michelle* in minutes. Howard was drinking a beer.

"Come on. Walk out to the strip with me. Something's up," said Jock moving only a little faster than his usual pace. Howard was quick-stepped, striding a few paces ahead of Jock until they got to the plane, out of earshot.

Jock explained what had happened while preflighting his plane and Howard, concerned over complications, said he'd get the Nest ready. Jock had fueled on the main province and had about four hours of flying time left in the tanks. Good enough.

The clock in the cockpit showed a few minutes to seven, the minutes ticking off fast. There was only a half-hour of legal daylight left and no runway lights on the strip. He'd have to hurry.

Jock flipped on the master switch, pushed the throttle and prop forward and turned the key. The engine sputtered, then turned over. He turned on the radio and heard a plane coming in to land.

Shit, he thought. That'll delay me. Woody'll be pissed. He taxied on the ramp toward the runway, noticing that Howard was

103

already gone, and glanced to see the plane coming in. It was turning final. He'd have to wait because there was no taxiway at Sandy Cay. The strip was too small and isolated. Planes used the runway as a taxiway, giving clearance to whatever plane was in the pattern first. It seemed like hours. 7:10. The plane landed and, as soon as it was clear, Jock inched onto the runway. He did his run-up as he taxied, spun the plane around at the end to face into the wind, gave it throttle and was on his way. He lifted off and headed southeast.

"I'm off at 7:20, Woody," he reported on a frequency they had arranged weeks before.

"You're behind schedule. Max's out there and can't find the damn boat. You see him?"

"Stand by." Jock began sweeping the water with his eyes. As he gained altitude, he could see Maxwell. Far beyond, about another eight miles at least, he could see a speck that looked like it might be a shrimp boat. Four quick red flashes confirmed the find. He flew over Maxwell, rocked his wings, and headed to the boat on the horizon.

"Woodpecker, you there?"

"Yeah, Jocko, go ahead."

"I got Max and I think I got *Seagull*. She's a good fifteen miles off Sandy Cay. Ohhh shit," he said slowly.

"What is it? What's the matter?"

"Police cutter to the north of us. I don't think it can see us from that far away, but I recognize the markings on her. Not positive, but...what do you think?"

"I'll tell Max to cool it on the VHF in case anyone's listening. We can talk 'cause no one knows the freq we're on. Besides, I doubt they'd have aircraft surveillance stuff."

Seconds later, Max did a quick sweep to the left, then to the right. He was aware of pending problems.

Jock had slowed the plane down to keep better pace with the boat. Now he gave it more throttle and headed toward *Seagull II*. From a thousand feet up, it looked like he had more daylight than was actually there. Think, Jock, he told himself. They're not on VHF radio contact and you're the only one to talk with Woody on this frequency. More important to stay airborne.

Worry about landing later. He circled the *Seagull II*, rocking his wings. In a few minutes, Max was alongside. The crew tied the small boat up and Max disappeared below decks. Jock flew a wide pattern a few miles past the boat, then back in order to avoid attracting attention. In what seemed like an eternity, Max came up from below and gave the no-go signal to Jock.

"Woodpecker. You copy?"

"Yeah, Jock, go ahead."

"Don't think Max can get the thing going. What now?"

"Shit."

Seconds passed.

"I can talk to *Seagull* on our special frequency. Tell him to unload what he can and have Max bring it in. It's risky, but we gotta move fast. Get the shit off as fast as we can. You head back, tell Howard, then go like hell in the red boat for some more. There's supposed to be a hundred bales on board. That's a lot of trips. We'll quit contact now till I see you. Good luck and don't fuck up."

"Roger. Heading back."

It was already dark, and Jock took a bearing on the island, flying a straight course in. By 8:30, he was turning base, then final. He flipped on his landing light and followed the beam to the runway.

Not exactly legal, but for everything else going on, it was probably the least significant act of all, he thought, hoping no one had seen him. It would look a little strange. He taxied to the tiedown area. The plane that had come in before was in his spot, so he taxied to the other side of the ramp. Howard met him with Manny's Jeep.

"Find them?" he asked, a load of gear next to him.

"Yeah. But that's not all. Police boat way to the north. Woody wants the load brought in. Max can't fix the ship. Doesn't look good."

"I've got the scope set up already. I'd go with you, but you're going to need as much room and weight as possible to haul that shit. Did the whole shipment arrive?"

"I guess so. Money's here and all that."

"Good. They'll get more when it's in our hands. Hop in. I'll

105

give you a ride to the marina to speed things up."

Jock jumped in the back of the Jeep and Howard headed for the road. Jock felt a little uneasy running out to the *Seagull*, but he didn't have much choice. At least he had a radio should he need it.

"What's the best way out there?" he asked Howard as they neared Conch Inn.

"Go along the south end, through the cut and head on out. That's the fastest and the safest way. Coming back to Smugglers, keep the big triangular cliff to your right. That's a good indication of where the cut is. At least we've got the beginning of moon tonight. You have a spotlight on that thing, but use it only if you have to so it doesn't attract attention. I'll be able to detect you at least ten miles away on the scope. If there are problems, I'll meet you on the company frequency. Good luck, old man. Know you didn't bargain for the sea part of this thing, but we'll take care of you. Everyone has to change roles when there's a screw-up." With that, he turned around and was off, past the village, across the airstrip to Osprey Nest.

Jock walked down the dock with unusually quick strides and jumped in the boat. It started right away, and with a roar he was off. He knew to keep well away from the shallows. He had seen the water channels from the air and vaguely knew he had enough under him to get around to the cut. High tide. Good. No problems with the shallows.

As he headed out the cut, he could barely see flickerings on the water created by a sliver of moon. The stars were out, the overcast of the previous evening gone.

Jock was a little uneasy at the wheel of a boat. He much preferred airplanes. He glanced at the compass and gave it as much as possible in the direction of the *Seagull*. The ocean was swelling, deep troughs inside of rollers a hundred feet apart. When he was on the crest of a swell, visibility was good, but in troughs, it seemed like he was the only boat in the ocean. About ten minutes of steady running and Jock could barely see the *Seagull*, her running lights bouncing on the horizon. Maxwell must already be on his way back to Smugglers by now. Another ten minutes and he could easily make out the big shrimper. As

Jock pulled alongside, he noticed a cargo boom rigged for unloading. The crew waved him to the other side and helped with the lines.

"Max get off with it okay?" he asked one of the crew.

"Si," he said.

The captain came on deck to direct the off-loading.

"The boat'll only hold about 10 bales. Manuel, get on board and put one up in the bow." The captain looked at Jock and shrugged.

"They understand English but sure won't talk it. Frustrating. I talk to myself all the time."

He swung the boom over and dropped another bale in the aft part of the boat. It took about twelve minutes before Jock's lines were cast off and he was on his way. He didn't really want to run out for the next load. The swells were much larger now so that he had to depend on his compass heading.

Time seemed to drag and he could tell the boat was heavy. The radio was silent.

Everything must be going okay, he thought, anxious to get back.

Scanning the horizon, he couldn't see another boat. Maybe the police cutter headed north and away from them. Or maybe it was sitting and waiting. Jock shuddered, scared for the first time.

If he were in his plane in the same situation he'd know what to do, but the boat was unfamiliar. The water was unfamiliar. And all the islands looked alike as he approached. What had Howard said? Big triangular cliff? He squinted as the dark island shapes began to form. Thank God for the stars, he thought. At least he could see something. It would have been disastrous last night.

"All right," he said to himself, noticing a rock peak. "That must be it."

"Right on target, Jocko," came a voice over the radio as if answering him. "Go north two degrees and you got it. Good luck. Max is already on his way back out. Don't answer."

Jock thanked God for Howard. He must be sitting up there big as shit enjoying this whole scene through the nightscope, thought Jock. He slowed down as he came through the cut, then turned south to the harbor entrance of Smugglers.

Woody was on the dock with an old push cart. As Jock pulled in, he could see that both Woody and Laura had been working hard moving the heavy bales. Bits and pieces clung to her dress and her face was smudged. She looked totally out of character.

"Nice going, Jocko," said Woody. "Didn't know you had it in you, ol' boy. Help us get this shit out. How's everything aboard *Seagull*?"

"Okay. Running smooth," said Jock. "Operation, that is...not the boat. They're still trying to get her started, but the captain wasn't holding out much faith. He's got a language problem on that bucket. Says he's the only one that speaks English."

"That's what the Colombians lead you to believe. They can talk pretty fast when they want to," said Woody. "Take it from me. I've been in these messes before. If it comes to saving their own ass, it's like the lord of tongues passes over them. Instant English, mon. Instant English. Throw me a bale."

They were heavy, and after ten were off-loaded, Jock was ready to call it quits. It had been a straining day.

"I'm going out for the next run with partial payment," said Woody, to Jock's relief. "Max gave me the headings. You help Laura load this stuff in the back storeroom. Jesus! Did you know this thing's almost out of fuel? Another mile and that's it. Come on. Help me haul down one of the fuel containers and make the transfer. Boy, it's a good thing Lucky made a fuel delivery this morning or we'd be shit out of luck. I sure as hell wouldn't want to go with my tail between my legs to Pete, and it would even raise a few eyebrows around Conch Inn this time of night."

They went back to the storeroom and rolled a large plastic fuel tank on its edge down to the dock. Woody rigged a transfer hose to the pump and began fueling the boat.

"We're losing time, but no sense going if I'm gonna run out of fuel. And I don't think we can push more than ten bales into these things. Damn. If it were Sunday we'd be all set. Now I gotta worry about storing all this shit until then. Could be tricky. What about that police boat?"

"Didn't see it," said Jock. "If we're lucky, it was heading north and away from us."

"Yeah, IF we're lucky. Not exactly something you should pray for, I guess, under the circumstances. There. That should do it. Have another barrel down here for Max when he gets back. We'll refuel each time out to make sure we can get out of trouble, if there is any. If we have fuel we can outrun them."

Woody started the boat and pulled away from the dock, another briefcase stashed under the seat. Jock and Laura began pushing the cart toward the storeroom.

What a spot to be in, she thought, but what could she do? She wanted the bucks as much as Woody and was well aware of the risks. He had told her when a deal went bad, it usually stunk horribly. She hoped they'd made the right decisions. Time was always critical. If you moved fast you could sometimes save a deal. But time was important. When deals were good they were very good and worth all the anxieties that went with them. But when they turned sour, even Laura knew to run as fast as possible in the other direction.

Woody headed out to sea, checking his course, pushing the boat and himself as hard as he could. The shorter the time involved, the less chance of a screw-up. He made it in twenty minutes to the *Seagull*, passing Max on the way back.

"Hey there, Cap," he said, coming alongside. "Bummer with your ship, huh? What the hell's the problem?"

"Don't know," said the captain, a gruff looking man in his fifties. "Crew's been in the engine room since early today. Think it's the fuel system. Don't really know. But we can't do shit till all this crap is offloaded. Can't exactly declare an emergency, you know. Come on board," he motioned.

Woody grabbed the small briefcase and climbed onto the aft deck, then followed the captain below.

"Here," said Woody. "That's half. Twenty-five. I'll bring the balance out on the last haul. Agreeable?" The captain indicated yes, opened the case and put the bills in his own safe place. Most of the money had already been disbursed. This was the last of it.

"Got something for your banker I'm supposed to give you,"

said the Captain. "It's good stuff. Guess it's part of his pay. Look."

He opened up another case. High grade cocaine. No wonder Howard hadn't said anything about what he was owed. He'd do well with this cache.

"He'll have it tonight," said Woody. "I'll deliver it personally, when everything's off this barge. I better get going. Think I'll make the next runs with this thing. It's getting late, and Jock isn't too quick."

"I noticed," said the captain with a sneer. "As long as he flies it's okay."

Before he got on board the red boat, Woody scanned the horizon looking for the police cutter, but nothing was in sight. Good. Must have gone the other way, he thought.

"Be back in about an hour," he said, climbing aboard and starting the engines. "Anything you want us to bring out?"

"Not till we're done. Then you might want to toss in a bottle of rum for the boys," he said. "Hurry back." The captain waved and Woody was off, back to Smugglers to offload the expensive cargo.

The next two trips for each boat were uneventful, but fatigue was setting in on everyone, including Jock and Laura, who had loaded the bales and put them into storage. They had completely filled the storeroom and another shed and were wondering what to do with the last two boatloads. Woody got off the boat to stretch. Maxwell had ended up on the same schedule, so the two were at Smugglers to do the last run together.

"You remember that warehouse over on Coral Cay?" asked Woody. "I checked it out the other day and it's totally empty. Island's deserted. Heard the owner died and no one's been back for years. Let's stash the last two loads there. Then we're a bit diversified too, if something should go wrong. All our eggs aren't in one basket, so to speak."

He looked at everyone for approval of his humor, but by this time, nothing was funny. Everyone was beat, yet the job had to be finished. And after all the bales were safe, Woody had to make the trip to Osprey Nest. Howard always had to know how a deal was going from his key man in the field.

"Well, you ready?" Woody asked Max, who hadn't said much all night. Max closed his eyes, tilted his head back and then nodded, his thin, wiry body almost quivering. One more load. Woody grabbed his briefcase with the final payoff, along with a bottle of rum, and within minutes, the two boats were traveling in tandem to *Seagull*. When they arrived, the crew was sweeping up any evidence, dumping excess weed and seeds that hadn't gone for joints for themselves, overboard. Woody paid the captain, toasted the crew, and in less than a half-hour from last leaving Smugglers, they were on their way back.

All one hundred bales accounted for, thought Woody. Everything paid for. And everything safe. So far. It was almost two o'clock in the morning. What a night. As they approached Smugglers, Woody indicated that Max should follow him. Instead of turning into Smugglers, they went a couple of miles past two other little islands, to Coral Cay. The warehouse stood out, bleak against the starry sky, and when the boats shut down, everything was quiet. Dead quiet, the type you'd imagine in the grave. It was spooky. At Smugglers, there was at least the sound of the generator. At Coral Cay there was nothing. Woody and Max beached the boats, and waded into the cool water to off-load, the bales seemingly heavier than earlier. The warehouse padlock had long been broken. They began storing the bales and had the load in the musty building in less than fifteen minutes.

"God, I'm tired," said Woody, leaning on his shorter leg. "You must be dead too. Good work tonight, Max. Didn't know you had it in you."

"It means money," he said, straight-faced, his glasses down on his nose. "That gets me going every time. If there wasn't the pot at the end of it — and THAT'S a funny to laugh at — I wouldn't have worked so hard. But it is a pot o' gold when it comes in, and that's good enough for me." He took a line for the black boat.

"Boy, do we stink," said Woody. "Beginning to get high on my own sweat. I better shower before going to see Howard. You going back to Sandy Cay tonight? I'll run you to your dock."

"Appreciate it. Pat's probably wondering. Didn't tell her where I was going. Maybe Marjorie told her."

They shoved the boats further into the water, climbed aboard and started the engines. The roar was deafening after the stillness. As they arrived at Smugglers, Laura was waving to them, looking like a wrung out dish rag.

"Woody," she shouted, above the engines as they came up. "Cap wants y'all on the radio, Ah didn't answer, like you said, so Ah don't know what he wants."

Woody hurried ashore, making sure the single sideband was on the code frequency. "Woodpecker to *Seagull II*. Come in."

"Good to hear you, Woody. All set?"

"All set. Every last bit."

"Good, 'cause I think we're going to get some company. Police boat has been sighted about five miles away. We're cleaned up, so we're going to throw some nets and lines over and enlist their help. We've got a bunch of fish already in the freezers. Not too much fun when a fish boat can't bring the catch in to market, right?"

"You devil. No wonder you're a rich old fart," said Woody. "Howard'll crack up over this one. Good luck. See you next time, but don't break down again. We're beat."

"Roger. Have a good one and give my best to Howard. I'm about ready to get company. *Seagull* clear."

"Woodpecker clear."

He turned the radio off and sat for a few minutes, looking at Laura, Max and Jock, until everyone but Max was grinning from ear to ear.

"I think we all deserve a drink for a good night's work. How about it? You want some rum, my crew? I'll even fix it." With that, he got up, headed for the bar, served up drinks for four, and opened a bag of corn chips. He was famished and so were the others.

"I'm going to take my drink right into the shower and get all this crud off me, then I'm going to take Max and Jock back to Sandy Cay and finish my business with Howard," said Woody, looking at Laura. "You're gonna have to stay here, Babes. Hate to do it to you, but we can't leave the island by itself until the load is clear."

"Ah know," she sighed. "Just keep the radio on in case Ah

112

have to holler help."

Woody headed for the shower, drink and towel and a change of clothes in hand, and glanced back. Laura was slouched in a chair, Max was lying on the pool table, and Jock was hunched over with his head in his hands. It was a long night. And it wasn't over.

A few minutes later, he was shaking Jock and Max awake.

"Hey, guys, time to go. Have another drink on the way out."

"Shit, Woody, where you getting your energy?" asked Jock, yawning.

"I can't rest till everything is straight. Come on." Max sat up, shook his head to rid himself of sleep, and slid down off the table. Woody was a hard one to keep up with. He poured another drink and walked out the door following Jock, and climbed aboard the red boat.

"We got enough fuel. Not going that far," said Woody, checking the gauge. "Besides, I doubt if we could bring another barrel down the dock. I'm gonna run this thing up to the point where Sandy Cay begins, then I'll put it in low gear so we just sort of whisper into the island. I don't want to raise any stink at this hour. Too hard to explain. Hold on. I'm gonna go like hell this first leg."

With that he put the throttles forward and the boat leaped. He almost made a record run to Sandy Cay, artfully going around the little rocks and avoiding the shallow areas. As he approached the island, he slowed down to an idle, letting the boat coast on the tide. He pulled up to Maxwell's dock and Max jumped out, pushing the boat off.

A few minutes later Woody was at Conch Inn, alongside the *Michelle*. He tied up on the outside and climbed over the schooner so it wouldn't be obvious he was at the dock. Jock opened the hatches on the *Michelle* to go aboard for the rest of the night, and Woody headed for the Nest, briefcase and a bottle in hand.

This would be some sort of celebration, he thought. In only a few days, they had pulled off a deal. Well, almost. Sunday would be the big day when it all left the island. Until then it could get a little hot.

Will have to guard the island closely, he told himself. Can't be too careful. He took a slug of rum from the bottle, walked through the sleeping village and turned down the runway. The moon had passed over the sky and the stars were still bright. The runway reflected a pale gray, and as he limped across, Woody could make out a light in Osprey Nest. When he came to the base of the ridge road, he looked up.

Good thing I don't have heart trouble, he thought. This climb would get him for sure. Bad enough with a bum leg. He took it easy up the steep incline, but by the time he got to the top he was panting, sweat rolled down his forehead and his shirt clung to his skin. Another hundred yards and he was at the Nest.

"Brought something for your open house," he said, as Howard opened the door before he knocked. "Little something from the captain for the good banker."

Howard smiled and took the package.

"Come on in. Been watching the whole operation. You boys moved okay," he said. "Got you right down to the last load, then lost you on the scope. Where'd you go?"

"We were full at Smugglers. Put the last twenty bales in the warehouse on Coral Cay — you know — that deserted building?"

"With the broken padlock where no one can possibly see anyone coming or going to it? Yeah, I know the spot. Don't like it. Make room up at Smugglers. There's no way to keep an eye on the stash down there and you don't know if anyone saw the whole operation."

His voice was authoritative and Woody nodded. "Come upstairs. You'll like this sight." Howard motioned, and Woody followed him up the steep stairs to the upper level. Howard had a nightscope mounted near the center of the room, aimed out to sea. He adjusted it, then moved away so Woody could take a look.

It made everything look like daylight. As he looked closely, he could see a police cutter with the *Seagull* in tow. "Unbelievable. That guy's got balls, I tell you. This scope is unreal, too. What'd you lay out for it?" asked Woody.

"Plenty of G's," said Howard. "But it's worth every cent.

I've been at a disadvantage in other operations, having to use the *Michelle* as base. This is great. Operation is coming together good. Real good. Should make us all rich. Give me a rundown on your conversations with the Cap, how the *Seagull* is doing, Max's and Jock's attitude and all that. I need all the details on communication, too, what was said and also what wasn't said."

Woody began recounting everything he could remember of the past hours. When he came to the end, about an hour had elapsed, a couple of rums were beginning to get to him and he was exhausted.

"One last question. Did you sweep the docks and area where you unloaded?" Woody looked at him with a blank stare.

"No, I don't think Laura and Jock thought of that. I'll check on it this morning."

"Good. Golden rule is always clean up behind you. Clothes washed right away, any grass or seeds swept clean and dumped. Check the boats too. There can't be one speck of evidence or the whole deal could sour. You never know who's watching, poking around or just plain curious. And you're not known as the quiet type, Woody. I want you to start shutting up. You get a few belts in you and the tongue starts wagging. Remember, diarrhea of the mouth usually indicates constipation of the brain. I won't tolerate it. Now, I think you ought to crash for a couple of hours. I'll wake you early so you can get back before anyone suspects you've been here. Pull out one of the sofas down below. I'm going to check on a few more things with this scope. Want to know where they're towing *Seagull*, and that the area's clear of strange boats. I noticed you used the fuel."

"Good move on your part," said Woody. "I would never have thought to get a supply this fast."

"That's why I'm the banker," said Howard, smiling. "It's to eliminate fuck ups. Another load will be coming in on Sunday to supplement the small boats. Get a few z's. You look terrible."

Woody went downstairs, pulled out a sofa and passed out.

What a night, he thought. What a sweet, sweet night. Another five nights and he'd be in the green. He drifted off to sleep thinking about packets of bills...sweet, sweet "Yankee dollars."

* * *

The next morning as Woody was coming down the steep road from Osprey Nest he almost tumbled into Helen, out for her usual morning walk, this day a little earlier than usual to beat the heat. She stopped, startled that anyone would be there at this time of day.

"Hello," she said, cautiously stepping to the side to avoid him. "Nice day."

"Yes, mam, a beautiful day," said Woody, squinting at the pretty woman in white shorts and yellow halter top in front of him. He hadn't thought to bring sunglasses in the middle of the night and he had slept longer than Howard liked. It was already seven-thirty and the island was stirring.

He smiled at Helen, both a bit bewildered, and said, "Have a good one. See ya." With that, he quickened his pace toward the village, hoping the red boat next to the *Michelle* hadn't aroused any curiosity.

Helen continued on her way, wondering if she should turn back to tell Pete what she had seen. But then, she didn't know why he was at the ridge house, and he wasn't doing anything unusual. She decided to continue her walk. She could tell Pete later. But Woody had sure looked strange. His clothes were disheveled, and he looked like he needed a good sleep. She walked on, not interrupting her routine.

* * *

Howard stayed at the Nest until he could see Woody heading back to Smugglers, then thought he better get back to the boat. Marjorie had given him hell because he wouldn't let her sleep in the house the first night and he had to pacify her, to tell her to bring the rest of her gear to move in. He almost slid down the incline to the road below, unaware that Helen was only a couple hundred paces behind him on her return walk. She stopped and let him get ahead of her, then took the back road to the club to see Pete.

116

Chapter 7

The Revenge

When Maxwell lost his job with the yacht club two years before, a curious mental progression followed. Prior to that time, he had been a relatively interesting, enjoyable individual who would joke along with the rest of them about his quest for a woman, always referring to the young ladies who came and went on the island as "birds."

He was pleasant looking enough, with a wiry frame stretching about five-feet-ten-inches, curly blonde hair and, lately, a mustache. He wore glasses when it was necessary to read a manual or work with tiny parts, but for the most part, he preferred getting along without them, although he found himself using them more and more often. In the years before, it had become a game among bachelor yachtsmen to find "birds" to ship over to Maxwell in hopes that one would build a nest for him and he'd live happily ever after.

The stories, both true and fabricated, were always part of the barroom banter at both the yacht club and Conch Inn. One story in particular recounted how a boat bum friend found two willing ladies hitchhiking in the States, told them about Maxwell and his little island paradise and how he was probably the horniest guy in the Western Hemisphere — and if they could see it in the line of charity — that it would be a good idea to fly over and take care of the poor love-starved Aussie. He had arranged for them to be "air mailed" with Charlie on his next flight. Charlie was clued in and couldn't wait to see what Maxwell was getting. When they arrived for the flight, he had to chuckle. Hairy armpits and legs, see-through sack dresses with no underwear and belongings in a canvas bag made an impression he'd never forget. He'd offered to take the girls free just so Max could have a little, but this was too much. They wore handmade leather sandals laced up the legs, had only one pierced ear apiece, and wore their hair in a multitude of braids, with not a hint of makeup on their faces. If Charlie had had an air mail stamp he would have labeled their foreheads.

The flight over consisted of the two girls in the double rear seat recounting all they would do for this poor guy, amusing, sometimes astonishing the other passengers: a mousy attorney who had never flown in a small plane before and whose seat was being paid for by a woman on a boat anchored off Sandy Cay; a gal who regularly commuted with Charlie while playing businesswoman in the States and boat bum aboard her vessel at Conch Inn, and a famous folk singer who had squeezed his large frame into the copilot's seat. The attorney, sitting next to the businesswoman in the middle seat, thought she was the stewardess, and she went along with it, keeping him well supplied with scotch as they listened to all the plans for sexual encounters the girls planned for Maxwell.

When the girls arrived on the island Max was there to meet them, having had plenty of warning the day before that all his fondest dreams were about to come true. He met them at the plane, saw past their obvious professional credentials and excitedly escorted them in his Jeep through the village to the club.

There, they had several drinks, the girls making a deliberate fuss over their "charge," egging him on. Max had invited several friends to have dinner at his tiny little house and cocktail hour began early after they left the club. Max, with an ear-to-ear grin, patted the gals on the butts and took a good look at what was in store for him. After dinner, his friends left so Max could have his fun. But alas, it wasn't to be. No one ever heard the full story, but it seems Max had too much to drink, had passed out and the girls went soliciting on the dock. The next morning, as Max came looking for them, Jackson informed him that the two ladies had gotten on board a big powerboat headed south. Max couldn't believe it and neither could anyone else. And while there was plenty of snickering behind his back, no one ever threw it in his face that he never got to first base.

Other incidents happened over the years, but when Pat said she would marry him, Maxwell settled into a family routine, content with the pretty girl who was willing to give up a job and Stateside comforts to join him in the small one-room house he lived in on the island. He never mentioned it to Pat, but planned to make use of her as an American wife. It opened doors in the States that were previously closed to him.

The wedding had been a quiet affair, held shortly after he left the yacht club. It should have begun new happiness for him, but his negative feelings were carried even to this event. Everyone was invited to the wedding with the exception of Pete and Charlie. Yet Charlie brought over many of the wedding presents and even the rings, which came special delivery to his home. Friends from the States flew to the wedding in Charlie's plane, bringing flowers and other decorations.

Neither Pete nor Charlie ever said anything about it, then or later, realizing it would do no good. Perhaps Maxwell would see that most of his vengeance was backfiring.

But that wasn't to be the case. The wedding took place on schedule and Max and Pat set up housekeeping.

Now, after almost a total of ten years in the vicinity of Sandy Cay, Max was a common word. Many people didn't even know his last name until they saw his shop sign. He was just Maxwell the mechanic with the Aussie accent. While he had always been a bit shy, which accounted for his lack of lady friends, he was still personable and likable. Until he left the Sandy Cay Club.

Then it was as though a screw was turned in his brain, creating a pressure that changed his personality. He became withdrawn, sullen at the mention of anyone associated with the club and vengeful, to the dismay not only of the club people, but the island as a whole.

After a while, his behavior became accepted. It wasn't a surprise when he'd make an obvious mistake, and for some reason yachtsmen — particularly those with money — expected to be "taken" by him. The theory was that Max was better than nothing at all and if you could limp home it was better than being dead in the water. A parallel could be drawn between Maxwell's mental deterioration and Pete's prior physical and emotional problems with drinking. The difference was that Max couldn't see himself, couldn't step outside of his skin to take a good look at Max, to see that he was hurting himself more than

119

anyone else in the world. Those he most hated came to accept him as a sick person and either ignored him or treated him accordingly. Aside from some verbal confrontations when a customer or friend was involved, the yacht club group kept its distance.

But it was difficult. There were times when Maxwell flagrantly solicited customers and worked right on the dock, knowing Pete would be upset but wouldn't say anything. Most mornings, Max would deliberately drive past the front of the club, eyes straight ahead, knowing Pete was inside having his morning coffee.

And then there was the boat.

Before leaving the club, Max had salvaged a small cabin cruiser with the idea of fixing it up. It sat, blocked up on the yacht club ramp, for the last year of his employment at the club, and was still there more than two years later. The bottom was missing planks, the paint had peeled to bare wood, windows were broken and, lacking a name, the boat had been designated *Maxwell's Revenge* by those who knew the story.

It was a constant, daily reminder to Pete, but since he couldn't do anything about it, he let it become a conversation piece. Pete always hoped the next storm would carry it away, but even though waves had crashed over the docks, throwing spray into the cottages and as far into the club as the pool table, the *Revenge* hadn't budged. Pete always joked it was because as water went in, it also went out, like a giant sieve. So it stayed, month after month, losing paint and deteriorating along with its owner.

But as Maxwell lost ground mentally, Pete became stronger in his ability to think, to have compassion even for Maxwell, and to accept things as they were, although his natural defense often prompted digs at Maxwell's incompetence.

The situation would have probably continued with Max sliding and Pete gaining if other elements hadn't cropped up. While Pete was willing to let things be, Max became an agitator, going so far as to publicly proclaim he was going to "get" Pete. When he set up shop at Conch Inn, Maxwell stealthily began building a wall that he hoped would divide the island people.

His ultimate goal was to have Pete evicted from the island.

While Maxwell's mind contrived various angles of attack, Pete went about his business, fully aware of the dissension building. In many instances, it seemed the island was split depending on where the natives worked, but as funds got tighter on the island, the club won economically. It wasn't a matter of siding with one of the white factions. It was simply a matter of getting paid.

The yacht club had proven itself in tough times before and the natives knew that ultimately their job was secure. Although Maxwell exhibited an attitude of devil-may-care toward the yacht club, he was miserable, unable to deal with the inner turmoil. An easygoing disposition evolved into fixed worry lines on his forehead. His once easy smile was now a strained, sullen look. His mind played games on him constantly, triggering ways to "get even," to win people to his side. But the more effort he put into his negative attitude, the more he lost ground. The natives, easily swayed, would nod in agreement when Maxwell was on a tangent, but quickly forgot the incident as soon as he finished talking. In this way Maxwell gained sympathy, then lost it as reality set in and people saw situations as they really were. Even the natives chuckled and said, "Well, dat's Max. Dat's him all right." And each year, he was given permission to work as mechanic on the island because he was better than no mechanic at all.

Only when Max saw another way out, a better way to get at Pete and also the island, which had begun to turn against him, did he start calming down. That's when he met Woody.

When Woody came to check out Smugglers Cay it was Max who showed him the island and equipment. Max knew Woody wasn't the average island owner and he saw the chance for the bucks he had been hoping for. He pledged himself to Woody's operation and agreed to be the support arm at Sandy Cay.

It was logical.

The yacht club people would never get involved and Max could gain the financial leverage he wanted. In any language, money talked. And in the Caribbean, the greenback went a long, long way when someone wanted something done. So Max changed his tactics. He became quieter, more withdrawn. After meeting Jock, the plot was complete.

In any war situation, the side that can cut off the enemy usually ends up the winner. Max planned to use the same strategy on the island. It would be a long, hard squeeze, but in the end, he would be victor. Being a pawn in someone else's game didn't bother him. He could handle it. As long as he got his sweet revenge.

* * *

"Hey, Max. Wake up! You gonna sleep all day? God, do you stink. You bring me any of that stuff or did you forget about me?"

Pat was standing at the edge of the bed in a pale pink bikini, dripping wet from a quick dip off the dock. She was towel-drying her hair, and Max watched every movement her muscles made, the suit clinging in all the right places. She had a good figure. And she was strong. Good woman for island life.

"What time is it?" he asked, ignoring her question, yawning and attempting to sit up. He fell back, content to lie in the light breeze of the ceiling fan.

"It's almost noon. What time did you finally get in? I went to sleep. Marjorie said you guys had something going last night. What did you do?"

"Can't tell you, but I'll be buying you a nice piece of gold soon. Don't ask any questions and you'll live like a queen. We're going to be rich. What's to eat? I could go for some eggs and bacon."

"Coming up." It was only a couple of steps to the galley-style kitchen. Pat was hungry too. She lit the compact gas stove and took out the eggs from an equally small refrigerator.

"Scrambled okay?"

"Anything. Just give me some food. You realize I didn't have dinner last night? I think Woody runs on fuel cells around his middle. Didn't even think of food until about two this morning and then he opened a bag of stale chips. How about some toast to stop the groaning inside?"

He was unusually pleasant, despite his fatigue, knowing that his reward for the previous night would come.

"We're on the last two slices of bread. You can have them. I don't need them," she said, making brunch as quickly as possible. Max got up, stripped, and headed for the shower. He had been so tired he had fallen onto the bed, clothes and all and had gone to sleep. He was amazed how Woody kept up his pace, especially with his limp. They had all run on pure adrenaline. As Max got out of the shower he put on a pair of jeans and a white knit shirt ringed with navy at the collar and sleeves.

"I better get down to the Inn," he said. "Told the guy on the *Sea 'n' Be* I'd help him with his exhaust system. It's not too bad, but Woody said it would be a good idea to check the boat out. Might come in handy."

Pat had the food ready and Max wasted no time eating. He was famished.

"What day is it?" he asked suddenly.

"Wednesday, why?"

"Oh shit. Told the boys from Rocky Point to come see Woody about jobs today. He's not going to want them on the island."

Max got up, turned on his VHF and called.

"Max to Woodpecker. Come in." Seconds lapsed.

"Woodpecker here. Switch over."

"Going."

"Max, what the 'H' is with you? Three natives came from Rocky Point about an hour ago. Said you sent 'em. I got no work for them right now. You know that."

"Sorry, Woody, but thought we'd talked about that the other day."

"Yeah, but that was before the change in plans, if you read me. Think I pacified them. Told 'em to come back on Monday and I'd see what work there was. Not the way I wanted it handled, you know."

"Roger. Sorry. Got the days confused."

"Well next time think. You rested up?"

"I'll make it. Heading to the shop now. Need anything?" He talked in his usual monotone.

"No, but I'll be there in a bit. You and Pat want to come here tonight so I can get Laura off this rock for dinner at the yacht club?"

"Okay, old man. Be there about six."

"Roger. Switching over."

"Gone."

"Woodpecker calling Sandy Cay Club. Come in."

"Sandy Cay Club. Go ahead," answered Jackson.

"Hi there, Jackson. Think you can put two down for dinner tonight?"

"No problem, Mon. Serve at eight."

"Roger. See ya later. Woodpecker clear."

"Sandy Cay Club clear."

* * *

Maxwell grabbed a few tools, climbed into the Jeep with its spreading rust and headed for Conch Inn, past the back of the yacht club. He saw Pete working on an engine in the shop out of the corner of his eye and kept going, speeding on the single lane road used by those walking or riding. Max was still tired from the night before, but knew he'd better get some work done today.

As he pulled into Conch Inn, he noticed the *Sea 'n' Be* was already tied to the dock. Three people were getting off another yacht, lugging suitcases, sea shells, straw bags and fishing poles to the open area between the buildings.

"Hello," said Max rather curtly, parking the Jeep and going about his business. Then he smelled revenge, walked over and extended his hand.

"I'm Max. You people leaving the island today?" They said yes, and asked if he was the island mechanic.

"Yes. I'm the one to see if you need anything done. How are you leaving?"

"Pilot by the name of Charlie's coming for us. Set it up with the yacht club last night. Didn't think there was such good service on this small island."

"Charlie, you say?" asked Max. "What'd he get you for?"

"Five hundred," said the tall man who was obviously taking charge of arrangements, tanned from his stay in the tropics.

"That much, eh?" said Max, fingering his mustache. "We've got a pilot here who'll do it half-price. You wouldn't even have to wait."

"Gee, that would be good, but we already arranged with Charlie...."

"Don't worry," said Max quickly. "I'll take care of that. Charlie comes and goes anyway. He'll just wait around to sucker someone else. Wait here and I'll be back." Maxwell almost ran down the dock to the *Michelle*.

"Jocko," he yelled, climbing aboard and shouting below decks. "Get out of the sack, for Christ sake. Got you a charter away from Charlie. Two hundred and fifty bucks to run them to the mainland. Get going. They're ready. I told you I'd put some extra bread in your pocket with my connections around here. Hurry up. I'll tell them you're on the way."

He leaped on the dock, walked over to the tourists and said, "All set. Put your bags in the Jeep and I'll take you to the plane. You'll be back to the mainland in no time."

As he finished loading their gear, Jock came up from behind, looking like he'd slept in his clothes.

"This is Jock, your pilot. He'll take you wherever you want to go," said Max. With that, he drove to Jock's plane, the passengers sitting on top of the baggage and holding on as best they could. As Jock checked the plane, Max loaded the gear and within fifteen minutes of meeting the people, they were in the air.

Score one for Max, he thought, pleased with his quick thinking. Jock would work out in more than one way.

He watched as the little single-engine plane taxied to the end of the runway, then took off. There was a lot of money to be made around here if Jock was willing to play the game, thought Max, almost smiling. Revenge was very sweet.

He started the rattling Jeep and drove back to Conch Inn. As he was walking down the dock to check out the *Sea 'n' Be*, he saw Charlie buzzing the club. Too bad ol' boy, he thought. You've been had. Get used to it. He quickened his step and climbed aboard the boat.

"Hi, Max. Think you can fix this thing? Been giving us some trouble and the fumes are pretty bad." Terry was dripping from a quick dive overboard to cool off, wearing a french-cut black suit. Juney was right behind him in a sexy purple one-piece cutaway that made Max stop and reorganize his thoughts.

Terry smiled, knowing the effect his pretty wife had on other men.

"Come on below," he said. "It's easy to get in the engine room on this thing. She's got some good design features."

Max followed Terry below decks, noting the spacious interior.

"What does she draw?" he asked.

"Five feet. She's got a long water line, too. Good for cruising."

"Good for a lot of things," said Max, noting the staterooms and salon of the custom trawler. "What's your range?"

"We can go a couple thousand miles without refueling," said Terry. "Carries a lot of water, too. Plus, we've just put on a watermaker."

Max went into the engine room. He could see where an elbow connection on the starboard exhaust system had come loose.

"There's your problem," he said, pointing. "We'll get you going again. I'll take some measurements so we know what we need and Jock will bring in the parts when he returns."

"We looking at much money?"

"Naw. I'll be easy on you. Any friend of Woody's gets a good price," said Maxwell, mentally calculating his share. Even an inexpensive part brought a decent cut for him. He wrote some figures down, then came out of the engine room.

"I'll be back to you after I talk to Woody. Meanwhile, enjoy the island. Good looking bird you got there," he said, shoving his glasses on his nose to get a better look at Juney.

Terry smiled. Juney had won several beauty contests and had been a cheerleader at the university they attended. Guys always gawked at her beauty wherever they went. Terry loved it. He followed Max onto the aft deck and handed over his tools when Max was on the dock.

"We don't plan on going anywhere, so this isn't an emergency," said Terry. "Anyway, this is a good place to be stuck. The water and beaches are incredible." He slipped an arm around Juney as Maxwell strode off toward his shop.

* * *

Max wrote up an order for the *Sea 'n' Be* and glanced at his watch. Four o'clock. Time to close up, get Pat and head to Smugglers. If he got there early, he could have Woody call in the order to Chubby for Jock to pick up.

Max straightened a few things on his workbench, pushed some paint cans into a corner and locked up. He looked at his hands. Hardly dirty. He could skip a shower. Max got in the Jeep and headed home, past the yacht club shop and up the hill.

Pat was making a cake.

"Hi. Smells good. We're going to Smugglers so Woody and Laura can get off the rock and have dinner at the yacht club tonight," said Max. "Forgot to tell you earlier. Don't know what they've got to eat — probably nothing — let's make a couple of sandwiches. I don't feel like fishing for dinner at this hour."

"Why does someone have to be at Smugglers? It never bothered anyone to leave the place before," she said, scraping the bowl. "Anyway, I need a half hour to get this thing done now that it's started."

"You'll know why we have to be there when we get there," said Max, not wanting to go into detail. "Look at it as an outing for us." Maxwell licked the spatula as Pat put the cake in the small oven.

She still had on her light pink bikini. With the summer heat, she wore as little as possible to take advantage of the refreshing sea. All she had to do was walk down a path cut in the brush to their dock below, where a small runabout and sailing dinghy were tied up ready to use. Many times Pat would just hang onto a line tied to the dock, letting the tide stretch her out, cooling her as the water swept by.

"I better change," she said, untying her top. "The no-see-ums might be out with the wind dropping and I don't want to get caught at Smugglers. I'm wearing jeans."

"Good idea. We'll go as soon as you take that cake out of the oven. We have any food around?" he asked, opening the refrigerator. He reached in, took an apple out of a plastic bag and bit into it, juice rolling down his chin.

"Where'd you get these?" he asked, somewhat surprised.

"Howard brought them from the mainland last week. Marjorie was cleaning out the galley and sorting stuff for the house. Have you seen the Nest yet? She says it's really nice, but I can't say I'd want to be that far away," said Pat walking toward the kitchen.

She had changed to light blue denims with a white oxford cloth shirt tied at the waist. As she brushed her hair, she kept sweeping it up, until she was able to put a band around it on top of her head. She then swirled it around and, with a couple of hair pins, formed a stylish bun to give her a pixie look.

As the buzzer sounded she turned off the oven and took out the cake. Then she made a couple of ham and cheese sandwiches with hamburger buns.

"Okay, I'm ready. You look tired again," she said, glancing at Max, now comfortable in an easy chair in the corner of the room. He finished the apple, dumped the core in a sack, and said, "Come on. Let's get going."

They walked down the path, being careful not to slip on the coral rock steps carved out of the hill, and got into the little runabout.

"Not as fast as Woody's boats, that's for sure," said Max, rather sourly. "Those mothers really go. Enough to give you a hernia."

He didn't want to admit to Pat now, but his sides ached from the work the previous night, not only from riding the bronco type boat, but from lifting all the heavy bales. The last twenty-four hours had been a bit much for him.

A little after five o'clock Pat and Max pulled up to Smugglers. Woody and Laura were sitting on the porch enjoying a cool drink with their feet propped up. Neither moved as Max and Pat got out of the boat, but motioned for them to join them.

When they climbed the few steps to the deck, Laura stood up, wearing a colorful wraparound skirt with a yellow knit top, her hair washed and blow-dried. Lipstick and eye makeup had completely changed her appearance since Pat had last seen her.

"Couple of rums for ya'll?" Laura asked, heading for the bar. "Sit down. Ya'll be comfortable. Looks better than the last time ya'll were here, Pat, wouldn't ya say?"

"Doesn't even look like the same place," she answered, peering into the clubhouse, now cleaned and showing a woman's artful touch. "You've got good ideas Laura. This place will be something."

Max sat down next to Woody and explained what part he needed for the *Sea 'n' Be*.

"How can I ask Jock to get it when he's here?" asked Woody, a little dumbfounded at Max's request.

"He's back on the mainland. I got him a charter this afternoon and he took it for a few bucks," said Max.

Woody stared at him.

"You WHAT? Who's paying you turkeys, anyway? Jock is supposed to stand by in case we need him. Now he's over there, we don't have a plane here and...what's the use of ranting. He's over there and there's nothing I can do about it. This time. Let's call Chubby and get the wheels rolling. Come on," he said, a bit disgusted.

Max followed Woody to the radio area and waited as he tuned in the code frequency. In minutes, Woody was talking to Chubby, telling him what was needed and to make contact with Jock. As he finished the transmission, the whole radio went dead.

"What the hell?" said Woody, a little bewildered. "Why would the damn thing quit just like that? You know anything about these wonder machines, Max? You used to putter around in electronics, didn't you?"

"Woody," he said in a sarcastic monotone. "If you'll remember, I told you I can fix these things. Get out of the way so I can check it out. Might be a loose connection or a circuit breaker." He turned the radio off and on, checking the power supply and trying to find out what was the matter. He couldn't

129

see anything and didn't want to open up the box.

"I'll have to look at it tomorrow. Need some tools and testing equipment," he said.

"Don't do anything until I check with Howard. I learned today I don't take a shit without letting him know what's going on. Got my ass chewed for putting the stash up at Coral Cay. I'm supposed to move it down here tonight, which is what I wanted to talk to you about. I've made some more room in the back of the club. Don't like putting it so close to where someone might see it, but Howard doesn't want it at Coral.

"Think you and Pat can move it tonight? I'd appreciate it. Otherwise, we might be in trouble. He can't see it from the Nest 'cause it's around a corner and blocked by the ridge on the next island over."

Maxwell looked at him in disbelief, his slight shoulders slumping at the thought. "Move all that shit? Those things are heavy, old man," he said, for once some expression to his voice. "We'll wait until you and Laura get back tonight. Pat's strong and all, but that's asking a lot of the girl. Let me rest up and we'll do it when you get back."

"Okay. Fair enough," said Woody, still trying to figure out the radio. "At least Chubby got the message. I better see Howard when I'm at Sandy Cay tonight. Let me tell you, he's not a man to cross up. Guess that's why he is where he is and doing what he's doing. Can't say I'd want his job. Too many loose ends. My part's bad enough. You want another rum, go fix it. I'm gonna get Laura and be on our way. Should be interesting. What's going on at the club?"

"How should I know?" Max growled. "You know I don't go near that place."

"Sorry, I forgot," said Woody, shrugging.

After Woody and Laura sped off to Sandy Cay, Pat turned to Max and said, "Okay, where is it?"

"Where is what?"

"The pot. I know you guys did something with pot last night and I want to try some of it. Is it good stuff or some of that crap like the guy peddled here a couple weeks ago?"

"Haven't tried it yet. You want some, you'll get some. Come

130

on." She followed him to the storeroom. "Whoopee!" she said as he opened the door.

Woody had hung a padlock on the latch, but hadn't bothered to lock it.

"Oh, Max. This is something else. Holy shit. It's enough to light up the world. Let's get high. How about it, huh? No one will miss a few joints," she coaxed, putting her arms around him.

"Okay, little bird," he said, contemplating the idea. "Woody won't be back for hours."

They soon were sitting on the same lounge chair Woody and Laura had occupied a short time before, overlooking the dock and harbor of Smugglers Cay, the smokey, sweet aroma escaping around them. They sat still, enjoying deep drags of top grade weed, and soon didn't have a care in the world.

* * *

As Woody and Laura approached Sandy Cay, they passed the yacht club and went straight to the *Michelle*.

"I have a couple of minutes of business with Howard, then we'll go to the Sandy Cay Club," said Woody. "You stay here. Be right back." He leaped onto the deck of the *Michelle*, his shorter leg dragging behind, and went below.

"Howard," he called, limping down the short stairway. "Howard, the radio's out. Was talking to Chubby and it just quit." Howard, dressed in an orange T-shirt and cutoff Jeans, was sipping rum and playing a game of backgammon with Marjorie.

"Max started to look at it...."

"Max doesn't touch the radios," said Howard, barely looking up from his game. "Max is good for some things, but not for radios. His hands aren't to mess up even one dial. Got me?"

"Yeh, Howard, I read you. But I think it would be good to get it fixed."

"It'll be fixed," he said. "You moving that load to the island tonight?"

"Yup. All planned. We're going to have dinner at the yacht club, then Max is going to help me."

131

"You're having dinner out? That's interesting," said Howard, looking up with a rather straight face. "I suppose you're now going to tell me you've got the mad mechanic and his tweety bird wife guarding the island."

Woody began to feel uneasy, leaning on his short leg.

"Yeah, Howard. Thought I was doing the right thing. Didn't want to leave the island unguarded. Just thought dinner in town would be nice. You know, Laura deserves...."

"You've got a lot to learn in this game, my boy. A lot to learn," he said, shaking his head. "We're going to the Nest. Don't expect me to do your fucking job, man. You read me?"

"Yes sir," said Woody, a little softly.

"And if I hear you were mouthing off at the club there'll be some shit to pay. You read me on that one too?"

"Yes sir."

"One more thing. From now on, don't think. It could be dangerous to your health, since you don't seem equipped to put all the pieces together. Check with me in the morning. The radio will be fixed by nine o'clock. Now get on with your tea party."

Woody turned and left, a little taken aback by Howard. Doesn't give me any credit, he thought. Not an ounce of credit. Screw it, he thought. We came into the village to have a little fun. We deserve it. He climbed into the red boat, gunned it, and within minutes tied up at the Sandy Cay Club, Jackson handling the lines. As they walked into the club, Woody noticed Pete behind the bar.

"Hey there, Woody ol' boy. How's your pecker?" Pete gave him a big toothy smile, cigarette hanging out the corner of his mouth, pencil over his ear and a cranberry juice in hand. The bar reaction ranged from quiet chuckles to a couple of loud laughs. Pete tucked his thumbs under the belt of his pants and continued. "What can I fix you two tonight? Beer, rum, some punch? Let me buy you one to celebrate your new island." His blue eyes looked straight at Woody and Pete grinned.

"Make it a couple of punches," said Woody, smiling back. "As to your question, it's just fine, ol' man. Couldn't be better, right Laura?"

She gave him an embarrassed smirk, nodded her head a

132

little, then smiled.

"Anything ya say Woody. Anything ya say. Ah mean, what CAN Ah say? Ah wouldn't get into a discussion on that one for anything," she drawled, reaching for her rum punch.

"Did your help leave or are you taking a stand behind the bar like in the old days?" asked Woody, trying for a comeback dig at Pete.

"Man, I'm just biding my time till Wanda gets here. She's running a little late. And those good ol' days you refer to weren't so good. I just didn't know any better."

He continued smiling, leaning against the bar, tugging on his graying beard.

"My motto is still to serve everyone. If they want a drink I'll fix them a drink. On the other hand, if they don't want to drink, I'll help them with that too. Just a friendly, helpful place here. Right?" Pete looked over to some customers and winked.

"I've heard you're pretty qualified," said one man. "Nothing like pleasing the public."

Pete turned back to Woody, catching the eye of Charlie, sitting a few feet behind him in a barrel chair, unnoticed.

"Hey, Woody, how's your pilot working out? Hear he's gotten into the charter business," said Pete.

"Guess he got a trip today," said Woody. "No big deal."

"Oh yeah?" said Charlie rather loudly from behind. He stood up, walked over to Woody, and said, "Let me tell you the facts of life. I don't know who you are or what you've got going with that pilot. But he's illegal and he stole a trip from me today that was set up in advance. I flew over here to find out your friend took off with my passengers. Don't appreciate it one bit. Now I'm overnighting for two nights before I take those old ladies over there back to the mainland," he said, nodding his head at the Cross party playing Chinese checkers. "I don't care what he does for you, but he had better stay out of my territory. If he doesn't want the heat on, he'd better lay off."

Woody shrugged his shoulders.

"Hey, man, I had nothing to do with it. Max set the whole thing up. Honest. I had nothing to do with it. Don't get so upset...we'll probably want to use your services too. Don't

133

sweat it, man. There's bucks for everyone."

"Just telling you how it is. If he's your personal pilot that's your business. But if he's operating commercially he's gonna be in trouble. Enough said. How about a Coke, Pete?"

Charlie, usually easygoing, was fuming.

"Sure thing. You say Max set him up? Interesting," said Pete, glancing at Charlie. "One other thing, Woody. I suggest you tell your pilot this field closes when the lights go out. He was out joyriding or some damn thing last night and came in after legal hours. That's also frowned on here. And don't tell me it wasn't him. I know where he last parked his bird and it wasn't in the same spot this morning."

Woody felt he'd been put in a vice, first by Howard, now by these two. It wasn't a comfortable position, especially not knowing what Pete knew.

"Hey, look, guys," he said. "I brought the wife in here to have a good time, not to get dumped on. How about it? I mean, it isn't my problem Jock's a jerk."

"Just want you to know how tings work here, as the natives would say," said Pete. "Let me give you a couple of refills to start your night over. That make you feel better?" His blue eyes looked intently at Woody as he drew on his cigarette.

Woody nodded his head. Laura was quietly watching the old ladies and listening to their conversation. Two more rum punches were served up, and Pete smiled.

"Well, here comes Wanda. Now I'm off the hook," he said, wiping his hands on a towel and walking from behind the bar.

As Wanda took her place behind the bar, hibiscus tucked in her hair and a black dress emphasizing her dark skin, Pete motioned for Charlie to follow. They walked out the door and Woody and Laura joined the bar crowd, glad that the mood had changed.

Woody pulled a bar stool closer to him for Laura and nodded hello to the couple across the bar. There was a pool game going in the far corner of the room and the ladies were still playing checkers, but other than that, the bar was relatively quiet. When happy hour ended, most partygoers had drifted out of the bar and down the docks to their boats. Woody motioned to

Wanda that he'd like another rum punch and turned to Laura.

"This is what we need, Babes, a quiet evening. I'm going to enjoy the shit out of it, have a few drinks and not worry. It won't be a late night, though. Still have business back at the island. Want another drink?"

"Ah sure do," she said, smiling. "What kind of business?"

"Tell you later. Not here," he said quietly. Then he glanced over to the couple at the bar who were getting ready to leave.

"Aren't you the engineer I heard about?" asked Woody.

"That's right. You need to be designed?" he laughed. "Tom's my name. This is my wife Sue. You must be Woody. How's your island coming? Heard it's looking good. Gotta give you credit. That's a big job to tackle. We poked around when it was deserted. Pretty little place. We followed those low stone walls around to the backside of the island where the old native shacks are about to fall down. Reminded us of other places in the Caribbean."

"Yeah. I've seen the wall, but haven't had the time to enjoy exploring. We'll get around to it. Buy you a drink?"

"No, thanks. We're heading out to our cruiser. Have a good dinner," he said, pushing on the screen door. "Maybe we'll come to Smugglers in a couple of days."

"Wait till next week sometime," said Woody. "Got a few things going on that should be done about Monday or Tuesday. Better if you come then," he said, not wanting anyone to visit Smugglers just now.

As the couple walked out, Woody asked for another punch.

"You really puttin' dem away," commented Wanda, smiling. "But I makes dem as fast as you kin drinks dem. Boss man says keep eberyone happy. You want me to makes up a pitcher full?"

"Why not? I know I'll want a couple more of these things and Laura will too. How about those nice ladies over there? Think they'd like to be treated to a drink?"

Wanda laughed.

"Dey goes for treats from anyone. You want me to ax dem?"

"No. Let me go see." He pushed off the stool and limped over to the Cross party, dressed in cotton sundresses for dinner.

"How about a round of rum punches for you ladies? It looks

135

like you're enjoying yourselves and I'm in a good mood. How about it?"

They were delighted. Not one of them would have turned down anything. So Wanda served up four punches for the ladies and another two for Woody and Laura, who cautioned him about having too many with work still to do.

"Quit lecturing, Laura," he said gruffly, in contrast to her soft voice. "I know what I have to do but I also know I'm here for a good time. Let me have a few drinks and unwind. I don't think you understand the pressure I've been under."

She was about to answer him when the bell rang for dinner. She knew she wouldn't get anywhere with him. Woody was on his way and there was no stopping. He asked Wanda for a couple more punches for the dinner table, then they followed the Cross party, already tipsy, to the dining area.

A few other couples were eating, but it was a sedate crowd.

Woody felt inhibited both by what Howard had said and by the nature of the people around him. No one seemed overly friendly so he and Laura chose to eat alone. After chowder, a salad, some grouper and all the trimmings of a native dinner, he was ready to leave, but only after hitting the bar first.

"Wanda," he said, perched on a stool and leaning toward her. "Is there such a thing as a pitcher to go? We don't have all the garbage to put in a punch and by God, gal, you got me hooked on those lethal things tonight."

"Sure ting. I gib you plastic pitcher, you brings it back next time you here, okay?"

"Okay. You're all right." He left her a ten dollar tip and followed Laura out the door.

"Ah have to admit it is a good punch," she said. Her words were beginning to slur, so she and Woody were now talking the same language.

"What time is it?" he asked as they climbed down into the red boat, lower now because the tide was out.

"About 10 or so," she said, yawning and almost losing her balance. Woody started the engines and they roared off the dock, sideswiping a small runabout anchored a few feet away. There wasn't any damage, but Woody found himself in a tangle of lines. He figured out the puzzle, then headed once more to Smugglers.

The moon had become a bigger ball in the sky and the stars were incredible. As Laura glanced back at the wake of the boat, she saw phosphorescence churning in the sea and flickers of light catching each little ripple. Woody, who knew the way almost blindfolded now, was inching closer to the little islands, trying to get to Smugglers the shortest way possible. As they neared their island, Woody could see lights in the club and what looked like Max and Pat on the sundeck overlooking the dock. As the boat neared the club they seemed frozen to their chairs so Woody and Laura docked by themselves.

"Hey, aren't you going to give us a hand?" shouted Woody, a little aggravated they hadn't jumped up when they saw him.

"Here," said Max, extending his hand in an exaggerated fashion. "You want a hand, Mon, you can have it. You want a foot, Mon, you can have it...." He had slowly stood up and was dancing on one foot, then fell onto the chaise as he lost his balance.

"I'll have your fucking head in about two minutes, the time it's going to take me to get out of this boat, walk up the dock and give you what you deserve."

Pat was giggling hysterically at Max, unable to sit up, and for the first time in a long while, smiling and laughing.

"Goddamn son of a bitch. What the hell's going on around here?" stormed Woody, revving up his madness. "What did you two do? Smoke us out of the entire load? I ought to...." He started to reach for Max, lost his balance and slammed his knee against the chaise. Max and Pat were higher than the dancing moon.

"Goddamnit," said Woody, holding his knee. "I'm pissed as hell. How're we supposed to move those fucking bales? I was counting on you keeping half a head together tonight. I can't even go and play around a little. You really fucked up. And quit your goddamn laughing. You're about as useless as tits on a bull."

Woody was shouting and even Laura was beginning to get the giggles over the helpless situation. She was bombed too, but somehow had enough sense to realize nothing could be done about what had happened.

"Look, ya'll," she said, laughing. "It's not going to do any good for ya'll to scream and holler and carry on. The best thing to do is for ya'll to get some sleep. Ya'll hardly had any shut-eye last night and Ah didn't either. Ah'm going to bed. Early morning is time enough to do whatever you have to do. Good night." With that, she took off her shoes and marched straight into the club, past the bar and up the stairs to where she and Woody slept.

"Well," said Woody, with a huff. "I guess she knows what the fuck she wants to do. Shit, Max. You realize Howard chewed my ass tonight?"

Max thought about Howard chewing Woody's ass.

"Bet he found your hide tough as leather," he said, in his normal monotone but still laughing from his high. "Which cheek did he get?"

Pat was now uncontrollable, with tears rolling down her face, a crumbled joint in her lap. The hairpins had come out and her hair now hung from the top of her head in all directions, down the back of her neck and straggling in her face. She was sitting yoga style on the chaise, rocking back and forth laughing, unable to stop.

"Piss on it," said Woody. "I'm taking my pitcher and going to bed."

"He's taking his pitcher to bed!" said Pat, laughing even more. "You gonna fuck the pitcher?"

Woody stood still, then limped over the same course Laura had taken, shaking his head and cursing under his breath. Good thing I'm thinking, he thought. Get some sleep, set the alarm, get up early and move the shit. He chugged some more rum punch and climbed the stairs, pitcher in hand.

Outside, Max and Pat were still high. She was holding her sides from laughing but beginning to wind down. Max sat back, mellowed out. He closed his eyes and listened to the tiny waves slapping at the seawall below the dock. In a few minutes, his mind was in never-never land, oblivious even to the hungry mosquitoes. Pat curled up beside him. Within a few minutes, both were asleep.

* * *

The alarm sounded for at least two minutes before Woody could even open an eye to see what was making the noise. Laura pulled the covers over her head to avoid the shrill sound penetrating her still-saturated head. After fumbling for the clock and alarm button, Woody brought silence to the small room. Six o'clock. The sun was streaming through the window, attacking his reddened eyes.

"Where's the aspirin?" he asked Laura.

A hand jutted out from under the sheet and pointed to a first-aid kit on the table across the room. He swung his legs over the side of the bed and kicked over the remaining rum punch.

"Oh God," he said, pitifully. "She must have put grain alcohol in that bucket last night. My mouth is awful."

Then he remembered Max.

He pulled himself together, took three aspirin out of the bottle and shakily headed down the stairs.

Max and Pat had come inside during the night and were entangled on the pool table. Woody limped over, still unable to maintain a straight line, and stood there, looking at the two of them before reaching over and shaking Max.

"Hey, what you doin'?" said Max, riled at the early morning call and back to his normal sullen disposition.

"We got business, if you remember."

"Ohhh," said Max, falling back on the pool table, holding his head, his blonde hair disheveled.

"Come on, dammit. You think I want to do this either? I'll make some coffee. Think you can figure out how to get away from her? God, she looks awful," said Woody, peering at Pat, clothes and hair a mess. She was only half-dressed, with her jeans down around her knees, bikini pants low on the hips and blouse undone. She opened her eyes and didn't bother to cover herself when she saw Woody staring at her.

"Oh," she said, with disgust. "It's YOU."

She sat up, buttoning her blouse and tugging at her jeans.

Woody shook his head and went to the kitchen. Black coffee

would cure all.

Max snapped and zippered his pants, walked into the kitchen looking like he'd been through the wringer of an old-fashioned washing machine and sat down. The water was almost boiling and Woody put down two cups with a generous spoonful of instant coffee in each one.

"We're gonna have to move fast," he told Max. "Promised Howard it would be moved last night. He's getting the radio situation squared away by nine this morning. Have to have everything in order by then." Max nodded, watching as Woody poured the hot water, went to the refrigerator, took out two ice cubes from the freezer compartment, and plopped one in each of their cups.

"We don't have time for it to cool off. Drink it and let's get going."

Within minutes, they were in the little red boat. The engines sounded like a clap of thunder in the early morning stillness, even though Woody kept them at idle.

He eased out of the harbor and slowly made his way to Coral Cay. As he came around the last little bend where the ridge blocked the view from Smugglers and the Nest, he could see the door slightly ajar.

"What the hell?" he said slowly, under his breath, noticing tracks in the sand from the beach to the building.

He glanced at Max.

The color had drained from Max's face and he was staring, like Woody, at the warehouse.

Woody gunned the boat onto the beach and both of them jumped out, tossing a line on the shore ahead of them. Woody stomped as he limped to the warehouse door and threw it open. He was stunned. Not a bale was there! Not even an ounce of sweet marijane remained.

Max stared too, unable to come to his senses on what had happened. They looked at each other.

"We've been ripped off, man. We've been fuckin' ripped off. And that's our profit, Max. That was worth a million bucks on the streets."

His voice was rising, his temper replacing the disbelief. "A million buck's worth, Max. We've been ripped off, Goddamnit. What do we tell Howard? We gotta find the bastards, Max. I'm not gonna put up with this shit. Come on."

Max still couldn't say anything. He followed Woody to the boat, helped him push off, then said, "Look." He pointed to a boat already a good mile off the island, riding low in the water.

"Come on!" shouted Woody. In no time, he had gunned the boat and was heading toward the larger vessel. It was the same type as his, only much bigger, with the sleek lines of an ocean racer and the power to go with it. But it appeared heavy in the water.

"We might be able to catch up to the bastards," said Woody. "They'll never be able to move like us with all that shit aboard."

He tore off after the modern day pirates, pushing the little boat for all it was worth, not thinking about what would happen if he did catch them.

As they neared, they could see a dark blue hull with two high-powered engines churning off the transom. A black man was at the wheel. As they got close, they could see another person in the rear of the boat, crouched low near the engines. As the gap began to close, the pirates let loose with gunfire.

"Holy shit," said Woody, ducking. "Under the console, Max. Reach under the console and then up. Give me that fucking carbine. I'll show those mothers who they're dealing with."

Max reached where Woody had said and, sure enough, pulled out a rifle.

"It's loaded," said Woody. "Fire at 'em."

"Shit, man, I've never handled one of these," said Max. "Here. You take it and I'll drive. That I can do." More gunfire was raining down, missing the boat each time. Woody took aim and let loose, four shots not even coming close to his target.

"Christ," said Woody. "We'll never get them at this rate. Keep following. I'll give it another try." As he tried to aim while watching a volley of gunshot fall short of their boat, the lead boat began to change course.

"Follow them," he said, and Max kept the speed in full gear.

"I can shorten our distance by cutting over there," he nodded, shouting above the roar of the engine.

"Then do it. We gotta catch 'em. At least get closer so I can shoot this thing with some accuracy."

As Max cut the arc of the circle, he felt a sudden thud. The boat came to a halt in about a foot of water, a sandbar acting as instant brake.

"Goddamnit!" shouted Woody, knowing he was beat. "Those bastards led us right into this fucking trap. High noon with the sun overhead we'd have been able to see that sand spit, but not at this hour of the day."

For the first time in many years, Woody wanted to cry. Max hunched over the wheel, not feeling any better than Woody.

"Well," said Woody. "Let's get this friggin' thing off this sandbar and over to Sandy Cay. We're gonna have to find out who those blackbeards are. Stole our profits, Max. They stole our profits. What am I ever going to tell Howard?"

Max shook his head in bewilderment, jumped over the side and tried to push the boat toward deeper water. It wouldn't budge.

"No use," he said. "We'll have to wait for the tide to come up." He got back into the boat and looked at Woody, seeming to age as he sat, gazing in the direction of his precious ripped-off load, sullen over the thought of facing Howard.

"Yeah," said Woody at last. "Tide will just slow down the music we're gonna hear. We're hard aground. No sense pushing it. God, would I love a drink."

* * *

An hour passed before the little red boat began to float on its own, then Max and Woody eased it off the sand shoal by hand.

"Better go easy with the props as you start it. Don't know what damage we did," said Woody.

He knew from examining the boat while aground that there was a problem with the starboard outdrive and that he'd have to take it easy. Max started the port engine and everything seemed to be all right.

"Good thing we're only a few minutes away," said Woody. "It shouldn't take too long." As they approached Conch Inn marina, the port engine started to run rough. Max eased the power, but it was no use. About three hundred yards off the dock, the engine quit.

"Oh shit," said Woody. "What now, for Christ sake? What else could possibly happen? Most people are only getting up and we've already been in enough trouble to last anyone a month."

Max spotted a couple of native boys looking for conch and gave a whistle, motioning them to come over to the boat.

"Got a few bucks on you?" he asked Woody.

"How was I to know I'd need any bread at this hour? I'm lucky to be in this thing myself, let alone with money. You got any?"

Max reached into his pocket and pulled out a worn wallet. "Yeah, I got a fiver I can give them. That oughta do it."

As the boys pulled alongside, Max tossed them a line.

"Mind giving us a tow to the dock? We want to tie up alongside that schooner."

The boys fastened the line, and smiling like they'd just caught a big one, began towing the speed boat toward the dock. Max gave them the tip along with a thanks, and they tied the red boat fore and aft alongside the *Michelle.*

No one was aboard the schooner.

"Must be at the Nest. Let's hike on out. Don't know about you, but I want to get this one over with."

"Might as well," said Max. "You want me to go with you? It really wasn't my mess-up, you know. It might be a better idea for me to look at the boat and get it running again. We're going to need it, and quite frankly, I don't want to listen to Howard. I'm just a worker in this scheme. We'll be in better shape if I can get the boat running."

"You're right," said Woody, "although I'd like the company."

"Good luck, old man. I'll get to work," said Max.

Woody headed toward the Nest, building up courage to face Howard.

Chapter 8

The Conference

As he left Max, Woody walked slowly toward the airstrip trying to organize his thoughts and put off the confrontation with Howard. He glanced from side to side, noticing how different the village looked early in the morning. One woman was washing clothes in a couple of big washtubs perched on a wood bench next to her house, while chickens scratched for feed in the yard.

He glanced at his watch. 8:30.

How did Howard plan on having the radio fixed by nine this morning, he wondered. On his right, some broken down playground equipment was a reminder of earlier island days, when there were more youngsters to swing and slide. The village generator emitted a low purr as he went by. Max must have gotten the power problem straightened out, he thought.

Soon he was crossing the airstrip and hiking toward the road to the Nest, his limp more obvious than usual. When he was just below the house he stopped, looked up and took a deep breath. Cardiac Hill. That's what we ought to call it, he thought, and began climbing. When he got to the top, Woody felt eyes on him although he couldn't see anyone in the house. As he raised his hand to knock, Howard opened the door.

"Why are you here?" he asked, suspecting trouble by the look on Woody's face.

"Gotta talk to you, Howard. Things are really fucked up." Woody was obviously agitated.

"Okay," said Howard, almost in a fatherly way. "Sit down, start from the beginning and tell me what happened. I know you were on the island for dinner last night. You get back okay?"

"Yeah. Everything went fine there. I kept my mouth shut just like you told me to and we left at a decent hour. When we got back, though, Max and Pat were out of it. If they're any judges of the stuff, it's damn good. Anyway, I realized we couldn't move the load in his condition and I set the alarm to

145

move it at six this morning."

Howard nodded, and Woody continued.

"Anyway, I got us going with a cup of coffee, then we went to Coral Cay. I was a little suspicious when we pulled up because the door looked like it had been opened. When we got there, the load was gone. I don't know what to say, Howard. Anyway, as we were standing there, Max saw a big racer on the horizon, riding low in the water. We jumped in our boat and took off after it."

"What color was it?" asked Howard.

"Dark blue," said Woody, "with a couple of big outboards. Even loaded, she really moved."

Howard nodded. "You want a cup of coffee?"

Woody nodded and Howard went to the kitchen.

"Then what did you do?" he asked, sitting down again and giving a mug to Woody.

"We tried to close on them and they started shooting at us. No shit, Howard. They started shooting. I had Max take the controls and got out the carbine, but couldn't get close enough to hit them. They started veering to the west and we cut in a smaller circle. We'd have had them if we hadn't run aground."

"You ran aground?" Howard said, matter-of-factly, looking intently at Woody, still flushed from all the excitement. "You ran aground. Then what?"

"Then we were fucking stuck, man," said Woody, impatient over Howard's calmness. "Had to wait an hour for the tide, watching our profits disappear on the horizon. Messed up the starboard outdrive, and as we limped in on the port engine it puked too. Had to be towed by a couple of kids. Max is working on it now. I'm sorry, Howard. Christ, I'm sorry. I don't know what else to say."

"That's it?" asked Howard.

"That's enough, isn't it?" said Woody, not knowing how to take Howard's reaction.

"Okay. You were ripped off by Juan. You're not the first and not the last. He makes a career out of stealing loads any way he can, pirating all over the Caribbean. He probably saw the whole thing when the *Seagull* broke down. We're lucky he only

146

got that much. He's a real pirate dating back to his great-great-granddaddy who ran with Blackbeard himself. Or so he claims. Flamboyant little bastard. Always flashing his profits. If he ever fell in the drink, his own gold would drown him. I'm not going to chew you on this because there's nothing we can do. Now that we know he's wise to our game, we have to cover ourselves better. Anyway, what can we do? Complain to the police? He's got us and he knows it so kiss the load good-bye. Big thing is to make sure the rest of the transfer goes okay. The profits went, but we didn't go in the hole. Let me handle it. We don't want any heat or any repercussions. Act like nothing happened."

Howard went to the window and grabbed a pair of binoculars. "Right on time," he said.

"Who's that?" asked Woody, hearing a plane.

"Jock, a new radio, the parts you ordered for Max, some other gear and a letter for me with all the latest info," said Howard. "I also put in a grocery order for you."

"Gee, thanks. Forgot about supplies."

"I know," said Howard, as if talking to a child. "I know. Come on. We'll meet Jock. Don't say anything about what happened this morning. That's a closed book. Just get that boat running again.

"By the way, you've got another fuel dump coming in with Lucky late Saturday. Don't want any boats limping out of fuel on the way to the mainland. It'll five hundred gallons. Store it in a sensible place, away from the main buildings."

"Got just the place," said Woody, thinking of the shacks Tom had mentioned the night before. They hiked down the hill and across the strip to the parking area as Jock's wheels touched down. He taxied over to where they were standing and climbed out of the plane with a big smile on his face.

"Hi, guys," he said. He was wearing his usual scrubby shirt over cut-off jeans. "What's going on? Got all the stuff you wanted, Howard. Everything cool?"

"Everything's cool," said Howard, taking the envelope Jock held out. "Everything's cool."

Chapter 9

Departures/Arrivals

On Friday morning, Charlie met the Cross party in the dining room of the club to see if the ladies would mind an early departure. Someone had come in on a boat the night before and needed to be on the mainland by noon.

"Sure, Charlie," said Mrs. Cross. "Whatever you say. Just fly us back safely and we'll not complain about a thing."

She and the girls were starting the day off right — a Bloody Mary with their omelet.

"Okay," he said. "As soon as you have your luggage together let me know and I'll help you carry it. Have a good breakfast and I'll see you in a bit."

He walked to the bar and motioned to Pete.

"You know that guy who asked about the flight last night?"

Pete shook his head no.

"Have a feeling about him," said Charlie. "Came off that powerboat that arrived late last night and left early this morning. Said he doesn't have much, just one little bag, and that he'll probably want to get back sometime next week. Is it my imagination, or is this island attracting a bunch of weirdos lately? Everywhere you turn there's a strange plane landing and taking off, or a boat from some mystery port, people walking around like their shadow's going to bite them and a lot of other strange things. And that shootout. You hear any more?"

"No, but Woody's little red boat sure isn't going anywhere," said Pete, smiling. "Max is working on it, so you know what that means. Woody's telling him to hurry it up and Max keeps running into problems, like he can't get it all together at the same time to make it run. Everyone's kinda laughing about it. Know what you're talking about on the feeling, though. Heard another plane late last night. Came and left. Don't want to make it my business, but it seems like this island's a new target for the funny boys. What do you think?"

"I've got the same feeling," said Charlie. "Here comes my

149

passenger now."

Pete looked over at a slender man dressed in jeans, a western shirt and leather boat shoes. He was carrying a briefcase. He didn't look unusual…dark hair, sunglasses, clean shaven…but it was rare that anyone traveled with just a briefcase.

"We don't get too many businessman types down here," said Pete, nodding to the briefcase and smiling. "Most people have chucked one of those before arriving."

The man just laughed.

"Well, business still goes on, even when you try to play," he said, making light of his baggage.

"We have to wait for those ladies to get their things together and then we'll be on our way," said Charlie, nodding to the Cross party walking slowly to their bungalows. As Mrs. Cross climbed the steps to the porch overlooking the water, she exclaimed, "My hat! Charlie, my hat! Pete, come here!" Sure enough. There, floating on the tide, was her hat, soggy from two days in the salt water, the flowery cotton band now bleached. But it was definitely her hat. Charlie and Pete hurried over, and Pete carefully inched down the coral rock to retrieve it.

"You lose this, lady?" he asked, chuckling. It was as though her stray cat had found its way home. She was delighted. Pete and Charlie helped the ladies load, dressed in their going-home dresses of pastel polyester, and they were soon on their way to the airstrip in *Cyclops*.

As they rounded the corner of the road near Conch Inn, Charlie saw Jock standing near Max's workshop. Jock glanced at him, gave a big toothy smile and waved.

Arrogant, thought Charlie, ignoring him. Really arrogant.

Pete brought *Cyclops* to the plane to simplify loading, and Charlie helped the ladies off the Jeep. In true form, Mrs. Cross had managed a carryout of Bloody Marys. Charlie chuckled and shook his head. How they managed, he didn't know, but manage they did. In less than five minutes, the plane was loaded and Charlie had done a thorough preflight, particularly checking his fuel.

"Be in again Sunday," said Charlie as Pete climbed onto the driver's seat of *Cyclops*. "Have two people for the cottages and four for some boat. I'll have empty seats going out, so see if you can fill them. I'll be in touch on the radio when I get back. The office seems quiet, though. Whole summer's been rather quiet."

"Yeah," said Pete. "I just have a funny feeling it's not going to stay that way. Have a good flight back. We'll be in touch. Say hi to Annie."

"Will do. It's about time I get the wife over here again. She thinks I have all the fun," said Charlie, laughing and closing the rear door of the plane.

Pete turned *Cyclops* around and headed back to the yacht club. Jackson had said something about needing help with the generator and two broken-down outboards. Charlie had both engines running and was taxiing as Pete turned along the back road to the club. By the time he was past the village well, he could hear the plane taking off.

* * *

A couple hours later, a sailboat came into the Conch Inn docks and tied up next to Maxwell working on the red boat, engine torn down and tools strewn everywhere. In overheating, the engine had seized and Max was now faced with rebuilding it. He was itemizing the parts he would need, when someone on the sailboat interrupted his thoughts.

"You know where we can find Charlie the pilot?" a woman in her mid-thirties asked.

"Took off a couple of hours ago," said Max, sullenly. Then he pushed his glasses on his nose and looked up. "You need to get out? We've got a pilot here who does the same thing Charlie does only cheaper. Can arrange it for you right away."

Two duffel bags were on the dock and a man obviously ready to travel by air rather than sail was making arrangements with the captain.

"Hey, Honey," said the woman, turning to him. "We just missed Charlie. If only the radio had been working. This man says someone else flies out too. You want to go with him?"

"Don't have much choice. We're already delayed with that breakdown. Gotta get back to work. How do we find this other

151

pilot?" he asked.

"I'll get him right away," said Max, wiping the oil off his hands on a rag. "Bring your bags and wait between the buildings in the shade."

Max jumped onto the dock from the red boat and went aboard the *Michelle*. Jock was making himself a sandwich.

"Got another trip for you. Will work out perfect for getting all these parts for the boat. They're ready to go, so eat fast and get your act together," said Max, ordering Jock in his monotone.

Jock nodded, stuffed the sandwich in his mouth and poured a glass of lemonade to wash it down. He took the list from Max, and in about five minutes, was greeting his passengers. They all climbed into Max's Jeep and headed for the strip, stopping next to Jock's small plane.

"Single-engine?" asked the man, a bit surprised.

"No sweat," said Jock. "Do it all the time. No sense wasting money. We'll get you there fine. "

The couple looked at each other, shrugged, and loaded their gear. They already were two days late and were pushing the clock.

"Get those parts as soon as you can," ordered Max, watching Jock preflight the plane. "In the meantime, I'll get the exhaust system done on the *Sea 'n' Be*. Let Woody or Howard know if there are any problems, but it should be easy to get them all. Gotta get that thing running."

"I know," said Jock. "Sure would come in handy this weekend. Well, I'll see you as soon as possible. Chubby will know where to get all this shit." With that, he climbed into the plane, waved and started the engine. Max turned back to Conch Inn to work on Terry's boat. No one was aboard.

"To hell with it," he said to himself, yawning. A nap would be much more sensible than work. He'd had only a few hours sleep, and with the excitement of the early morning, Max was ready to call it quits.

He packed up his tools from the red boat, then went to close up shop as Manny was coming around the corner.

"Hey, Mon. What happened to you dis mornin'? Heard you had it out wid de down-island boys," said Manny, looking at

Maxwell suspiciously.

"What's goin' on, Mon? We can't hab all dat shit on dis island. Dis a happy place. People gits scared and dey no come."

"Don't believe all you hear, Manny," sad Max, crisply. "Had a little problem running aground this morning. I'm getting the boat fixed and no one should be concerned. Don't know about the down-island boys. If I hear something, I'll let you know."

"You look like a tired old mon," said Manny, noting how listless Max was for mid-afternoon. "You better gits some sleep. Dat wife o' yours keep you goin' too strong, Mon. Gotta eat more conch. Keep you manhood goin' strong," he chuckled. Max almost smiled. Whatever the problem, conch was the cure. The natives wrapped the raw shellfish around babies' arms for teething. Children swallowed the slippery innards to grow strong. And men swore raw conch increased their families.

"Conch cures all, I know," said Max.

Manny smiled and disappeared into his little marina office. Max could feel fatigue setting in and wanted to get home. As he was driving up the hill past the yacht club he saw Pat.

"Nothing like forgetting about me," she said, dryly. "Hitched a ride with Tom and Sue after they brought Woody back to Smugglers. What happened, anyway? Where's the red boat? Woody said it ran aground. How can you navigate at night with no problem, then run aground in the day? That's pretty stupid. Anyway, Woody got them to give me a ride back to the island. I couldn't get anything out of him on where you were or when you'd come get me, so he shipped me back with them."

Max rested his head on the steering wheel as Pat carried on, wanting to climb into bed and ignore her questions. When she was done with her barrage of words, he said, "Glad you got back okay. I'm dead. Let me rest and we'll talk later. Where are you going?"

"I WAS looking for you," she said, flipping her hair back. "I'll get a few groceries. Did the freight boat get in last night? They were out of lettuce."

"Haven't heard. But then, I didn't ask anyone," he said, wanting to cut the conversation short.

"Okay. Get some sleep. You look pretty bad. See you later."

Pat hiked off, looking completely rested and together. Probably slept all morning, thought Max, watching her a little enviously. A few minutes later he was home, stretched out on the bed, shielding his eyes from the sun streaming in the front porch. He couldn't remember the last time he was this tired.

* * *

"Woodpecker to Max. Woodpecker to Max. Come in Max...."

Vaguely, in the back of his subconscious, Max heard Woody calling on the VHF. He rolled over and slowly came to. Six o'clock. Still daylight. Pat wasn't back, he noticed, looking around the tiny bungalow.

"Woodpecker to Max. Come back, Max. Woodpecker to Max...."

Max walked over to the radio, picked up the mike and answered back.

"Max here. What do you want, Woody?"

"Well, it's about time you answered. Just want to know the status of the red boat. You get it running or you just sleeping the day away?"

"Very funny," said Max dryly. "I sent Jock back to the mainland for parts. Don't expect anything great until Monday. Even Chubby doesn't have the connections to pry those parts loose on a weekend."

"I'll be coming there in the black boat," said Woody. "Have a few things to take care of. You gonna be around?"

"Yeah. Not going anywhere," said Max, stretching and yawning as he talked to Woody.

"Okay. See ya. Woodpecker clear."

"Max clear." Max stood for a few seconds, still not completely awake, wondering how Woody kept up the pace. Must be on speed, he thought. No one has that much natural energy. He walked slowly toward the bed and flopped back down. As he was about to drift off to sleep again, Pat walked in, loaded down with groceries.

"Were in luck," she said. "The freight boat got in, we've got

154

lettuce, tomatoes, even some native pineapples. What a mad rush. Everyone's starved for freshies lately. Ought to have Jock bring stuff in on his trips seeing as he's making so many. Want a banana?" she asked, pulling one out of the bag and laying it on the counter.

"No," he said, sitting on the edge of the bed and yawning again. "Christ. I feel like I've been run over by a bulldozer. "

"You were from all the rumors floating around in the village," she said. "I told everyone you guys just misread the water. Were you really shot at? I mean, you can tell your wife, can't you?"

"Less you know the better," said Max. "We got any lemonade or soft drinks around?"

"How about a beer?" He screwed up his face at the thought.

"Well, I'm going to have one," she said, opening a can. "Keeps me going. Had a couple in the village with Manny this afternoon. He's all concerned about the island and some of the things that have been happening. Did you hear about the plane that came in the other night? Someone gave it fuel before it went on. Manny was trying to figure out who did it."

"Why is Manny so goddamn concerned about what's happening all of a sudden? He probably fueled it himself and is trying to pass off the blame," said Max. "Business hasn't been all that great for him lately and you'll notice he's not screaming the poor cry like he used to. Bet he's mixed up in something too. Never can tell with the natives, you know, not even living here as long as I have. They always know what's going on. Think they beat the drums. Toss me that banana. I'm starving."

She held back, smugly asking, "Say please...."

"For Christ sake, woman, toss me the damn thing. I'm not in any mood to play around."

She tossed him the banana and gave him a smirk.

"You never are, Max. I'm beginning to feel it...."

"Oh shove it," he said angrily. "You're taken care of, aren't you? When I ask you to do something, you can do it."

"And if I ask for a little consideration you can give it," she said, putting things in the tiny refrigerator. Max was fine as long as she kept her place, an unliberated one as far as HE was

155

concerned. Oh well, she thought. Play him along.

"Chicken okay for dinner?" she asked, faking a smile.

"Fine. Anything's fine. The mood I'm in, with no sleep and all, anything's fine. It would all taste the same anyway."

"Then I shouldn't bother to cook it," she said, snapping back.

He looked at her in disgust. "I'm going down to the dock. It's hot in here."

She watched as he walked out the door. Typical, she thought. I do the shopping, come home and now have to cook dinner alone.

The situation was becoming more predictable. As long as Max had everything his way life went along smoothly. But the minute he didn't, Pat caught the backlash. No wonder it took him so long to get a woman, she thought. And how totally dumb of me to marry the SOB.

She split the chicken and reached for a baking pan. Life wasn't easy on the island. She thought of how convenient supermarkets were in the States, how easy it was to get in a car and go somewhere, how you could walk into a place and not have everyone know who you were, who you were married to, where you lived, what you ate for breakfast, who just sent you a letter, who got drunk or high the night before and who was sleeping with who else's partner.

At times the island confinement, masked by its semblance of total freedom, smothered Pat. It took looking out the front porch to bring her back to the beauty of the island, to its simplicity, its rugged features, its natural charm. When she put the chicken in the oven and had it set, she walked to the porch, curled up in the old-fashioned swing Max had hung for her before they were married, and looked out over the incredible water.

She could peer down to the bottom of a reef from the porch, and could almost see fish swimming. Once, they had baited a shark off the dock and she had seen the huge beast take the bait, its dark hulk reflected in the moonlight as it struggled for freedom. She could see Max now, dangling his feet in the cool water, probably thinking about the nasty mood he was in. She thought of how he would come back to the house with a better

156

attitude and they would start all over.

The first few months the scene was sporadic, but lately, it was becoming routine. Sort of a kiss and make up, she thought. But the beauty was there on the island, and she knew no life was perfect. She kicked the window sill, letting the swing rock her. It had a tiny squeak to the chain as it went back and forth. As Pat got up to put some rice in a pot, Max came up the hill.

"Water's nice," he said. Pat nodded, turning on the stove, knowing that his comment was as close to an apology as he could manage.

"I took a dip earlier, after a nap," she said. "Boy, did I feel like shit this morning. How about you?"

"Like that pool table was my tomb," he said, recalling their bed. "You look good now, though, and I'm beginning to feel human again. I'll have a beer with you."

He walked over to the refrigerator and pulled out a can.

"Not very cold."

"We haven't had much power," she said. "Are we ever going to get a decent generator?"

"You're talking money," said Max, dryly. "I'd rather steal what I can off the yacht club and use our generator in an emergency."

Money again. She knew he had the bucks for whatever they wanted or needed, but Max hated to part with money. He was often teased about being Scottish, rather than Australian. But it didn't matter. He bought only what he absolutely needed and hoarded like a modern day Scrooge. He wasn't dumb, he told Pat. He had enough saved to take care of them should anything ever happen, and he had promised to buy her a home in the States as soon as they found a "good deal," whatever THAT was. So Pat hung in, living on his promises and hoping they would come true someday.

In the meantime, she lived rather Spartanly, swimming and sunning at will, with very few responsibilities outside of keeping the house clean, fixing meals and doing laundry without a machine.

The little house was beginning to fill with the aroma of baked chicken, and Pat set two places on the divider bar between

157

the kitchen and living area. She washed a head of lettuce and made a salad. She always tried to have the ingredients of a well-balanced meal, but with supplies in short order, it wasn't always possible.

They relied on the sea for their protein, but vegetables, fruit, flour and rice had to come from the mainland, often taking days to reach the island via the weekly freight boat. As she took the chicken out of the oven, Max sat down. "Good dinner," he said, helping himself as she put the pan on a trivet. She smiled. everything was okay again with Max. They'd have a good evening.

* * *

About eight o'clock, Max could hear the high pitch of engines. He looked out and saw Woody pulling up to his dock, looking up to see if he was home. Max waved, walked out of the house and down the path to the dock. It was almost dark. The engines were still running as Woody began talking over the low roar.

"Going up to see Howard about the weekend plans," he said. "If everything's on schedule, that load will be off by midnight Sunday. You want to come with me? Might not be a bad idea. There won't be a screw-up if we both know what's going on."

"Didn't know I was supposed to be a part of that end," said Max, pushing his glasses on his nose.

"Need some muscle," said Woody. "The boys will have had a long trip and face a longer one back. Want to give them all the help we can. Also, want the whole thing over as quickly as possible. The two of us can move those things pretty fast as a team. What do you think?"

"You're probably right. What does Howard say?"

"Don't know. Going to see him now. Come on. Think it's important, especially with Jock gone. Hop in."

Max turned and looked up toward the house. Pat waved. He waved back, indicating he was going with Woody, and they headed for Conch Inn marina.

Manny had moved the red boat to make room for a sailboat

and Woody eased the black racer to the inside dock. He glanced over. The hatches on the *Michelle* were closed and padlocked. Howard was at the Nest. As they were walking down the dock, Terry and Juney were returning to their boat.

"See you got the parts, Max. Think you'll get to it tomorrow?" asked Terry.

"Planning on it. All depends on the schedule. Do you have to get going right away?"

Terry looked at Woody.

"Fix it first thing in the morning, Max," said Woody pointedly. "I'll talk to you later, Terry. May have a job for you, but I'll let you know. Come on, Max."

They walked on, Max beginning to get the picture. Osprey Nest looked like a beacon against the evening sky on the ridge above. "What do you have planned for them?" he asked coyly. "That boat isn't very fast."

"Something different," said Woody, limping at a quick pace. "We're going to send her south. The kid's made a few runs before and knows the ropes. Juney speaks fluent Spanish and knows her way around too. Just get the *Sea 'n' Be* in top shape before I send them off."

"Will do. Never know, do you?" he looked at Woody.

"Nope. Think we're probably in for a few more surprises along the way. Only one thing wrong with this damn place of Howard's," he said, stopping and looking up. "It's gonna kill someone some day. Look at that road. It's almost perpendicular."

"We could walk the long way if it's easier for you," said Max.

"Waste of time. Better to just take a deep breath and pant when it's over."

They climbed the path and were soon at Howard's door, already opened to greet them. They could smell something cooking, and Howard had poured a couple of drinks for them.

"Evening, gentlemen," he said, motioning for them to sit down at a table near the kitchen. Max hadn't been at the house since it was built. The view was still incredible. Even from the lower level at night, he could see along the top of the ridge and

159

below to the ocean where the beach stretched almost a mile, interrupted only by coral formations indenting several private beaches. At low tide, beachcombers could walk from one to the other, but at high tide, each beach was snugly cut off from the next, making ideal lovers' hideaways. Sunbathers always used caution approaching the far beaches, and if someone was already there, courtesy demanded they walk on to the next one. The moon was gaining altitude, revealing the sandy shore below with the surf gently glimmering as it caught the moonlight on white-capped waves.

Howard took the envelope Jock had delivered earlier and spread the information on the table.

"Okay," he said, tapping a pencil. "Here's the plan. We have six boats of varying size due into Smugglers from dusk through tomorrow night. We're staggering the arrivals so it's not obvious something's happening. The first boat will be a thirty-six foot sport fisherman. Load her down as best you can. Code name for her is *Blue Fox* on the radio. Every vessel will be on the six-eight code frequency. They'll make initial contact on five-six, then switch over to six-eight. Got it?" he asked Woody, then glanced at Max.

"Got it," he said, and Max nodded.

"Okay. Next boat will be a high speed racer, twenty-five feet, code name *Alpha*. She's not due until ten o'clock, and will approach from the ocean side into the inner harbor. She'll leave through the dredged cut after she's loaded down."

Woody and Max nodded, and Howard continued naming the boats, code names and estimated times of arrival.

"All boats will need fuel, some more than others," he said. "Give them what they want. You should have three hundred gallons left from last week and Lucky's delivering another five hundred between eight and nine Sunday morning. If it looks like we'll need more, I can get another load late that afternoon. I'll be in touch, but according to the fuel requests, you should be okay. Is the *Sea 'n' Be* ready to roll yet?" he asked Max.

"Tomorrow afternoon," he said. "I plan to work on her first thing in the morning."

"Good. Woody, tell Terry to come up here when you go

160

back. After this load is gone, we're going to use a couple of different tactics. Too many people on this island. We're going to lay low, particularly after this morning's incident. But there are other ways. Also, we're going to hit on some coke. Easier to transport and higher profits. Big thing is to get this load done and then I'll let you know the future plans. Any questions?"

"No. Think I have it in my head okay," said Woody. Max nodded in agreement.

"Good. I'm giving you a copy so there's no question. Destroy it when the job's done. Now get back, get some sleep, keep your mouths shut and remember the details. One thing. Clean up after each boat as if it were the only one coming in. And be careful to be on the right frequencies. You never know who's listening, even though those channels are never used. Good luck," he said, and rose to let them out.

When Howard was done with business, he was done. Neither Woody nor Max had ever heard him engage in small talk. He was business all the way.

As they walked out the door, Marjorie was setting the table for a candlelight lobster dinner. Howard knew how to live.

"We should have good weather tomorrow night," said Woody. "Clear skies, a good moon and plenty of stars."

"Works two ways," said Max. "No one can see what's going on when it's pitch black and overcast." He slipped as they went down the path, grabbing a scrubby bush to stop his fall.

"He'd better improve this path if we're going to be visiting at night," said Max. "It's murder."

As they approached the airstrip, they saw a plane at the end of the runway where a little creek connected to deeper water. There was a small boat in the muddy shallows and a few people going between the boat and plane.

"Keep walking and pretend you don't see it," said Woody. "We don't want to mess up someone else. Has a way of turning around. Can you see who it is?"

"No," said Max, sneaking glances down the airstrip. "Twin-engine plane. Small."

When they were out of sight of the runway, they heard engines starting, then the plane rolled down the strip, lights off.

It took almost two-thirds of the runway before lifting, then turned its running lights and strobe on as it headed north.

"She was pretty loaded down," said Woody. "Let's get out of here."

Max nodded, and the two walked a bit faster to Conch Inn. As they reached the dock, a little boat was headed in the opposite direction, toward Rocky Point. Woody went to tell Terry to see Howard, and Max climbed aboard the black bomb, as they referred to it. In minutes, they were heading for Max's little dock. As they came alongside, Pat was looking down from the porch. Max waved, got out, and shoved Woody off.

"See you tomorrow," he said. "I'll be on the *Sea 'n' Be* if you need me. Should be finished by noon."

"Okay," said Woody, gunning the boat. He was anxious to get back to Smugglers.

* * *

The next morning, Tom and Sue came to Smugglers and invited Laura and Woody to go snorkeling in the hope of getting something for dinner.

"Well," said Woody, hesitantly, "I'm pretty busy. Into a project I really can't leave, but Laura can go. Wait here and I'll be right back."

As he walked toward the clubhouse, Laura came out, drying her hands on a towel.

"Hey, Honey, want to go diving with Tom and Sue? Would probably be fun for you. Get into your suit and grab some gear. You'll have fun."

"Ya'll have to wait a second," said Laura, waving to them. Woody sat on the dock talking, not wanting to invite them ashore. Laura came out, a two-piece suit showing a white middle.

"You'll get some sun on that belly today," said Woody, giving her a pat on the butt. "Have fun, all of you. maybe you'll get something for dinner. Good luck."

They started the dinghy and were off. Laura welcomed the invitation. She had been staring at the clear blue water, wanting to peer underneath to glimpse the wonder below. Now was her chance, without Woody pressuring her and making cracks about her snorkeling ability. She'd enjoy learning from this energetic couple.

As the tiny dinghy disappeared, loaded down with bodies and gear, Woody went inside, fixed himself a drink, and decided to check the radios to make sure all was in order. He fiddled with the VHF, listening to a couple of boats, and keyed the transmitter. No problem with this one. He turned on the new radio Jock had brought in. He switched to the code frequency. No one was on, as expected. If someone had been talking, he would have had to switch frequencies once contact was made with Chubby.

"*Naughty Lady, Naughty Lady.* Woodpecker calling *Naughty Lady.* Come in *Naughty Lady....*" He adjusted the squelch and tuned the clarity knob.

"*Naughty Lady,* Woodpecker calling *Naughty Lady.*"

"*Naughty Lady* back. Hi, Woody. Everything okay?" Chubby came in loud and clear.

"Everything's great. Good reception. Better radio than the other one. How do you copy me?"

"Five-by-five," he said. "Everything's on schedule. If you need me, I'll be here. If you miss me, check on the even hours until six tonight. After that I'll be here through midnight. Then I'll be on at six in the a.m. Got that?"

"Sounds good," said Woody. "I'm not going anywhere. Just taking care of everyone."

"Good luck. Talk to you later. Too bad about yesterday morning."

"You heard?" he asked.

"Drums beat, you know. That's it for now. *Naughty Lady* clear."

"Woodpecker clear."

How had Chubby heard, he wondered. No one had talked too much to Jock yesterday but somehow Chubby knew something had happened, that they'd been ripped off. Howard may have told him. No, Howard was too cool, thought Woody. He wouldn't pass that sort of thing on the radio, even on the special frequency. Jock would have told him.

With Laura gone, Woody was bored. He wanted to take the black bomb and go see how Max was doing, but he knew he couldn't leave the island. He fixed himself another drink and decided to take a walk back along the old slave wall, as it was called from more than a century ago, and to take a look at the old shacks Tom had talked about. He put on some rubber soled shoes and limped toward the generator shed.

The wall began on the other side and followed the contour of the island. Woody wondered about the people who had painstakingly built the wall. Coral rock had been set in ancient cement, making it about a foot wide and two feet high, outlining where cotton once grew, or sisal, from which hemp was made.

Woody had read how a hurricane years before had devastated the island group, wiping out the few crops and washing the topsoil into the sea. Bleak islands of porous coral rock remained, along with the slave field walls, cemented to the rocky foundation of the islands.

It was hot. Woody could feel the sweat trickling down his spine, soaking his white T-shirt and dripping down his navy shorts.

In the decade that followed the great hurricane, scrubby plants had replaced more useful crops, and vegetation slowly crept back. But the precious topsoil was gone forever. Only deep down, in potholes carved by nature in the limestone rock or blasted by some ambitious natives, were tiny crops grown — a few scraggly banana trees, some corn stalks, a lemon tree.

Woody could see how the beach had receded, then built up, time after time as the seasons came and went. He reached a point where the tide had totally washed away part of the wall. He imagined the shallow bay was probably once part of the island, but with the onslaught of nature, had been carved to hold the water that came and went on its rhythmic cycle. He found the wall again about twenty feet away and followed it around a curve to the old native shacks, long open to the elements, a combination of rubble construction and wood. The paint had gone years ago and the two little shacks now had the appearance of two gigantic pieces of driftwood.

164

Woody speculated the little buildings were probably used during Prohibition and the old "wracking" days when the natives survived by picking the bones of ships wrecked on the outside reefs. Smugglers Cay had earned its name decades ago.

Woody walked into the first little structure. There was still a semblance of a roof, and the floor was rough concrete. It was a good place to store fuel containers, he thought, but rather inaccessible. The best way was probably by boat on the high tide, he thought. It would be all right to store surplus here, but not the fuel they would need right away. The second structure was more overgrown, about twenty feet away. It wasn't worth getting stuck by the thistles and thorns of the hostile plants, and he decided these shacks would only be used in time of surplus or emergency. Even though it was hot and he was about a quarter of a mile from the club, he decided to learn the lay of his land beyond. He hiked along the shore, sand sometimes giving way to mangroves, then coral rock formations. He climbed up an embankment that marked the end of the island and could see the tip of the club. He made a mental note of it. Good place to spot anything if he needed an outpost in the future.

He tried walking further, to circumnavigate the island back to the club, but the terrain forbade the intrusion of human steps. Woody realized he needed a machete to cut through the growth, and it was both unnecessary and totally stupid to consider going on. He turned and walked back the same way, following his uneven footprints already made soggy by the incoming tide. It was a pretty island, he thought. How grand a place it must have been when the plantation was in full swing and a community of natives worked the soil. How different from now, he thought. The island was almost bleak when compared to the fields, rain forests and mountains of other Caribbean islands.

But one aspect of beauty surpassed anyplace Woody had been in the tropics. The water around Smugglers and the vicinity was a natural wonder in itself, the beauty capturing even the heartiest of souls. The varying blue hues, the varied bottom of sand, coral reefs — both alive and dead — grassy patches and different depths played a constant game of changing colors.

Woody had seen the same water look pale green at low tide,

aqua blue at higher tide in the sunlight, then almost steel gray as an approaching storm churned the waters. The sea was always changing.

Woody chuckled. How maudlin of me. I should be worrying and planning these two days instead of being sentimental over the goddamn scenery, he thought. As he came to his more prosaic senses, he limped past the generator shed to the docks. He had to figure where to put the excess fuel. The shacks were too far away. The storage areas were already crammed with bales, and he didn't want to chance using the club.

He remembered some heavy tarpaulins lying next to the generator shed, and limped back to where the engine kept humming out kilowatts. The tarp looked huge. Best thing to do is put the containers in the bushes behind the storage shed where the brush had been cleared away and cover them up, he thought. Woody considered the problem solved.

As he was about to go into the club, he saw Laura and their friends heading back to Smugglers. She waved and he waved back. In a few minutes they were tied alongside. Laura, now sunburned, held up two lobster.

"Look at the bugs Ah got all by mahself," she shouted proudly.

"You didn't get 'em, did you?" asked Woody, teasingly.

"She sure did," said Tom. "Taught her how to use a sling and she took to it right away. She's got good eyes. I didn't even see these two. Found them all by herself."

"Good dinner tonight," said Woody. "We'll have those things in the pot before they know they've been caught."

He gave Laura a hand, then asked Tom and Sue if they wanted a drink.

"No thanks. We're done in by the sun. Best we head back to the boat and rest. Thanks anyway. We'll be back in a couple of days. Know you guys are busy, but if you want to come out to the boat anytime, Just give a holler on the VHF. Always love company."

He put the boat in gear and Laura and Woody watched them motor away from the dock.

"Max to Woodpecker. You there? Max to Woodpecker...

Come in Woody...." Max's voice sounded frustrated as Woody walked into the club. He went to the radio.

"Woodpecker here. Go head, Max."

"Thought you'd abandoned the place," he said, back to his usual twangy monotone. "Got the *Sea 'n' Be* running. Just left the dock. I'll be leaving here shortly. What time is it, anyway?"

"About two," said Woody, looking at his watch. It didn't seem like it should be so late.

"I'll be there by four. Need anything?"

"Just you," said Woody. "Bring your portable VHF."

"Roger. Clear."

Woody limped outside to where Laura was cleaning the lobsters.

"Don't suppose we could consider eating them right now, could we?" he asked. "Max will be here for dinner and with the upcoming schedule, lobster might not fit in. Besides, we haven't had lunch. There's probably enough there for salad as well."

"Sounds good to me," said Laura. "You know me. Ah could eat lobster all day long. You finish cleaning them and Ah'll put a pot on. Ah can taste them already."

Woody carefully took one of the antennae and with quick motion, cleaned the insides of the tail. Laura had already removed the heads. He took off the legs. They were large enough for snacks. When he carried the lobsters into the kitchen, Laura already had water on to boil and was cleaning a head of lettuce. Some tomatoes, lemon wedges and melted butter would complete the feast. He put his arm around her as she stood at the sink.

"Oh come on, Woody, you know how Ah hate to mess around when Ah'm in the kitchen. Save that fo' later. You've been so pooped lately...."

"Just you wait," he said, giving her another squeeze. "We're gonna have our second honeymoon affair yet. Just let me get rid of all the shit floating around here and we can be together more. I'm going to get some workers here next week so we don't have to do anything heavy, and baby, we're gonna play around — on the beach, out in the boat — you name when and where."

"Promises," she said, smiling, knowing that he really meant

167

what he was saying. "To tell ya the truth, Ah'm getting squirmy with all those bales here. Ah almost died when our friends arrived today. Ah wanted to go, but even if Ah didn't, Ah would have so they wouldn't come ashore. That's a lot of pot out there. Ah think Pat managed to snitch a good share. Ah didn't say anything to Max."

"Couldn't have been that much," said Woody, unconcerned. "Let her have it. Then she'll be off Max's case. Anyway, it's pretty well known that she's hooked on it, so I'd rather supply her than have her go begging. It's only peanuts, anyway, and it's important she stays happy. Max says she gets fed up with island living every now and then and he ships her back to the States periodically. If she's happy she stays longer on the island, so that keeps him content. He doesn't like taking care of himself."

"So Ah've heard. He's not all that nice to her, ya know," said Laura, going to the stove. "The water's boiling. Can you give me those tails?"

She dumped them into the pot and within seconds, the lobsters turned bright red. She set a table for two with a colorful checkered red and white cloth with matching napkins, and tossed the salad.

"Ah hate to say it, but Ah see trouble ahead for Max and Pat. Can't blame either one, but Ah do see something down the line," she said as they sat down.

"What a smell!" exclaimed Woody, tasting the lobster and ignoring her intuitions. "We're living like kings, Bunchy, and it's going to continue. Just you wait. It's not long now before we're really rolling in it. You'll have lobster at will."

She smiled. Woody and his promises. But we're getting closer, she thought. Definitely closer.

* * *

Max arrived on schedule, a few minutes past four o'clock. He notified Woody on the portable radio as he left Conch Inn, and talked on a little-used channel on the way to Smugglers, testing the radio's range and output. As he arrived at the dock, Woody was waiting.

"Fun should begin in a couple of hours," said Woody, grabbing a line. "I've already made contact with *Blue Fox*. She's on schedule. Due in by six. Captain figures he'll need a hundred gallons, but wants to take it in drums. He'll give us two empties in return. The *Sea 'n' Be* get off okay?"

"Yeh. They're already headed south," said Max. "What's their game plan?"

"Don't know and Howard's not saying. That means we better not ask questions. When we're supposed to know he'll tell us."

"He must have cast iron stomach muscles," said Max, shaking his head. "Nothing seems to bother him. Like he's been through it all before."

"Don't think he hasn't," said Woody. "Won't talk about it, but I've heard stories. He's an old timer in this business, and the control strings are not that far above him. Moves around a lot. Guy I talked to knew him in South America about eight years ago. Handles a lot of funds for the big boys."

"Haven't heard much about him around here," said Max, keeping pace with Woody's limp to the club.

"He kept a low profile for about six months," said Woody. "Think he was on some sort of sabbatical, if there is such a thing in the business. Now he's back in full swing. When this operation closes, he'll probably reappear someplace else. Some life, eh? All I want is to make enough for Laura and me to enjoy the fine things of life right on this little island. Have a beautiful sailing yacht picked out. Gonna buy her, sail her over here and enjoy the shit out of it."

"I just want to bank it," said Max, dryly and pointedly. "Bank it and watch it multiply."

"That's the difference between you and me, Max. Shit. I want to enjoy the hell out of it. Spend it and forget it."

"When I spend it I CAN'T forget it," said Max. "But when the whole world's in financial trouble, I'll be on top."

"Yeah, like the Germans pushing their wheelbarrows full of marks for a loaf of bread. Not me. I'll spend it. Easy come, easy go. That's what they say and I don't want to disappoint anyone who would come up with such a wise remark. Spend it. To hell with putting it in the bank. I like my fun, right Laura?"

She had caught the end of the conversation as they came in and readily agreed to whatever he was saying.

"When Woody's in the chips the whole world knows it," she drawled. "It's kind of fun, 'cause we've been at both ends of the scale. When times are good, they're very good, and when times turn — well, Woody gets another act together."

"Let's get a couple of full barrels ready," said Woody, turning to Max and changing the subject. "That boat will be in before we know it, and I don't want it here any longer than necessary. The faster we move the crap off this island the safer we are. Come on."

With that, Max followed Woody to the warehouse, realizing it might be another long night ahead. Once the marijuana's gone from the island it would be someone else's problem. Then it would only be a matter of waiting to hear it got to the final destination to determine the money he'd make. They began organizing the transfer.

* * *

About 6:15, the *Blue Fox* appeared on the horizon, her tuna tower rocking gently back and forth as she rode the slightly rolling sea. Through binoculars, Woody saw two men dressed in dark clothing standing on the bridge. He wouldn't talk on the radio. They were too close for the sideband and Woody didn't want to stir up suspicion on the local VHF channels.

"Hey, Max, want to look?" He gave the glasses to Max, and he scanned the boat.

"She'll be able to carry it easily," he said. "What's her allotment?"

"At least twenty. Don't want to push it. If she goes out too low in the water it could raise some flags as she approaches the mainland. We'll just give them what they're supposed to get, especially since we're short twenty bales. I think Howard cancelled a boat after our incident. Good lines to her, what do you think?" asked Woody, watching the *Blue Fox* approach.

"Nice," said Max. "Looks like she's been fishing. That's

170

good."

"Howard said no boats would arrive during daylight hours that would arouse suspicion. The fast boats will be in after dark."

"Good planning," said Max, a little edgy. "You want a drink before we go down to the dock? I'll fix. What's your gut-level prediction on tonight?"

"Okay," said Woody. "If someone doesn't fuck up, it should be okay. See if Laura has a lime to squeeze into the rum. Sure would taste good."

Max went to the bar and Woody kept looking through the glasses. As the *Blue Fox* came close she slowed down, and they went to meet it. As lines were tossed ashore, the crewman only nodded. Then the captain came from the bridge.

"Any chance of getting some food?" he asked. "Have to wait a little before we load. Too light out. Any yachtsmen or strangers poking round?" He was dressed in black, like his deck hand, but wore white sneakers, black beret and dark sunglasses. The crewman had a quick smile, sandy hair and blue eyes that made him look like a modern day Viking.

"Haven't seen anyone," said Woody. "Been pretty quiet. But then, we haven't exactly put out the welcome mat on the VHF."

"Good," said the captain, rather soberfaced. "We'll take on fuel now and baggage later."

"Got it ready. Hundred gallons, right?"

"Right," he said. When the empties were exchanged for full drums, he relaxed and looked around.

"Nice place," he commented.

"In a month or two it'll be a lot nicer. We only arrived last week. Lots of debris has to be hauled away, a new cistern built, some more cottages for guests — haven't figured out what the plan is yet."

"Don't bring in outsiders if you can help it," he said. "Bad for business. When a place becomes known you can't have the freedom in moving shit. Keep it private and forget about being a people-pleaser."

"Want a drink?" asked Woody.

They both shook their heads yes.

"Rum's fine. Just swirl in a little water and squeeze a lime or a lemon."

Laura came out to greet the crew and Woody gave her the bar order. They all sat on the deck above the dock, the crew stretched out on chaises.

"Long ride," said the captain, who typically avoided any type of introduction. If no one knew names, no one could be implicated should there be a problem. "We took a few days to get here, but it'll be a fast one back. Thanks," he said as Laura gave him a drink.

"Bet the fishing's good around here. What do you catch?"

"Well, lately, only square grouper," said Woody, laughing. "Not much time for anything else. Expect to do some fishing next week. Laura went out this morning and got a couple of lobsters. Had a good lunch. Think she's planned a ham for tonight. Easy for sandwiches, but we'll have a full dinner for the two of you. You're our first company," he said, smiling.

"Good company, huh?" he said, smiling back with a bit of a smirk.

"The best, when you get right down to it. All you boys make it possible." They continued with small talk, not naming any mutual acquaintances and avoiding anything connected with the overall plan. As it got dark and dinner was finished, the men walked to the storeroom and began loading bales onto a push cart. Within a half hour, the *Blue Fox* was on her way. It was only 8:30. Time to try radio contact with the *Alpha*, thought Woody. Max began cleaning up the dock and Woody headed for the radio. He checked his code book again on the frequencies, and went through the contact procedure. The *Alpha*, too, was right on schedule. Woody was thankful that the unloading had begun and that the place would be clean by the next night. He fixed another drink and joined Max and Laura on the dock.

"Everything's right on schedule. *Alpha* will be in by ten, if not a few minutes before," said Woody. "He's chugging along at 50 miles an hour. That's moving, but there's a calm sea. Some swells, but nothing to slow them down. She's supposed to take ten bales and a hundred gallons. We better have a fuel transfer pump handy."

"That'll still leave fifty bales. What's coming in next?" asked Max.

"Thirty footer for fifteen," he said. "Most of it will be gone tonight. Tomorrow night three small boats are coming in to finish it off. They get back faster, but the bigger boats draw less attention. It's a combination of speed versus size. The sport fisherman might not be back till the others make it, depending on sea conditions. Lot of factors to consider. I'm just glad I'm sitting where I am and not beating my brains out in one of those boats. The boys have to be a little crazy to fight the elements like that. Much better to be here, doling it out and drinking rum." He smiled, getting up to fix another round.

The arrival of the *Alpha* was relatively uneventful. She was fueled, loaded and on her way by eleven o'clock, with a cooler of beer and sandwiches for the journey to the States. She was low in the water but would make good time.

"One more," said Woody, watching the running lights of *Alpha* disappear in the night. "One more to go. Where's that list, Max?"

"Left it by the radio. Next one is *Green Streaker*. She only needs one drum of fuel. Let's talk to her."

They went to the radio room, and Woody called on the contact frequency.

"Woodpecker to *Green Streaker*. *Green Streaker*, come in." They waited, but there was no answer.

"Maybe they're too far out," said Woody.

"Doesn't make sense," said Max. "This radio is for long range, remember? Is there an alternate?"

"Not for contact. This is the contact frequency, and it worked for the first two. Let's try again. *Green Streaker*, *Green Streaker*, this is Woodpecker calling. Come in." Nothing.

"Her ETA is midnight," said Woody. "That's only a little while from now. Wonder if Howard's heard anything. Hate to call him though, unless we have an emergency. There's no sense bothering him yet. He'll be watching the whole thing anyway. Did you get chance to look through that nightscope?"

"No. Not his, anyway. Some bloke passing through had a pair of binoculars he let me look through. Nice piece of equipment," said Max. "Expensive."

"We'll wait a few minutes and try again," said Woody, nervously shifting on and off his shorter leg. "What do you think of using the VHF?"

"I wouldn't," said Max. "Whole world listens to that thing. Now even the island telephone bleeds over to the VHF, so everyone hears one side of the conversation in addition to what's normally going on. No, forget the VHF."

Woody tried the sideband again but there was no answer. He switched to the frequency for Chubby and gave that combination a try.

"*Naughty Lady*, Woodpecker calling *Naughty Lady*."

"Chubby said he'd be on till midnight. He should come back," said Max. He did.

"Woodpecker. *Naughty Lady*. What's the problem?"

"No problem, Chubby, just waiting to hear from your friends. First two came to visit, but the third hasn't made contact."

"Roger. Sit and wait. They'll be there. Good crew," said Chubby. "*Naughty Lady* clear."

"Boy, he sure doesn't want to talk, does he?" said Woody, a little indignant. He was about to try the *Green Streaker* again when Laura walked in.

"Ah see a boat heading this way," she said. "Is that the next one?"

Woody and Max rushed to the dock. Woody looked through the binoculars but it was impossible to determine who it was in the night. The boat was coming in cautiously. God, he hoped it didn't mean trouble. Everything was going so smoothly. As it entered the harbor, he could see a green stripe painted alongside. Had to be the *Green Streaker*, he thought. Suddenly, above the purr of engines, a loudspeaker hailer bellowed, "Looking for Woody."

Max, Laura and Woody looked at each other in surprise, then began waving the vessel in. As Woody took the lines, the captain apologized.

"Sorry, old man. We could receive you but our transmitter went out. Frustrating as hell, but here we are. Got everything set?"

"Yup. Just give us a hand. Fifteen, right?" The captain gave the thumbs up and came ashore. The crew began making room for the load and fuel. Woody already had the fuel drum on the dock, ready to hoist aboard. Then they went to the warehouse for the bales.

"Didn't skimp on these, did they?' said the captain, examining the cargo. "Last load we hauled they shorted the bales. Only made eighty percent of what we anticipated. These are good and full. No problem. Nice place you got. Good entrance to it, too. Picked it up on radar and chugged right in. We could almost have homed in on your distressful call to us. Wanted to answer, but couldn't. How you fixed for a bite to eat?"

"Have it all set. Been giving out care packages," said Woody. "Laura's getting it ready now. Just wanted to see how many were on board."

"Normally it's just me and one other guy. Have a greenhorn along tonight. He'll learn. We've found that an internship doesn't hurt. Profit stays up better when they know the game."

No one said much as the heavy bales were loaded onto the boat, and as soon as everything was secure, the captain had the engines turning. By 12:45 he was heading for the States. Woody and Max shook hands, congratulating each other on the dumping of forty-five bales.

"Let's have a drink, Max. Goddamn I feel good. Hey, Laura, how about another round while we clean up?"

"Better not party too much," said Max dryly. "Tonight went smooth, but we don't know what's in store tomorrow, especially with Lucky coming in. Can you run me back? It's late, but Pat's expecting me."

"Sure. You're right. Tomorrow night we can let loose. Tonight we'll play it cool but shit, I feel good. Come."

They took their drinks and headed in the black bomb to Sandy Cay. As they approached Max's dock, they could see a light above. Pat was waiting. Max jumped out and waved as Woody headed back to Smugglers. Pat would be the perfect end to a good night's work. He quickened his step to the little house.

Woody and Laura slept late the next morning. They had sipped a few rums together after Woody came back from taking Max home and neither had been able to fall asleep. The sun was already bright when they awoke, and the heat was setting in. At about nine o'clock, they were jarred by the roar of engines overhead. Woody jumped up, looked out the window, and said "Ho-o-o-ly shit!"

Lucky had done a low pass and was now coming straight into the harbor with his huge seaplane.

Woody ran his fingers through his thinning hair, grabbed a pair of pants and rushed down the stairs. Laura was right behind her limping husband.

As they reached the dock, Lucky was taxiing the big bird to the mooring buoy. Woody got into a runabout to help secure the plane. As he pulled up, Lucky opened the door, smiling ear-to-ear, dressed in cut-off jeans and a T-shirt that boasted "Mile High Club." His light brown curly hair was tousled and he wore his favorite hunk of gold on a heavy chain around his neck. As usual, he was barefoot. "Hiya, Woody. I'm back. Never say good-bye to ol' Lucky!"

"You're getting to be a Sunday habit," answered Woody, smiling. Then he saw them. Two of the most gorgeous chicks he had ever laid eyes on came out of the main cabin where Lucky had his king-size waterbed. The brunette wore only little white bits that barely rated being called a string bikini, and the blonde wore a one-piece lavender cutaway that showed as much as the bikini. Lucky gloated as he watched Woody size up his girls.

"Nice, huh? If Laura wasn't around I could share my wares, but...."

The girls stepped into the little boat as if modeling their skin. Lucky made sure the mooring was secure, then climbed in too.

"Meet Olga and Cookie," he said. "Olga doesn't speak English too well but that isn't one of my requirements. Anyway, nothing really needs translating. Cookie, on the other hand, talks real sweet. Don't you, Honey? Anyway, girls, this is my friend

Woody. He owns this little island."

They smiled, knowing nothing more was required of them. As Woody pulled up to the dock, Laura was surveying the boarding party with skepticism, wondering how any woman, even in the hot tropics, could run around naked — or almost.

"Hi, Laura. Good to see you again," said Lucky as he stepped off the boat, kissed her hand and made a low bow.

"Why do Ah feel overdressed?" she asked, a slight smile and look conveying her feelings.

"Now, now," said Lucky, still holding her hand. "You look lovely in your Sunday best."

"Oh knock it off, you old Casanova," said Woody, laughing. By this time Laura had to laugh too. Lucky was something else.

"How do you like my shirt?" he asked, taking in a breath and puffing up his chest. "Do it over 5200 feet and you're entitled to it. Anytime you two want to join, let me know. Let you romp in that waterbed right over the island."

"Ya'll are too much," said Laura. "Anyone want a drink? Coffee? Bloody Mary?"

"You just hit on it," said Lucky. "Fix a pitcher full and then you won't have to make so many trips."

"You're the only pilot I know who gets away with such shenanigans," said Woody. "How you do it, I'll never know."

"No one will," said Lucky, patting Olga on her tiny bit of bikini. Cookie just sat, not saying anything, taking in the island scenery.

"Talked to Howard on the air frequency," said Lucky. "Said to tell you he's pleased about last night. What do I hear about the down-island boys giving you a chase? You should have more sense than to mess with them. They're pros, man. But I've got them right where I want them. Bailed them out once. Literally. Police boat on their tail and all. Almost had to dump the load when I told them to come into Crab Cut. Landed this bird, off-loaded the crap into the plane and took off. I ended up with the load and the profits. Police couldn't do a goddamn thing to them. Gotta be smart in this funny business. God, is it a kick!"

Another story about Lucky, thought Woody. The man was incredible in his feats of skirting the law. Always with flair.

177

Nothing shy or bashful about Lucky. He was faster and smarter with more sophisticated equipment than any government agency. And he loved the thrills he created.

Laura came out with a pitcher of Bloody Marys and a tray of glasses and Woody poured, sticking a celery stalk and lemon wedge into each drink.

"Yup," continued Lucky. "Gotta hand it to you, Woody. You'll do all right after a little practice. At least you know you can always count on Lucky, here."

"Yeah, but you're not always available," said Woody. "From what I hear, you're all over the world."

"True, true," said Lucky, "but I keep myself cloned in these parts. Sort of a phantom Lucky. Never know when I'll show up, but I've got the knack of being at the right place at the right time when someone else isn't. Being a doper is easy. Being a doper's doper is more for me. And I never let it get to me. It's a game. I laugh like shit when I've got a tail on me and I can outrun 'em. You should have seen what I did to a police chopper over in the States. Guy was on my tail and I knew it. Let him come up just so, then gave him the impression I was landing on a little strip in the middle of nowhere. As I came in to land I did a loop and the chopper guy was so intent on following he almost crashed the son of bitch. I flew over him after he had to land the thing and saw him puking his lunch. No shit. Talk about funny. Guy still probably doesn't know what happened."

He had everyone laughing, even the two girls who had probably heard the story several times.

"Not to change the subject, but I presume you brought the fuel?" asked Woody.

"First of all, never presume," said Lucky. Woody's face fell, and Lucky smiled. "Of course I brought it. Just have to pump it out of the tank and into your drums. Howard thought that would be the best way since you haven't checked on your underground tank yet and I was goddamned if I was going to carry a bunch of jugs into this bird. I can pump it ashore in a matter of minutes with a high-pressure hose. Won't be obvious, either, if someone comes near the island. Always feel queasy when I'm lugging those goddamn blue jugs for someone. I mean, what else comes in those friggin' things but scammer fuel, huh? I like being cool about it. I'm also lazy," he said, smiling at Olga and Cookie, and making all sorts of little kissing signs to them.

Laura looked at Woody with her I-don't-believe-him look and Woody shrugged. That was Lucky Daye's style.

"We should probably start the transfer," said Woody. "If we're gonna have a problem it's best to know early."

"You never have problems with Lucky, man. Only other people fuck you up. I've got the best equipment you'll find anywhere. I am where I am 'cause I don't have those kind of dumb problems. Make sure everything works before I get into a mess, then I know I can get out." He smiled at his crew.

"You girls want to go to a nice little beach and sun? I'm sure Laura can find you a towel to lay your beautiful bods on." He turned to Laura and she nodded.

"Ah'll get two beach towels."

Woody and Lucky went to the dock.

"This little boat will do just fine. I'll get in the plane and hook up the hose and pump and we can use the boat to bring the hose ashore. Let's get the drums ready, 'cause when this pump starts, it's only gonna take a few minutes for each barrel."

They went to the storeroom and began rolling the drums to the edge of the dock, still out of sight from anyone arriving by boat.

"What a way to make a livin', huh? This is the boring part," said Lucky. "Necessary evil. Like putting toilet paper in the executive washroom when the maid's not on duty. Gotta have it."

As Lucky predicted, the fuel transfer only took a short time. They were just finishing when a plane flew overhead. Lucky and Woody both looked up, shielding their eyes from the bright sun.

"Charlie," said Lucky. "Good ol' innocent-as-a-virgin Charlie. Just keeps truckin' to the island hauling people and their baggage. Doesn't know the fun he's missin'. Bale of pot can't talk back to you or tell you where to go and normally doesn't miss its flight. People, on the other hand, are a pain in the ass and cheap as hell. Give me my pot and my coke and all that other good stuff any day of the week. No way would I be a head-hauler except to maybe scare the shit out of some little old lady who's never flown before. That would be a gas."

Woody laughed.

"Don't think Charlie's too happy with Jock," he said. "He took a couple of trips from him and Charlie let us know he's pissed."

"Don't worry about Charlie. He's a pussycat and a good chap. Don't screw him up too badly, though. Like it or not, he's done a lot for these islands. Go back a long way with him. He's straight, but he's okay. And dependable. About as dependable as they come. Even brought a couple of cuties over to me when I had gone a night without one. He's okay."

Still, Woody didn't like anyone seeing anything happening on his island, and there was no mistaking the big bird in the harbor or who it belonged to.

"You look worried, man," said Lucky. "Shit. I'll just fly to Sandy Cay and make it look like I'm visiting everyone today. These chicks will make anyone forget anything. Even Charlie. He never minds looking over my inventory." They both laughed. Lucky had an answer to everything.

* * *

About noon, after Lucky and his girls had gone for a swim on one of the isolated beaches of Smugglers, they decided to be on their way.

"Church will be letting out up the road at Sandy Cay," said Lucky. "Don't want to disturb the holy rollers, especially since the natives don't want gals in bikinis walking through the village. Can you imagine the Reverend's reaction to these two dolls? Whooee! We'll swoop right into the yacht club. Come on gals. Gotta show you another little island. Better give me some Bloody Marys to go, Woody. You know how they are on Sunday. Be damned to have them cramp my style."

Woody went to fix a takeaway pitcher while Lucky got his girls into the boat. In a few minutes they were aboard the seaplane and Woody untied the mooring.

Lucky waited until Woody was back at the dock before

starting the engines, spraying water with the props. He waved, taxied into the wind and roared off. Woody could feel the fine mist as the plane lifted. Lucky rocked the wings, then turned back toward Smugglers, swooping down just a few feet above Woody's head. That's Lucky, he thought, as he intuitively ducked. What a character.

In a few minutes, Lucky buzzed the Sandy Cay Club. Pete and Charlie were on the dock, along with some people Lucky didn't recognize. He made another pass, then came straight in, skimming the surface and touching down just short of the boat ramp. Pete and Charlie walked over as Lucky, then the two girls, stepped out into the knee-deep water. Lucky held the pitcher and steadied the girls as they walked ashore.

"Hi guys," said Lucky, grinning. "What's up?"

Charlie took in the scene, then looked at Pete with his cigarette hanging out of his mouth, staring at Lucky, the two girls with almost nothing on and the Big Bird. He started laughing.

"Where are the film crews, Lucky?" asked Charlie. "You can't be for real. But I know my eyesight's in order 'cause I just finished a physical. How the hell are you?" He extended his hand and Lucky took it, still smiling.

"Haven't been by for a while and thought I'd keep in touch. Besides, I told you I'd drop in so you could see the new bird. Oh. Meet Olga and Cookie. Either one will do ya, what do you think?"

Pete and Charlie looked the gals over, nodded their heads with just a tinge of a give-the-guy-credit smirk and said "hi" to each of them.

"See you brought your own," said Pete, pointing to the pitcher. "That's good. Sunday, you know."

"How could I forget? All those dry seventh day flights I made in here hungover at my island hoping for a beer to set me straight and you not serving? I remember, Pete. No, Lucky watches out for Number One in every possible way. That's survival, man. Survival."

"There's a friend of yours sitting in the club reading the paper."

"Yeah? Who?" asked Lucky, slowing down. "Not a broad, Pete. I mean, not with what I've got going today."

"Not a broad," said Pete, smiling, his blue eyes dancing. "Better than that." He swung open the screen door and the five of them walked in to see Captain Ned Kilpatrick with his head buried in a newspaper. No one said a word, then the captain looked up at Lucky and muttered, "Well, if it isn't Bullshit. Goddamn pirate's still alive, huh? Biggest bullshitter in the world, you are. They're gonna get you one of these days, you son of a bitch."

"Well now, Ned. I think time has passed."

"The only thing I want to see passed is you. Got no class. And look at what you got in tow."

"Come on now, Pops. No need to still put me down. Just because..."

"Don't just because me and don't call me Pops," said Captain Kilpatrick, rising from the barrel chair, his face obviously resurrecting memories he would rather keep forgotten. "You married my daughter against my will. Not even a decent church wedding. No. You gotta drag her off to Vegas before anyone could talk some sense into her. You're a son of a bitch. You know it. I know it. And it won't be long before the whole world knows it, the rate you're going. I'm leaving. Lucy's due in today. If anyone sees her tell her I'm on the boat."

With that he turned, walked out the door still favoring his leg and didn't look back.

Lucky was a painful memory to him, but those who knew the situation tended to think both men had met their match in each other, with the only difference being forty years between them. Lucky was the colorful, wild, cunning and notorious alleged doper. In his time, Captain Kilpatrick had run guns, rum, fugitives, and had deserved the name buccaneer.

The day Lucky met Molly, Ned's youngest daughter, was a day the island would not soon forget. Lucky had come into the club in his usual style from a nearby island he owned, swooping to the beach in a small sea plane. He had walked into the club, taken one look at Molly with her long red hair, quick blue eyes and perfect figure in a black bikini, asked to be introduced and

182

that was it. He proposed two hours later, convinced her to fly to Vegas the next day, and then had the courtesy to invite her parents to go along. Captain Kilpatrick had declined in a huff, never thinking Molly was serious.

It was a very quick wedding and the two were back on Lucky's island five days after meeting. The upshot was that Lucky had two mistresses, one a French stewardess, another a Playboy bunny, living on the island. He didn't bother to tell either of them he was off getting married until he came back, at which point one punctured his waterbed after strewing all his important papers on the floor, and the other tried to burn the house.

While he managed to stop the fire, the papers were destroyed and the two women left in a huff on Charlie's next flight out.

He and Molly then settled down to a very erratic life that lasted exactly two months. It didn't take Molly long to realize the marriage was another one of Lucky's wild charades and she left him, to her father's delight. Only later did Lucky realize Molly was probably the only woman worth his flamboyant lifestyle, but by then she had found someone who truly appreciated her and had settled down. As to Captain Kilpatrick, no matter what the old man thought of him personally, Lucky cared for his ex-father-in-law, if for no other reason than he knew the old man had his number. As everyone watched Captain Kilpatrick walk down the dock and step aboard his schooner, Lucky looked at Charlie and Pete and shrugged.

"I'm almost ready to open the bar on that one," said Pete. "I wonder if he'll ever forgive you, Lucky."

"We'll discuss it in the devil's parlor some day. Till then, I'm not going to let the old coot get me. You got any glasses and some ice? That's not out of order for Sunday, is it?"

"No," said Pete chuckling. "Be glad to help you there."

"Who are those people on the dock?" asked Lucky, nodding to a couple getting into a small boat.

"You don't know? That's Joe Jenkins, the guy who bought your island after you did your disappearing act," said Pete. "He's the guy who made sure Molly got her share of the

183

proceeds. Smart man. Not your kind of smart, Lucky. Just smart."

"Square smart, you mean?"

"Yeh. Square smart. Loves the place. Did a lot to it, added rooms, enclosed the porch, built quarters for the help."

"It's a nice little island. Still wish I had it at times. But shit, I got enough responsibilities. I'm renting a mansion overlooking a gorgeous lagoon a few miles south of here. Just like on Fantasy Island without that little man in the white coat. Got the plane, a big yacht, all this shit to keep up the style I've become accustomed to. Hey, girls, help yourself to this stuff. We've gotta be on our way."

"Man, you're always on your way," said Pete. "When you going to slow down, take it easy, enjoy life and all that shit?"

"When they bury me," laughed Lucky. "I sit in one place for more than ten minutes and I gotta get going. Don't want life to pass me by. Want every inch I can take and I'm getting in the mood to take it. If the autopilot wasn't giving me a hassle I'd take it right after taking off," he said, looking his girls over top to bottom and back up. "Just had to stop in and say hi, you know, for old times. Still one of my favorite spots. Been everywhere and somehow this place still remains special. Lots of good memories." He began chuckling, the real Lucky pulling out of a sentimental slip. He looked at Pete and Charlie. They were chuckling too.

"Next time you drop out of the sky see if you can bring back the radio you borrowed from me. Remember?" asked Pete.

"I remember, but that one took the deep six. I'll bring you another one. Good reason to come back. Come on girls. We got some territory to cover. Can you make sure that pitcher gets back to Smugglers?" Pete nodded.

"Saw you there as I flew in," said Charlie. "Must be nice not to need a runway."

"At times I don't even need a plane," said Lucky, laughing. "When you want to check out in it, let me know."

"Really?" asked Charlie. "It's gotta be a thrill."

"Everything's relative," said Lucky. "Everything's relative. I guess you'd call it a thrill. Dynamite when you're coming in at night and all you can see is the white surf beyond and you don't know when the bottom's gonna fall out of it. Yeah, it can be a thrill."

Pete and Charlie waded out to the plane with Lucky and his crew to see the inside, and before the island had a chance to realize Lucky had arrived he was gone, swooping over the village like a giant albatross eyeing an old nesting ground.

After Lucky took off, Charlie told Pete what he had seen while flying over Smugglers.

"Lucky will never change," said Pete, "and I can't say I'd want him to."

"You're right. He's surpassed his own legend," said Charlie.

A motor yacht was coming into the dock and Pete went to handle the lines. Charlie went into the club.

Pete helped secure the vessel, an 85-foot beauty that carried a crew of three for its rather well known but elusive owner. The yacht came in often and the owner spent a lot of money at the club, but books had been written on his high jinks in the securities racket and his whereabouts were generally kept secret from the press. Pete had come to know the owner well, servicing the yacht's various generator and watermaker systems. The owner was well protected as long as he minded his own business in his country of exile.

The captain, a tall good-looking native who had been educated in the States and who had managed to conquer his "th's" and "v's", thanked Pete for his help.

"Back again, eh Captain Knowles? How long this time?" asked Pete. "Need anything special?"

"No, mon. Just the usual. Boss's party would like dinner ashore tonight, but that's all for now. Don't want to ask for too much on Sunday. We're goin' fishin' for while, then be back. Anything new around here?"

"Naw. Same old bullshit. Lucky just dropped in to say hi with a couple of babes," said Pete, smiling and shaking his head in bewilderment.

"Saw his plane leave," said the captain. "Makes you wonder, Mon. Makes you wonder." He coiled a line and laughed with the soft chuckle characteristic of the natives.

185

"Well, we'll see you. How many for dinner, six?"

"Yessir."

As Pete walked back to the club, Charlie pointed. Pete turned round and saw a small yellow boat being towed by one of the club's runabouts. As the two boats neared the dock, Pete and Charlie went to take the lines from the troubled boat.

"Ran out of gas about five miles out," said the tall, slender man with a neatly trimmed dark beard. He had a good sunburn on top of a tan, and was wearing a white T-shirt and red bathing trunks. "Thought we had it made, but no luck. Any chance of getting some fuel?"

"Pumps are closed on Sunday," said Pete. "Would love to help you, but can't until tomorrow morning."

"Gee," said the guy, scratching his head and looking at his crew, a short stocky fellow with wavy blonde hair. "We need a few gallons right away. I'm willing to pay double for enough to get me a few miles."

"Sorry," said Pete, tugging on his pants at the waist. "The other marina might be able to help you. Got a VHF aboard? Call them and see. I'll give you a ride down that way in a few minutes when I go home, if you'd like."

"Thanks. We'll let you know."

Pete and Charlie walked back into the club. There were a couple of people playing pool and some others playing cards.

"I'll wait a bit before going to the house," said Pete. "Helen's probably busy with some project right now anyway. When's your trip out?"

"Not until Tuesday," said Charlie. "People off a boat. Still have open seats, so I might as well hang around and try to fill them."

Pete walked back toward the kitchen, checked on a few things, and Charlie picked up the paper Captain Ned had been looking at earlier. In about ten minutes, Pete came back.

"Where's that boat?" he asked Charlie.

"Gee, I don't know. Heard something running a couple minutes ago, but didn't bother to look to see who it was." He stood up and looked out. "By God, they're gone. Wonder who gave them fuel."

186

"Don't know," said Pete, pushing the screen door open. "Let's go see."

Captain Knowles was getting the small fishing boat ready for the owner to use.

"How'd that guy get fuel?" asked Pete. "He bum from you?"

"Yeah, Mon. Only wanted five gallons. Didn't think you'd mind us helping him out. Said he had to get to Smugglers and that five would do him."

"Hell, I don't mind," said Pete. "Smugglers, huh? Didn't know Woody had reopened the fuel pumps. That's interesting. What was the name on the boat, did you see?"

"Called it the *Y-Not*," said the captain. "Fast little thing. I've seen the type before." He looked at Pete and Charlie and they looked back, not saying anything, but definitely communicating.

"Well, I wish him all the luck in the world," said Pete. "I'll be back about five o'clock if you need me, Knowles. Take it easy and make sure the boss catches something this afternoon. Come on, Charlie. Let's get out of this heat."

They walked back to the club. Pete told everyone he was locking up for a while, and after they were out, the two headed for Pete's house.

"Five gallons," said Pete, shaking his head. "And he's gonna get fuel at Smugglers. That's very interesting."

"Fits with what I told you earlier," said Charlie.

"Sure does," said Pete, lighting a cigarette. "Sure does."

* * *

The *Y-Not*, scheduled to arrive at approximately 8 p.m., pulled into the dock at Smugglers Cay at 3:30, limping on one engine. Woody and Laura were puttering around the club and didn't notice the boat until the two men walked up the dock. Woody rushed out, not knowing who they were.

"Hi," said the bearded man. "We're early. Hope you don't mind. Ran out of fuel five miles off but we bummed some from a big yacht at another island. Mind if we fish awhile and go for a swim?"

"Go ahead," said Woody. "We've got some extra snorkeling

gear and slings if you want to go diving. Where did you get the fuel?"

"Sandy Cay Club," he said. "Guy wouldn't sell to us on Sunday so the captain on a big motor yacht helped us out. You've got fuel for us, right?"

"No problem. Just arrived this morning. As I recall, you're supposed to take on a hundred gallons, right?"

"You got it," he said "Good. That's a load off my mind. Pardon the pun." He smiled, showing a straight set of teeth and a sparkle to his eyes. "We won't bother you. Just want to check out that beach and the reef as you come into the harbor."

"Go ahead," said Woody. "We're just messing around trying to get a few things done. We'll plan on you for dinner. Don't mind grouper, do you?"

"Sounds great. Thanks."

"You didn't say anything to anyone at Sandy Cay, did you?" asked Woody, a frown creasing his forehead.

"Just told a native captain we were headed this way. That's all," he said.

Again, there were no introductions and the two men went their way to explore the nearby waters. Woody limped back to help Laura clean a guest cottage, and explained who the new arrivals were. Max wasn't due at Smugglers until seven-thirty. Woody hoped Pete hadn't been involved in the fueling of the yellow boat. Five gallons wouldn't make much sense to Pete, especially believing Woody didn't have fuel available at Smugglers.

Laura was finishing up, so he went to the radio room to double check the names and estimated times of arrival for the other two boats. Nine and eleven-thirty. Good. He'd be done by midnight, he thought. Then the four of them could let loose and enjoy the sweet rewards of success. They would hear about last night's boats from Chubby, and would hopefully have cause to celebrate. Woody made a mental note to make sure he pulled some grass out of the shipment for himself. Might as well enjoy it, he thought. Don't know when the next load will be in or where it will come from. Howard hadn't specified anything in the future.

Woody walked over to the bar, fixed himself a drink and went out on the sundeck. His company was coming back, a lobster dangling on a spear. "Nice catch," said Woody as they pulled up to the dock. "Clean it and take it into Laura to add to dinner."

"Thanks," the bearded man said. "Any chance of bumming a rum?"

"Help yourself. You know what's ahead of you better than I do," said Woody.

The two men joined him on the deck a few minutes later, drying off with some towels Laura had given them. They talked about the good weather and their boat, skirting anything personal or controversial. By seven o'clock, they were sitting down for a seafood dinner, and by seven-thirty Maxwell and Pat arrived.

"One thing about you, Max," said Woody. "You're a hell of a lot more dependable than these guys. Arrived mid-afternoon instead of tonight. Think they just wanted to do some fishing. You guys ready to take on fuel? It's beginning to get dark and I haven't seen anyone around. Might as well get on with it. Go on out, and I'll make the radio contact."

According to Howard, all boats were supposed to arrive at the specified hour. He wanted to check with Chubby on the *Y-Not* before releasing any of the goods.

"*Naughty Lady*. Woodpecker calling *Naughty Lady*." In a few seconds, Chubby answered.

"Switch over."

"Going." He switched to the second code frequency. "How do you copy, Chubby?"

"Good. Go ahead."

"The *Y-Not* arrived early this afternoon. Two guys. Was that planned?"

"Tall guy with a beard and shorter guy with blondish hair?"

"That's who."

"They're okay. New at the game. Probably thought better early than to mess up. Let me know when they leave. Already know about their fuel shortage today."

"Now, how would you know that?" asked Woody, a bit surprised.

189

"Howard saw the whole thing," said Chubby. "I don't have time to yak. Switch over, then make contact as planned when company arrives."

"Roger. Woodpecker clear."

"*Naughty Lady* clear."

Woody joined the men near the fuel drums, and helped rig the transfer pump. The crew brought the boat up closer to the fuel supply, and in only minutes, the *Y-Not* was fueled.

"Give us about fifteen more minutes, then we can load you," said Woody, looking at the sky. "If you want another drink now is the time, because as soon as you've got ten bales aboard I'm going to cut your mooring lines. Want you on your way as soon as possible. Keep to your schedule going back. None of this arriving by day if it's supposed to be night."

The bearded man nodded, getting the message. Woody felt good to have the upper hand, knowing they had screwed up in the afternoon. Another round of rum and the sun began its race for the horizon. They stood, watching the bright orange ball sink.

"If you look real close, you can see the last bit of sun throw off a green flash," said Pat, a sunset lover. "I've only seen it once." They stood and watched, but no green flicker was to be seen tonight. The sun sank like a fiery ball of lead. The sky kept a pink hue for a few minutes, then a dull gray set in.

"Time to load," said Woody, walking to the push cart and easing it over to the warehouse. They worked fast, and in fifteen minutes, ten bales were loaded on the *Y-Not*, her engines were running with the fresh flow of fuel and she was off. Woody made the radio contact with the time to Chubby, then joined the rest to wait for the next boat, a 40-foot speed racer called *Mooner*, scheduled to take fifteen bales.

While Laura, Woody and Max had their rum drinks, Pat smoked, enjoying the weed and lying on a comfortable chaise. Max wished she'd drink with the rest of them instead of smoking to get high right away. Pat easily embarrassed him, and he wondered if she did it on purpose.

"I think the worst goddamn part of this game is waiting. It would be much easier to get them all over at once," said Woody, beginning to pace, his limp obvious.

"Get it over with and get on with it. Right Laura?"

"Whatever ya say," she said. She'd been sipping a few rums in the kitchen since afternoon and was feeling no pain. While Woody tended to get loud, she withdrew into her own shell, mellowing out at an easy level.

About nine-fifteen, they could see the lights bobbing on a boat far out, headed toward the island. It loomed larger and larger until it was roaring into the harbor. The bow nosed down parallel to the water as the engines were cut, and they could see two men aboard.

"They have to be old-timers at this," said Woody. "Look how she came in."

"She gets a hundred and fifty gallons, right?" asked Max. "Hundred in her own tanks and fifty in drums."

"Think you're right," said Woody, rising. "Let's take care of them. Is it my imagination, or are those bales getting heavier as we approach the finish line?"

"We're getting anxious," said Max, matter-of-factly.

The boat came to a stop, and when the engines were turned off, the air echoed the silence. The captain secured a second line to the stern, allowing the boat to rest its aft end at the dock where it would be fueled.

"You make it easy for us," said Woody. "One fifty, right?"

"Right," he said, poker-faced, dressed in dark clothes. He opened the fuel tank and Woody connected the hose. Max and his crewman humped the fuel drums aboard.

"Okay, now the crap," said the captain. He was definitely the no-nonsense type. Within twenty minutes, all fifteen bales were stowed away. He waved off the offer of food or drink, saying they were all set, and *Mooner* was off, ironically in the direction of the rising moon. Her wake spread the dancing flickers of light to either side, as if carving a path to another galaxy.

Woody helped Max clean up, the women relaxing in the coolness of the evening. It had been a hot day, but as usual, the sun had turned down the thermostat as it greeted the other side of the world.

"You don't smoke, Laura?" Pat asked, lazily.

"Only tried it once. Still prefer the booze. Ah can follow it more closely."

"Yeah, but sometimes it takes forever."

"Depends what ya looking for, Ah guess," said Laura, yawning. "Right now, Ah'm just content. It's been a long week with all this stuff sitting here and Ah'm glad to be rid of it. Be glad for a few dollars, too."

"Yeah. That's the best part. The bucks. How Max loves his dollar bills. The bigger the better."

Max and Woody came on the deck. Woody continued into the club to make another radio contact.

"One more boat to go," he said, disappearing inside.

"You can tell he's happy about it," said Laura, sitting up. "Ah am too."

"That warehouse looks empty now," said Max. "Didn't realize we'd crammed so much into it. It's bigger than I thought."

They sat in silence for awhile, listening to Woody in the background talking to Chubby. It was a short conversation and he soon joined everyone.

"Boy!" he said. "Talk about a schedule. Everything's right on guys, right on. One more boat and then Woody, here, is gonna let loose."

"Promises, promises," chuckled Laura. "Loose with what?"

"Every goddamn thing possible. I'll run naked along the dock, I'll dive in for a swim...."

"And a shark'll get ya," interrupted Laura. "There ya'd be with your behind chewed. Let's celebrate quietly tonight, okay? Ah can't take another scene like last week. Ah'm still tired from it."

"Who asked you to be so goddamn sensible?" asked Woody. "Shit! Am I on edge!"

"You don't say," said Max, stretching his wiry frame out in a chair.

Woody limped back and forth across the deck area and down to the docks. He was like a caged circus animal, ready to jump through a hoop if anyone had the energy to hold it. After fifteen minutes, he joined the group, sat down and stared out to sea. It was almost eleven o'clock.

"Time to start looking for the next boat," he said.

"It's a small one. Only twenty-six feet," said Max, not moving. "She'll be here before we have a chance to track her."

"You're probably right," said Woody, still staring. "Might as well fix another one. You still smokin', Pat?"

"Like a California forest fire in dry season," said Laura.

"Very funny," said Pat. "Ve-r-r-y funny. But I'm past the point of caring." Her words were a bit slurred and she kept her eye on Max in a dreamy stare.

"There she is!" shouted Woody, rising and going toward the dock. "Come on, Max. Let's get this last one over with."

Like the previous boat, it came in with full steam, stopped short of the dock, requested fifty gallons for the internal tank and a thirty-gallon drum. A soon as it was fueled, the last bales were loaded and the boat was ready to leave.

"Hold on," said Woody. "Almost forgot. Need to keep a little for ourselves."

The crew pulled some grass from one of the bales, rewrapping the plastic, and handed it over.

"Won't miss it," the captain said, smiling. "As long as they count ten on the other end I don't care. Let's go."

In no time, the boat was only a speck on the black horizon, headed for the final payoff.

Woody and Max stood on the dock watching it disappear and Laura and Pat did the same on the upper deck. It was almost a let-down. Instead of feeling raring to go, Woody was suddenly very, very tired. The week hit him like a wall and he wasn't prepared for it.

"Jesus!" he said. "I can't believe it's all gone. You think Howard's watching with his scope?"

"Sure of it," said Max. "What do you have in mind?"

Woody looked over to the girls.

"Come on, gals, get down here. We've got a celebration to conduct and by damn, we're gonna do it. Get your sweet asses down here. We're gonna do a dance for Howard on the hill. Come on!"

He grabbed one of Laura's hands and one of Pat's and Max did the same. They went round and round, laughing like children playing ring-around-the-rosy.

"How's that, Howard?" shouted Woody to the Osprey Nest, a couple miles way. "How you like them bananas? Whooee! We did it!" He was jumping up and down and running round, comical with his short leg, hugging the girls and shaking Max's hand. They were all laughing.

"Ah think this is what's called comical relief," said Laura, as they suddenly stopped, exhausted.

"Let's fix another drink and settle into this situation," said Woody. "Pat, smoke your head off if you want. I feel good."

* * *

At Osprey Nest, Howard chuckled. Crazy fools. Not a hitch in almost forty-eight hours. Those guys deserved their fun. Tomorrow they'd be even happier. Even though part of the load was stolen, a good share of bills would be passed around. Crazy crew, thought Howard. The last link would be closed when all the bales were accounted for on the other end. But the last leg was the least concern. Only a rare boat ever got caught. Chubby had all the protection in the world for them on the other end. Last night's boats were already safe. Good deal, thought Howard, going downstairs to where Marjorie was still reading a book. Good deal.

PART TWO

Chapter 10

Rainy Day Blues

It was the most oppressively hot August Pete could remember and the eighth week of no rain.

The watermakers couldn't keep up with the demand of the club, and he was desperately trying to figure another way to produce more water. He was already recapturing what he could off the generator heat, much like a still produces liquor.

Now, as a last resort, he was trying to reopen an old brackish well that had been shut down due to pollution many years before. It was a messy, rough job. No one could work long before sitting in the shade. Jackson and another native had helped Pete for two days. The salinity of the well was tested. If he could filter the water sufficiently prior to it entering the reverse osmosis watermaker, the well could possibly keep up with the demand, provided rain came soon.

It was the first year Pete could remember where the afternoon storms continually bypassed the island, dumping torrents on open waters but not a drop on land.

The natives could no longer drink from their own wells because the salinity level was beyond their tolerance. They came to the Sandy Cay Club with jugs to be filled with drinking water. The catchment system, consisting of eaves on the club roof, normally funneled water into a series of cisterns, but the concrete holding vaults and vinyl-lined children's play pools were totally useless without rain. The roof was now littered with fallen leaves and Pete realized that when the rain finally did come, he would have to clear the gutter in order to catch every available drop. He also knew the docks needed repair if the club was going to survive another season of harsh northwesterly winds. With the summer heat, too, cottage guests complained that the paddle fans were barely keeping up with the no-see-ums in the still of early evening, and were losing the battle completely during the day when no wind blew. Guests had begun to sit in the ocean off the nearest beach, water up to their

197

necks, during the heat of the afternoon to avoid too much sun and the horseflies that loved to attack hot, sweaty bodies.

As Pete walked back from checking the generator, Jackson met him near the front porch of the club.

"Nudder day widout de rains," he said, shaking his head and looking at the cloudless sky. "Don' know de las' summer it dis bad. You gits dat ol' well working?"

"To the point where we can start pumping after Charlie brings in the filters. He should be in later today. Had him make a special trip for them," he said, drawing on a cigarette, his face showing concern over the impending crisis.

"Last time we were without water we almost didn't survive financially. Those big yachts won't come here and people certainly aren't going to stay in the cottages if we don't have water. They can only drink so much booze, but for some silly reason, they don't like to shower in the stuff."

Jackson laughed. "Whole village prayin' for rains," he said. "Good Lord maybe not see dis tiny island. He better come trough soon, or we be in bad trouble. Bad trouble." Jackson shook his head slowly, knowing that it was far worse for the village than for the club. Pete at least had a fancy watermaker to produce drinking water. The natives couldn't possibly afford to buy water even if Pete had it to sell, yet there wasn't a cistern in the village that had more than a few days' supply.

As they stood silently looking over the harbor and the yachts, Maria came out of the club.

"Hey, Jackson. Can you dip dis kettle into de sea?" She smiled, showing a beautiful set of white teeth, warm, friendly eyes and a winning grin. "I use sea water to cook de wegetables an' fish, not fresh water," she said, giving Pete an explanation where none was necessary. He knew the natives had survived times like this before and that all the little tricks had been passed on through the years, generation to generation, about what to do should the summer storms not come.

Jackson took the big pot, walked down the dock, tied a line to its handle and tossed it into the sea. When it began to sink, he pulled it up and carried it back.

"You needs some more?" he asked, smiling. "Gits you

anyting you need."

"Tanks, Jackson. I know dat. Dis good for now. You gits de final count for dinner?" she asked, turning to Pete.

"Fifteen, including family," he said. "Anther boat made reservations, but I haven't seen it yet. Might not make it here today. Who knows, right?" He turned to Jackson, who shrugged his shoulders in agreement as he stared past the boats at anchor.

"Look like Tom out dere still hauling de water in his cruiser to Smuggler's Cay," he said. "Made a deal wid Conch Inn, only I don' tink it too smart. Manny selling dem his water and he don' ewen know how much he hab. His cistern is low, but dere he is, selling de water so Smugglers can keeps afloat. Don' make no sense. He habing too good a time to mind de store dis summer. Woody and dem keeps him goin'. And dere go his water. Tinks he gits rich, but he be poor man soon."

"Yeah," said Pete. "I heard that they were getting supplied by Manny, but I thought his cistern was still okay."

"No," said Jackson. "I checks it de udder day and tell Manny it be low. He don' listen. Can't make a mon listen iffen he don' wants to. But he runnin' out o' water fast just to keep all dose people happy at Smugglers. Lots o' people 'round dat island lately. Cheap dinners, you know. He charge only half what we do. Don' know how he doin' it. Do you?"

"Got my own thoughts on that one, Jackson, judging from the type of people there. I don't think we're missing any business we'd want anyway. Let him play the wining and dining game. Sooner or later he'll find out you can't give stuff away for less than it costs you. He thinks he's getting all my business, but I'm the one who'll be here next year and the year after. Let him play his games."

"You right, you know," said Jackson. "We be here long after dat Woody. You see his friend's new plane? Nice one. Twin engine. He bringin' all de supplies dey need. 'Tween him and Jock dey no rely on de freight boat. Brings it in from de States."

"The expensive way," said Pete, grinding his cigarette in the dry sand. "Doesn't add up. Planes cost money. Fancy dinners cost money. But he's not charging. Maybe he doesn't have to. Maybe he's so successful with that new plane and all his other

199

deals that he can afford a big giveaway. All I know is he's sure living the life for someone who didn't have a pot to piss in a year ago. But then, who can say?"

"We maybe no say, but we sure can tink," said Jackson, the two men communicating. "He been a little quiet lately, don' you tink? For awhile, dere, it was go, go, go all de time. Now he stayin' on de island and more comin' to him. Like he jis sit back and let all de udders do de tings he was doin' before."

"I think you're right. And when you're not minding your own store, so to speak, you can expect trouble. The party can't keep up like this. Something's happening, I suspect, but the trouble with Woody is he's closed-mouth on what he does and talks big on stuff that doesn't matter. He knows that we know he's up to something, but he's not going to let us in on it. He's cooled with that Howard character, too. Howard left the island for a few weeks and told everyone to stay away from his house, that he'd be back shortly. Haven't seen him, but I overheard he's anchored off another island to the south."

"And I hears dat Jock flies dere pretty regular," said Jackson, nodding his head. "Last time Lucky here he mention Howard. You tink dere's a connection?"

"Who knows?" said Pete. "But that's an interesting possibility."

"Well, I gits back to work," said Jackson. "Den I go do some tings on my house. You wants me I be dere."

"Okay, Jackson. It's going to be slow with no water for awhile. When Charlie gets in maybe you can come and help us put in those filters. I'm going to do it in series to make sure no solids hit that membrane on the watermaker. If we can get the brackish well going we can survive longer with no rain. But we'll have to be careful on pumping that, too. I'm sure it's limited."

"Fresh water no like dis island," said Jackson. "Maybe de good Lord nebber tought any person be here."

"Could be, Jackson, but here we are and we need water," said Pete, smiling. "Don't worry. The man upstairs will send us a gusher one of these days." He looked up and laughed and headed for the generator shed.

Pete sat on the front porch of the club in the shade, but the couple of degrees didn't make much difference. It was hot. And humid. Humid without rain. He could just see Tom's boat rounding the point before it would be out of sight on its way to Smugglers.

Ever since Woody had gotten the resort going, some of Sandy Cay's regulars had changed watering holes, and with boat people being notoriously cheap, Smugglers had gotten the bulk of the live-aboard as well as transient traffic. That didn't bother Pete so much as the fact that Woody was giving everything away.

Stories were plentiful on the wild parties, the smoking and drinking and the late hours. He mused over what was happening, how Jock came and went frequently with Maxwell keeping a steady flow of passengers for him, cutting into Charlie's business. He could feel tension building on the island, with the natives as well as tourists. Those flying were tugged between a cheap flight with Jock and a legal flight with Charlie. Although it was basically Charlie's problem, it was felt at the club. Fewer people came in asking about the next flight, thought Pete. While flying people began to be profitable for Jock, suspicion clouded his short flights to islands for no apparent reason. He carried only a briefcase, and often departed and returned within a short time. He never talked about where he went; he simply smiled.

Pete thought how Maxwell had kept up his hate war against him, fueling it every chance he could in little, subtle ways. More and more, he had been working on the Sandy Cay Club dock, eyes straight ahead avoiding contact with Pete whenever he came. Pete glanced over to *Maxwell's Revenge*, still deteriorating on the club's ramp. The summer sun had scorched the remaining paint even more and the planks and decks had shrunk in the hot sun. If it were launched today, thought Pete, it would act like a giant sponge before ultimately sinking on the spot.

It was three-thirty. Charlie would be in shortly. And, he hoped, the brackish water would be turned into fresh by tomorrow. He picked up an old magazine and began to read, then heard a boat sputter. He got up and looked. Just beyond the

201

club dock, Woody and his red boat were both limping, the engine running hesitantly. He shut down one engine as he babied the other toward Conch Inn. Pete chuckled. It was becoming a weekly occurrence. Maxwell would have to work on it again. Ever since the fabled shootout, the boat hadn't been the same.

"Sandy Cay Club, Sandy Cay Club. Charlie here." Pete walked back into the club and answered. "Sandy Cay. Go to our frequency."

"Going."

"Hey, Charlie. You got the filters?"

"Roger. You'll have them in about fifteen minutes. Have a couple of passengers that need transportation to the club. You got a big 65-footer called *Dreamer* at the dock?"

"Roger. She's here."

"Might tell them their people are here. Called as I was about ready to leave. That's why I'm late. Didn't want to miss them."

"Okay. meet you at the strip. I'll tell them they have guests arriving. Sandy Cay clear."

Pete locked the cash box, walked down the dock to tell the *Dreamer* it had company and walked back to where *Cyclops* was parked. Pete hoped Charlie would have a new fuel hose for the groaning vehicle as well.

As he drove toward the village, Pete felt a stillness in the air. The natives rested in the afternoon to escape the heat. Dogs lay alongside the road in whatever shade they could find, and the few chickens walked around the yards in slow gear, heads moving slowly in time to their feet. The lizards waited until the last second to scurry off into the brush as *Cyclops* drew near.

Charlie was landing as Pete drove up. He sat and waited for him to taxi to the ramp. The engines were shut down and Charlie opened the rear door.

"Hi," he said, waving, wearing light blue jeans and a white club shirt with the logo on the pocket. "What a time for the air-conditioning to go. At eight thousand feet it was nice, at sea level forget it. Can't remember a summer when it's been this hot." He helped a couple out of the plane.

"They've got a lot of gear," he said, walking to the forward luggage compartment of the plane. "The yacht decided to resupply at this point rather than on the main province. Good for me they did."

He and Pete began loading cases of wine, groceries and gear on *Cyclops*. Charlie looked around at the few airplanes on the ramp.

"See Jock's back. Who's he flying now?"

"Don't know," said Pete. "He comes in and heads for Smugglers right way. Heard he's making friends with Tom and Sue — particularly Sue. Woody just came back to Smugglers with the red boat. Sounds like he's got problems again."

Charlie shook his head and chuckled. "Keeps Max busy. Better he's messing with Woody's boat than one of our customers. Thing never will run right. You can't work on a precision engine as if it's an old washing machine. Max will never get it right. He doesn't have the tools or the facilities and can't even time it properly. You know and I know, and in the end, Woody's going to know, too. As long as it keeps Max busy, what the hell." He shrugged and smiled, as Pete took the back road to the club.

"Have some good reservations coming in next season," said Charlie, handing Pete the mail packet. Lines creased his forehead.

"Hope I can make it until then. I can't compete with the son of a bitch. How do you tell people about insurance premiums, hundred hour inspections and all the other shit I have to go through when all they want to know is how cheap can they fly? My back's against the wall. And the authorities know it. If I did what he's doing I'd be out of business. He doesn't even own the plane he's flying. He's got nothing to lose. I'm gonna ride it out, Pete, but I need help. If Max wasn't such a vindictive bastard nothing would have happened and this would still be a sleepy little island that tourists remember. Look at it now. I can feel the pulse changing."

"I feel it too. Different type of people coming around now," said Pete, a serious look on his face. "A younger, faster moving crowd. See that runabout at the dinghy dock? Notice the new motor. Carlton just bought it from me. Three thousand bucks. All cash."

"Carlton?" said Charlie, mouth agape as he stared at the shiny new engine. "Carlton the native?" he repeated. "Where the hell did he get the bread for THAT?"

"Don't know," said Pete, "But he's sure happy with it. I'd be too. He's the big honcho with the native boys now. It's his hotrod."

"I heard an interesting comment at customs the other day," said Charlie. "Agent there said the new pastime in the islands is ripping off the scammers. Find the stash and you're instantly rich."

"Now that you mention it...." Pete looked at Charlie as if he'd just discovered there was no Santa Claus. "It fits. It honest to God fits. The native boys were talking about a cave south of Rocky Point when I walked in on their conversation the other day. Place went dead quiet. I didn't think much of it 'cause they always stop talking when boss man comes around anyway. Kinda like the old wrackin' days, huh?" he smiled.

The islands had survived for years off shipwrecked boats and sailors, and today was no different if the opportunity presented itself.

Charlie laughed at Pete's realization.

"As the natives would say, it's a different ting," smiled Charlie. "This place wasn't any virgin during Prohibition when it harbored the rum runners. Why should these times be any different? Survival is based on what's at hand, and from what I'm beginning to see, a lot is at hand." He lit a cigarette and the two sat for a few minutes in silence.

Ripping off the dopers, thought Pete.

"That means they're selling and someone's buying," he said, tugging on his beard. "Or they could be playing a little game of blackmail on the side, selling the stuff back to whoever stashed it in the first place."

Charlie raised his eyebrows and nodded.

"All different kinds of possibilities," he said.

"Well," said Pete, as if tired. "I think we better install those filters to see if my gambling is going to pay off for a few more days of survival. You want to get Jackson? I'll meet you behind my house on the hill. Ran pipe all the way to the club. Spent a fortune, but what am I going to do? We need water."

They walked out of the club.

"I'll take your Jeep and drop you on the way," said Charlie. "We need anything else?"

"Just manpower and a lot of prayers."

They climbed into the open vehicle, a plywood top protecting them from the sun. Charlie dropped Pete and the filters off and continued to Jackson's house. After more than three years of building it was almost finished, everything carefully done by Jackson and a few helpers. It was a beautiful four-bedroom house that overlooked the little lagoon near the airstrip. In a few months, Jackson would move in.

In the meantime, everyone was taking bets on whom he would choose as a wife. Tradition held that a man didn't take a wife until he had a house. Jackson had the house, but there were only rumors on the wife. Whoever it was would be the equivalent of the First Lady of the island, with the finest of everything. Jackson had put tremendous pride into the home, with ceramic tile and wood parquet floors, beamed ceilings and spacious rooms.

The cistern was constructed to hold two-years' supply, and the house had all the modern conveniences. His wife would not have to wash clothes by hand. She would have a new washer. She wouldn't have a cook house out back. She'd have a modern kitchen with microwave oven and double stainless steel sink. And fresh water in modern toilets. Charlie smiled. The bets were favoring Maria, the cook at the club, but there wasn't a hint of anything beyond casual friendship that she was special to Jackson. It would be kept a secret, Charlie knew, but it was fun to speculate.

As he rounded the village road past the church and generator, he could see the house, an imposing ranch-style home complete to stone chimney, bay windows and front porch. No other house on the island had grass in the yard, but Jackson had nurtured it even in the dry, hot season, so that the young blades were surviving.

The house was a credit not only to Jackson but to the native culture. In his own persistent way, he had shown that an island-

205

born man could raise himself in stature and respect through perseverance and hard work.

There wasn't a person — white, black, native or foreigner — who did not think the world of Jackson. Generous tips for hard work had made the home possible.

As he pulled up, Jackson came out.

"Hey, dere! You bring de filters?"

Charlie nodded. "Hop in. We're going to see about making some water. How've you been, Mon? House looks fantastic. Soon as you finish it that's where I'm staying when I'm here. None of this brackish water business at the club. When I want a decent room with a good shower I'll bunk in with you."

Jackson laughed.

"Dat okay, you know. You welcome. But don' tell nobody, eh? Don' want all de riffraff tourists."

They both laughed. The men were good friends, and between Charlie and Pete, Jackson had been encouraged to learn the many facets of business, to feel that he was on an equal footing with those who had learned by books.

The house was a symbol of his future. It was a monument of hope, to the dream that the lowliest person could become a success. The house was Jackson's statement. When he was ready, it would be said out loud. In the meantime, the symbol would do.

They headed back toward Pete's, each hoping silently that the well had enough good brackish water to make the project worthwhile. Time and close watch would tell.

As they approached the hill, Pete was already working on the pump. It took until midnight, working on and off with a torch in the darkness, before the first gallon of brackish water passed the drinking test, but by morning, Pete and the villagers were happy. The ancient well was producing enough water to ward off a crisis...at least for another few days.

* * *

The next morning as Pete and Charlie were congratulating each other on the new source of water, Woody came to the dinghy dock with his black boat. He tied up and limped toward the club, carrying a briefcase and wearing a colorful Smugglers Cay T-shirt, cut-off jeans and rubber sandals.

"Well, if it isn't Mr. Successful," said Pete, a bit mockingly as Woody walked into the club. "Tell me. How do you possibly do it? I'm beginning to think I ought to come by boat with the family for dinner every night. Let them get a little bit of class." He winked at Charlie who was sitting on a barstool, hand over his mouth hiding a grin. Pete could say anything in his own place.

Woody laughed.

"Gimme a beer and I'll give you the secrets — providing you can tell me how to make water."

"Oh. You've got a water problem, huh? You hear that Charlie? Man's got a water problem. He's human, just like the rest of us. I'll be damned. Man's got a water problem." He shook his head and pulled out a beer.

"Cut the shit, Pete. I've been getting it from the natives ever since I hired the bastards and I don't need any lip from you. I'm not asking you to make a rain cloud. I've got hard cash. I want to buy a system since you're the dealer for the damnable contraptions...."

"How many gallons you want?" said Pete. "Or should I ask how much money you have and then tell you how much water it will buy?"

Woody looked at him, not wanting to be made a fool.

"I would think six hundred gallons a day should be enough," he said. "Damn it, Pete. I'm serious. I've been barging it for the past few days on Tom's cruiser but that gravy train's just about over. Had a hard time pumping any into the boat yesterday."

"I hear Manny's cistern is about dry as a result," said Pete, more seriously. "You can't just turn on the tap. It takes newcomers like yourself a long time to realize it. Let's see what a watermaker will run." He went to the radio room and reached for a manual stuffed between catalogs and other advertising flyers. As he leafed through the pages, Woody turned to Charlie.

"How's the pilot doing?" he asked, as if forced to make conversation.

207

"Not bad under the circumstances," said Charlie, wanting to avoid a confrontation about Jock.

"Fuel's pretty expensive now," said Woody, continuing the small talk.

"Tell me about it," said Charlie, a bit stand-offish.

Pete walked out of the radio room with an opened manual.

"Six hundred gallons'll run you seven thousand installed," he said. "You want two?"

"Shit. Should think twice about one," he said. "Order it up. When can I get it?"

"Well, we can put in the order and Charlie can probably bring it on his next trip if it's expressed from the factory. You got the money?" he asked, looking him square in the eye.

Without saying a word, Woody reached for his briefcase and opened it. He carefully counted out seventy crisp one hundred dollar bills, laying them in seven neat piles of ten on the bar.

Pete looked at Charlie.

"The man's got the money." Charlie shrugged, making close eye contact with Pete.

"Now," said Woody. "Just tell me where to pick it up and I'll have...." He stopped, thought about what he was going to say, then changed his mind. "That sounds okay. The sooner the better. Now, what did you want to know about running a resort?"

Pete picked up the money, opened the cash box and dumped it in the bottom drawer, making sure the padlock closed. Both Pete and Charlie ignored the reference to Jock.

"Well, I just want to learn how to be as successful as you are," said Pete, pulling on his pants with his thumbs. "I mean, here I am, years in the business, and I've never been able to make ends meet without charging the prices I do. Now in a few weeks I see you've gotten the place going and everyone's raving about how reasonable everything is. I just want to know the secret."

"Well, it sure as hell isn't in the help," said Woody, avoiding the digs. "You got no idea what I've been though, Pete. Those black bastards were supposed to build a cistern. They went and cracked the rock or whatever damn thing they do to make cement, laid the whole thing out and started pouring it. Half way through, one of the women had to birth a kid or some other such nonsense and everything stopped. Right in the middle of the thing. Two days later they came back to finish the pour. Then I found out the last cement was made with brackish water 'cause Tom hadn't arrived with the fresh water and they heard boss man was mad. Christ! Now I've got a cistern that holds only half what it's supposed to, with water leaking over the damn island. And the roof. You want to hear about the roof on the new shed?"

Pete and Charlie were laughing. A cistern made with brackish cement. In two pours. It was too much.

"Tell me about the roof, Woody, if I can stand to hear," said Pete between chuckles, his blue eyes twinkling to listen to someone else's problems for a change.

"You've heard about tin corrugated? You know, the stuff you can get anywhere in the world? The stuff that houses are made of in the back jungles? The crap that looks a million years old before it gets nailed into place? Well, let me tell you. It may be the universal poor man's roofing material, but you best know which country it comes from. I found out the hard way that American and European corrugated doesn't match. You know those little grooves that are supposed to fit together so you can slap the shit in place with no problems? The fucking grooves are different. Either has to be one or the other. And I got the last of both from the main province. Quit laughing. I'm serious. What am I supposed to do? I can't think for the goddamn purchasing agent. No shit. Two different size grooves. And now I hear the whole country's out of cement block. I tell you. Laugh, will you?

"Give me another beer. At least you know THAT'S gonna be the same. Sometimes colder than other times, but it'll still help you forget where you are."

"Welcome to the tropics," said Pete, still laughing.

"And my dock. You want to hear why it's no bigger or better than the day I stepped on the island?"

"We're listening," said Charlie, enjoying Woody's tale of woes.

"Ordered up the pilings. You know, those thirty-foot things

you have driven into the muck and coral? Well, would you believe they were out of the thirty-footers and sent me two fifteens for every thirty-footer ordered? Now what the fuck does fifteen feet do you? Top of the friggin' dock would be underwater even at low tide." He opened the beer Pete put on the counter. "I tell you, it sure ain't all they say it'll be."

"And I thought you were successful," said Pete, pulling on his pants, shaking his head and still laughing. "Man, you're dumb! You sure you're not drinking or smoking too much? You've got all these expenses and problems going on and you're sponsoring a free lunch program. Who's gonna pay for those pilings even if they ARE the wrong size? And the freight on all that shit? That costs, man. And nothin' down here is returnable."

Somehow it wasn't funny any more. Woody sat, fondling the sweating beer can. After a few minutes he regained his composure and said, "Well, can't win 'em all, folks. Back to the drawing boards, I guess. You get that watermaker for me and I can forget the cistern. As to the shed, well, looks like we'll design a new roof line and patch it with tar. The docks..." he sighed, "the docks there's no hope. You wanna buy some good, new fifteen-foot pilings cheap?"

"No thanks," said Pete, chuckling. "I've got my own problems. May have bought some time on the water, but I'm looking at a new dock, too. It never ends, Woody, it never ends. Get used to it and get used to being used. The tropics get you man. You never win. But you can have a hell of lot of fun trying. By the way, I see you're still having problems with the red boat. What's up?"

Woody squirmed on the stool and squeezed the empty can.

"You had to mention it, huh? Another worm in the can. I'm beginning to know why Max is working on this stupid island rather than in a big reputable shop somewhere. He doesn't know shit about what he's doing. The money I've spent I could have shipped the thing to the States and had new engines installed. He gets one thing done and something else goes. Story of my life lately."

"Just don't bring it to me to pick up the pieces," said Pete. "I don't touch anything he's laid hands on anymore. People have to learn the hard way. It never will run, Woody. Mark my words. Not like you want it to. It's a sad fact of life. If Max has touched it consider it cursed, or 'Maximized' as we say now. You're not alone. He's messed up a lot of people."

Woody sat thinking, not saying anything.

"Maybe I'll have this yachtsman look at it who visited the other day," he said finally. "He seems to know about boats."

"Be careful on that, too. He doesn't have a permit to work in the islands, and Max isn't selective when it comes to doling out vengeance. You got yourself in a bind. Just do the best you can under the circumstances."

"Guess you're right. Gimme another beer, will you?" Woody pulled another hundred dollar bill out of his briefcase and laid it on the bar. "Put that toward the tab."

"Glad to," said Pete. "They all feel new. You printing them now?" He winked at Charlie as he unlocked the cash drawer and added the bill to the watermaker money.

"Nope, but making it just as fast," said Woody, a little of the braggart returning in his voice. "You ought to come visit, Pete. I'll even buy you a drink. Wouldn't want you to just go on hearsay about my place."

He picked up the can of beer Pete had put on the bar and eased off the stool. As he reached for his briefcase, he turned to Charlie.

"Got a couple of passengers for you if you want to go back today to get that watermaker going," he said. "What time can you leave?"

"Whenever they get here," said Charlie, dryly. "Good thing I'm not proud."

Woody ignored the remark and limped out to his boat, tossing in the briefcase before untying the line.

"Be back in an hour," he shouted. "Three people."

Charlie nodded. Three passengers was worth a trip back, even from Woody.

* * *

Later, as Charlie left the island for the States and gained

211

altitude, he could see a weather system building that he had been cautioned about earlier. In the distance, swirling clouds built to high peaks, blocking out the summer sun. More than an hour later, he landed on the mainland with no problem, but the wind had begun to blow. Once back in his office, he put in a rush order for the watermaker, sent off a purchase order and checked the weather for the next day. It didn't look good. Winds of forty miles per hour were predicted, enough to keep him grounded, and there was talk of a hurricane. There already had been several tropical storms since the season began, but nothing serious. He hoped this one would blow over like the others.

* * *

The next morning the sky was black, giving the impression that clocks were several hours off, that daylight in fact was not yet due. But it was eight o'clock, time enough for the sun to already blister the earth on a normal August day. Charlie went to the radio to call Pete.

"Sandy Cay, Sandy Cay. Base calling Sandy Cay." There was crackling and static, as if recording bursts of thunder and lightning.

"Sandy Cay. Base calling Sandy Cay."

"Sandy Cay to base. Can hardly read you, Charlie. What's going on? Weather's awful."

"Looks like a hurricane building in your back yard, Pete. According to the coordinates and report, it could hit with full force by tomorrow night. Watermaker's due in late today, but I can't deliver it in this weather."

"Don't worry about THAT. Keep me posted. We better batten down. Hurricane, huh? What are the winds?"

"Still blowing forty and fairly stationary. Weatherman predicts it will be on the move again later today, heading northwest. But it could go northeast at this point, too. Warnings are out. I'll keep you posted."

"Thanks. I better get to work. Sky's pretty black and winds are around thirty. Talk to you later. Sandy Cay clear."

"Base clear."

Charlie looked outside. The trees were flinging their branches wildly against a gray sky, as if totally confused. The waterway in front of his house showed dark patches as the wind scurried the tide in different directions, creating zig-zagging designs and rocking boats tied to docks. People were putting up storm shutters. He'd better do the same.

* * *

As soon as Pete signed off, he went to look for Jackson.
Hurricane.
It was a bad word in the islands, even though it was several decades since one had hit with any severe damage. But the prediction of high winds and rising water was not to be taken lightly. A warning was just that. And Pete took it seriously. He walked to the work area behind the club.

"Jackson!" he shouted above the roar of the generator. Pete motioned for Jackson to come outside.

"That's more than just a passing storm that doesn't want to rain on us," he said, nodding to the sky. "Charlie said there are hurricane warnings. Go to the village and warn the people. He'll give us the updates as he hears them in the States, but let's get things ready for a blow. Always something, right?"

"Right, Mon. Hurricane, eh? Dat's real bad news, eben if dey jis' warnin' us. Storm can be bad. Ol' lady here 'member de one dat wipe out dis island before. People climbed in pot holes so de wind not carry dem away wid dere house. Hurricane dangerous. Eben little one. I go tell dem to tie tings down. Den I be back and we clear de dock."

"Let me handle the cottage guests," said Pete. "I don't want anyone panicking. I'll tell Helen and Johnny to take care of the house. Meet you here in fifteen minutes."

"Okay," said Jackson, and he was off, heading toward *Cyclops*. The natives had heard stories of past storms, when the heavens engulfed the tiny rock in the middle of the Lord's seas, raining terror on its people and all their earthly possessions. At least in these times there was some warning. Years before, no one knew the measure of a storm's fury or its potential threat to

213

life. Now they did, and Jackson knew the word was already out as he reached the village. Windows were being boarded up and children were picking up toys and loose objects in the yards. He could feel the temperature drop between leaving the club and arriving in the village. Jackson spread the word, encouraging everyone to "batten de hatches," then continued to his home. A worker was out front, picking up pieces of wood and drywall. As Jackson pulled up, he walked over.

"Heard bad storm comin' dis way. I clean up de yard and lock all dis loose stuff in de back room. Den I gots to go to my house. Don' worry, Mon. I take care."

"Tanks, Shorty," said Jackson. "Don' look good. Charlie say blowin' on de mainland good. He keep us posted. Look at dat sky," he said, glancing above. "Clouds look funny. Like dey don' know what to do. Yet dey all lined up like dey want to form a bridge across de sky. Don' look good. You hurry here an' gits to yo' house. I be back after I help at de club. We gots lots to do if dis ting gonna hit. Could be bad."

He put *Cyclops* in gear and headed back toward the club, feeling the stiff breeze freshening. He noticed the people from the cottages were already packed and ready to leave for the airstrip. At least they had their own plane to head for safety, he thought.

As Jackson drove through the village, he could see the signs of restlessness in the animals. Dogs were stalking back and forth and chickens were strutting nervously. The wind was picking up, but at the same time, there was a stillness in the air, a hesitance in the face of what would come next.

As he neared the club, he could see boats leaving, heading to find shelter where they could ride it out. Boats on moorings would probably stay, hoping the permanent anchors would hold. Jackson made a mental note that notice of the storm was short. Normally, a hurricane stewed in its juices for at least a few days before whirling into a spin. This storm had built on their doorstep. The warning left little time to prepare. He pulled up to the club, got off his perch on *Cyclops*, and headed inside. Pete was on the radio with Charlie to the mainland.

"Okay, base. Thanks for that info. We'll keep in

communication. If you lose us you know it's the storm. Good luck."

"Just keep good sense," said Charlie. "Base clear and standing by."

Pete shook his head, a serious look on his face as Jackson came in.

"Doesn't look good. Winds are building on the mainland, but we're going to get the blow first. It's a steady thirty knots now, with higher gusts. She's still a tropical disturbance, but gaining intensity. Weathermen figure by early tomorrow it'll be a full-fledged hurricane. Earlier they were talking tomorrow night. It's definitely gaining, and looks like it's veering our way. I sent the bigger vessels to Coral Cay to get protection in the creek at high water. If they can anchor in those deeper holes and tie onto the mangroves they can probably ride it out. We'll worry about floating them later if they become landlocked. Important thing is to save what we can. Boats and buildings can be replaced, but lives are another story. The cottage guests already are gone. If the water rises, tell the natives to come up the hill to our house. We're filling water jugs now, and Helen is getting the girls to gather food at the house in case we can't get back down to the club. The docks, well, hopefully they'll weather the blow. The club — everything could be rebuilt. Important thing is to be able to stay on the radio with Charlie, because after it's over, he'll be our link for supplies, emergency medical help or whatever we need. Let's make sure we have enough fuel in drums near the generator in case we can't get to the spigot later on. Listen to that wind. It's hard to think with that blow boiling out there. Look at the water."

He and Jackson stared past the docks to a buoy marking the channel into the club. It was bobbing up and down, often swallowed by a whitecap. The water had turned a menacing steel gray to match the sky. The cloud line puffed itself into a uniform mass spanning the sky, and seagulls were screeching at the wind, landing on one piling then another. The wind was approaching gale strength, and someone walking on the dock was nearly blown into the sea. But the rain had not yet begun. Jackson shook his head and turned to go.

215

"I'll gits all dose tings done," he said. Then he caught himself staring at the famous *Maxwell's Revenge*. "You tink dis storm finally be de one to carry dat ol' lady to a decent grabe in de sea? If dis one don' do it she outlast you and me bote."

The teasing glint was back in his eye, replacing the fear Pete had seen moments earlier.

"We should be so lucky, eh? I think she's anchored to the good earth forever, but we'll see. THAT would be a blessing. I'm not looking forward to the next few hours. Barometer is really dropping now. Feel the temperature changing? I think we ought to drag out the foul weather gear. We're going to need it."

"I tink you right. Good idea. Well, I gits goin' before I blows away."

As Pete headed toward the kitchen, he heard someone calling Sandy Cay Club on the VHF. He walked to the radio room and answered.

"Sandy Cay here. Who's calling?"

"Pete. It's Woody. What the shit's happening, man? We're about to blow off this rock. No one told me we'd have to weather a blow like this during the summer except if a hurricane came. What do you hear?"

"Just answer one question, Woody. Are you sober or drunk?"

"I'm having a few. What difference does it make?"

"Because hurricane warnings went up hours ago and the thing could hit by tomorrow. You see all the boats going by your island? They're looking for a place to hide, Woody. I suggest you get off the hooch or the marijane or whatever your drug of choice is at the moment and get yourself ready for a blow. Look. I've got things to do. Just get your crew together, tell them the world may end within the next twenty-four hours and maybe that will snap them into reality."

There was silence on the radio. "You still there, Woody?"

"Yeah. I'm here. Sounds like a good excuse for a party. I'm gonna get on the other radio and find out how serious this thing is and get back to you. I wanted rain, but this is ridiculous. Oh God. The tin roof just blew off. Talk to you later. Woody clear."

"Sandy Cay clear." Pete chuckled as he headed back to the

216

kitchen. Thank the good Lord he was sober or he'd be stammering and stuttering worse than Woody and the club would probably fall down on top of him. As he entered the kitchen, he saw Maria and the girls stowing canned goods in boxes.

"You takes dis to yo' house so we know we eats if de club all wash away," said Maria matter-of-factly to Pete. "Don' know what de wederman say, but I feels it in me bones dat dis be some blow gonna hit dis island. Dose clouds mean, Mistah Pete. Jis' plain mean. Reberend up de church now settin' up prayer meetin'. We gonna ax de Lord to help us. Dis storm goin' ta be bad."

"I think your feelings are right, Maria. Take whatever the village needs. Don't worry about it. The important thing is that we all use our heads if this storm does reach hurricane strength. You need something and the club has it, just take it. We're all one family in a time like this. Make sure the kids understand what to do. A wind could snatch them away. My house weathered the famous hurricane of three decades ago. I think it's safe for this one too. Tell everyone they are welcome. We'll be scared together."

"Tanks, Mistah Pete," she said. "We knows you take care." The other girls nodded in agreement.

"Now get on home," said Pete. "This place isn't important. Get going."

In a few minutes Pete was left alone in the club, staring at the sea now lashing at the dock pilings. He glanced at the barometer — 29.45 and falling. The wind indicator still showed gusts of 35 to 40 knots. He better get to the house with a load of supplies. Helen would be worried.

"Sandy Cay Club. Come back, Pete."

That had to be Woody. He answered.

"Sandy Cay here. Go ahead, Woody."

"You weren't shittin', man. That damn storm's headed right for us. What're we going to do?"

"Well, as the natives say, Woody, batten de hatches. I got my own problems. Do what you can. We'll be here when the hell and high water hits. Just use your common sense." To

217

himself, he added, if you have any.

"Okay. I better get all this crap put away. Stuff flyin' around could cut a man's head off."

"Roger. Sandy Cay clear."

"Bye." As he was getting into his Jeep, Pete felt the first drop of rain. It had begun. A gray sheet was moving in across the water, giving up the precious liquid they had waited for all summer. Pete shook his head, then had to chuckle. What was the saying? When it rains it pours? He finally understood.

* * *

The next morning Pete noticed the winds had reached a steady forty-five knots, with the barometer still falling. The village had weathered the night of constant rain and wind with only minor damage to trees and unsecured household items. There was an anxious fear penetrating everyone as stories of past Big Storms kept the old folk wailing to the good Lord to save them and the children wide-eyed with frightened wonderment. Dogs and chickens now paced inside homes, and seagulls shrieked as their hiding places were invaded by erratic rains and slashing winds.

There was a steady, high-pitched hum as if a fiddler had clamped his fingers around the neck of his instrument while his bow arm mechanically kept up the mournful sound. As everyone else stayed inside, Pete worked his way to the club to make radio contact with Charlie and to check things over.

"Sandy Cay calling base. Come in Charlie. Come in."

"Base back to Sandy Cay. Thought we'd lost you. Been waiting for your call. The weatherman says you're really catching it. Can you give an update?"

"Wind steady fifty knots. The sea is breaking over the docks and the cottages are flooded. There's spray on the pool table and there's a fine mist over the bar. Everyone's okay, but there's a lot of praying going on. What's the prediction?"

"Continued strengthening, with hurricane status about one this afternoon and winds around a hundred miles per hour. It's moving about twelve miles an hour, which puts it at your coordinates about four this afternoon. Wish I could do something. We're just feeling the blow here, but it's more of a spinoff of what you're getting. The eye is to the west of you, and that's in your favor."

"You're beginning to fade, Charlie. Lots of static. Talk at noon if I can get back down here. If not, make it on the even hour thereafter."

"Roger. Good luck, Pete." Charlie's voice sounded concerned even with the poor connection.

"Just pray," said Pete. "I mean it. Talk later. I'm getting drenched."

"Base clear and standing by."

"Sandy Cay clear."

As Pete walked out of the club, garbed in a yellow hooded parka, the wind caught the screen door and almost tore it from the hinges. He put it back in place as best he could and left the padlock open. No sense locking the place, he thought. No one would want to be in the club during a storm. It wasn't all that stable. And then there was the termite theory, that if they drowned in the storm the place would fall down, thought Pete. He began to chuckle, remembering an old piano. Someone sat down to play honky tonk one day and as he pounded out a tune, the piano disintegrated, totally claimed by termites.

A branch from a casuarina tree swept across the path, and as Pete looked down to protect his head, he saw a lonely hermit crab seeking shelter, dragging its shell as if carrying the whole world. As Pete reached the hill to his home he felt the wind strengthening, coming in gusts as if some imaginary boxer were trying to knock him down. The rain followed him inside, spraying a fine mist into the living area. Helen and Johnny were playing checkers, a blessed candle lit on the table. As Pete unzipped his parka, there was a loud knock on the door.

"Jackson. Come in. How is the village doing?"

"It bad down dere, Pete. Real bad. De water, it lashing at de freight dock bad. We gonna hab to bring de ol' people to higher place. One lady wailing in de rocker, praisin' de Lord for all she wort'. Her two sons bring her here if dat okay. De little ones too. Maria want to know if de back room o' yo' house could be used

219

for de children. De womens bring dem here."

"Of course," said Pete. "I'll help you. Talked to Charlie, and according to reports, this isn't anything yet. Hurricane will be here by late this afternoon with winds twice what we have now and a lot of rain. Come on," he said. Turning to Helen, he added, "Honey, I'll help with the children and be back soon. That back room will be safe for them."

"I'll get it ready," she said. "We'll try to keep them busy with stories and games. Tell Maria if she and the other women want to come they're welcome too."

"Tanks Miz Helen," said Jackson. "You hab a houseful pretty soon."

He and Pete left, leaning toward each other for protection from the wind and rain, walking toward the village. Jeremiah, the town drunk, was huddled at the well, totally oblivious to the storm, sipping a bottle of rum. Pete and Jackson looked at each other, and without talking, each took an arm. Jeremiah didn't argue. He had practically embalmed himself. He stumbled as they helped him to the nearest little house. He was taken in and Pete and Jackson continued the short distance to Maria's.

About twenty youngsters ranging from toddler to teen had gathered, their wide white eyes contrasting a sea of dark faces. They were scared and showed it, but when Pete told them they were all going to Miz Helen's, there were smiles. They all loved the house on the hill.

* * *

At ten minutes to four, a clap of rain hit the side of Pete's house like a wrecking ball. Everyone became silent, listening to the howling wind shaking the rafters. The little children began crying, some sucking their thumbs for security. The hurricane had arrived.

Pete left the women and children and walked to the front of the living room where he could look out to sea. It was a spectacular sight. Great walls of water waltzed by the wind, lifted, then dropped, in rhythmical fancy. He could see the club dock swallowed, then heaved up by the water, but still intact.

220

Leaves and twigs and debris flew in a steady parade past the house, sand spun into miniature tornadoes whipped by the wind. Rain fell like thundering hail, huge drops splattering on the cement porch. The noise was deafening. For hours, the thrashing went on, then gradually, as night masked the fury, the wind began to die from a raging hundred knots to seventy. Pete thought it strange that hurricane winds could actually be comforting, but after the peak of the storm, the aftermath seemed tame.

Helen and the women had rocked the young ones to sleep and the older children contented themselves with games, books and projects. One by one they fell asleep where they sat, little curly heads bobbing until fear subsided and gave in to dreams.

By two in the morning, Pete realized the eye of the storm had missed the island. The worst was over. He fell asleep, listening to the wind and rain batter his house. Morning would tell the extent of damage, but for now, he needed the sweet relief of sleep.

* * *

Morning came too quickly for Pete. The sun was rising like a light bulb glowing in a smoke-filled room. The wind blew at a comfortable twenty knots and the sea had given up its fight. The children were laughing and playing as the women fixed breakfast for the hungry houseful, and for the first time in many hours, he felt relieved. As Pete dressed, Jackson came to the house, reporting that all had survived the night.

A few windows had blown out and water stood in some of the homes closest to the sea, but the natives were in good shape. Many had started to repair and clean up, knowing the storm had spared them again.

"Dis storm almost like de one six years back," said Jackson. "De eye o' de storm passed by to the west. Dead quiet o' de eye didn't come."

"That's the only thing that saved us, Jackson," said Pete, pulling on his deck shoes. "If the eye had passed over and the winds come from the other direction the whole village could have been wiped out. We were lucky. Have you been down to the club?"

"No. I figures we go togeder and gits de bad news as a team," he said, now smiling. "I see de docks still standin 'cept for one piling, and dat one gib us trouble befo'. Couple o' days' work and she be back in shape and people partying at de bar."

"Don't be so sure. We haven't seen the inside of the place yet," said Pete. "It was pretty wet the last time I was there. I better call Charlie. He's probably sitting by the radio waiting."

They stepped over tree branches and skirted puddles of water as they walked to the club. The beach had changed slightly, where rocks and sand had switched places. The cottages still stood, a couple of shutters loosened from windows and a balcony railing dislodged, but aside from being drenched inside and out, the little buildings had stood up quite well. As they neared the clubhouse, Pete could see his roof cleaned of all the leaves, and aside from a few torn screens and pervading dampness, everything was in fairly good shape. There was a film of fine sand strewn across the floor, piled in miniature drifts along the wall, and a few burgees and miscellaneous mementos lay on the floor against more permanent chairs and tables.

"We'll have to fix that hinge," said Pete as he opened the screen door. "Let's hope the radio works."

He walked to the small room, turned on the radios and waited for them to warm up.

"We still have power. Better check the generator, though. It'll be out of fuel soon. I'll double check the radio antenna."

As he walked outside around the far corner of the club, he saw it. Pete stood as if in a trance, a smile on his face. He had never seen anything so beautiful in all his life. There, on his ramp, was nothing. Nothing at all. He continued to stare and smile, watching the sea spill over the slanting cement slab. *Maxwell's Revenge*, that hulk of an eyesore, that leaky Noah's ark, was gone. Completely. Not a trace remained. Washed away. Forever.

Suddenly Pete felt light-headed. He glanced at the antenna as he scurried past the back of the club. All was in order. Jackson was just entering the generator shed when he turned and saw Pete. He couldn't imagine why he was so happy, then Pete told him to follow him. They stared where the Great Obstruction had stood, chocked up on the ramp, now gone. They giggled like children, slapping each other on the back.

"Poor Max," said Pete, laughing. "What will he do next?"

"You tink he hab it insured?" asked Jackson, almost straight-faced. They laughed some more. "I better tends to dat generator before it quits. Den we be sure o' no problem," he said, walking back toward the generator shed. In a few minutes, he and Pete went back to the club. Pete wiped down the counter of the bar and began laying things out to dry, picking up soggy magazines and old papers and tossing them into a trash can.

"Well, let's give Charlie a try," he said, tuning in the frequency. "It's eight o'clock. He should be on. Sandy Cay calling base. Sandy Cay calling base. Come in." A few seconds passed, then Charlie answered.

"Base to Sandy Cay. How is everyone?"

"Whole island is fine," said Pete. "Storm is winding down now and everyone is okay. How'd you fare?"

"Okay. Had winds up to eighty but everything's fine. Thought the tide was going to wet our feet but it stopped before reaching the house. How are the docks?"

"Surprisingly, still there. We'll give you the details when you come over, but the *Revenge* is gone."

There was silence, then Charlie said, "That's a good omen, the best news I've heard in months."

"When's your next flight?"

"Later today if the wind dies. Have the watermaker," Charlie said, dryly.

"Just what we need after what we've been through," said Pete chuckling. "I'll tell Woody. Sandy Cay clear."

"Base clear."

Pete looked at Jackson, a glint in his eye and a smile creasing his cheeks. He switched to the VHF.

"Sandy Cay calling Woodpecker. Come in, Woody." He looked at Jackson and shrugged. "Maybe they've got trouble." The smile began to fade. Then, as he turned up the volume, Woody's voice came booming in.

"Woodpecker to Sandy Cay. We're all still here. How about you?"

"Island's fine other than the mess you'd expect. Did clean up one bad corner, though. The *Revenge* became one with the sea. I've got a boat ramp again. How are you?"

"Other than my head splitting and me seeing double I'm okay. The *Revenge*, eh? Wonder if Max knows. How's my boat?"

"Your what?" asked Pete.

"The red boat. Max said he tied it to the dock at Conch Inn so it could weather the blow. Can you see it?"

"Hold on." He walked out the club, down his own dock, and looked toward Conch Inn. He could barely see some lines, but as he squinted, he saw the boat. Pete walked back to the radio to tell Woody.

"It sunk," he said.

"It WHAT?" shouted Woody.

"It sunk. The lines go to something strung out under the water that looks pretty red to me. I presume it's your boat. No one else took the chance of leaving something on the dock."

"I'll have Max's.... My head is splitting, Pete. What other great news do you have for me?"

"Your watermaker will be here this afternoon."

"My WHAT?"

"Your watermaker. You know, six hundred gallons a day and all that?"

"Yeah. All that being seven grand. Any chance of canceling?"

"Negative. Bought, paid for and on its way. I'll install it before your cistern goes dry."

"You better work fast, man. She's leaking like a sieve. But water is my last concern right now. We're out of beer. How're you doing?"

"Plenty here. But you gotta come get it. No delivery today."

"I'll send someone. Watermaker, huh? Just what I need. Oh well, story of my life. Get back to your mess and I'll look at mine awhile."

"It'll get better, Woody. Honest," said Pete, chuckling.

224

"Sandy Cay clear."

"Woodpecker clear. I think."

* * *

The next day Charlie helped Pete install the watermaker at Smugglers and Howard arrived with Jock to check his home and to touch base with Woody. The *Sea 'n' Be* had gotten caught in the storm and needed parts and bail money before being allowed to leave an island where they had sought refuge. Certain officials had to be taken care of to allow them to continue with their illegal cargo, and so two hours after he landed, Jock was again airborne with a briefcase. He put it behind one of the wall panels especially designed for it and headed south. He bought fuel with no questions asked at an island on the way and continued.

He found Terry and Juney with minor engine problems, a soggy interior with the exception of the well-protected bales, and rather low spirits. The ride from the airstrip to the harbor was strange, with no one, not even the taxi driver, talking to him from the time he landed to the time he arrived at the harbor where the boat was anchored. Terry came into the dock with the dinghy, told Jock to stay with Juney, and that he'd be right back. About three hours later he returned, face sullen.

"Okay. We can leave now. What a goddamn mess. Tell Howard the cargo's okay and that we'll hurry the time schedule. We didn't lose too much on this deal, but if the heat's on, we might have to unload someplace other than Smugglers. This trip is making an old man of me."

"Heard that's what it does," said Jock. "I'm not supposed to be involved, but have no choice. Howard says fly the bread or otherwise you're out of business. I'm getting the heat now for carrying passengers, too. Oh, well. They'll never stop me. Been around these islands too long doing this sort of thing. The bureaucracies actually protect guys like me. It's the legitimate boys who do everything by the book that get screwed. Anything I should tell Woody?"

"No. Just that we'll see him soon. Our radio's working okay now. Storm really played hell. Doesn't look like it now, but

225

Juney was sick as a dog as we were tossed about. Not a pleasant experience. Well, you better get going if you're going to land before dark at Sandy Cay. Take care."

"You too," said Jock. "Don't worry. Bastards will never get you."

Jock headed back to the plane with the same silent driver, climbed in and took off. Daylight was fading, but he'd make it back in time. He smiled. Who cares if I don't? All anyone can do is slap my hand. As long as I can find the island I got no problems. No problems. He took his time, and as official sunset was at least one-half hour past, he landed at Sandy Cay. No one was at the strip when he came in. Got 'em again, he smiled.

* * *

Five days later, the *Sea 'n' Be* anchored off Smugglers in a beach-ringed cove. Woody told the few boats moored at the club that he had to make room for a larger vessel and asked them to leave. After a few protests, the dock was cleared the following morning, and late afternoon, Terry eased the *Sea 'n' Be* alongside the dock nearest the warehouse, Woody handling the lines.

"That's good," said Terry, as the spring lines were secured. "What a trip, Woody, a bad trip. Would have come in earlier, but didn't want to leave the boat for one second with this shit aboard. Learned how to deal with the local officials a few days ago. I really sweated it. You never know if you can buy them or if they're going to rip you off before or after the payment is made. Juney played it real nice with this fat black with all the stripes on his shirt. Didn't have to sleep with the jerk, but almost. That probably upset me more than anything. She handled him good, crying over the fact that she was still on her honeymoon, that if she ever came back she'd look him up when she had more experience. What a pickle. Your own wife on the line. How's it going?"

He looked around and could see the club was in fairly good shape, even after the storm, looking legitimate as a resort.

"Had a few minor catastrophes, but you'll hear about those

226

over a few rums. Makes you wonder. We were damn near out of water so I ordered a fancy machine from Pete. He no more than had it ready to fly back over when that fuckin' storm hit. Now we've got more than we need with a watermaker all hooked up. Story of the tropics, from what I hear. Pete says it never ends."

"I'd believe him. Heard a few of his stories, too. Normal people leading nine-to-five lives would think they were made up. It's different when you actually live here. Even making this run...well, that's a story too, but like you say, it'll be more tolerable over a few rums. What's the plan now?"

"Met with Howard last night," said Woody, limping aboard. "We have two boats coming in tonight that will take the majority of the stuff off. I don't want to use this island for storage and Howard agrees, so we're going to gamble on the Coral Cay warehouse again, only we'll keep a closer watch on it. How's the boat running?"

"Not real good. Had some more engine problems which I'm hoping Max can solve. We were supposed to turn around for another load, but after this storm we need a little time off."

"No problem," said Woody. "Howard already arranged it." He smiled, looking beyond Terry. "Well, look who just came out. Hi, Juney. Boy, you sure have the knack for looking like a million dollar doll. Bet the official's eyes popped if you wore anything like THAT!"

Juney was dressed in a see-through knee length white gown, braless but wearing white bikini pants. Her dark hair hung loosely to her shoulders, a gentle curl to the ends.

"Hi, Woody," she said. "That guy was a pig. Don't mention him again if you care about me."

"Okay, doll. That bad, huh? I'll forget it and hopefully you will too. Just takes time. Let's have a few drinks and talk over other stuff." He heard the whine of an outboard and looked out the harbor. "Well, here comes Max. Guess he can start looking over your boat now so he knows what to tell Jock to bring over."

They watched as Max came into the dock, a frown creasing his face, navy work pants and oil-stained white shirt indicating he'd been working.

"Hi," he said, somewhat curtly to everyone as he pulled up.

227

Turning to Terry, he nodded. "Welcome back. Heard you had problems. Anything I'm supposed to do?"

"Man, you sound like a bear in a bee hive," said Woody. "I know the red boat's a problem. Pat not taking care of you?"

He glared at Woody.

"Hey, Max, I'm sorry. Didn't mean to upset you, really I didn't," said Woody, backing a couple of steps. Max was in one of his moods. "Let's have a drink. You can dump your problems with the rest of us. Come on, man. Don't look so damn down and out. You're not fretting over that old boat finally being washed away, are you?"

Max creased his forehead, and with a set jaw, shook his head no, although most thought he was upset over one of his thorns being removed from Pete's side.

He followed everyone inside and listened as Terry explained his engine problems. After a few drinks and with the evening's game plan laid out, Maxwell offered to keep an eye on the stash up at Coral Cay the first night.

"Hey, Max, you don't have to do that. Pat will be a little miffed, don't you think?"

"Would serve the little bitch right. I'm taking the first night. Let her wonder where the hell I am."

"Something tells me Max is upset with Pat," said Laura, rather quietly as she joined the group. The rumor mill had been churning out some choice ones lately. Maybe they were true.

"Listen, Max," said Woody. "Your woman will always give you a hard time. Just forget whatever it is. This is a screwy place to be, remember, and we don't always keep our wits about us. Look at the wild parties we've had. No one's been perfect."

"Just forget it for now," said Max, grumbling. He got up, fixed another drink and came back. The conversation was being led by Woody, recounting in detail how the natives had done him in and all that had happened since Terry and Juney had left. Max had heard it all before and was bored. After Laura served a cracked conch dinner and some more drinks, they settled into a routine, Woody making radio contacts. At exactly ten o'clock, two sport fisherman-type yachts arrived, and within less than an hour were on their way. About ten bales remained, and they loaded them into the black boat. Woody made a snide remark about how much nicer the red boat would be to use, and Maxwell ignored him. Woody and Max took off, the almost full moon glistening the way to Coral Cay. The bales were secured in the warehouse and a new padlock barred the door. It was decided that Max would stay up all night at Smugglers, listening for the sound of boats or anything unusual. By midnight, everyone was in a partying frenzy except Max, who sullenly sat on the open deck overlooking the harbor. He smoked a cigarette and sipped his rum, purposely not thinking about Pat. Keeping watch was extremely convenient for him tonight.

* * *

The next day, Woody, Laura and Max took turns keeping an eye on the warehouse. Then, about seven thirty, just as it was beginning to get dark, Max and Woody loaded the bales back into the black boat. They went out to sea, and about eight thirty, just as the sun was going down, headed toward the north end of Sandy Cay, easing the boat into a small creek that ran parallel to the airstrip. The meeting was planned for high tide, the only time the boat could get within ten feet of the airstrip. As they came into the little cut, Chubby was overhead, flying a twin-engine plane. He didn't bother with a normal flight pattern and came straight in, landing to the north and taxiing to the end of the runway where they waited. He kept one engine running and opened the rear cargo door. Woody and Max quickly lugged the bales from the boat through the water to the plane.

"Nice work, boys. Give my love to Howard," said Chubby after the last bale was on board.

"Will do. Have a good flight," said Woody.

"Always do," he replied, smiling, his stubby beard a bit grizzly. "You take care, now." And with that, he pulled the cargo door shut, climbed into the pilot's seat, started the port engine, taxied and took off into the almost breezeless evening .

Woody looked at Max and Max at Woody, and Woody slapped Max's hand.

"Another one down," he said, "but look at us." They were

drenched, with loose marijuana stuck to their clothes. Their faces were smudged and they looked like they'd been through an ordeal.

"We better go back and get cleaned up," said Woody.

"You don't want to check with Howard first?"

"No. Don't want to leave the boat in any conspicuous place 'cause it still has some crap in it and besides, Howard watched the whole thing anyway. Let's get out of here. Don't want to be seen."

They sped off in the black boat around the south end of the island, past the village, Conch Inn and the Sandy Cay Club.

* * *

From Pete's point of view, looking through binoculars at his house, he could barely make out the plane that had come in, taken on questionable cargo and the little boat that had supplied it. But as he saw it leave, disappear around the island, then appear a few minutes later going past his home, the pieces of the puzzle fit. Woody was still up to his funny business.

Chapter 11

Pretty Pat

It began mid-June when the house felt like a kiln with no air-conditioning. The sea was the only thing that could bring body temperature to a comfortable level. Pat rose early every day, did the few household chores she'd planned the night before, and by eight o'clock, after Max left the house for the shop at Conch Inn, she would walk down the little path to their dock. She loved wearing a skimpy bikini and was conscious of her beautiful tan. It was the only benefit of the summer, so far. Max spent long hours at the shop and Smugglers.

One Wednesday, as she laid her dripping body on a towel, she saw a tanned sailor coming closer and closer on a sailboard. He made a quick pass, waved, and went on sailing. Pat sat up and watched, his slender, muscular body acting like mast and mainsheet as he tacked back and forth across the wind. He wore a brief red, white and blue bathing suit, had a light brown beard and longish hair. On the second pass, she waved, smiled and watched him pull up to the dock.

"Hi," he said. "Name's Sam. I'm on that ketch out there." He pointed to a boat about 28-feet long at anchor. "You live here?"

"If you can call it that," she said, a bit sarcastically. "I'm Pat Hynes. Is it hard to sail one of those things?"

"Not if you have a good teacher. Want to try?" he asked, smiling.

"Sure." She smiled back, a big, wide grin, her eyes locking to his.

"First of all, you have to learn to stand on the board and get in what's called the ready position. Then I can show you how to handle the sail."

She stared at him. Blue eyes, nice teeth, a gold earring in one ear. His tan almost matched hers. She felt very sexy in her pale pink bikini. Sam demonstrated the basics as she watched, hardly hearing what he was saying. A few minutes later, she was trying the board herself. In only seconds, she fell, the sail on top of her head. Sam swam over, helped her get untangled, and held her shoulder a little longer than necessary.

"Try again," he smiled. "But don't run me over. Just stand on the board and once you're comfortable, you can lift the sail out of the water. Make sure the board is at the right angle to the wind or it'll dump you again. Hey, not so fast!"

She had stood on the board, reached for the line to hoist the sail, and toppled into the water again.

"I've heard it's the toughest sport going, but I really want to do it," she said, smiling as he helped her again. Her wet suit subtly revealed what it was supposed to be covering. She could feel Sam's eyes examining her. She craved the attention, her moves emphasizing her long legs, her hips, her squared shoulders. After several more useless attempts, she gave up.

"This is hard work. I'm exhausted. Wanna come in for a cool drink?"

"Of course," he said, smiling, tying up the board and sail and following her up the path. Nice ass, he thought, looking at Pat as she climbed the irregular coral rock steps in front of him.

"You want a rum, beer or an iced tea?"

"Better make it tea. The rum will blitz me instantly in this heat. Maybe I'll have one later, after I unwind a bit. Windsurfing taxes the body." He smiled as she handed him a glass of tea, then watched as she filled two trays to put back into the freezer compartment.

"You the mechanic's wife?" he asked.

"Guess you'd say that," she said, dryly, "although he's never around much. How about you?"

"I'm single. At least now. Had an old lady but she didn't like the sailing life and I couldn't settle down to a land-locked house. So we split. I put an ad in a newspaper for a companion, but the chick who came aboard left me on the main province. Turned out she was still married and her old man came for her. Glad I wasn't aboard when he arrived. The stories I hear he would have killed me, and I'm basically full of chicken shit."

Pat laughed. Somehow Sam gave the impression he could whip the world. It didn't seem possible he'd cower before anyone, even if it was the husband of a girlfriend.

"You're just a pussy cat, huh?" she teased, putting her feet on a driftwood table. She eased back into the sofa, settling into the cushions, sipping her tea. Sam was beautiful.

"What do you do all day?" he asked. "Place isn't that big to make a slave of you."

"You haven't met Max, have you?" she said, dryly. "There's plenty to do. I'm on strike with him right now. Wants me to sand a boat he's working on but it's too damn hot. Told him to shove it. So he hired a native. Anytime his pocketbook is hit he's a bastard to live with, but I'll be damned if I'm going to work like that."

"Thought that stuff went out years ago with women's lib," said Sam. He moved a bit closer on the sofa, under the pretense of examining a huge helmet shell Pat had found and placed on the table. "This is beautiful," he said, turning it over to reveal the vivid markings.

"I found it off Coral Cay where the sandy bottom slopes down about twenty feet. Only one little point was sticking out of the sand."

"You like to dive?"

"You bet," said Pat, smiling. "I'm good at it, but you probably won't believe me after my klutzy moves on that windsurfer."

"Oh I believe you," he said. "How else would you keep that gorgeous shape?" He let his eyes wander over her body, from the top of her head, where she had coiled her hair to get it out of her face and off her neck, to the pale green eyes, high cheek bones, completely natural face, freckled shoulders, bikini top hiding small firm breasts, a flat stomach only slightly creased as she sat, bikini bottom tied in bows at the hips and long, slender legs. He could feel himself being taken by her. Gazing at her eyes, he could sense the same desire. Neither said a word as he moved a bit closer, then leaned over to kiss her cheek.

"You're beautiful," he said, stroking her arm. She could feel the hair rising slightly, and her heart began pounding. She hadn't felt this way in a long time. Even Max had never stirred her insides this much, and she felt weak all over. She let Sam's eyes

233

roam over her body, and she studied his. Disheveled, wind-blown hair, a ruddy complexion, sunburned nose, straight jaw, blue eyes and callused hand went with a body about six feet tall. She welcomed his arms around her, wanting him like she had never wanted Max.

He was gentle but determined as he caressed her, kissing her neck, her arm, her lips. She put her arms round his neck and drew him closer, her own temperature now rivaling the mid-morning heat wave. She let him undress her, and she instinctively tugged on his swimsuit as well, feeling his firm buttocks, until their bodies were working together, tanned, sweating and tense. The overhead fan meant nothing now, two bodies generating internal heat, fueled by their basic desires.

It was quick and passionate, and when it was over, both sat silently looking at the other.

"I feel I've known you all my life," he said, "like I was directed here by some great force."

Pat giggled. "That's a line if there ever was one. The Almighty doesn't look with grace upon his children that fuck total strangers."

They laughed, dressed, and Pat went to the kitchen.

"You want a rum now or a beer?"

"Beer if it's cold," he said. "Max work all day down at Conch Inn?"

"All day," she said, returning with two beers and a big smile on her face. "And he doesn't come home for lunch, and sometimes not even for dinner. Sometimes, I wonder why he even comes home at night. Do you know what I know about engines?"

"No. What do you know about engines?" he asked, thoroughly enjoying his visit.

"Everything. I mean it. Diesel, gas, inboard, outboard, with cruise generator, with separate generator. Know how I know?"

"No. Tell me."

"Maxwell talks in his sleep."

Sam laughed out loud.

"I'm not kidding. He talks about engines in his sleep, and could care less about my own lower unit."

Sam chuckled.

"Well, maybe you need to crank his shaft."

"That only works when you've got gas."

The two laughed, Pat relieved to confide in someone.

"You want to try the sailboard again?" asked Sam. "Looks like the breeze died down a bit. Then we can come back here and relax. I don't want Max to find me here, though. He's a madman from what I hear."

"I can handle him," said Pat. "You smoke?"

"Yeah. Got some?"

"The best. We'll enjoy it when we come back."

They walked back down the coral rock path to the dock, and Sam gave her Lesson Two, followed by many, many more lessons.

* * *

After a fun summer with Sam and the August storm, Pat became despondent, silently mourning the disappearance of her lover, who left seeking shelter when the first tropical storm warnings went up. She hadn't heard from him, and now acted like a love-sick schoolgirl. She knew he was probably gone forever from her life, already seeking a replacement for her on another island. Sam was a free spirit, and Pat knew that as long as he was being loved by some woman, ANY woman, he'd be happy. They had gotten high together and drunk together, and he had told her he didn't want commitment — his or someone else's, so when he left, he merely waved from the boat, pulled up anchor, hoisted sail and was gone, heading into a sunset.

Each day she felt herself drifting from the stranger who shared her bed. Maxwell had found out about her affair with Sam, and had been the butt of a few comments during late barroom hours at Conch Inn. Even Manny had teased him about keeping his woman "happy so's she no go lookin' for it someplace else."

Max spent more and more time with Woody and Jock and ignored Pat, who would have repented, and been happy for any bit of kindness he could show. But instead, it whiplashed.

Max continued his cold war against Pete and now his wife as well, and Pat relied more and more on her pot and booze to survive the island life. At night, she went to Conch Inn, where she danced and laughed with the natives, freely letting them stroke her body to the beat of a persuasive drum. Manny especially loved to see her come in because it always meant more business and he got his kicks out of watching her suggestive movements. She became the object of American scorn and native delight, but to herself, she was merely surviving in the only way she could, trapped, lonely and desperate for attention.

During the day she led another life, a more straightforward existence. It was at night that she couldn't bear the pain of loneliness. Eventually she could only remember faces in the morning-after stupor, and Maxwell stopped talking to her completely, his silent treatment shrieking in her mind. As the pressure of daily living and Pat's affairs increased, Max's work got less dependable, with boat owners accusing him of shoddy workmanship, rip-off and incompetency.

Instead of getting hold of himself, he found that painting an engine was a lot easier than tearing it apart to see what was wrong, and that as long as the parts list showed he had done work and that people had seen him, he could get away with it.

The vicious cycle began: Max lost touch with his wife, then his work, then himself, still carrying the grudge against Pete. After Sam left, Max began coming to Conch Inn at night to make sure Pat didn't make a fool of him. But often he made the fool of himself, falling asleep on the bar after a smoke or a few drinks.

What bothered Max the most, though, was the thought that Pete probably knew what was going on, that he was gloating on the hill, sober and straight, high and mighty, waiting for the Final Fall. It was this thought that made him plead with Pat to begin a better way of life.

Reaching a strained level of communication, Pat told Max she wanted to go back to the States to live normally, to get her thoughts together, to escape Fantasyland. He admitted he needed time to himself as well. Pat had married into a hate war, camouflaged under the guise of falling in love, and had not anticipated the lengths of Maxwell's irrational behavior. She only saw his love for her at the time, never associating that love and hate were bedfellows in his mind and that there was nothing in-between to mellow the extremes. It had to be one or the other, so that by the time Maxwell had some idea of what was happening, he was on a mental and emotional teeter-totter that would not let him stay up or down. Somehow, in Pat's grasping for reality, she had instinctively moved on the seesaw so that the ups and downs began to level off. With the promise of a stay in the States, she began changing her ways and looked forward to staying with her mother while finding an apartment. Two weeks after the hurricane, Pat left the island, flying with Jock and two other passengers who originally were scheduled to fly with Charlie.

Chapter 12

Everyday Happening

After Pat left, Max was still faced with Woody's boat problems. He had replaced practically every part and it still wouldn't run. Maxwell raised it after the storm, but in the short time it was submerged, the paint had begun to deteriorate, the windshield showed pitting and the chrome revealed rust spots from salt water feasting on the fittings. He had removed the vinyl seats, and in a few days the hot sun dried the foam stuffing, but the engines were still torn down. Woody delighted in calling him every day to get an ETA — estimated time of arrival — for the boat back at Smugglers. Jock came and went several times, bringing in parts as well as tourists, and it was pretty well decided among those who knew the situation that the boat would never again run properly. Even Woody let go of it.

As Max puttered with the engine, grease up to his armpits, scowl on his face, Jock came down the dock with Sue, off the cruiser that had brought water to Smugglers from Conch Inn.

"Hi," he said, sitting on the dock and dangling his feet over the side. "How's it coming?"

"Hi, Sue," said Max, nodding. "You had to ask, huh? Terrible. Can't figure this thing out. You just get in?"

"Yeah. Took Susie to the states to do some shopping for a few days. Got quite a bit of stuff." They smiled at each other.

"I bet," said Max, taking a cue from her suggestive look. "Guess I'm not the only one around here with problems."

"Aw, come on. What do you mean by that?" said Jock. "Saw Pat one night, by the way. She's looking pretty good and sends her love."

"I had some long talks with her," said Sue, quietly. "She's happy to be off the island for awhile. I think she's looking forward to coming back, though. Maybe you could visit her. It's a totally different environment." Her deep brown eyes had a penetrating depth, and when she spoke, which wasn't often, it was with total sincerity.

"Yeah," said Max. "I'm going to have to get off this rock myself, but right now I've got too many responsibilities. Chap from Spoon Island is due in next week and expects everything working. Last time I was there I couldn't turn over the generator and I haven't been there since the storm."

"I thought you were supposed to check the place each week," said Jock. "At least that's what the Frenchman told me when I flew him out. Said he didn't need any more help, that you were taking care of his island."

Max didn't answer. He felt that as long as the island was still there, the buildings hadn't fallen and the dock was still usable, he could survey it on his way to Smugglers each day without going ashore. The fact that he was paid to make a weekly trip didn't make any difference to him. He just worked frantically before Pierre arrived, usually with guests. Pierre would explode in a temper, Max would work feverishly into the night, and by morning everything would usually be in order, Pierre calmed down and Max smiling over a big tip.

Max looked Jock in the eye and said, "I take care of his bloody island, but I wasn't aware people checked up on me when it's none of their business."

"Don't take it that way," said Jock. "Didn't mean to upset you. Can't help it if Pierre talked about you."

"I know," said Max. "I'm on edge with Pat gone. This goddamn boat's a mess and three other jobs are overdue. I've got yacht owners screaming at me, Pierre coming in the end of next week and a whole lot of other problems I don't care to talk about." He wiped his hands on a rag and said, "Let's go to the Inn for a drink and forget it."

"Let's call Tom and tell him to come to Conch Inn with the dinghy," said Sue, anxious to see her husband after a few days with Jock. "Then I'll have a ride out to the boat and Tom can catch up on all that's happening. Guess the storm put a few things out of whack around here."

"A few things would be putting it mildly," said Max. "Washed my old boat right off the club ramp. The generator went out again and the village has no power. Everyone's on me. Conch Inn doesn't have power either except for about four hours

240

a day, just enough to keep food from spoiling. Sometimes I wonder why I stay here. Maybe Pat is right. At least by marrying her I can get a job in the States."

Jock looked at Sue and raised his eyebrows. Most people who knew Max thought he stayed on the island because no one in their right mind would hire him in the States. He was a backyard mechanic who could be king on the island, but who would have a hard time making it elsewhere, even with the proper papers.

They walked into Conch Inn, dark even in the middle of the day, and sat at the bar. A couple of native boys were playing pool and a radio blared out a steady beat of Caribbean music. Manny came in behind them.

"Eh, dere, how you be? Jis' gits back?" he asked Jock. "Sue," he said, going behind the bar while keeping his eyes on her. "Do Tom know he send you to de mainland wid a mad man? Don' trust dis character. I know de type. You do better."

"He's harmless," said Sue, smiling. "Besides, Jock's our regular guest. Saves him from running to Smugglers every time he comes in."

Jock, wearing sneakers with no laces, khaki pants and a Conch Inn T-shirt, had made a good arrangement with Tom and Sue. He'd fly them for nothing back and forth and they'd give him free room and board on their boat. That way, no one could accuse him of "stealing" them as customers from Charlie, and Tom and Sue had enough friends and boating contacts to give Jock a good link to passengers. He had come up with a formula. People paid cash, were led to believe they were only sharing expenses of the plane, and were willing to stand behind him if anyone asked questions. It was only fair in return for the cheap rate. Jock suddenly had a whole new set of "friends." It was the perfect cover, and Tom and Sue played the game with him. Ironically, Charlie still brought their mail, and after he realized what was happening, that Sue was spending time with Jock on the mainland on the pretense of working part time and obtaining supplies, the picture began to unfold. Rather than confront Tom, Charlie continued to haul his mail and packages as a favor, knowing that at some point, it would be to his advantage.

241

After a few drinks at the bar, Tom arrived.

"Hi, Hon," he said, leaning over and kissing Sue. "You get the tapes I wanted?"

"Sure did," she said, smiling. "How's the boat?"

"Couldn't be better. Got those cabinets done in the galley for you. Look real nice. Also changed the refrigeration around so it's a little easier to store things."

"Good. We needed that."

"Manny," said Tom, shouting above the music. "How about a rum here? You gonna leave a man high and dry on such a hot day?"

"Hey, Mon. Didn't see you come in. Watchin' de boys play dere game. Got a couple o' pool sharks in de makin' here. Could make de island famous if dey eber got de chance. You want a punch or rum an' Coke?"

"Make it a plain rum with water and a squeeze of lime if you've got it. I've had enough caffeine for the day, but not much rum. Thanks," he said, as Manny gave him the drink.

"Well, let's finish here and get back to the boat. Woody wants you for something, Jock, and he's still screaming for his red boat, Max. What are you going to do? That thing's in worse shape now than ever. Need a hand?"

"No thanks," said Max, a bit curtly. "It's my job and I'll do it. Did you bring in the parts, Jock?" Jock nodded. Max swallowed the last of his drink, waved at everyone and left, heading down the dock to the red boat. Jock went to the airstrip for Max's parts.

"Max isn't looking too good," noted Tom to Sue, who sat quietly. "I'm actually worried about him. Ever since the mess with Pat and Sam, and all the problems Woody's thrown at him, he's been worse than ever. And the way he acted at the town meeting the other night. Whew!"

"What happened?" asked Sue, who hadn't heard any news on the mainland.

"Well, he publicly talked about how Charlie was ripping everyone off and that everyone should fly with Jock, and that all the natives could go free and that the whole island should see how Pete had gotten Charlie to grab all the money he could. It was really rotten. The Reverend stood up and told him to be quiet, that he was disrupting the meeting."

"Good grief," said Sue. "Did anyone stand up in Charlie's defense? I mean, we might not fly with him because of Jock, but he's still legal and all and has a lot of expenses Jock doesn't have."

"Well..." he began, then stopped. "Finish your drink and we'll talk as we go." They both swallowed the last of their rums, waved to Manny and walked down the dock to their dinghy. Tom picked up the few bags of groceries and supplies, and Sue carried her bags, dumping them into the dinghy before climbing down the ladder. Tom started the motor, but kept it in low gear. They sat next to each other, supplies and groceries forward, and Tom told her how Manny had drunkenly stood up for Max and Jock.

"I tell you, Sue, we're going to see an upheaval on this little island. It can't survive all this rivalry, jealousy and tension. Pete and Charlie seem to be minding their own business, but I'll bet there's going to be hell to pay with Charlie over this last meeting. The natives don't know what to think. They know Charlie and Pete have always been there in emergencies and that they've always helped them, but now Jock is carting them wherever they want to go and everyone thinks he's a great guy. You and I know that can't last forever. The only reason he's doing it is because of Max. We're in a rather precarious position. Pete is trying to get me a work permit. If I screw him up he can hardly endorse me."

They were nearing their boat, sitting majestically at anchor behind a rocky little island boasting one of the most outstanding sea gardens in the Caribbean. People came from all over the world to photograph and swim in its wonders. They pulled up alongside, put their gear aboard, climbed onto the deck near the doorway to the main salon, and secured the dinghy on a cleat, letting it trail behind with the tide.

Sue stowed the groceries while Tom rummaged through the bags looking for his cassette tapes. They hardly heard Jock arrive in another boat. He climbed aboard, waved to the native boy who had given him a lift, and stepped into the main salon.

"Hi," he said, shuffling his feet and rubbing his beard. "Not interrupting, am I?"

"No. Come aboard," said Sue. "Want a rum?"

"Sure. Not flying anymore today."

"Since when did that matter?" asked Tom, noting how he looked at Sue. "I saw you toss a beer can away before climbing into that bird last week. Don't think we don't notice that sort of thing. Be careful, 'cause that's what could get you in deeper trouble with Charlie."

"Shit, I've forgotten all about him," said Jock, grinning from ear to ear, sipping the rum Sue had just given him. "Nothing he can do to me. Got the boys wired at the other end. They just pull the tickets when I come in and there's no record for him to go after. Cost me a few bucks and a few favors, but I'm covered. He can scream and holler all he wants."

"Glad you feel that way, 'cause I heard the heat's really on to stop you from carrying people," said Tom. "I don't fully understand the situation, but I can't see a problem if you're just charging for expenses."

"You're right. Just expenses," he said, smiling cunningly. He'd never quite defined expenses to those stepping into the airplane, and each one-way trip was charged as round trip, so that he was actually making more money than anyone knew — even Tom. Charlie was the only one who would be able to figure it all out because he knew how much fuel it took and what the actual costs were. But if there were no records, his knowledge was useless.

"Mind if I crash awhile?" asked Jock.

"Go ahead. I'm going to listen to my new tapes. Don't know what Sue's doing. Thought you were going to Smugglers."

"Later," said Jock.

"I'm just reading," said Sue. "Crash on the waterbed, if you want. That's where it's nice." She gave Jock an extra long look and smiled.

Jock smiled back and headed below decks. It was a nice life.

* * *

About five o'clock, Jock came up from the main cabin, stretching and yawning. Tom and Sue were listening to the ham radio as yachtsmen chattered about what was happening in their lives. It was like Bible Hour. Whenever the boat people were on the air, Tom and Sue listened, often chiming in with events in the islands.

"Can I borrow the dinghy to go to Smugglers?" Jock asked, running his fingers through his hair. "Told Woody I'd meet him late afternoon."

"Go ahead. We're not going anywhere," said Tom. "We need some time together."

"Just like asking Daddy for the car," Sue teased.

Jock pulled the little boat alongside, lowered himself down, started the engine and untied the line. He headed toward Smugglers. Something was brewing. When he had gone back to the airstrip for Max's parts, Howard had met him. He wanted to see Woody, Max and Jock at the Nest about ten o'clock, as inconspicuously as possible. Max already had the word, but Jock didn't want to broadcast it on the VHF to Woody.

As he ran the little dinghy into the harbor at Smugglers, he could see Woody and Laura entertaining Terry and Juney.

Howard hadn't said anything about telling them to come to the meeting. As he pulled up, Woody came down to greet him, took the line and threw it around a piling.

"Hey, Jocko, how's it going? Hear you got a regular commuter line going. Before you know it, you'll have graduated from our business, you'll be all uppity and won't even talk to us. Come ashore. A rum punch? Hey, Laura, fix a good one for the pilot, here. Jock's not going anywhere tonight."

"Don't count on it," said Jock, taking Woody's arm and pulling him aside. "Howard wants you, Max and me at the Nest at ten."

"Gotcha," said Woody, rather quietly, winking at Jock. "Have a feeling I know what it's about. Terry and Juney are shoving off so I guess we'll get ours tonight. Have a feeling it's also pay day."

245

"Oh yeah?" said Jock. "That would be nice. Nothing like a little incentive."

"Right on. Come, let's join this crazy group." As they walked over, Woody pointed to Juney. "Get a load of this gal, Jock. Isn't she gorgeous?"

Juney had outdone herself, wearing a clinging black terry jumpsuit slit down the front to below the navel. Jock smiled as he looked her over.

"Nice, Juney. Really nice."

Terry beamed. Laura ignored the looks and began picking up empty glasses. Woody saw her hint of scorn and followed her into the club.

"Hey, Laura. It's all in fun," he said. "She's a gorgeous young chick, just like you once were. Let her enjoy it."

"Ah know. Ah can't help but feel old. Guess Ah can still remember those days," she said, a touch of nostalgia to her voice.

"Hey, Babe," said Woody, putting his arms around her and holding her close. "You're just right. I got a big mouth, but you're all right. Kiss?"

Laura looked at her stout, middle-aged husband and smiled. "Kiss," she said. "Dedicated to growing old together."

As they were embracing, Jock walked in, a little embarrassed.

"Hi, folks. Sorry. Just wanted a drink. Go ahead. Don't mind me. Hey, Laura, where's the ice?"

She let go of Woody, shook her head and laughed.

"No one ever takes old people seriously when they're having fun," she drawled. "The ice is in the trays in the freezer in the kitchen. If you are going to be a regular around here, Jock, you gotta do your share with the ice." She fixed a couple of drinks for herself and Woody, and gave Jock his rum.

"Isn't Pete designing a block ice maker for you?" asked Jock.

"We talked about it, but I don't want too many boats coming in for all that stuff. I'd have to hire a boy to run the docks, and someone to pump gas and diesel, and before you know it, people would run me ragged. Gotta save this island for the original

246

purpose, which is not to encourage the public to live aboard our little rock. We'll continue carting the ice from Sandy Cay when we need it in quantities. When's dinner, Laura? Jock and I have to shove off about nine-thirty."

"It's almost ready. We're just having spaghetti," she said. "The garlic bread's warming in the oven and the pasta is cooking. Ask Juney to help set the table. Ah'm about to strike like Pat did with Max. Too much work lately, Woody. Ah'm running mahself ragged."

"And loving every minute of it," he said. They smiled at each other, mutually kidding.

* * *

At nine-thirty that night, Jock and Woody fixed a rum, got into the black boat and headed for Sandy Cay. There was a fine film of clouds making wisps out of the moon, but the night was relatively clear. The stars seemed closer in the late summer day than in the winter, and the islands could easily be seen with bits of reflection from the sky.

Woody took the long way to Sandy Cay, coming into Conch Inn from the ocean rather than along the small chain of islands. He found the markers into the marina and followed them. The water was smooth, with hardly a bounce as they cruised along at good speed. Max was waiting for them on the dock. He took the lines, secured the boat, then they walked in silence past the hotel rooms and onto the road to the airstrip, Woody limping beside Jock's and Maxwell's strides.

"Think I'll have the red boat going by tomorrow night," said Max, finally, as they crossed the runway.

"Promises, promises," said Woody, turning to him with a smile. "Don't give it top priority, but I'd appreciate it whenever you get it. What did the *Sea 'n' Be* need?"

"Just new fuel filters after that shakeup she had in the storm and a couple of minor adjustments. A minor job," said Max. "She's ready to go."

"Bet you didn't mind working on that vessel with Juney aboard. Hell, she'd be an inspiration for doing more. What a

247

gorgeous chick," said Woody, loosely shaking the end of his hand. "Terry better keep close reigns on THAT one."

"I don't think I'm one to comment," said Maxwell, "but she's some bird."

"Well," said Jock, stopping and looking up. "Here we are again. The impossible hill."

"It's so we appear groveling to Howard by the time we arrive on his doorstep," said Woody. "What's this meeting all about, anyway?"

"Don't know," said Jock. "He just met me and told me to tell you."

"He never tells me anything," said Max, grumbling. "Guess we're about to find out. I can hardly talk while climbing this path."

"Then don't," said Woody, and the three proceeded in silence, step-by-step to the Osprey Nest. As usual, Howard opened the door before they could knock.

"Evening. Come in. Drink? Foolish question." He walked over to the small kitchen, made four rums, and returned to where the men already sat around the table. It was becoming a familiar seat of conference. "Marjorie stayed in the States this trip. I'm batching it as you can see. Nothing like a woman to clean up after you."

"Tell me about it," said Max, dryly.

Howard ignored the comment and launched into what the meeting was about.

"I'm ticked off over two ventures going sour even if we didn't lose everything, but we've now got to step up the schedule if we're going to take advantage of the remaining months before the northers start blowing. Terry and Juney are leaving tonight to head south for another load."

He looked at the three men intently watching him. "I was going to give them some time off but can't afford the luxury right now. He'll move some coke as well as grass this next time round, so the boat won't have as much bulk to give her away. On the way south, he's going to work on some internal hiding places on the boat for the coke, but that's not our concern tonight. By the way, one of the sportfish boats that took part of the *Sea 'n'*

Be load had a problem coming into the mainland the other night. They dumped the bales, but not in time. They now owe us on the next run. Bailed their butts out of jail. We're also going to be fueling a couple of helicopters within the next few days. Lucky's bringing in the fuel. That's going to make up for the screw-ups of the last two loads, and it's a way to pull ourselves into the black. How do you feel about making a run in the single engine, Jock?"

He looked straight at him, jarring his attention.

"Not too good," he said, squirming in his seat and sipping his drink. "That's a long way and I don't think…"

"You're not paid to think. Anyway, it's part of the plan. I've got you covered on fuel and have good support set up. You won't be going all the way to Colombia, so don't freak out. I need a transfer plane and you'd be a good cover because they're looking for twin engines, not singles lately. The chase plane is too fast to cover a pokey single, so from that standpoint, you're pretty safe. I'll go into that later, but wanted to prepare you."

Howard got up, walked to the kitchen, grabbed an ice bucket, bottle of rum and some soda and brought them back to the table.

"Here. Fix it yourselves," he said.

"Okay. Next order of business. We're getting a lot of freelancers in the area lately, fueling and transferring at Sandy Cay. Natives are getting restless. They're not dumb, even though they won't say anything, so we have to be more careful now. They're starting to put their fingers in the pie. Some local boys ripped off a stash in the bushes the other night when a plane dumped it to go for fuel. It was gone when they came back. Place is going to start getting jumpy if it follows the normal pattern. Have to beef up security and communications. It's the only way to survive the game.

"I've got some multi-band aircraft radios coming tomorrow with Chubby for use with the helicopter fuelings. We'll need them down the line with a couple of other quick deals I've planned. I'm making the fuel connections now.

"Suppliers are getting squirrely lately with so many amateurs trying to make it big. We now have to post more up front and they're checking credentials pretty close. It's not like the good old days when you just went south and came back with a load. You have to be connected now. I'm only bringing this up in case any of you decide it might be nice to branch off on your own. Forget it. I'll butcher your credit and you'll wind up in the pokey — someplace."

He looked at the three faces staring at him. "Fix another drink, boys. You all look like you need one."

"Hey, Howard, we wouldn't cross you," said Woody.

"Not for a million dollars, Woody? Come on. I'm no virgin. The best of them have tried to do me in. Wouldn't blame you if you tried. I'm only giving you the facts of life. Take them or leave them, but keep in mind you're always better off with a connected banker than you are farting around on your own. It's deep water out there, both on land and the sea. Just remember that."

He stopped, lit a cigarette and poured himself another drink after Jock poured for himself, Woody and Max.

"You're pretty quiet, Max. Any problems?" he asked.

"No. Just minding my own business."

"Good. Does that mean the red boat's fixed and ready to go or shouldn't I ask? You were hired as a mechanic, you know. We expect you to perform."

"It's almost done. Should be running by tomorrow afternoon."

"Good. What about you, Jock?"

Jock shrugged and shook his head. "I'm just flying wherever anyone tells me to."

"So I've heard. Also heard the authorities are watching you. Cut down on your passengers. Just because you've beaten the rap before doesn't mean you'll escape it the next time. By the way, I know all about your little mishap with customs and know who bailed you out. That's not exactly healthy either, considering the game we are in. You may have to compromise, you know, but you better not mess up this operation to save your ass. You could wind up dead. And speaking of dead, have you noticed the down-island boys cruising these parts again? They're armed to the teeth now and have boarded a few boats coming north. They'll raid even the legitimate tourist if they think there's anything worthwhile on board. Just warning you. Keep a lookout and keep your wits. And don't go firing at them unless it's in total self defense."

He looked at Woody. "Keep your cool, men."

He sat for a few seconds, rocking on the back legs of his chair. "That's it. Any questions? No? Okay. Drink up, fix another one, then get on with your business. One of these days I'll get to Smugglers to see what you've done, Woody. Hear it's shaping up. Tell Laura I appreciate her efforts."

"Will do. Would love to have you for dinner sometime," said Woody. "Laura fixes great cracked conch."

"It'll probably just be for a quick drink and to check the area for the fueling process," said Howard. "Don't want to make it look like we're real friendly."

"Gotcha," said Woody, drinking the last of his rum and pouring another.

"It's eleven o'clock. The *Sea 'n' Be* should be leaving your dock, Woody. Let's take a look."

The four climbed the steep steps to the lofted room and took turns looking through the nightscope. They could see the *Sea 'n' Be* going out the cut as easily as if it were the middle of day instead of night, heading south to open water.

"This thing is unbelievable," said Woody. "What a toy."

"You'd say the same thing about a loaded gun," said Howard. "Let's hope they're successful."

They could see the frothy wake being made by the *Sea 'n' Be*, her running lights like Christmas ornaments reflecting on the calm water off the bow. She'd be many days at sea before Terry would head back, carrying the cargo that would put everyone in the chips.

"She'll do okay this time. Have a feeling in the gut that everything will go all right," said Woody, glancing through the scope. "Max. You're pretty quiet tonight."

"Not much to say," he said. "I just do as I'm told. What does one of those run?" he asked Howard.

"Too much for you right now," he said. "Do a good job and you won't have to ask. You know the saying 'If you have to ask how much a boat costs you can't afford it?' Same thing with this gear. We do have some expenses, you know. It isn't all gravy. Come on. She's on her way. No sense sitting up here."

They went back downstairs, finished their drinks, and Jock, Woody and Max got ready to leave.

"Keep in touch, boys. Jock, I'll see you later this week. After that, I'll be gone for awhile."

The three stood, waiting. Howard began walking toward the kitchen, then stopped and turned around.

"By the way, there's no bread tonight. Sorry," he said. "Too many screw-ups, ripoffs, payoffs and bail-outs."

"Aw, come on, Howard. Nothing?" asked Woody.

"Not tonight. I'll see what I can do in the next couple of days. Don't worry. Sometimes it takes awhile for the ship to come in."

"You forgot we sent the ships out in good shape. Why should we take the rap for someone else fucking up?"

"Yeah," said Jock. "That isn't fair."

Max acted like he'd been stabbed.

"No money? No money?" he said. "What am I slaving over that bloody boat for if I'm not going to get paid?"

"You didn't hear what I said, boys," said Howard. "You'll get paid, but not tonight. If I had it I'd give it to you, but right now the dough went to skinny a couple of butts out of jail. I'm sure you'd want the same consideration from your fellow workers if you were in the same spot."

They stood, shuffling their feet, looking from one to the other.

"Well? Either you believe in what we're doing or you don't. But let me clarify one thing. If you're not made of what it takes to accept a few knocks then you're in the wrong game. I thought I was dealing with guys who had a few guts as well as brains. I'm beginning to think I'm a loser on both counts. You boys want out? Tell me now while you have the chance. There's the door. You want out?"

"No, Howard, don't get us wrong. We just wanted some bucks if they were available. We understand, don't we?" Woody turned to Maxwell and Jock, as if encouraging them to agree.

252

They nodded their heads. "See? We understand. Don't want anyone sitting in the klinker on our account. No sir, Howard. We understand. Come on, guys. Let's head on out."

They grumbled a bit to themselves after they were out of earshot from the Nest, but knew there was nothing they could do. Howard was the controller, the man who said yes, no, or forget it.

"Well, I guess we gotta go back to the original assumption in life that nothing good comes easy," said Woody, "but right now I don't feel like being toughened up."

"I better get some money by the end of this week," said Max, muttering angrily. "When I do something I expect to get paid for it."

"Oh shit, Max, even when you DON'T do something you expect to get paid for it," said Woody, slapping him on the back and laughing.

Max saw no humor in his remark. The three became silent, thinking about what Howard had said. They walked through the village toward Conch Inn, where Max had parked his Jeep.

"See you tomorrow," said Max, climbing in.

"Night, Max. Don't take everything so seriously, okay? Bad for your health," said Woody.

Jock and Woody walked down the unlit dock, climbed into the black boat, and started for Smugglers.

"Shit," said Woody. "You still have to go back to the boat tonight with the dinghy."

"I know," said Jock, wearily.

It was a quick ride over the smooth water, and Woody was soon waving good night to Jock as he headed back toward the anchorage. The lights were out on the cruiser, and Jock silently climbed aboard, anxious for a good night's sleep.

* * *

Two days later, on a walk to the far side of the island and back on her routine after the storm, Helen enjoyed a cool breeze for the first morning in weeks.

The stones crunched underfoot as she took the easy incline

to the top of the ridge. She glanced over her shoulder as she passed the Nest, but didn't see anyone. Ever since the day Woody almost fell on top of her and she had seen Howard, she used caution at this part of the path. Everything was quiet today, except for a few gulls enjoying morning playtime, swooping down on the beach below, and the hermit crabs that lugged their homes across the path. Someone trying to identify the tracks would be totally confused. There were a few seagrapes still hanging on the stunted trees, and the wild morning flowers with their sky blue petals crept across open areas on both sides of the path. Some red poison berries hung in clusters from a bush, and she heard lizards scurrying off as she came near, sounding like much larger creatures as they rustled the underbrush.

At the top of the ridge, between the Nest and the far end of the island, Helen stopped to take in the view. It was one of her favorite spots, because she could see the sprawling beach below, the rocky cliffs of the northern end, the rooftops of the tiny, colorful village homes, the airstrip, the little cays, rocks and islands stretching around the compass rose. It was a breathtaking sight, well worth the jaunt.

She hadn't been to the far end of the island all summer, and since it was cool, decided to go as far as her winter walks usually took her. Sand gave way to more substantial dirt, and the path became more overgrown with weeds, thistles and what everyone called "dammit" vines because it was so easy to trip on them. The brush was still stubby, as if starved for nutrients, and she felt the salty mist even though she couldn't see it. Toward the end of the path she looked for her favorite rock. Some brush had grown near it, but it was still there. She sat down and wiped her face with a tissue, feeling good about the exercise. She poked a hermit crab as it walked past her feet, watching it dodge inside its top shell, then continue on its way. As it crawled, she followed it with her eyes. Then suddenly she felt a chill come over her and her heart began thumping wildly.

The crab had climbed over a dark piece of metal that looked like a pipe, and Helen followed it to each end. She sat frozen, the hair rising on her neck as she realized she should not have come this far today.

A shotgun with a shiny barrel and varnished stock was next to a box hidden behind some weeds. She glanced around, then peered closer, realizing the box was a radio. She began trembling, knowing she had to get back unseen to tell Pete. Her knees gave way as she tried to walk nonchalantly along the pathway, fearing someone had seen her. But it was before eight in the morning, and time was on her side. The scammers usually kept night hours and didn't hang around the island in the early morning. At least that's what Pete had told her. But a gun and a radio. That was serious stuff and she felt uncomfortable.

The coolness she felt on the walk earlier gave way to a gnawing fear inside that she might have been seen. Someone might know that she knew. She walked faster, hoping she could slip past the Nest with the same stillness as before. She glanced from side to side, instinctively expecting someone to jump out at her, to grab her, to threaten her, to make her reveal her secret knowledge.

Her mind raced as she thought of the consequences of seeing a gun and a radio in a place where neither should have been. She glanced ahead. The Nest still looked quiet. She quickened her pace, putting her toes down before her heels to walk as quietly as possible. The gravel still crunched, but she stepped on sand or weeds as much as she could. She held her breath, hurried past the upward path to the Nest, and felt like running once it was behind her. But that would have given her away. Walk slowly, Helen, not like you're being chased by an invisible mad man, she told herself. Slow down, take it easy, don't worry. As soon as she was out of sight of the Nest she ran down the rest of the sloping path to the airstrip. At least there she would be in the open. It didn't stop her terror. She kept up a quick pace along the back road leading to the club.

As she walked up, panting loudly, Pete took one look at her, quickly stepped to the screen door to open it, and asked, "What happened? You're as white as if it were the middle of winter and you're shaking all over. Come in. What happened?"

Helen, relieved to the point of tears, pointed to the dining room.

"Let's go over there," she said. "I'm okay. Just frightened."

They sat down and Pete waited as she caught her breath. Then she told him what she had seen. Pete was concerned and worried.

"Firearms are only used by bad guys in these islands," he said. "Let's hope no one saw you. Keep quiet about it. Charlie and I will check it out later. On second thought, we'd better leave it alone. You never know who's involved. I'll talk with Charlie and see what he says."

"I was so scared, Pete. I can't tell you. My whole life went before me. I was afraid someone was lurking in the bushes. For all I know someone WAS there, but I don't think so." Tears welled up in her eyes, and she held Pete's arm as he comforted her.

"Go ahead, Babes, cry it away," he said. "You'll feel better if you do. Don't go on any more of those jogging jaunts, okay? In this case, walking could be dangerous to your health, huh?"

She managed a little smile and wiped her tears.

"I just got so scared, thinking of you and Johnny and all that we've worked for here. What gives those people the right to come in and ruin it?"

"Nothing, Helen. Nothing. But they are managing to put a good dent in our tranquil bit of paradise here. It's a new ball game, one that we don't have the rules for. I'm worried too, but all we can do is keep our heads together."

"I think it would be a good idea to pray," she said, putting her hand on top of his on the table. The two sat in silence.

"You want coffee Miz Helen?" Pete and Helen looked up to see Maria with a couple of coffee mugs and thermal pitcher, a little embarrassed to see Helen had been crying.

"That would be nice, Maria. Thank you."

"Anyting I kin gits you? Is Johnny okay?"

"He's fine, Maria. Don't worry. You know how sensitive I get," said Helen, smiling in reassurance. "Thank you anyway."

"Okay. I jis don' want you feelings bad." She left the pitcher and went back to the kitchen to get breakfast for the cottage guests. A couple in their mid-thirties came in and Pete stood up.

"I better be getting on with business," he said. "Why don't you go back to the house and get into a project with Johnny. I'll finish up here and come home. After a scare like that I don't want you to be by yourself, okay?"

"Okay, Pete. Thanks." She took her mug of coffee and went out the back door of the club. Her trembling had stopped, but she still felt a hollow pit in her stomach.

* * *

The next day brought more boat people to the island. Mid-August was when the touring crowd wound down the summer months, partying up the last few days in and around the Sandy Cay Club before heading back to the States to get the kids in school. The afternoon showers came quite regularly now, and no one complained about empty cisterns. Instead, there was talk about the pilots who came and went, the fast boats that dropped in for fuel and the number of people around who didn't bother to bid anyone the time of day.

Pete was in the club behind the bar talking to Charlie who had brought in guests for the cottages earlier in the day, when two rather scruffy men walked in, laid a ten on the bar and ordered two beers.

"You fellas on a boat?" asked Pete in a friendly way, putting two beers on the counter.

"Naw. Have a plane," said one, his dark glasses emphasizing a ruddy complexion. He was wearing a heavy gold link chain around his neck and a fancy gold watch on his wrist. The other man sported similar jewelry and had an almost identical look, with dark wavy hair, a couple days' growth of beard, T-shirt advertising an outboard engine company, navy shorts and boat shoes.

"Oh yeah? What you flying? Got a Cherokee, myself," said Pete, trying to make conversation.

"Aerostar," he said, almost as if he didn't want to talk.

"That's a pretty fancy bird to fly around in," said Pete. "How fast is she?" Out of the corner of his eye he caught Charlie giving him a stern look and shaking his head.

"Fast enough," he said. "Got any room for us tonight?"

"Sure. Cottage number three. You want it?"

257

"Yeah. We'll have dinner, too, but skip breakfast. We'll be leaving early."

"Okay. You can catch me after dinner to pay the bill. Let me get your names for a tab."

"Don't bother. You want cash up front?" He looked at Pete and pulled out a roll of bills.

"No. Catch me later," said Pete. "You got a brother or some buddies who look like you that came in here a few days ago?"

"No," said the other man. "Why?"

"They were flying an Aerostar too and took off early in the morning. Just wondering, that's all," said Pete. "Guess you're not connected."

The two men looked at each other and quietly went back to sipping their beers. A few minutes later, they walked out, turned toward the village and were gone.

"Tell me that isn't your typical doper profile," said Charlie. "Aerostar, huh? Bet if we walked out to the strip we'd find all the seats gone."

"You're probably right," said Pete. "We'll do that later just for fun, okay? Weird bunch. I'm surprised most of them even find this stupid island. What I can't figure out is why they come here if there's no fuel available."

"It's a good rendezvous and transfer point," said Charlie. "Whenever you have a strip this close to water you're going to attract the wild scammers. Ninety-nine percent of the shit they're carrying winds up trouble-free so it's worth a gamble. They can afford fancy equipment because there aren't enough agents or even agencies to stop them. And it's getting worse. Now even the enforcers have their own share of corruption. Too much money in it. The scammers start spreading it around and you don't know who they're buying."

Just then Jackson walked in.

"You see dose men who comes tru' de willage? Dey's de ones de down-island boys talks to early today before goin' off in dere fast boats. What dey want?"

"A cottage for the night and dinner," said Pete. "You see their plane?"

"Yeah. I looks at it after dey head into de willage. No seats in it. Jis' a few o' dem blue bags and no seats. Anuder funny plane, you tink?" he smiled, but it wasn't with the usual sparkle in his eyes.

"I'm sure," said Pete, "and Charlie's sure. You saved us a walk to the airstrip. Charlie was just saying how there probably aren't any seats in it. Guess they're on their way down."

"Yeah. Better watch who dey talks wid. De las' plane to come tru' empty like dat tried to gits me to arrange some fuel. I told dem no plane fuel on de island. Dey ax if I kin gits it. I tell dem no. We don' do dose tings here."

"What did he say?" asked Charlie.

"Told me dat not what dey hear. Dey said dey were told to see a native and dat all would be okay and dat de fuel would be waitin' when dey come back tru' in a couple o' days. I told dem no, tain't tru'. No fuelin' here."

"Bet they got their signals crossed somewhere along the line," said Pete.

"No. Dey ax if dis island Sandy Cay. Dat's why I come here before goin' to de willage. I wants ta know what to say widout makin' any wrong tings agin' someone."

"Anyone in particular, Jackson? You seem to know what's going on," said Pete.

"I no wants to talk 'bout it," he said. "I got me own feelin's on it but it don' inbolbe yo peoples. It's my people's problem, dis one. I'm goin' ta check around. Gotta be sly as fox as you say or I be in trouble too."

He stared at the floor for a few seconds, then glanced out on the dock.

"Big boat comin' in. I better go handle de lines. Don' say nuttin' 'bout what I tells you, okay? I let you know iffen I hear anyting." With that he walked out the screen door and down the dock to secure the big motor yacht. He'd worry about the airplane boys later.

As Jackson walked out, two couples came in, ordered rum punches, and launched into sea stories on their cruise aboard a sailboat they had chartered for a week out of the main province.

Pete fixed the drinks and smiled at Charlie. Typical charter party, he thought, trying to do all the islands in one week when

259

one snug little harbor or bay with a few good reefs would give them all they were searching for.

"You didn't charter to go around the world, did you?" asked Charlie, smiling. "Everything you want is here, within a couple of hours' sail. You want to relax or play hero? There're no records to break, you know."

"Yeah, but when you've only got a week you want to see as much as possible," said one man, dressed in a yachty outfit of white knit shirt, white duck shorts and deck shoes. His nose was peeling and his sunburn had not yet turned to tan. "You know the area?"

Charlie laughed. "Yeah. I know the area. Ran a charter boat for several years in these parts. Everything you want is right here. This is where I brought people. You've got the club for the barroom excitement and all kinds of little islands, deserted beaches and reefs within an eight mile radius. Do yourselves a favor. Spend tomorrow poking around in your dinghy."

"Bill wanted to sail about ten miles tomorrow," said one of the gals, wearing a light blue bathing suit top and white terry jogging shorts. "I'd like to stay put. There's a gift shop here, isn't there?"

"You had to ask, didn't you?" said the other man, a bit irritated. "All she wants to do is spend money. As if this trip isn't costing enough." He puffed on a cigar, then chewed on it.

"Honey, I just want to buy a few things for the kids and our moms. I'm not looking at breaking the bank." She looked at the other woman and the two shook their heads at the man.

"Listen, gang," said Pete, tugging on his jeans with his thumbs at the belt. "Tell you what. Next drink is on the house. Then I'll have Jackson open the gift shop for you and you can see the few things we have. There's no way this place will break you unless you want a gross of T-shirts. That way you can get the spending out of the way and you can enjoy your cruise a bit more. How about that?" he asked, directing the question to the man irritated with his wife.

"Okay," he said, cigar smoke circling his head. "Sounds good. Think this heat is frying my brain. Can you show us where some good snorkeling areas are?" he looked around the club, as if taking it all in for the first time. "This place does look kinda nice. Maybe we ought to stick around."

Pete poured rum punches, and gave the man named Bill a tab to fill out.

"Here," he said. "If you're going to stay, just put it all down and pay up before you leave. That way you don't have to worry about walking around with money."

"Sounds good," said Bill. "You want to share it, George?"

"Yeah. We'll divvy it up later."

Bill turned as Charlie brought over a chart of the area.

"Here are a few good spots to anchor," he said, pointing to a couple of islands. "The reefs are everywhere. When you're in your dinghy, look for dark spots in the water against the sand. Some heads are small, but have good fish and a variety of coral. Also look along the rocky edges of the little islands. You can usually find a few interesting fish."

"Like barracuda?" asked George, who seemed to be the volunteer pessimist of the group.

"They won't hurt you," said Charlie. "Just don't trail any bloody fish when they're around and you'll be okay. The sharks haven't been too hungry lately, with the exception of a resident nurse shark that lives right about here," he said, pointing to a spot on the chart. "It feeds on the lobster that live under the rock shelves along that tiny island. The current's strong there, anyway, so it wouldn't interest you. Best time to snorkel is at low water, slack tide if you're not used to depths. Do you have a guidebook?" They nodded. "Check the tide tables in the back and you'll get a good idea on timing."

"Where would be a good place for anchoring tonight?" asked George. "Looks like this cove right here might be nice," he said, pointing.

"That's okay if you take less than six feet of water," said Charlie. "What does your boat draw?"

"Five. So that would be all right. Okay. Let's do that," said Bill, turning to the others. "Everyone in agreement?" They nodded. "Okay. Drink up, let's go to that gift shop and be on our way."

As he finished talking, Jackson walked in.

"Think you can open the gift shop for these people?" asked Pete.

"Sure ting. You wants to go now?" he asked, looking from one to the other in the party, not knowing who was making decisions.

"Soon as we down these punches," said Bill. "We'll be right behind you."

Jackson nodded, went out the screen door and headed toward the tiny gift shop. There wasn't enough help or demand to keep it open all the time. They finished their drinks and followed. When they were out of earshot, Pete turned to Charlie.

"Looks like another bunch that got aboard, turned right as they left the harbor marker and followed the yellow road. What's with people who charter a boat to such novices?"

"Don't knock it," said Charlie chuckling. "Maybe it'll be another salvage job for you."

"Just what we need," said Pete. "That would sure pull me out of the hole right now. Slow crowd this afternoon. Everyone's probably at Smugglers."

"Heard them talking earlier on the VHF about free drinks at happy hour," said Charlie. "Just for kicks we ought to take them up on it."

"You can if you want to, but being around that group drinking like they do would be bad for my mental health if not my sobriety. No thanks. They can all get sloshed down the drain. They don't need me to watch."

"I didn't think you'd take me seriously, Pete," said Charlie, pulling a soda out of the bar cooler. "The last place in the world I'd like to be is Smugglers with Jock and Max and all that bunch talking about what a shlump I am. No way. I like my own peace of mind, too, to say nothing about the seat of my pants."

Pete chuckled. It was almost five o'clock. Time to head home.

"Wanda should be here in a few minutes. Want to come up to the house? I'll fill you in on what's happening, then we can ride to the airstrip and see if there are any new arrivals. If it keeps up, we'll need a control tower for this place."

Charlie laughed. "Just something for one of those fly-by-night pilots to hit. Bad enough there's a radio tower sticking up a hundred feet. You think they'd agree to landing fees?"

"Come on. Let's get out of here. Wanda just came in the back door," said Pete, grabbing his keys. Pete waved to her and they left. At his house, Pete told Charlie about Helen's discovery the previous day.

* * *

There were about twelve people for dinner that night, including Pete, his family and Charlie. Maria outdid herself with lobster tail, conch chowder, barbecue ribs and a big tossed salad. No one said a word the first few minutes after being served, enjoying the good food. The cottage guests had been at the club before, and were talking to some people at the next table who were on a boat, comparing the best beaches and snorkeling areas, and whether or not barracuda was edible.

As Pete and Charlie overheard the conversation, they had to laugh. The natives told people it was okay to eat small barracuda, but that the big ones were poisonous. What constituted big and small was measured by hands used to telling fish stories.

"I think the natives scare everyone out of eating barracuda so tourists will give the fish to them," said Pete. "Not a bad deal, really. Barracuda's good eating. If they're small." He dipped a piece of lobster in butter.

"What's small?" asked Charlie. Everyone laughed.

* * *

Later that night, as Helen and Johnny were playing a game of monopoly and Pete and Charlie were talking, the drone of a plane interrupted the quiet.

"Sounds pretty close," said Charlie. "What time is it?"

"Almost eleven," said Pete, looking at his watch. "What do you think?"

They heard an engine sputter as the noise got closer. A few seconds later an explosion brought Pete and Charlie to their feet.

"Come on," said Pete. "Something's happened." Helen seemed paralyzed, a look of fear on her face.

"Pete, don't go. You don't know what you'll run into. You know they're probably up to no good."

"Don't worry, kid," he said. "We won't do anything stupid. Sounds like someone's in trouble. We'll be back."

Pete started the Jeep as Charlie climbed in next to him and they rushed along the back road of the village to the airstrip.

Jackson was already watching a huge ball of fire that was blazing short of the waterway near the airstrip.

"I sees de plane comin' in and heard de engine sputter. She come down fast," he said, almost out of breath. "De landin' light swept across de brush as de plane come in, den she fell outa de sky. Looked like de gear grabbed de brush."

Everyone rushed to see what had happened. There were explosions as fuel tanks burst and pieces of hot metal flew like fireworks, searing the blackness. The plane became a giant bonfire in the night, the heat from the flames so intense it was felt a hundred feet away.

"There's nothing we can do," said Pete. "Nothing. A few more feet and the plane could have hit the water. But there's nothing we can do where it is."

"Who dey be you tink?" asked Jackson. Two native boys who had come with him stood gazing in horror at the flames, the whites of their eyes like lights glowing against their dark skin.

"Don't know," said Pete. "All we heard was the crash. Can't tell what kind of plane, how big, the numbers, can't see anything now. We better get on the radio and see if we can raise rescue service to at least report the accident. No sense sending for help. It'll just be a blob of molten metal by the time anyone gets here."

"You smell what I smell?" asked Charlie, looking at Pete, Jackson and the boys. He had been standing as if mesmerized by the flames and the heat, feeling helpless at the sight of a fellow pilot dying, even if he didn't know who he was or what he was up to.

Pete took a whiff and nodded. So did Jackson.

"Dat marijuana, no?" he asked.

264

"That's marijuana," said Pete. "I've never smoked it, but from what I'm told it smells like rope burning, and from what my nose tells me, it's got to be pot."

Charlie nodded in agreement.

"Well, the boys in authority will have fun with this one," said Charlie. "All the evidence gone, the plane probably unidentifiable and the body or bodies burned beyond recognition. I wonder if they radioed for help when they knew they were in trouble or if they thought they could make it. They were probably scared to call anyone with the cargo they were carrying."

"Didn't think to listen on the portable," said Pete. "It would have been too late anyway. They must have come in fast, lost an engine and experienced a downdraft. When the pilot figured he had the runway made, the bottom dropped out."

"I've had to give more power many times coming in to land," said Charlie. "If he had an engine out, the guy didn't stand a chance."

He shook his head, still gazing at the fiery mass shooting toward the sky. Little "pops" kept punctuating the still night, as if summoning the entire island to the scene. Curiosity over the bright glow from the end of the strip even brought Helen and Johnny to see what had happened. As she moved toward Pete, she shuddered, taking his arm and holding Johnny's hand.

"How awful," she said. "How awful that anyone should have to die like that. What's that smell?"

"Pot," said Pete. "That's what it is."

"Someone's going to be mad tonight," said Charlie. "Wonder what the load was worth? You know how those guys view a loss of the goods. Never mind the pilots, but that cargo is not considered expendable."

"That's awful to say," said Helen. "Do you really think they'd care more about the pot than human life?"

Pete and Charlie both nodded, still gazing at the flaming plane.

People began asking what happened and speculating on all the possibilities. No one expected a plane this hour of the night and if anyone did, was not admitting it. The plane had crashed

265

on landing, but the airstrip could still be used. There would be an investigation and the runway would probably be closed temporarily until the debris was sifted through and moved to the side of the approach. It took more than half an hour for the flames to subside, but the intense heat kept everyone away much longer.

"Well, there's nothing we can do tonight," said Pete, "but I think we better make a report on the radio. The police will have to determine what happened."

"With all that sputtering, he was probably low on fuel," said Charlie. "Think someone on the island was supposed to receive the goods?" No one answered as they climbed into the Jeep, Jackson and the boys hitching a ride on the bumpers to the village. A plane crash was a devastating sight, because there was nothing the bystander could do but stand back and watch. There had been no time to help, no time to do anything but watch.

As the people left the crash site, Howard kept watch from the Nest. He had seen the plane come in, knew it was in trouble and had focused the nightscope. As it crashed, the light exploded in the scope and he switched to regular binoculars. He couldn't see the numbers on the plane as it had come in and couldn't tell what type of plane it was. When he switched back to the scope, he scanned the airstrip on both sides of the runway. After everyone had gone, he saw a native slip out of the bushes and sneak back to the village. He kept a close watch, not moving from the scope, as if knowing the next moves. He wasn't disappointed. A Jeep came over the back road, quietly drove down the strip, two natives loaded fuel drums, then headed back to the village. Amateurs, thought Howard. Stupid amateurs. Probably the pilot's first haul, too. No one would ever know. The accident would be investigated but Howard knew that like so many other such incidents, no one would ever know all the details.

* * *

Pete and Charlie dropped Helen and Johnny off at the house, then continued to the club. There were still a few people sitting around the bar, the radio blaring out the standard Caribbean beat. Pete was going to tell someone what had happened, then looked at Charlie and said, cynically, "Why bother? They've got their own fire in all those liquor glasses. They'd never understand a crash and burn. For them, it's more like burn and crash." He unlocked the radio room and tried to call. No one answered.

"Better try the marine operator," said Charlie, and in a few minutes a connection was made. Pete tried to explain about the crash.

"Marine operator. This is Sandy Cay, the island of Sandy Cay. We are reporting an airplane crash. Do you copy? There is an airplane crash. Do not send help. Send police in the morning. Do you copy?"

"To the vessel calling. Please repeat who you wish to speak to. You are broken."

"This is the island of Sandy Cay. Island Sandy Cay. Do you copy?"

"Roger. Island Sandy Cay. Go ahead."

"Send police in the morning. Airplane accident. I repeat. An airplane accident. Send police in the morning to investigate."

"Roger, Sandy Cay. I read you loud and clear now. We will notify the police of an airplane accident and for them to come first ting in the morning...Is that a roger?"

"Affirmative. Roger," said Pete. "No survivors."

"No survivors. Tank you for that information. Marine operator clear."

"Sandy Cay clear."

As Pete turned off the radio, he had about eight faces intently staring at him, trying to focus on what had just been transmitted.

"What you talkin' about, Pete? Where's there an airplane crash?"

"Out at the strip. If you boys weren't so intent on cleaning me out of booze you would have heard the crash. A big mess. Can't get near it, so don't go trotting out there. Morning's soon enough. Drug deal. You could smell the bales of pot burning."

"What a shame," moaned one man, his arm around a gal

267

helping him stand up. "Wonder how good it was. What a waste. All that good shit into the atmosphere."

"This is too much to take," said Charlie. "Come on, Pete. This place is sicko tonight."

Pete looked around at the crowd and shouted.

"Okay, everyone, closing time. Drink up cause we're closing down."

"Aw come on, Pete. We're having fun," said another somewhat inebriated soul.

"Closing time," repeated Pete, then in a quieter voice he told Wanda she could leave, that he'd close up.

"Tanks, Mr. Pete. Dis crowd wild tonight. Anyone alibe in dat accident?"

"No," he said. "Whole plane was on fire. There was no way to get anyone out. I just called to have the police investigate in the morning. You go home. Everyone will still be talking about it and you can learn as much as anyone else knows."

"Can we buy a bottle to go?" asked one of the patrons, swaying on his feet.

"Haven't you had enough?"

"No, man. There's never enough."

"That's what I used to say," said Pete.

"Huh?"

"Never mind. You want rum?"

"Yeah, man. Rum's fine. Any kind."

Pete grabbed a bottle off the shelf, took the man's money and started nudging people out the door. In a few minutes, the place was quiet except for the grumbling drunks trying to find their dinghies and their yachts.

"People in the cottages turned in early," he said, noting that the little bungalows were dark except for porch lights reflecting on the water.

"Let's go home and get some sleep. This is the latest I've been up in a long time," said Pete.

"Me too. Quite a night," said Charlie, following silently beside Pete as they walked to the Jeep. When they arrived, Helen and Johnny were already in bed. Only one light was burning.

"Well, thanks for all your support, Charlie," said Pete.

"I didn't do anything," he said. "Just glad for a place to stay."

"One of these days you'll have a place here too," said Pete. "Good night."

"Hope you're right," said Charlie. "Night."

He went into the little den that was used as a guest room and almost fell onto the sofa. He was exhausted. The fire had mentally and emotionally drained him.

* * *

At six the next morning, he heard a knock on Pete's front door. Charlie pulled on his pants and went to see who was there.

"Jackson," he said, opening the door. "What time is it? It barely looks like the sun is out."

"It only six in de mornin'," said Jackson. "Nurse from Rocky Point, she broughts woman habin' a baby and hemorragin' to de island to go out wid police when dey comes, but it don' look like she gonna makes it. She pretty bad. Jis' happen las' night. She gonna lose dat baby iffen she not in hospital quick. Nurse say she in labor and losin' blood. Kin you helps? We kin gits her to de plane real fast."

"Yeah, Jackson. Get her over there. Let me find my keys, tell Pete what's going on and I'll meet you there in a few minutes. Can the nurse go along?"

"She plannin' to. Don' know what's gonna happen, she says. So she goes in case dere a problem. I better gits goin'. Tanks, Charlie."

Before he realized Jackson had come he was gone. Charlie knocked lightly on Pete and Helen's door, trying not to wake up Johnny in the next room. In a few seconds, Helen came to the door.

"What is it, Charlie?" she whispered. He could hear Pete snoring. He told her what had happened and she reached for Pete's Jeep key.

"Here. Drive yourself so you can get there faster. It must be Marabella. She was expecting soon. Tell her I'm praying for

269

her."

Charlie nodded and was on his way. The Jeep sounded like a tank in the still morning hour, and he took the back road to the airstrip. The Aerostar was just taking off with the two men as Jackson arrived with the nurse and woman. Charlie parked the Jeep, unlocked the plane and did a quick preflight inspection.

"Help me with these seats, Jackson. We'll take three of them out so she can lie down. It will be easier on her. If she delivers the nurse will have room to work," he said, nodding at a big sheet of plastic.

They unfastened the seats, laid the plastic down and helped the woman into the plane. She was in pain, biting on a piece of cloth, her eyes rolling as they lifted her. Charlie told the nurse where to sit for takeoff and how to secure the pregnant woman, then waved at Jackson as he closed the door. Within minutes the engines were running and he was taxiing to the end of the strip.

The wreck was still smoldering as he turned the plane around for a quick runup. Seconds later, he was off, gear up, heading for the main province. As he put the plane into a steady climb, he turned around to see how his passengers were doing. The nurse was attending the woman, but put her thumb and finger together for the A-okay signal to Charlie.

He hoped there was time to get her to the hospital. He remembered a similar incident two years before. Another nurse had come with him. They had gotten to the main province, expecting to be met by the ambulance he had requested. But as the natives say, tings move slowly in the islands, and as they waited, the woman gave birth to a baby girl on the airport ramp. Now Charlie knew to hail a taxi instead of an ambulance. From experience, he knew a good tip would beat an ambulance ten to one on time. He'd radioed for both today to cover the odds.

The islands looked misty in the early morning sun, the waters gray as the sun's rays had not yet begun to reflect the varying depths. As he neared the mainland, he explained the emergency to the tower and was assured an ambulance would be waiting. Luck was with them. As he landed, he caught an emergency vehicle in the corner of his eye near the tower. He taxied toward the ramp, and within a few minutes, his passengers were whisked away to the hospital. As he filled out the necessary papers, a constable approached him.

"You just come from Sandy Cay, right?"

"Yeah. You got a good one down there," said Charlie. "Plane landed short of the runway with engines sputtering and burst into flames almost instantly. There wasn't any way we could reach the pilot or passengers," he said, shaking his head. "That's why we radioed for you to come this morning. No one could have done anything last night."

"We're getting ready to go to de island now," he said. "Were dere any witnesses?"

"I don't think so," said Charlie. "It all happened pretty fast. I think it's best if you get all your information at the island. You know more about those things than I do."

He didn't really mean the last statement, but wanted to make the man feel good about doing his job. At the island he would determine the cargo. Charlie didn't want to give conclusions before they had a chance to investigate.

"It was so late no one was listening to the radio, so we don't know if the pilot called for help. For that matter, we don't even know how many people were on the plane or what kind it was. Twin engine. That's all I can tell you," he said.

"Tanks. We see you at de island. Was dat woman from Rocky Point?"

Charlie shook his head yes.

"Hope she makes it. She didn't look good," he said.

"Hope they BOTH make it," said Charlie, finishing up his paper work and following the constable out to the ramp. "See you at Sandy Cay."

"Okay," he said, walking over to the police plane.

In about fifteen minutes, both planes were heading toward the island, chatting on the radio. Before the rest of the village had eaten breakfast, Charlie had been to the main province and back. A jaunt that used to take ten hours on the freight boat had been cut to less than an hour, enough time to help someone — hopefully two people — live.

As he landed, Charlie saw Jock get out of his plane with a briefcase. The police plane was about ten minutes behind, coming in to land. He wondered. Jock's plane was there when he left this morning. Now, a couple of hours later, he was returning from somewhere. It didn't look good.

Chapter 13

Care and Feeding of Whirlybirds

The plane crash couldn't have happened at a worse time for Howard. The choppers were scheduled to arrive the next night, needing fuel at Smugglers Cay to ferry the load from a mother ship to a drop point in the States. He watched the police plane arrive the day after the crash and was glad Jock was back from his errand. With the island crawling with cops asking questions, he didn't want to be around. When everyone went into the village, he walked the back road to Maxwell's house, and "borrowed" his runabout. In a few minutes, he was at Smugglers.

"Howard!" shouted Woody, as he finally recognized who had arrived. "Pull in here. That Max's boat?"

Howard handed him a line and stepped onto the dock. He glanced around, noting the changes that had taken place, and nodded approval.

"Give Max a call on the VHF and tell him not to be concerned about where his boat is," he said. "Don't tell him I have it. Play it cool."

He followed Woody into the club, commenting on how nice the place looked.

"Tell Laura," said Woody. "She's the one who's been working her tail off around here."

Hearing her name, Laura came out of the kitchen, a little surprised to see Howard.

"Hi," she said, wiping her hands on an apron. "We've been hoping you'd come see the island. Can Ah get you anything? Tea? A beer?"

"Tea's fine. On ice, if you have it," he said.

Woody went to the radio and passed the word for Max not to worry about his boat and sat down at the table next to Howard.

"Place has really changed, huh? See those fishnets? Laura found them on the beach. She's gonna put some shells and glass balls into them and hide the rafters," he said, looking at the ceiling where the nets hung loosely.

"Nice," said Howard. "A firetrap, but nice."

"What's going on at Sandy Cay? Saw a bunch of planes this morning and wondered if something happened. And now you're here...is there trouble?" Woody moved nervously as he talked, almost cowering in the presence of Howard.

"Plane crash last night. Some amateurs," he said. "Place is covered with the fuzz from the main province. Not that they'll find anything. It was a good crash and burn. Could smell the grass all the way to the Nest."

"REALLY?" asked Woody, wide-eyed and wondering who was operating in their territory. "Could you see what kind of plane?"

"Happened about eleven o'clock. Couldn't see anything. But that's why I'm here. We've got those choppers coming in late tomorrow night, and Lucky coming in early morning. I'm going to move Lucky to late tomorrow afternoon about happy hour time. The cops will either be gone from Sandy Cay or enjoying their free rums at Conch Inn. They won't suspect the plane if it comes in during daylight hours and there aren't too many boats available that could bring the cops here. Besides, Lucky's fast. He can off-load before they even know he's landed. He'd probably relish a delivery with the heat on anyway. I think he works better under pressure from the authorities no matter where he's doing business. I want to use your radio to contact Chubby. Everything working?"

Woody nodded and pointed to the radio room.

"You want to do it now?"

"Yes." As Howard stood up, Laura brought him a tall glass of iced tea. "Thanks," he said, and followed Woody to the radio. Woody showed him how it was set up, and stood as Howard checked it out. Then Howard nodded for him to go to the other room. Woody felt miffed at being excluded from the conversation but Howard was the boss. He walked over to the bar and pulled a beer out of the cooler. Howard's voice was muffled by the partition and he couldn't hear what was being said. In a couple of minutes, Howard walked back to the table, sipping his tea.

"I'll be getting a call within the hour, as soon as we hear from Lucky," he said, stretching his long legs out, jeans rolled up at the cuff over handmade leather sandals. A plaid shirt was unbuttoned to mid-chest, showing tanned arms and a gold necklace. He tapped his fingers lightly as he looked around the clubhouse.

"You ever get your watermaker hooked up?" he asked.

"Yeah, now that we don't need it. Goddamn cistern leaks, though, so it's probably good we have it. Just in time for the off-tourist season. After the next couple of weeks no one will even be around to drink rum, let alone water," said Woody, nervously squirming on the seat as he talked with Howard. For some reason, the man totally intimidated him, giving him anxiety and a feeling of inferiority. Yet he wanted to do everything right, to please Howard, to be rewarded for work well done. What he didn't realize was that it meant nothing to Howard, who saw Woody only as another cog in the wheel of making the megabucks in a crazy but organized business. As they sat silently for a few minutes, they heard Chubby calling Woodpecker.

"I'll get that," said Howard. "Be right back." He put his hand gently on Woody's shoulder as he rose from the chair, indicating he didn't want company. In a few minutes, he returned.

"Lucky will be in at five-thirty. He'll be off-loading several plastic drums of fuel. Transfer them into the black boat and haul them to Coral Cay. The choppers will land there so they won't draw attention to Smugglers. They'll come in from the east so it's possible Sandy Cay won't even know they've come and gone. The key is to get the fuel there. Let's go so I can check the landing spot. I can't see it from the Nest and I haven't been on that rock for a few months. Have a couple of ideas," he said.

Woody stood up, short of Howard's shoulders, and limped behind him to the black boat. As Woody started the engines, Howard uncleated the lines and soon they were in the little harbor of Coral Cay, facing the warehouse. As he inched the boat onto the beach, Woody tossed out a stern anchor and Howard stepped off the bow.

"These your footprints?" he asked, noting the many tracks above the high water mark. Woody jumped off the boat and examined the sandy ground.

"I don't think so," he said. "We usually wear deck shoes. These prints are bare feet."

"Look at the shape of the foot," said Howard, crouching down. "These feet aren't used to wearing shoes. See how the toes are spread out, and the foot is flat? These are native footprints. I was afraid of the down-island boys. They've gone wild lately, infringing on territories. After the fuel is delivered I want someone to stand guard until the choppers are fueled. How are you doing on ammunition?"

"About fifty rounds," said Woody. "Do you really think...?" His voice trailed off as he looked at Howard's face, answering the question. Howard walked to the warehouse, unlatched the door and peered inside. It had the dank, musty smell of a building with a leaky roof that had been closed up too long. Large sheets of plastic were crumpled on the floor and lizards squeezed in and out of the cracks in the two small windows. Droppings in the corner indicated that something larger, perhaps a rat, also called the abandoned building home. Although the door squeaked on the hinges and the window frames were full of dry rot, the building itself was sound, made of rubble construction with large rocks plastered and held together with cement. With a little effort, thought Howard, the building could be usable again, either for dry storage or as a hideaway. A primitive privy was a few steps away, the door hanging on unpainted and rusted hinges, a weathered one-holer visible inside.

Howard nodded toward a clearing to the east of the warehouse, and Woody followed, noting that the barefoot prints were all over the area, not just at the warehouse. Howard looked over the landing site, about twenty-five feet across the diameter of a crude, irregular circular area, completely devoid of plants except for a few thistle weeds, with a fine film of sand covering an almost solid coral base.

"Perfect," said Howard. "Just as I remembered it. Nothing can grow on this hunk of rock. It's one of the flattest spots in the islands. Whirlybirds will wipe it clean of sand and you'll have a rock pancake. We'll need a good spotlight to shine on the center. Someone can easily climb to the roof of the warehouse and hold it as the choppers approach to give them the target. If the wind keeps on this course, they'll be downwind of Sandy Cay and no one will hear the noise. Wish there were some way to quiet those damn things. They're loud."

Woody hadn't said a word, but followed Howard's hand as he pointed out what he wanted done. With any luck, it could be a quick deal.

Howard looked at his watch. Almost one o'clock.

"You have any lunch back at Smugglers?" he asked.

"Sure," said Woody. "Laura probably has something ready. Anything else you want to do here?"

"No. This will work out fine. We'll be in good shape. Anyway, the choppers will be clean when they come in, so you won't have to worry about a load being ripped off. I wish I knew how fresh those footprints were. When did it rain last?"

Woody scratched his head and thought.

"Two afternoons ago," he said. "I remember someone commenting yesterday that the clouds passed us by, just like earlier in the summer. That means someone was here recently, right?"

Howard nodded and walked toward the boat.

"Is Jock with Max?" he asked.

"I wouldn't know. He's at Sandy Cay, probably at Conch Inn. He hangs pretty thick with Maxwell when he's on the island."

"So I've gathered," said Howard, with a smirk. "Those two okay or a little funny?"

Woody chuckled a bit hesitantly and said, "Who knows? They are a pair though, aren't they? Wouldn't be surprised either way. Jock always makes like he's after the girls, but I've never seen any great action, just a lot of leading up. Some of the gals have talked about him being safe, but again, who knows? Tom sends Sue to the States with him quite regularly, yet he doesn't seem worried. What do you think?"

"I'm not too thrilled at the possibility of pansies on the

payroll, but we're stuck with them, for now anyway. Let's not jump to conclusions. I know Pat wasn't too excited about Max in the bedroom and no one really blames her for running around. Who knows?" He shook his head and helped Woody shove the boat into the water. The tide was down, which meant Lucky would arrive at high tide later in the day. Howard took a closer look at the small harbor entrance.

"I think Lucky can put that son of a bitch down right in here," he said. "That way you won't have to transfer fuel so far. Let's get back so I can radio some new plans."

Woody nodded, hopped into the boat and started the engine. He picked up the stern anchor as he backed down, and they headed for Smugglers. Laura had lunch waiting, but Howard walked past the dining area to the radio. Woody told Laura the tentative plans, and by the time Howard returned, he was ready to eat.

"All set. Lucky'll be into Coral Cay at five-forty-five tomorrow. Be sure to have the boat there, along with an extra pump."

"Gotcha," said Woody, biting into a ham sandwich. The chips were stale, as usual, but no one complained. "It's quiet today. You run everyone off?" asked Howard.

"Don't know where they all went," said Woody. "Over the weekend there were a few boats. Party boys. Drank all night."

"Did they have chicks along with them or was it just guys?" asked Howard.

"Mostly guys. I haven't seen many cruising couples lately, just bunches of guys who don't seem to be on a timetable."

"They are," said Howard, matter-of-factly. "Just waiting for their loading orders."

"You think so?"

Howard put down his sandwich, stopped chewing and looked at Woody.

"How can you be in the business and be so goddamn naive?" he asked. "Half the yachts around here are just waiting for someone to piss or get off the pot. Usually it's to get onto the pot. Christ, Woody. Wise up. Look around. The place is crawling with scammers, but they're mostly amateurs. That plane that crashed was probably delivering to the joy boys you were entertaining. Start using your head, or you'll be a dead man, Woody. Funny business is damn serious."

Woody ate the rest of his sandwich, putting together pieces of conversation he had heard from the crowd the other night, wishing he had been more attentive.

"Another thing, Woody. I don't like bringing it up, but it's not a good idea to booze it up or sample the product when you have people around. Keep your head clean and it'll stay on your shoulders."

Howard stood up, thanked Laura, and turned to Woody as he pushed his chair into the table.

"I'm going to head back and have Jock take me up for a spin over the area. I'll let you know if I spot anything. Just want to know the game before we start playing tomorrow night. We can't afford to mess this one up because this is the one that pays."

Woody nodded. Money always talked.

Howard left, pulled up to Max's dock and tied up the boat as he had found it. Then he walked the back road behind the Sandy Cay Club to Conch Inn. Max was in his shop working on Woody's red boat again. Howard shook his head as he looked around, marveling at Max's mechanical inabilities. But Max was still better than nothing, he thought, and another warm body in the operation.

"How're you doing?" he asked.

Max was so startled to see Howard in his shop that he dropped a nut and washer.

"Okay," he said, bending to pick them up in the sand, shoving his glasses back on his nose. "Should have this thing running by the end of the day."

"We've heard that before. Where's Jock?" he asked, looking around.

"Flew some blokes to the States," said Max, fitting the nut and washer on an engine bolt. "Said he'd be back later today. "

"Charter flight?" Max nodded. "Since when is Jock the self-appointed tour director of the island? Did anyone tell him what he's here for?" Howard was talking in a low voice, but it was threatening. Max put the engine part down, wiped his hands, and began defending Jock.

"Some people were looking for a ride back, he was here, he figured you wouldn't need him today 'cause he hadn't heard anything, and he wanted to pick up an extra buck or two. He'll be back."

"He may be out of a job, too. He's supposed to be part of the operation. Part of the deal is to be available for the boss. Just because I haven't flown with him doesn't mean I never planned to. I suggest you get through on the telephone and tell him to get his ass over here. I don't care what time he has to arrive, but if he isn't back today he's out of the operation. And that isn't all." Howard turned and walked away before Max could answer. He put his wrench down and followed.

"Howard," said Max, catching up to his long strides. "Jock's planning on coming right back. I don't think I need to call him."

"Do you always stick up for him?" Howard stopped walking and looked Max straight in the eye. "Because if you do, you may be out with him."

"He'll be back. I'll call now," said Max.

"Good," said Howard, turning and heading for the Nest, fuming inside that Jock had taken another flight. It wouldn't be so bad if he'd cleared it with him beforehand, thought Howard, but all Jock saw was the chance to make a buck with no concern for anyone else in the operation. Howard stomped up the steep hill to the Nest, venting his mounting anger. He had a slow burning point, but once ignited, his vengeance could be lethal. He decided a rum would cool him down. As he entered the house, his eye caught a sign Marjorie had hung on the kitchen wall: "It's difficult to soar like an eagle when you work with turkeys." How true, he thought, and almost smiled. Jock and Max. Two turkeys. Maybe a couple of peacocks. And Woody — a turkey for sure.

* * *

Max knew he couldn't reach Jock by phone and hoped that he had the sense to turn right around and head back to the island.

As two hours went by, he became concerned. By five o'clock, the last person he wanted to face was Howard, yet there he was, watching him close up shop. Neither said anything, but a plane could be heard in the distance. Max hoped beyond the wrath of Howard that it was Jock. He wasn't disappointed. In seconds, Jock did a low pass over the marina, almost grabbing a mast with the landing gear. "Not too smart," said Howard, "but then, I'm finding this out all along. He's not too smart."

"You want a ride out to the runway?" asked Maxwell, relieved, locking his tool box. "He'll probably take you wherever you want to go."

"Tomorrow will have to do. It's too late now to do what I had in mind," he said, climbing into the Jeep. They arrived at the airstrip as Jock was taxiing the plane to the ramp area. As Jock got out, his face dropped when he saw the stern look on Howard's face.

"Hi," he said, getting out of the plane and drumming up a smile. "Didn't expect a welcoming committee."

"And you didn't get one," said Howard, still sitting in the open vehicle. "The next time you fail to file a flight plan with me you're fired. Done. Finished. Understand?"

The smile left Jock's face and he shook his head to answer.

"Max, take me to the bottom of the hill," said Howard. "I'm going to the Nest. Jock, I'll see you at seven o'clock tomorrow morning ready to roll. Hopefully you boys don't have any hot dates to interfere with business?"

His voice mocked them and they knew it. Max backed up and sped Howard across the runway to the path leading to his house. Neither said a word as he got out and walked straight ahead to the Nest. As Max came back, Jock jumped in, handed him a hundred dollar bill, smiled and shrugged.

"Tomorrow's another day," said Jock. "Let's go have a drink." He whistled as Max drove to Conch Inn. Howard would be in a better mood in the morning, he thought. Nothing like a good day's worth of flying. As they walked into Conch Inn, they could see three policemen and a pilot sitting at the bar. No one seemed to be working.

"Hello," said Max, recognizing one of the authorities. "You

281

find out what happened?"

"Dose boys did a good one on dat plane," he said. "Nuttin' left. Two pilots an' all dat shit dey was carrying burned total. No sense eben sabing a bone. Dere mudders will neber know what happened to dere sons." He shook his head and set the empty glass down hard on the counter, indicating he wanted another one. Manny took it and refilled it.

"Where'd you get ice?" asked Max, knowing that Manny's freezer wasn't producing any.

"Sent a boy down to de yacht club. Told dem dat's dere share o' puttin' up dese dummies." He smiled as the police looked at him, and everyone laughed. A native could get away with a whole lot more than a white man in this bar, and they all knew it.

"We's goin' back to de main prowince as soon's he's ready," said the constable, nodding his head toward the pilot finishing a beer. "You 'bout done?"

He shook his head and got off the stool. In the islands, native pilots did as they pleased. In this case, it included a toddy on the job with the boys.

In a few minutes, the four were headed to the airstrip to fly back to the main province. As they left, a few boat people started coming back ashore. Visiting yachtsmen felt uncomfortable around the police, carrying their weapons as if they knew what to do with them and drinking on the job. It was better to stay away and let them do their business.

* * *

That night the island rocked with partying and summer goodbyes. Conch Inn bar had a band for the evening, and the yacht club served up a buffet of cracked conch, grouper, chowder, peas and rice and some fresh fruit. Most tourists headed back to the States felt compelled to live up the last couple of nights in the islands. Charlie helped Pete tend bar before Wanda arrived, and during happy hour, he counted a crowd of forty people.

"Good turnout," he said to Pete as he put a couple of beers

on the bar. "Haven't seen this many live souls in a long time."

"They'll all clear out as soon as the price of drinks goes up again, and they aren't all that alive," said Pete, his five o'clock pessimism rising. "Bar does all right during this hour, but I'm glad I don't have to stay and entertain people. At least now I can keep track of the tabs instead of buying drinks on the house. Christ! You should have been here a few years ago. I could outdrink every person in the place." He shook his head, remembering some of the shenanigans. "I ever tell you about the ten-foot boa constrictor that decided to make a visit along that rafter up there?"

"No," said Charlie. "That's one I haven't heard."

"Christ, one night I looked up and this thing was staring back. I thought I'd had too many rums. Place was packed. Didn't want people panicking you know. Anyway, there were a lot of people in here that night. Fan was going and I was afraid the damn snake would get its tail caught in the blades, but he was just settin' there."

Pete was raising his voice and the crowd began quieting down, eager to hear another of his stories.

"The girls rang the dinner bell and everyone went in the dining room. I sat there, drinking my rums, trying to outstare the snake. Then Jackson came in. I couldn't tell him about it because the natives go wild even at the mention of a snake, so I talked with him keeping one eye open out the back of my head." He put his cigarette down and poured a cranberry juice and soda.

"What happened?" asked Charlie. "That can't be the end of the story."

"No, hell no," said Pete, chuckling. "After everyone had dinner and Jackson had locked up the fuel and gone home, I announced drinks on the house for fifteen minutes. Did they chug down the rum punches! Then my old friend Chester came in, the one who has the old motor yacht with the barn paint on the sides? You know — Chester the molester, the virgin tester? Well, I took him aside and pointed to my nonpaying guest in the rafters, and he just rolled his eyes. Then the snake moved about six inches, which was like twenty feet, and all I could visualize was screaming old ladies and the natives running for their lives.

After fifteen minutes of free drinking I told everyone I was closing. They never knew what to expect from me after a few drinks so no one thought it strange that I was closing early. I was pretty unpredictable. But let me tell you about removing a ten-foot snake from the rafters." He took a sip of his juice and looked at all the wide eyes staring at him. He smiled and asked if anyone wanted more to drink. After a promise he'd finish the story while fixing the punch he continued.

"Well, after everyone was out, Chester and I realized we weren't too bright to be tackling this situation. Shit, I'd never even SEEN a snake that big before let alone wrestled with one. So we decided Chester would continue the stare game while I went and found a stick, some heavy gauge wire and some hose clamps. Well, between the two of us looking cross-eyed at this snake, we got some sort of trap stick rigged, but then we didn't know how to get the snake into it. That was when the radio room was more of a storage room for the original kitchen. Anyway, this rafter, see how it goes?"

He pointed, and everyone around the bar followed his finger.

"Well, that rafter goes right out under the eaves. I went outside on the roof, laid down and hung over the side, and Chester sat in here, poking that damn snake until I saw his head come out. Then I snagged it in the wire loop. Do you have any idea how much a ten-foot snake weighs when your arms are outstretched and it's dangling almost to the ground? A lot, I'm here to tell you.

"Anyway, here I was, this goddamn snake half dead but still swinging in the snare. We hadn't thought about what we would do when we had him. I started hollering for Chester to come help me and he wouldn't get anywhere near the thing. I told him to go get the bang stick for killing sharks, my arms damn near coming out of the sockets and this snake not giving up. It was strong. Well, after forever, Chester came back with the bang stick and somehow we got me and the snake down from the roof. We took the snake over to the dock, still wriggling away, right on the edge of the concrete and...hey, does anyone want another drink?" He was booed and told to get on with the story.

"Well, I held the snake's snared head and Chester let him

have it with the .22 bang stick. Shot his head off, but somehow, the rest of the body wasn't told it lost an important connection. It kept right on wriggling all over the place, Chester and me jumping out of the way, until it finally wriggled itself off the end of the dock. Last we saw the snake it was a gourmet dinner for some shark and barracuda. They used to hang around the docks early evening. Too many people now. They stay away till the dead of night."

"Now we'll take some more punch," said a man who was staying in the cottages. "I knew it had to end up being a fish story."

Pete turned to Charlie, chuckled and shrugged. "No one ever believes these things. Remind me to tell you about my parrot."

"You have a parrot?" asked a woman, slightly slurring her words.

"Did have. Oh, great, here's Wanda. Well, folks, see you later. Enjoy yourselves. Anyone wanting dinner reservations better see the cook now. You comin', Charlie?"

He nodded, waved and followed Pete out the door.

"Have you ever seen another snake like that on the island?" asked Charlie. "I'm not too much of a reptile lover."

"No, but I know there are coral snakes around here as well as the harmless kind. They help take care of the rats," said Pete. "And they don't like people, so don't worry about them. Let's go listen to the news, talk with Helen and Johnny and come back for dinner. We're all eating at the club tonight with such a big crowd anyway. Almost like the middle of the winter season, huh?"

They climbed into the Jeep, the engine protesting before it started.

"Glad your business is doing well," said Charlie. "Ever since Jock came mine is down. Saw him take some more people off the island today. Didn't get back until after five."

"Wish I could help you on that one, but I don't know what to do," said Pete.

"I don't know either," said Charlie. "Let's wait and see, but I can't make airplane insurance payments and maintenance bills if he's going to continue undercutting me. People don't know

285

what they're doing. The public is basically stupid. If it's cheap they'll take two, and that's the same theory they use getting in an airplane with a jerk pilot. Oh, shit, let's forget about him and enjoy ourselves. Look at that sun going down."

It was almost seven o'clock. In about fifteen minutes the giant orange ball would sink into the horizon, seemingly holding onto the edge for a few seconds before tumbling to the other side of the world. The sky would then have pink veins and puffy light pink clouds interspersed with the slightest twinkle of stars trying to wake up.

"Dinner's about eightish tonight, a bit late," said Pete. "Boys were still getting conch out of the shells a half-hour ago. Should be a good dinner."

"Maria does all right," said Charlie, holding on as Pete drove the Jeep up the hill to the house.

Helen was reading a book and Johnny was playing solitaire as they walked in.

"What excitement do you have planned for tonight?" she asked, smiling. "Don't tell me, but please, not another airplane crash. I couldn't take it. Hi, Charlie."

"Hi. I think the big event tonight is cracked conch at the club. Let's hope that's all."

Pete turned on the television news, a snowy reception that defied detail, but the sound worked. They were too far from the States or main province for anything better. The only reason anyone had a television on the island was that sometimes, though rarely, the atmospheric conditions were perfect. Then the set was a welcome link to the outside world. Video movies also raised the number of television sets on Sandy Cay.

To Helen's satisfaction, the evening meal was pleasant and nothing out of the ordinary happened. Everyone welcomed a good sleep.

* * *

Howard awoke the next morning grateful the police plane had left the previous night. He rose slowly, peered in all directions from his glass-walled bedroom, scratched his chest, stretched and yawned. He pulled on a pair of jeans and went down the stairs to fix a cup of coffee, mentally rehearsing the possible events of the day.

It was only six o'clock, but the sun already was creating heat as it rose from the horizon. The tide was up and the beach was deserted. He enjoyed the solitude of early morning from Osprey Nest. It gave him a feeling of power as he lorded over the scrubby land and the far reaching sea. The colors of the water had not yet begun to differentiate in the rays of the sun. Only later, toward noon, would the dark patches of the deep ocean reef show their mottled colors beneath the blue waters. When his coffee was ready, Howard continued to sit and stare. This was when he missed contact with the States, the morning paper and someone to cheer him up. He turned on the sideband, only half hearing the jumbled talk of others, and decided to double check arrangements with Chubby. He turned to their pre-arranged frequency, then halfway through the conversation switched to a third frequency. Anyone listening would not know their code, and Howard felt secure with the system. It was the only way it could work without a telephone to avoid the marine operator and the common ham radio system. Everything was a go. Lucky would be on schedule and so would the choppers.

Now Howard's only fear was the unknown whereabouts of the down-island boys. Hopefully, he'd know if they were a threat in another hour.

Jock better be on time, he thought. Cocky son of a bitch. He sipped his coffee and noticed the first stirrings in the village — Jackson checking something at his house and a native woman carrying a water jug on her head to one of the community wells. A small runabout was coming toward Sandy Cay from Rocky Point, probably carrying a worker for the island, he thought. In a few more minutes he saw Jock walking around his plane, checking the fuel and getting it ready. Time to go, he thought, and poured out the remaining coffee in his cup. He gave it a quick rinse and locked the door behind him. In a few minutes, he was walking across the runway to the plane.

"Morning," said Jock. "Ready? Where we going?"

"Just in the area," said Howard. "I want to check out the

whereabouts of the rippers."

"All right," said Jock with enthusiasm. "Want to fly low or do any passes or anything like that?"

"Just fly the plane and I'll let you know as we go, but I don't appreciate acrobatics and if you scare the shit out of me, you're fired. I'm only flying with you because there isn't anyone else but Charlie available and I don't think he'd understand the mission."

"That's for sure," said Jock, chuckling. As soon as they were buckled in, he started the engine. Jock looked to see if anyone was coming in to land and taxied to the end of the strip. He took off, and as soon as he began gaining altitude, banked the plane to the south, toward Smugglers.

"Keep it about this high," said Howard. "This is good for looking around without raising any suspicion."

"Anyone seeing us at five hundred feet at seven in the morning will wonder what we're up to," said Jock, challenging his decision. "This isn't the usual tour, you know."

"Sweep back and forth over the islands so I can scan the coves and creeks."

They were over Smugglers and heading toward Coral Cay. Jock did some turns so Howard could get a good look at the water below. About five miles south of Coral Cay, Howard pointed. "Just as I figured. Down there. See, between those big rocks at the entrance to that cut? There are two boats almost hidden under the mammoth rock shelves. It's the down-islanders, sure as shit."

He took a pair of binoculars from behind the seat and focused on the boats.

"Don't go so fast, or turn around or whatever you have to do," said Howard. "I want to get a count on these guys if I can."

Jock slowed the plane to maneuvering speed and made a couple of wide sweeps over the islands Howard pointed out.

"Only four of them. One looks like little Juan. Two boats with two bastards each," he said. "Okay. We can head back. He put the binoculars away and looked forward.

"That's it?" asked Jock. "That's hardly worth burnin' any fuel. Can't we go someplace else while we're up? I do a great

288

tour of the islands at about fifty feet off the deck."

"I'm sure you do, but not with me in this contraption," said Howard. "Back to Sandy Cay."

"What are you going to do about those jokers down there?" asked Jock. "Think they might screw us up?"

"Tonight's pretty foolproof because there's nothing to rip off, but they don't know that. They might assume the choppers are carrying dope and try to make a play for it. Do they ever come into Sandy Cay?"

"Yeah. Saw them the other day. Buy fuel all the time, just as if they fish for a living."

"They do," said Howard, with a sinister smile. "Only problem is, the grouper are square." As they approached the runway of Sandy Cay, Howard came to the conclusion to let the down-island boys in on the plan rather than risk losing a chopper. After they landed, he told Jock to notify him if their boats came anywhere near the island.

"I'd rather talk here than to visit them where they are," he said. "I'll tell Woody to let us know if he sees anything. In the meantime, I'll keep watch from the Nest. That's still the best lookout. Thanks for the ride. You flying people today?"

Jock shook his head no.

"Good. Have a bag that has to get to another island later in the day. I'll let you know if you're the one to do it. Tell Max to get that friggin' boat going."

"Will do," said Jock. "I know he's working on it."

"By now the whole world ought to know he's working on it, and the designer and manufacturer are probably constipated at the thought. See you later." Howard turned and took long, slow strides across the runway to the Nest. He needed another cup of coffee. Hopefully, the down-island boys would need fuel or something to eat or drink during the day.

* * *

Charlie was at the club early in the morning, relaying his flight schedule to his office on the radio. He had been lucky the previous night, booking six people to return to the States. He was scheduled to fly at noon and was busy making a list of things various people needed. He went over an outboard parts list with Jackson.

"That's it?" he asked, after Jackson had checked on the year and serial number of a motor.

"Dat's all. Not too much dis time, eh?" Jackson had come to work about seven-thirty, fueled a few boats heading back to the States, told a couple of native boys what to do around the club and was now ready to sit down and enjoy his morning cup of coffee.

"Dey neber find out who dose pilots were dat crashed," he said. "Dat's real sad ting to hab happen 'round here. You tink it goin' ta keep gettin' worse, or do you tink it gonna clean up?"

"I don't know what to tell you, Jackson. The authorities questioned me the other day on Jock and I had to be honest about what's happening. He'll probably have the heat on him and I'll be blamed. I tried to let him know he'd only hurt himself, but that type never cares. Besides, I think he's flying people as a cover for what he's really up to."

"I tink you right," said Jackson, nodding his curly head. "You see him come and go wid nuttin' but a briefcase? He goes and come back fast so's you know he don' go far. He up to sumptin'. An' dat Woody. What a wild man he be. Dey call at Conch Inn las' night. I goes in to git a soda and dey all carryin'' on like crazy, all de dancin' an' drinkin' goin' on." He shook his head and rubbed his chin with one hand, a coffee mug in the other. "Less dan a year since dose funny boys start comin' here and look at de changes. I ain' friendly no more right away till I sees de type person I talkn' wid. I neber use to be dat way. I likes bein' friendly, but you don' know what de people wants no more. Dey ax you crazy tings to do, like fuel at night and to look out for dere buddies in such and such a boat. I don' wanna get inbolbed wid dat stuff, you know. It no good."

"You have the right idea, Jackson. It isn't easy. Guy offered me fifty grand the other day to make a run. Said he'd give me more the next time, but I don't want to live that way, always looking over my shoulder and wondering if I'm going to see the year out. No thanks," said Charlie.

290

He didn't want to go into it with Jackson, but he'd been offered a lot more if he'd use his own plane for the job. Still, he wasn't about to put himself or his family in jeopardy. He'd sooner plug away at a legitimate occupation and struggle along with the rest of them, paying bills month by month and hoping business kept up. Jock had hit him hard this summer, taking at least fifty percent of the business he would normally have booked. It was only a matter of time, if he could hold out financially, before justice would be done, he hoped.

"Those guys with the Aerostar come back through here yet?" he asked Jackson.

"I haben' seen dem, but I 'spect dey be tru' one o' dese days," he said. "I don' know who gonna fuel dem, but dey probably made some deal wid one o' de boys 'round here. Hard tellin'. Nobody say nuttin'. But dey all got new fancy tings. You notice?"

"I notice, Jackson, and it's not good. The young boys think all they have to do is rip off a doper and they'll have it made, but it's going to catch up with them and they'll wind up in the pokey. In the meantime, they forget about bettering themselves in school, drop out and then what do they have? It's happened on other islands, Jackson. I hate to see it here."

"Me too," he said, a slight frown between his eyes. "Speak o' de debil, look who comin' in here. Dose de down-island boys and dey's bad. Been hangin' 'round lately. You know dat Juan, de little one wid all de gold 'round his neck? He always buyin' fuel and cigarettes and rum. But dey don' go nowhere it seems. Dey come, stay 'round a while, den disappear for a few days, den dey back. Crazy. Wonder what dey want now." He got up from the stool, took a last sip from the mug, shook his head and pushed the screen door open, heading for the docks.

"Hey, Juan, what you wants 'round here agin'? Taught you boys long gone agin. What you up to?"

"Hey, Jackson. What you cares 'bout us long's we pay fo' what we buy, eh? We'se jis' 'round de area, doin' little fishin' 'n' such." Juan opened the fuel cover and said, "Need gas. You gots some? 'Bout forty gallons'll do. Saw de tanker come in las' week, so's I knows you gots it. Cash today. I's got cash."

291

"I'll gits it for you, but I don' see no fishin' poles in yo' boat. You hidin' dem, eh?" Jackson gave Juan a big grin. No one was going to fool him on the type of fishing going on.

"You tinks you pretty smarts, island boy. We's all smart, eh?" Juan turned to his crew, a teenager with a fancy gold watch on his wrist and black beret on his curly head.

"I's smarter 'en you 'cause I's here wid a good job," said Jackson hauling the fuel hose to the boat. "I works for a libin'. What you do?"

"You ax too many questions and you ain' gonna gits no answers," said Juan. "You too tight wid dem honkeys. An' speakin' o' honkey, see whose comin' down de docks?"

Jackson turned and looked up from passing the fuel hose down to Juan. Jock was shuffling his feet back and forth, smiling, and running his fingers through his thinning hair.

"You Juan?" he asked.

"Dat' me, Mon. What you wants wid me?"

"Someone at Conch Inn wants to see you about something."

"I no goes at de beck an' call o' no honkey," said Juan, filling the tank. "Mon want to talks wid me he can come here."

Jock looked around nervously, wishing Jackson would go back to the club, but he took his time coiling a water hose, listening to what was being said.

"Look, Juan," said Jock, crouching down and talking in confidence. "My boss man wants to see you. I don't know what it's about. I'm just here to pass the word."

"Who is you boss man? Dat big tall fella dat lib up de ridge?"

Jock nodded his head yes, noticing Jackson watching out of the corner of his eye.

"Yeah, man. Hey, don't get me in trouble, huh? These guys round here...." He took his hand and rolled it back and forth, indicating he didn't trust anyone at the yacht club.

"Okay. I be down dere after I drinks a beer or two here. Wouldn't want ta jis fill de tanks an' run. Dey gots good rum here an' we almost dry. Need cigs too."

Jock nodded his head and stood up, smiling at Jackson as he walked by.

"You want dis on de tab you gots goin' o' you gonna pay today?" asked Jackson, scratching his head, then reaching for the fuel hose from Juan.

"We hab a few drinks and den pays de whole bill. We's goin' down islands for a few days and won' be back till I don' know. Don' want nobody chasin' dis black ass for no bill. Don' you worry, Jax. We not goin' ta stiff ya. Come on, Junior, let's gits a drink."

The two went to the club as Jackson reeled in the fuel hose, then followed. Charlie tried to read Jackson's face, but it was totally blank. If a native, even one close to you, didn't want you to know what was going on in his head, he would erase all emotion and any indication of what he knew. Jackson grabbed a bottle of rum and a couple of beers from the cooler and put them on the bar.

"English cigarettes?" he asked Juan.

"Right on," he said, then turned to Charlie.

"Eh, mon. How's de flyin'? I mights hab to go to de States one o' dese days. You hits me up de same price as eberyone else?"

"Same price, Juan," said Charlie. "I wouldn't want anyone to think I was prejudiced."

Juan laughed.

"What you goin' to de States fo'?" asked Jackson. "You gots no business dere." A twinkle in his eye and the teasing tone of his voice baited him for an answer.

"What you knows 'bout my business, mon? I gits lots o' business ober dere. I knows lots o' people. Big peoples. Dey trust dis black mon, here. See all dis gold stuff on me? You gits dat workin' for rich mon. You jealous, mon. You jealous."

Now he was teasing Jackson. The banter continued, Charlie adding a few insignificant comments, then Juan and Junior got up to leave.

"I see you later, maybe," he said, turning to Charlie. "All depends on business. But I mights go anyway. You gots a seat open goin' out?" Charlie nodded yes. "When you goin'?"

"In about fifteen minutes, but I'll be back in a couple of days." Juan nodded and went out the door to his boat, followed by Junior. The two climbed aboard, undid the lines, and started the engines. A few minutes later, the dark blue boat pulled into Conch Inn marina where Howard sat on the docks, dangling his feet over the red boat, watching Max work. Max looked up in disgust as he saw Juan. If it wasn't for him and the chase a couple of months ago, the boat wouldn't have had all the problems.

Howard took a line as they came in, then helped Juan up on the dock. Comparison of the two men was almost comical. Howard, at six-and-a-half feet totally dwarfed Juan, who stood a little over five feet. Juan looked straight up at the big man.

"So, what does de boss mon hab to say to dis boss mon?" he asked cockily. Howard smirked. Juan was everything he had heard him to be.

"Choppers coming in tonight are clean, so don't try anything," said Howard, looking him straight in the eye and not volunteering any more information.

"Dat's it? Dat's why you calls me all de way ober here?"

"That's it," said Howard. "Just a friendly warning, that's all. Thanks for stopping by." He smiled at little Juan, who didn't know how to take the white boss man but who got the message nonetheless.

Howard turned back to the red boat and handed a wrench down to Maxwell. Juan peered down to see what Max was doing.

"You sure do got problems wid dat boat," said Juan. "We ain' seen it goin' at any speed for a long time. You got troubles wid it?" Max almost boiled as he glared at Juan, but didn't say a word and went on working.

"Guess ol' Max don' talk to Juan no more. Too bad, Max. You be fixin' dat boat in hell someday." He started laughing and motioned for Junior to follow him. They walked down the dock toward Conch Inn. A few minutes later they came out with a couple of beers.

"Dey ain' cold but better den nuttin'," said Juan to Howard as he and Junior climbed back into the boat. The engine started with a roar, and Juan gunned it a few times, looking over at Max. He laughed, then sped off at top speed, the wake rocking the red boat and catching Max off balance. Bastard, thought Max. Little black bastard. He went on working, consciously ignoring Howard, who rather enjoyed the scene.

When Juan had gone and Max regained some composure, he looked up.

"You think they got the message?"

"They got it all right," said Howard. "I just hope they're smart. He's a squirrely little bastard. Uses too much of his own stuff. He even shot at the police boat further south of here. Didn't know what he was doing. Well, I'm going back to the Nest. Be at Smugglers no later than five. Woody's going to need help. Tell Jock to go too. Where is he?"

"Said he was going to crash at my house for awhile. He doesn't like getting up early," said Max.

"Poor baby," said Howard, mockingly. "Tell him to get his ass up to the Nest by three. He's got some flying to do today and I'm tired of listening to you boys complain."

"I'm not complaining, Howard, just trying to get this bloody thing running. As to Jock, well, you can talk to him."

"Since you're such good buddies, I'll depend on you to get the message through and also the one between the lines. Had to get up early. Christ. What does he think we're running, a day care center? I'm going home."

Howard stomped down the dock past the hotel rooms and onto the road to the airport. He was tired of tolerating his mediocre crew, and decided to talk to Woody about his nephew. He wanted a steady flying job pretty bad. Maybe he'd fit into the scheme of things. Having thought of a way to bring in new blood to the organization, Howard took long, fast strides toward the Nest. As long as you stick to family, he told himself, you can bring in someone new. It's when you bring in someone who may have connections with another company that you run into problems. Woody's nephew would be fresh, unknown to the competition and could be taught right from the start how to survive and make it big in the trade. He had already flown in supplies with Chubby. He'd talk to Woody after the choppers were long on their way.

At four-thirty, Jock landed at Sandy Cay after making a

delivery south for Howard. He suspected what he was carrying, but never asked questions, just took the locked briefcase and gave it to whoever was supposed to pick it up. He was paid well — much better than the others by comparison — and didn't want to mess up this part of the job. He parked the plane, blocked the wheels and ambled over to Conch Inn, where Max was nervously pacing back and forth waiting for him, the usual scowl on his face.

"You could speed it up a little," he said as he saw Jock with a big smile on his face coming from the airstrip. "We have to be at Smugglers in a few minutes. Come on. I've got the red boat going."

"Don't sweat it, man," said Jock, bending over to tie a worn sneaker. "We'll get there. Did you test run the thing?"

"Just at the dock. Let's take it for a spin."

Jock followed Max down the dock and climbed into the boat. Max started it and the engines turned over right away.

"I'll be damned," said Jock. "It actually runs."

"I don't need bullshit from you, Jock. It's bad enough I get it from everyone else on this bloody island." Maxwell turned the boat in a sharp bank to the south as he came out of the channel and gunned it toward Smugglers. About half-way there one engine sputtered, then ran all right the rest of the way. Dirty gas, thought Max. He hadn't flushed the tanks after the storm. There was probably some salt water seepage. He'd take care of that another time.

As they rounded an island just north of Smugglers, Max saw Woody looking to see who was coming. He waved both arms in the air when he saw Max and the red boat. As Maxwell pulled up, he admired his favorite toy.

"I'd forgotten how great that thing looks skimming over the water," he said. "Glad to see it's running. I'll take you back in it tonight so I can bring it back here. Needs a bath."

"Didn't have time to clean it up," said Maxwell, noting all the greasy fingerprints and scuff marks. "Won't take long to get her pretty again."

"Thought you'd do that," said Woody. "It's not my fault the thing got so screwed up. Come on. Toss me a line and let's get down to business. We made up some rum punch, and Lucky should be here within the half hour. We'll grab a cooler and some ice and glasses to give him a proper welcome."

Jock and Max helped carry the refreshments, and Woody went for his carbine.

"What's that for?" asked Jock, a bit surprised. "I don't want to be in the middle of any of that shit."

"Relax. I'm going to stand guard on the fuel till the choppers come in. They're scheduled for midnight. Howard doesn't want Juan and his gang coming anywhere near the place. I got orders to blow them to hell if they try. They got the word to stay away, so they probably will. They're just looking for loads to rip off and Howard told them there wasn't anything coming in. Ready?"

The three climbed into the red boat and waved goodbye to Laura on the dock. She watched until they were out of sight. These were the nights she wished she were back in the States, comfortable and secure in a home. Even though Woody told her not to worry, she instinctively did. She would be uneasy until the choppers were well on their way and Woody back at Smugglers. She fixed a rum, sat on a chaise, and soaked up the late afternoon rays. She had a good tan now, and her hair had become sunbleached. She felt healthy and young, the hot summer agreeing with her. Today, like most days, she wore only a two-piece bathing suit. Shorts and top were donned when it cooled off in the afternoons, but for the most part, Laura enjoyed the natural warmth of the sun on her body. She dozed in the silence, then woke as she heard an airplane coming closer. She put her hand over her eyes to shield them from the sun and tried to see what kind of plane it was. The big bird had to be Lucky. She watched it sink lower into the sky, heading toward Coral Cay. She mentally crossed her fingers that everything went as planned, then lay back to catch a quick nap.

* * *

Jock had no more than fixed a round of drinks when they heard Lucky coming in from the east, as planned. He came straight in, seemingly not bothering with the wind direction, and dropped between two little rocky islands before skimming over the water and landing just short of the harbor. He taxied the big bird almost to the beach at Coral Cay, shut down the engines, opened the door and stood up, smiling, as if waiting for the trumpets to blow "Ta-Daah."

"Hope you guys brought a glass for me," he said, noting the cooler. "Let's not waste time, though. Help me get the shit off this bird. Someone asked me what I was hauling today. I said bird shit. That's what it is. Bird shit. This bird's full of it."

The three looked at each other and even Maxwell had to smile. They pushed the red boat into the water toward the plane, unloaded fuel drums into the boat, pushed it to shore and off-loaded to the warehouse. In about twenty minutes, the fuel was stashed away. Woody hooked the fuel pump to one of the containers. Everything was ready for the choppers.

As drinks were poured, Woody turned to Lucky with a blank look on his face, fuel streaking his arms and white T-shirt.

"Where are the broads, Lucky? You never go anywhere without the broads. You hiding them in there?"

"No broads today. Have them resting up for when I get back." He smiled, a big toothpaste commercial grin. "Didn't anyone ever tell you women have big yaps? I don't mind cruising around with them, but I like to think of Lucky Number One when I start meeting up with folks like you. This ain't no Sunday morning hello. Besides, Juan's in the area. Flighty little creep. He shouldn't be any trouble tonight cause Howard's given him the word, but you never know."

Lucky finished his drink, tossed the remaining ice and put the plastic cup back in the cooler.

"I'm enjoying your little picnic but something tells me to get my butt in the air and get that bird back home."

"Where you hanging out now?" asked Jock.

"You know I don't broadcast my campsites," he said. "I'm not too far away. Don't worry about ol' Lucky. I'm always within earshot of what's going on and always know what's happening. I got more communication gear than all the agencies put together. Sometime when you get a chance, come visit. I even put a radar detector aboard my yacht. Anything or anyone

298

comes within a hundred feet of the thing it triggers an alarm. My mechanic came in late the other night drunk as a hyena stuck in a mud bath laced with booze, trying to get aboard without me knowing what was going on. He opened the hatch and I had a double barrel pointed right at his crossed eyes. He yelped and jumped overboard. Fastest I ever saw the bastard move. Anyway, it's a nice toy. Got all that new weather scan stuff too, to tell me what's happening anywhere in the Caribbean — or world for that matter. Helps me plan the load factors. Well, you boys have fun tonight. Just play it cool. You staying here, Woody?"

Woody nodded, lifting the gun.

"Good. You want to take me out in the boat, Max? I'd hate to get my shoes wet." They looked at him and laughed. Lucky was wearing rubber zoris, the kind sold in discount stores around the world. He hopped in the red boat and Max started the engine, backed down and swung over to the plane. Lucky stepped aboard, waved as he closed the door behind him, then put on a Red Baron hat and goggles to give the boys another laugh. He pretended to throw a scarf over his shoulder as he started the massive propellers, first the left, then right, and as quickly as he swooped down, Lucky took off into the setting sun, downwind in what little breeze was blowing. He banked to the east and departed the same route he had taken on arrival.

Max secured the red boat, stepped ashore and fixed another rum. Finally, when all was quiet, Woody said, "You guys can head back whenever you want to, but I'd appreciate company for a while yet. Laura said she'd fix dinner about eight. Maybe you can bring some chicken back to me. I'll probably need some more rum and ice, too."

"We can stay awhile," said Max. "We go back there and we might have to answer to Howard or something else might bloody well happen."

Jock walked around, poking at lizards along the base of the warehouse.

"You bring a flashlight?" he asked Woody.

"No. Bring one back when you come. Also bring that portable aircraft radio so I can talk to the choppers as they come in. Howard said the freqs are the same as on the last deal. I think it's great they're using choppers this time. They can land, pick up and drop anywhere."

"But they can't outfly the reconnaissance plane they've got cruising around searching for dopers," said Jock. "They're using a jet now."

"That's the point," said Woody. "A jet's too goddamn fast. The choppers would know if they were being tailed 'cause they'd have to circle to keep them in sight. The choppers can set down in a remote area and let the jet record the whole deal. By the time they can get anyone there the deal's gone down and the authorities have lost again. Actually, a chopper run gives them the bird when they're onto what's happening."

"Anyone live on this island?" asked Jock, noting the footprints leading in all directions.

"Abandoned house over the ridge, but no one's lived here for years that I know of," said Max. "Old couple who was here, well, he died and the widow didn't want to sit on this rock by herself. Her kids didn't want any part of it, so now the bloody place just sits. You can go over there if you want to, but it's been vandalized so often nothing's worth seeing. Wouldn't be surprised if that's where Juan and the boys have set up camp."

A little while later, the ice sloshing in the bottom of the cooler and a good dent put in the rum bottle, Max and Jock decided it was time to head back to Smugglers. They'd be back in a bit with a flashlight, radio and food for Woody.

"We're not bringing any more rum," said Max, looking at Woody's eyes. "One more drink and you'd probably shoot yourself if a bloke came near. Watch it, huh?"

"Yeah, I'll watch it. Truth is I'm scared shitless," said Woody, sitting on the coral rock, gun across his lap. "You're probably right. Don't want Howard mad at me. When it's all said and done I can let loose."

Max and Jock shoved off, the port engine giving him some trouble on starting. Woody shook his head. Damn boat still wasn't right.

* * *

300

After Max and Jock went back to Smugglers, Woody had the feeling he was not alone, that somewhere, someone was watching him, lurking in the bushes, hiding, waiting. A lizard scurried past and Woody pointed the gun. This is stupid, he thought. No one's here. But the door suddenly squeaked on the warehouse, and the breeze picked up, rustling the brush. Woody sat back down, shook himself as if throwing off a load of fears, and was quiet. A lonely seagull cried as it glided overhead, and he watched as the ball of orange sun disappeared into the horizon. The sky took on a grayish cast and the island lost its vibrant green in the scrubby but hardy bushes. He found himself staring at the barefoot prints, wandering all around him with no sense of order or purpose. The locust-like insects began their loud whirr into the night, and what seemed to be complete silence when Max and Jock were with him turned into bedlam. The slightest move of a tiny insect amplified a hundred times in his head. Woody put his hands over his ears and stood still, hoping to squeeze the anxieties away, but no matter what he did, he was still gripped with the fear of the unknown, of what he was, in fact, doing. He welcomed the sound of a boat in the distance and stood up to see if it was Max and Jock coming back. But the sound disappeared and he could see nothing in the darkness.

He walked over to the warehouse, nervously pacing, and looked at his watch. Eight-fifteen. They should have been back with his dinner, the light and radio, he thought. Woody walked to the shore and looked toward Smugglers, but the ridge and a neighboring island blocked the view. The insects continued their trilling symphony and Woody, gun in hand, sat down on the same rock as before to wait. It bothered him that they weren't back. He began biting his nails, the gun laid across his lap.

It was a clear night, with the Milky Way spreading a magic carpet across the sky and the moon almost full. The lights were bouncing off the water, flickering signals back to the heavens, the little islands standing out like mountains on a desert floor. Even after walking around, Woody could not shake the fear of being left alone on the island. He mentally went over the planned course for the night, trying to bring peace to his insides.

301

I'm hungry, he thought. That's what's making me feel this way. He wanted a drink, but there was nothing left, just an outline where the cooler had been and a damp spot in the sand where it had drained. Woody took a stick and started poking in the sand, writing his name, then Laura's, and drew a big heart, just like a child would do in a sandbox. How far away from life's normal humdrum he was, he thought, and imagined that a lonely mountain climber or hunter waiting to stalk the first buck of the season would feel the same way, enveloped in nature's amphitheater. He wiped out the heart and started doodling with the stick. He was just getting comfortable with the surroundings when he felt something poke him in the back. It was as if a bayonet had pierced him. He sat quietly, deathly afraid to turn around. He broke out in a cold sweat and began groping for his gun, not moving his head or any other part of his body.

"I wouldn' touch dat iffen I's you," a voice said. The effect was like cymbals crashing in the middle of a violin solo, a cherry bomb exploding in an empty fuel drum. Then the laugh started, the object in Woody's back moving as the person giggled.

"Eh, mon, you scared shitless. Nuttin' like a scared honkey. You' got a right ta be scared, too, cause iffen you not honest wid me I blowed you a tousand ways. Shobe yo' gun ober dere." Woody felt the hard object move across his back to the right, and tossed the gun aside. "Now trow yo' bullets. An' don' tries ta act smart. I knows what ya gots dere." Woody tossed the ammunition next to the gun and felt the object in his back being taken away. His eyes were smarting in fear and he blinked to get rid of the wetness welling up. He was shaking visibly.

"Dere, now," said the voice, as its source walked around to face Woody, the barrel of a 12-gauge automatic shotgun pointed at him. "We meets agin', eh?" said Juan, dressed in drab U.S. Army surplus shirt and cutoff pants. He was barefoot, his toes cutting a wide arc in the sand. The barefoot prints, thought Woody.

"Hi, Juan. What do you want?" he asked with as much composure as he could muster while still shaking. His voice was a bit higher than usual and Juan knew he was scared.

"I jis' want to know I bein' told de trut," he said. "It wouldn'

302

be nice, now, iffen dem choppers came in wid stuff and you didn't' share it wid yo' fellow smuggler now, would it?"

"They're coming in clean," said Woody, a little more relaxed, even though Juan brandished the gun across the level of his chest. "We're only giving them fuel. What do I have to do to prove it to you?" His confidence was returning.

Juan laughed. "You know I not believes a word from no honkey mon, 'specially one wid a funny leg. I's gonna see for meself when dey comes in. You by yoself now, but I knows de udders'll be back. Gimme yo' gun."

Woody reached down to pick it up, Juan following his every move with the shotgun.

"Dump de ammo," he said. Woody let the bullets fall to the ground. "Gimme de gun." He handed it to Juan, who double-checked that it was empty. He gave it back to Woody, then pointed to the rest of the ammunition. "Gimme de rest." As Woody picked up the rounds, Juan stuffed the bullets into his pockets, looking like a mini arsenal bulging at the seams. He walked over, kicked the sand around to make sure Woody had given him all the bullets, then turned and smiled.

"Now you nots pull anyting funny on me," he said, "or you be de sorry one. Don' tell yo' buddies when dey return. I's gonna be right here, lookin' on likes I been all night and you not gonna tell dem I's here. Iffen I even see you roll dose honkey eyes toward me I pull de trigger. Iffen de choppers clean I won' mess wid yo' deal. Iffen dey's got anyting at all wort rippin' off you gits nuttin' but maybe a blast o' dis gun. My boys all surroundin' here. You don' stand a chance. You hear, honkey mon?"

Woody looked at the cocky little native and said, "I hear you."

"Good, den I assumes you unnerstand, too. Sits back down an' enjoy de beautiful night, or goes back to writin' lub letters to yo' white bitch. Jis' don' forgets anyting I tells ya. You know my reputation?"

Woody shook his head. "Yeah, I know it. You proud of it?"

"Bet yo' white ass I am. No one messes wid dis black mon. No one. Not eben annuder black mon."

"I believe you, Juan. That's it?"

"Dat's it. I be watchin'. Don' fuck up." With that he was gone, into the bushes, invisible even in the bright moonlight. He was like a weasel, cunning, ruthless, with a will to kill. Woody held his empty gun and sat back on the rock. Nine o'clock. He finally heard Jock and Max returning, and stood up as the boat rounded the corner of the island. As they came up to the beach, he noticed they were in the black bomb.

"What happened to the red boat?" he asked as they tossed him a line to tie onto a bush on shore.

"Broke down again," said Jock. "Would have been here an hour ago. Had to nurse it back to Smugglers and get this one." Max was silent, not wanting to hear any more words about the red boat.

"I oughta just kiss it goodbye," said Woody, almost as a question to Max.

"I'll get the bloody thing running, don't worry," said Max, angrily. "It's something stupid, like dirty fuel or something. I'll look at it tomorrow. Want some chicken?"

"I'm starving," said Woody, feeling a wave of relief now that he had company. He reached for the foil-wrapped package and opened it. Laura had put in a couple of legs, a thigh and a plastic cup with some peas and rice, fixed native style.

"No drink?" he asked.

"Just a soda," said Jock, handing him a can.

He ate while Max and Jock carried the radio and a big flashlight off the boat and laid them next to the warehouse.

"Anything happen?" asked Jock.

"Nah," said Woody. "Pretty quiet." He spoke in a louder voice than usual, knowing that Juan would get the message.

"You know what frequency this thing's supposed to be on?" asked Jock.

Woody walked over, not wanting to say the numbers out loud, turned on the radio and tuned in the special frequency.

"This should do it," he said. "They won't be calling until almost eleven-thirty, though, so no sense in leaving it on. Did you get the new batteries for the light?"

"Yeah," said Jock. "They're fresh." He flicked it on, the

powerful beam showing the landing area. "We can shine it from here. No sense climbing up there unless we have to," he said, glancing to the roof of the warehouse. "You bring some cards, Max?"

Maxwell finished securing the boat and tossed an anchor off the stern.

"Yup. Right here." He patted a shirt pocket and waded ashore, raggy jeans rolled up, carrying his sneakers. He sat down on the rock Woody was sitting on earlier and put on his shoes. "Here, Woody. You want to deal?" He gave him the deck and the three got comfortable.

"Might as well play poker as talk about nothing," said Woody, glad something would pass the time away while Juan lurked in the bushes. The gun was across his lap, useless, but keeping up a good front.

"Look at that moon," said Jock, glancing up. "Can even read the cards."

The game began and went on through several hands, the cards getting damp from the sand and evening dew. Woody kept the conversation "safe," knowing that every word was being mentally recorded by Juan. Before they knew it, the moon was almost overhead and the choppers were due to arrive.

"It's eleven o'clock," said Woody. "Let's fold and get on with what we're here for. We better start getting the fuel out so we can work the pump easier."

They went to the warehouse and began carrying the plastic containers outside, lining them up along the wall. The first one was ready with the pump. It would be a matter of switching from one to the next until the choppers were fueled. Woody turned on the radio and waited.

At eleven-forty, he heard a call.

"Whirly One to Woodpecker. Come back."

Woody grabbed the mike and answered back, the adrenaline flowing and Juan almost forgotten.

"Woodpecker to Whirly One. Come in."

"Whirly One is twenty minutes out and on time. Number Two is fifteen minutes behind us. You ready?"

"Come on in. Everything's a go," said Woody, the

excitement mounting in his voice.

"Lights on at eleven-fifty-five."

"Roger. Woodpecker standing by."

The next few minutes dragged as they checked over the fuel supply, the pump, the light. But at ten to midnight they could hear the low hum of the chopper, coming in from the northwest. At eleven-fifty-five, Jock turned the light on the landing area, and in what seemed like only seconds, the chopper was hovering over the site, easing down for the landing. The pilot gave the thumbs-up signal, the copilot pointed to the fuel tank cover, moving around in the obviously empty chopper, and Woody crouched as he went to open the fuel tank. Max brought the hose and Jock made sure the fittings were tight. In only minutes, the fuel was flowing. As one container was emptied, Jock moved on to the next, Woody helping him to keep up a steady flow. In about ten minutes, the chopper was full. Woody tightened the cap, gave the thumbs-up signal to the pilot, and joined Jock and Max at the warehouse. The chopper spewed loose sand in a clockwise sweep and they could see Whirly Number Two coming in behind. The second chopper was fueled just as fast and everything went without a hitch. They congratulated each other, Woody especially happy that Juan had not interfered. Jock grabbed the light and radio and Max and Woody each picked up a fuel container. The tide had gone out and the black boat was resting on the sand, so it was easy to load. When they were ready to shove off, Jock noticed Woody's gun.

"Where's your ammo?" he asked. "You had a bunch earlier."

"Stashed it back there in case we need it some other time. I got more at Smugglers," he said, more reassuredly than he felt. Now was not the time to tell them about his encounter with Juan. "Let's go back and celebrate. Made us some big bucks, boys. Some big bucks."

"Any chance of meeting Howard tonight to get our share?" asked Max, somewhat eagerly.

"It can wait till tomorrow," said Woody. "What I want right now is a drink. A good, tall glass of rum with some water and a squeeze of lime. Tomorrow's soon enough for the green stuff. I want a drink."

They headed back to Smugglers, the wake of the boat bouncing like fluorescence in the moonlight, the choppers on their way to finish the job.

* * *

Once back at Smugglers, Woody hit the rum hard, trying to wipe out the fears and tensions of the past few hours. When he was mellowed out and Max and Jock were feeling no pain with him, he told them how Juan had watched the whole deal, and about how he had threatened Woody's life. They sat wide-eyed as he blew the encounter out of proportion, Laura horrified at what he had been through.

"You gonna tell Howard?" asked Jock.

"Think I better, since he already talked with the little bastard," said Woody.

"So he got your bloody ammo?" asked Max.

"Yeah, but you can see why I couldn't tell you, right?" asked Woody, looking for support. "You'd have done the same thing. No, on second thought, you'd be telling us you'd have it fixed tomorrow, Max. That's what you'd be telling us."

Everyone got a good laugh but Max, who sat with a scowl on his face, downing rum on the rocks. He was particularly miffed with Jock.

"Thought you were my friend," he said, looking him in the eye.

"I am, Max, but that was too much. Aw come on. See some humor in it."

But Max could see no humor. He continued to drink as Woody expanded some more on his story, Juan's gun getting bigger, his language fouler and the threats more dangerous. It was almost three in the morning before the booze leveled everyone out, happy the fueling was done and that Woody was there to tell about it.

* * *

The next morning Woody, Jock and Max tied the red boat to

307

the black boat and headed for Sandy Cay. Woody was hung over and didn't want to talk to anyone. Max and Jock weren't too wide awake either, but Max had more of a purpose, more direction than anyone else that morning. He wanted a pile of money and he wanted it bad. Woody held his ears as the motor ground out a dull roar and Jock perched himself so he wouldn't bounce too hard. As they pulled into Conch Inn marina they could see the village already in full swing for a weekday. Wash was being hung, children were heading to the small school, and workmen were painting the outside of the church. They tied the black boat up, and eased the red boat over to Max's working dock. They didn't say anything as they passed Max's locked shop on the way to the airstrip.

"Why do we always have to climb this goddamn hill when we're half dead?" asked Woody, groaning and limping more than usual. "This is going to finish me off."

"Come on," said Max. "There's money at the top of that bloody hill. Like the end of the rainbow. Come on." He walked twice as fast as Woody and Jock, and reached the Nest first. Howard obligingly opened the door.

"Well, look who's here first. And Woody. What did you do to yourself? You look like death," he said. "Hi, Jocko. Come in, boys. Come in." He let them sit and get comfortable before saying anything.

"Coffee?" he asked. Woody moaned yes, Jock and Max nodded their heads in agreement. Howard grabbed three mugs, poured and brought them to the table.

"How did it go? I know they got the fuel all right and everything went well on the other end. Any problems?"

"Had a visit from that little black bastard Juan when Jock and Max went back to Smugglers for the radio and light," said Woody. "Scared the shit out of me but I handled him okay. He said if there was anything worth ripping on the choppers we were dead. I was glad you had talked to him, Howard, or he would have probably blown us to hell after finding nothing on board. Could have been a bad scene. As it was, it wasn't too pleasant."

"I'm surprised he didn't give you more trouble," said

308

Howard, thinking. "Consider yourself lucky. We all can. He's the meanest, sorriest, most ruthless of all the rippers. His granddad didn't come close as a wracker compared to Juan. What weapon did he have?"

"Twelve gauge shotgun. Automatic," sad Woody. "You ever look down the barrel of one of those things or have one waved across your chest? The old heart really flipped out. Jesus, was I scared."

"Last night you were telling us how brave you were," said Jock, teasingly.

"You can sit there and say that," said Woody. "You weren't looking that little fucker in the eye."

"Okay, boys. Knock it off. Anything else I should know?" He looked from one face to the next, everyone shaking his head no.

"Then is it my imagination that I saw a black boat towing a red one?" He looked at Max.

"It'll be running later today. Think it's in the fuel tanks," said Max without expression.

"Uh huh," said Howard. "Am I wrong, or does that sign by your shop say you're a mechanic?"

Max glared back at Howard but didn't say anything for fear his share would be cut.

"Okay, boys. I'll divvy up the cash. The big load is still on the way, though. Terry and Juney made it south and picked up the shipment. They should be back in a couple weeks or so. They're taking it easy, cruising so they don't look suspicious." He went to his briefcase and pulled out three stacks of bills held together with rubber bands. They could see ten individual packets in each bundle.

"Ten grand apiece for now," said Howard. "You'll have at least fifty when the *Sea 'n' Be* returns and the load's safe. Any questions?"

"I thought we were supposed to get fifteen today," challenged Max.

"Look who's talking," said Howard, mocking him. "You're not even doing your job. You're nothing but a warm body, Max. I'd take the ten and shut up if I were you. You really piss me off, you know. And I don't like to be pissed off, especially by scrawny Aussies who think they're hot shit. Understand?"

Max shook his head yes.

"Any other complaints?"

"No sir," said Woody. "I'm happy as shit with ten grand right now. But I'll be happier when the next load goes down."

"We all will be. What about you, Jock. Okay?

"Fine," he said. It was especially fine since he'd gotten another two grand earlier for the short flights he'd made for Howard, but he couldn't talk about that to the others.

"Okay. Here's what's happening now. I'm leaving and I don't know when I'll be back. I'm taking the nightscope and a few other things I consider personal, so don't go poking around up here. I'll be in touch, but it may be awhile. Any questions?" He looked at the three, totally out of touch with the day. "Okay. Then I guess this is goodbye for now. Should I call the meat wagon?"

Jock looked at him and chuckled. Even Max almost smiled. Then they looked at Woody, who stood up and ran for the bathroom.

"At least he's alive," said Jock.

"For now," said Howard. "If he keeps it up he might as well kiss his sweet ass goodbye. He'll end up drooling and rolling his eyes in some nut house."

Woody came back, his face red and puckered.

"You got a beer handy?" he asked.

Howard went to the small refrigerator.

"You finishing yourself off?" he asked, opening the can. Woody took it and guzzled half.

"I'll live I guess. We better go," said Woody. "Sorry about this little scene, Howard. I couldn't help it."

"I know," he said. "Okay, boys. Out of here. I'm packing and clearing out. Jock, I'll expect you at the plane at noon. You'll be taking me back."

Jock nodded, and picked up his money. Max had already counted each individual stack to make sure it amounted to ten grand and had stuffed it in his pants and shirt pockets. Woody took his and tried to figure out where to put it. He didn't have any pockets in his shirt and his pants were too tight. Howard went in the kitchen and found a small brown sandwich bag.

"Here," he said. "Take it easy now."

"Yeah, Howard, I will," he said, and followed Max and Jock out the door and down the path, happy to be taking some bucks back to Laura.

PART THREE

Chapter 14

Slow September

September was always a quiet month in the islands. Vacationers were home grinding out weekly paychecks for another holiday, and the islands fielded the predicted series of tropical storms, mostly false alarms.

It was the time to fix the docks, the generators, to patch up the cottages and clean out the kitchen. Helen called September "bankruptcy blues" time, when extra help was sent home and the island readied itself for the coming winter tourist season. Only a little money dribbled into the Sandy Cay Club at this time of year, mostly from stragglers or delivery crews wanting to fuel on their trip south. It was a lonely time for Pete, with Helen and Johnny in the States for school.

This year seemed especially dreary, he thought, sitting on the front porch of the club. Captain Ned Kilpatrick had gone north with his schooner, and Charlie flew in only about once a week. Pete had heard that Maxwell was talking about joining Pat in the States. Jock kept up a steady flight schedule, prompted mainly by Max feeding him what business there was and by free-lancing on his own, delivering briefcases and transferring people whenever asked. Howard had mysteriously left the island three weeks before. No one heard anything about him since. It would be a slow fall, Pete thought, and decided to check the generator.

* * *

Even though the Sandy Cay Club was quiet, Smugglers Cay was still alive. Woody delighted in wooing the few remaining cruising yachtsmen and by contrast, Smugglers looked like boom city, as if a shipwreck discovery had lured every sailor around with tales of pieces of eight and gold doubloons. Smugglers was the place to go because Woody didn't charge dockage, drinks were usually on the house and a good dinner the price of a

315

welfare lunch on the mainland. Woody decided that if he was going to be open during the slow months he was going to have what little traffic there was. The giveaway attracted those seeking a fake fortune.

Since Howard left Woody hadn't received any orders, and he needed people around him, lots of people, to keep up the excitement, to whirl the merry-go-round at a pace he'd become accustomed to, with the partying and the carrying on that Caribbean living was supposed to be all about. One thing he didn't have, however, was fuel. When the outboards needed juice or the generator coughed or the boys needed diesel or gas to make their runs, they went to the Sandy Cay Club.

The weather had cooled off a little, but the afternoon thunderstorms were still taken for granted. Maxwell had asked Jock to get more parts for the red boat and Woody was furious that it hadn't run right since June.

* * *

Back at Sandy Cay, Pete put in an order for a barge to drive some more dock pilings and was going over receipts from the previous month when he heard a plane overhead. The radio room was locked so he walked outside and looked up. Charlie. Good, he thought. We can get some other things done while he's here.

He grabbed his keys and walked to the Jeep, now starting to show the wear of only six months on the island. The body was rusting, the plywood top was warping from the rains and it groaned more and more on starting. Pete took the back road to the airstrip, not wanting his bad muffler to disrupt the quiet of the village, particularly with school in session. Even the little sign tacked to a tree at the picnic grounds advertising the yellow house as a store looked weathered from summer heat and rain.

As he pulled into the tiedown area, Charlie was taxiing the plane. Pete recognized Joe Jenkins and his pretty wife, owners of Lucky's old island. Charlie would be loaded with a variety of gear and supplies. As he opened the rear door of the plane, Charlie waved.

"Boy, am I glad to see you," he said. "This guy even has me

316

hauling cement today. Can you believe it?" Pete chuckled.

"Sure. When you can't get it in the islands you have to be resourceful. If you've got the bucks to fly it in, why not? What else is there?"

Charlie handed out boxes to Jenkins. His wife Mary watched the scene, impeccably dressed in white pants, a navy and white knit top and white scarf tying her long blonde hair at the base of her neck.

"A radial arm saw, some chair cushions, a cooler of meat. You name it," said Charlie, "and Jenkins will put it on the plane."

"Just trying to do it the easy way," said Joe. Some people called him by his first name, others by his last. It made no difference to him. "I tried to get a barge and they wanted too much money. The smugglers have the corner on cargo planes and you can't get one at a decent rate. I figure as long as I come to my island every weekend I might as well have Charlie bring in as much as he can each time. Makes sense. You don't mind, do you, Charlie?"

"Hell no," he said. "Makes my payments. That's all I'm concerned with right now. Just making the payments. Jock come in?" He turned to Pete.

"Saw him yesterday, then he took off. He'll probably be back today or tomorrow if he follows the pattern," said Pete. "You hear any more?"

"Heat's really on him. He's violating every rule in the book — in both countries. But you know the bureaucrats. Also, they suspect he's got someone on the take."

"Real cool," said Pete, shaking his head. "You can't compete with that kind. He'd sell his mother."

"Only after putting her on the streets first," said Jenkins. "I talked with him a couple of trips ago. He's got one of those plastic smiles you'd like to bust. I wouldn't trust him for a second. I told Charlie he should hurry things up a bit."

"I don't want to invite trouble, but he's jeopardizing my right to earn a living. If Jenkins keeps me going in the off-season, I'll be able to hang in and fight. We'll see what happens. Aviation authorities are going bananas because everyone who flies with Jock says they're sharing expenses. You and I know what he's doing and so do they, but it has to be able to stand up in court, if it comes to that. So they want to be damn sure when they nail him. Can't blame them at all."

They loaded as much as they could in the Jeep, then Jenkins and Mary said they would walk to the government dock. Pete drove their gear ahead. Old Conley, the caretaker for Jenkin's island, had been notified he was coming in. As usual, he hadn't "reached" yet, but they could see a boat in the distance.

When Pete and Charlie had Jenkins' gear stacked on the dock and ready to go, they chatted with him for a few minutes. "You don't have to wait for Conley," said Jenkins. "That's him for sure. Go back Sunday?"

"You're calling the shots," said Charlie. "Sunday's fine. Gives me a chance to help Pete out. Have some business to discuss." As they talked, a plane flew overhead, buzzing Conch Inn.

"Isn't that the police?" asked Charlie, looking up. "That's the same plane that came to investigate the crash. Wonder what they're doing here."

"What you really mean is you wonder what took them so long," said Jenkins, laughing. "It's about time the authorities started poking around and finding out what's going on. This place isn't the same anymore. I thought by buying out Lucky it would be different, but I guess that was just the beginning. They're all crazy." Jenkins waved to Conley as he pulled alongside the dock and Pete and Charlie turned to get in the Jeep. Manny was starting his Jeep to pick up the police when they drove by Conch Inn. Pete stopped.

"Isn't that the constable?" he asked Manny, who nodded yes. "What's he doing here? Something going on?"

"How do I know, mon. I jis' know dey gettin' fed up wid all de reports o' stuff goin' on here. I take care o' dem and send dem on dere way. Don' want dem pokin' 'round here."

"Why not?" asked Pete, looking him square in the eye. "A lot of crazy things have been going on and it's not good for the island. You know that. I see Max is still squatting in that shop. He ever pay you any rent?"

Manny didn't want to get into the Maxwell-Pete situation and he steered clear of making any judgments.

"Nah. Told him it okay. He gonna fix de generator."

"Just like he's gonna fix Woody's red boat?" Pete and Charlie smiled.

Manny couldn't help but smile back. "Le's hope he do better at de generator. Well, I gots ta pick up de constable, gits him drunk and maybe gits him laid. Dat should do it."

"Lovely, huh?" said Pete, waving to Manny and looking at Charlie. "Get the constable's mind off his business so the dopers can run circles around him. It's a losing battle, my friend, a losing battle." He shook his head and wrestled the transmission into first gear.

"It's only a matter of time, Pete," mused Charlie. "The locals will only put up with it so long. Look at Maxwell. He's digging a hole for himself. The natives hardly even talk to him anymore. He's like a mad man and they know it. Look at Jock. The authorities know about him. We need patience, my friend. Lots of it. What do you always say? You can't control people, places or things? Well, Pete, no matter how you cut it, we can't change the bastards. But we can work within what little system there is. Max fired off another hate letter, by the way. This time I answered in defense because it was to someone high up in the ministry. All I did was explain who I am and why I am here and why it's important I continue to operate. Brought in all the mercy flying stuff. I don't expect an answer, but at least I've stated my rights."

"Good. I've thought it would come to that and I'm glad it's happened. Max's house must look like a pigsty since Pat left."

"From what I hear it wasn't much better than a whorehouse before," said Charlie. "I understand that Sam, the sailor who was here this summer, arrived back in the States and that she's keeping company with him."

"Oh yeah? Well, I heard that the crew off the three-master that was anchored here in July took her on too. When's Max planning on heading back?"

"I don't know. You aren't the only one no one talks to, and for some reason I can't hear the drums beat. When he leaves I

319

guess we'll know it. Three days on this rock," said Charlie, shaking his head. "I have to be as crazy as the rest of you."

Pete laughed. "Well, I hate to tell you, but there must be something here or you wouldn't go through the pain of trying to stay. You had lunch?"

Charlie shook his head no.

"Let's go raid the kitchen. How does that sound?"

"Great," said Charlie. Both of them were hooked on the chocolate brownies and Maria obligingly ordered double what she would need for dinner guests. She knew they disappeared from the freezer when she wasn't around, and she loved teasing Pete and Charlie about stealing them.

Pete parked and they headed for the kitchen.

* * *

As the local representative for the political party in power and the owner of the native hotel, it was Manny's job to make sure visiting dignitaries, no matter what level, were housed and entertained. So when three policemen in uniform landed, they automatically headed for Conch Inn. Their pilot, dressed in dark pants and a green and yellow striped shirt, was not known for his protocol and flew the police more as a hobby than an occupation. No one ever told him to dress otherwise, so he didn't, enjoying himself like a tourist with carte blanche privileges wherever he went.

"Hello dere," said Manny, as they walked over to him. "You know sometin' we don'? Who send fo' yo?"

"Hey dere, Manny, how's it goin'? You gots ice in dat place yet o' did dat mad Australian still sidestep ya?"

"He's still working on it. You on business or jis' here to fool 'round? No one's on de island. Like it dead, so don 'spect no fancy womens or anyting likes dat," said Manny .

"No, mon. We's on business," said the chief constable, with the accent on "ness." "We needs some infomations from you 'bout dat man dat bought Smugglers Cay. You know him?"

"Woody?"

"Yeah. A mistah Woodrow Cameron. Hab some udder

320

names, too, but we talk ober a cold beer, eh? You send a boy down to de yacht club and hab 'im bring back ice. I wants my drinks cold. Got lots o' business dis trip. Hate it when dere's sometin' goin' on. I no likes to work, ya know."

"I know, jis' like de rest o' us," said Manny. As they were getting comfortable on their barstools a plane buzzed overhead and the chief constable went out to take a look.

"Yeah. Jis' as dey told us. Dat guy in dat plane. What he do?" He turned to Manny.

"He jis' fly people in an' out. Max sets 'im up. He also fly de parts and tings for Maxwell," said Manny.

"Dat ain' all he fly," said another policeman, the youngest in the trio. "He fly shit all ober de place. He been caught before. He also bring' stuff in wid no duties paid. He not what we consider de type o' person to better de islands."

Manny got quiet, not wanting to stir up more trouble. It wouldn't help him and could easily backfire. Just then Maxwell started his Jeep near the workshop. The head constable motioned the younger one to follow him and they began walking the short distance to the airstrip, beers left on the counter. They arrived just as Max and Jock were leaving, loaded with a few things Jock brought over in the plane.

"Oh shit," said Max under his breath, recognizing the burly constable with the billy stick and hand gun. "Wonder what that bloody bloke wants. Thought it was the heat that landed but I wasn't sure. And this one is straight — not like a lot of the others."

"Play it cool," said Jock, and he put on his best grin for the gendarmes.

"Hi," he said. "Anything we can help you boys with today?"

"Dat depends," said the constable. "I'd like to sees yo' paperwork."

"Sure," said Jock. "No problem. Left it in the airplane."

As Max turned the vehicle around, Jock confided that duty hadn't been paid on the parts for the boat, nor had he declared everything in the Jeep.

Jock climbed into the plane and pulled out a crumpled transire.

321

"Here," he said, handing it over. "Most of that stuff I picked up at another island. Duty was paid a long time ago."

"Do you hab de paper fo' it from de udder island? An' I don' see where you been dere before you comes here. Dis paperwork not in order at all. What's in dat case?" He pointed to a briefcase stuck under a seat.

"Can't remember. Just some old charts and things. Never look in it," said Jock, mentally beating himself for not stashing the case in the hidden compartment. "I forgot to take it out of the plane the other day." Jock smiled a wide grin. "You know how you forget about things."

"No, I don' know," said the constable. "Let me see it."

Jock nervously reached for the black case.

"It's locked," he said, "and I don't have the key with me."

"Den we breaks it open, don' we?" said the constable, noting that Jock had become a bit nervous even though he was keeping up a smiling front. He took the case and picked at the lock. It was a combination and wouldn't budge. The constable took out a knife and began slitting the case. Jock kept quiet, not saying anything. He had a feeling he knew what was inside, but on Howard's orders, he had picked it up to deliver to an island further south. They were expecting it tomorrow. He doubted now if he would be able to make the connection.

Beads of sweat formed on his forehead and under his nose, giving his scruffy beard and mustache a wet look. Jock kept smiling, but inside he wanted to get in the plane and fly away. He knew he'd have to let the scene play itself out. The briefcase was rugged, but the constable's knife was sharp.

"I woulda blowed de lock off but I neber knows what's inside dese tings and I don' wanna blast anything dat might be useful, no?" He looked at Jock as he worked on the case. He took his time slicing through the top and down one of the sides. He pried it open. Jock began nervously scratching his head and shifting from one foot to the other. Maxwell stood firm, not knowing what was in the case and comfortable that he wasn't part of the deal. In minutes, the constable was gazing at stacks of bills.

"You look like poor mon to hab all dis bootiful green stuff

in here," he said. "How much in de case?"

"I don't know," said Jock, convincingly. He really didn't. He was just glad it was money and not cocaine or some other substance. Money was an easy one to beat. "Let's count it. Hell, if I'd known it was there I'd have opened it up a long time ago. I can always tell the boss it got ripped off." He looked at the head constable, raising his eyebrows for a response.

"I sho yo' could," he said, fingering the money. "We's goin' ta see 'bout dis. We'll take it back and count it and gib you a receipt. Den we's goin' ta de main prowince and yo' gonna 'splain yo'self. We tryin' ta clean up de act and boys like you jis' mess it up for eberyone else. You not too smart takin' sumpin' you not eben know what it gots in it. Who yo' boss mon?"

"Don't know his name," he lied. "All I do is get paid for flying."

"You got a license to do dat?" He looked at him questioningly, white circles around piercing black eyes.

"I got a license," said Jock, reaching for his wallet.

"Big deal," said the constable, looking at the certificate Jock showed him. "Dat jis' say priwate pilot. No commercial, no nuttin' else. You not legal nowhere iffen you puts a warm payin' body in dat bird. You knows dat?"

Jock didn't answer, but started kicking stones in an arc around his foot, still with the pasted smile on his face.

"Okay. Don' wan' you leabin' till dis straighten out, you unnerstand?" Jock shook his head yes. "Good. Dere's no jail here an' I not goin' to handcuff you to a tree in dis hot sun. I sugges' you tinks 'bout dat man's name you works fo' 'cause dat be an important ting to report. No funny business, yo' two, o' you bote be sorry white mons. Unnerstand?"

Max and Jock nodded. "Good. Now you gib us a ride back to Conch Inn so's we kin counts dis money."

"Need any help?" asked Jock, back to his brazen self.

"No. We no need yo' help. I kin counts dis stuff widout you starin' at me. I let you know what I's come up wid. Neber you mind. But you's in trouble, mon. Don' mind tellin' you dat. You's in big trouble. Stick 'round. We mights be here longer dan we plans."

Jock and Max drove the constables to Conch Inn, then Max backed down to his workshop, picked up parts for the red boat and walked down the dock, not saying a word to Jock.

"Hey, man, you mad at me?" Jock had to walk fast to catch up with him. Max continued walking down the dock, then stepped aboard the red boat. He was mad. Anyone looking at him would know he was mad.

"What the fuck you trying to do to us?" he finally growled at Jock. "How much bread was there? You know damn well you'll never get a right count on it. And you know your ass is in a sling. What do you plan to do about it? Those bloody guys stick around and we'll ALL be in trouble."

"Hey, cool it," said Jock. "Don't worry. So we pay them off and go about our business. He's been paid off before. I recognize him from a bad deal further south. Besides, that was peanuts compared to what's stashed in the nose compartment."

"What?" asked Max, pointedly and slowly.

"I got five kilos of coke up front, all sealed in. Just picked it up to go with the cash, but now I've got to change my plan. The money they got was nothing," he said. "As long as I can scoot out I've got it made. So play their silly games, let them think all I had was the money and let it go. Shit, Max. Don't worry about those assholes. Just get this boat fixed, will you? I'm tired of bringing in parts. The shop in the States thinks I'm crazy too. I finally told them it was for another boat because I was too embarrassed to let them know you still haven't got this one running."

"Thanks a lot," said Max, dryly, wiping his hands on a rag and reaching for another part. As he looked up, he said, "Oh shit."

Jock looked, too. All three policemen and the pilot were walking toward them. When they reached the red boat, the head constable said, "You got a boat to take us to Smugglers?"

"This thing isn't running yet," said Maxwell. "You check with Manny? He has a boat."

"Jis' dat puny ting," said the constable, pointing to a little runabout. "We wants to go see dat place. Unnerstand dat Woody

324

mon dumped lots o' money into de island. We wants ta see what he did. Maybe we gits a boat from de yacht club. Tings seem to run better dere. Hope de owner not payin' yo' by de hour fo' dat red boat," he said, shaking his head. Max was becoming legendary.

With that, all four walked back to Conch Inn.

"You notice he didn't say anything about the bloody money?" asked Max, looking up to Jock on the dock.

"Yeah," said Jock. "I've kissed it goodbye. Just play it cool, huh? You tend to get a little hot under the collar and they can sense that. Keep cool, let them leave and we'll get back to business. I think Woody should be warned, don't you?"

"Yeah. Give me a second here, then we'll drive to my place and take the boat up there. Cops won't even know we've left. They're probably still drinking Manny's beer."

"You mean Manny's WARM beer," said Jock, chuckling. It was so easy to get to Max. He ruffled at the slightest implication of his incompetency.

"Let's go," said Max, closing his tool box, ignoring the comment. "This will have to wait for tomorrow. I can't work under such bloody pressure."

The two gathered up the parts and tools and walked nonchalantly down the dock, locked up Max's shop and climbed into the Jeep. They waved as they drove by the bar, the four gendarmes enjoying themselves. Pete and Charlie were at the club workshop when Jock and Max drove by. Max stared straight ahead but Jock turned and smiled.

"What a pair," said Pete, softly laughing to himself and shaking his head.

"They deserve each other," said Charlie.

"I've heard they think so too," said Pete, and they both laughed.

As Pete and Charlie walked back to the club, they heard Jackson approaching on *Cyclops*.

"Hey, Jackson. What's the good word?" asked Charlie as he pulled up.

"You know de constable's here?" he asked rather excitedly.

"Tree cops and dere pilot. Dey hassle Jock, den dey carry bag to

Conch Inn, and now dey lookin' fo' a boat to take dem ta Smugglers. You wants me ta offer ta take dem in yo' boat?"

Pete and Charlie looked at each other.

"Go ahead Jackson. This may be an answer to a prayer," he said, smiling. "Give them a good tour. The longer they're in the area the squirrelier Max and Jock will be and Woody will go insane. He got Jock on something, though, huh?"

"I don' know de full story. Dey neber say, but I can tells by de way dey talk dat dey onto sumpin'. We see, eh? I tells dem dey got boat yo' compliments."

"Good thinking, Jackson. Let us know what happens," said Pete.

Jackson got back on *Cyclops* and rode toward the village to tell the constable he would take him to Smugglers Cay. Jackson smiled. He hadn't been to Smugglers since taking Woody and Laura the first day, but he had heard plenty about what went on at the white man's play patch. Jackson could now get a first-hand glimpse at what had been done since old man Miller went mad and left. The natives had talked about it being nice. Now he'd get the chance to see. And by taking the constable and his party, Jackson would be in good light with the authorities. He parked *Cyclops*, jumped down, and went into Conch Inn, a big smile on his face.

* * *

As soon as Jock and Max arrived at his house, they walked down the path to the little runabout. In minutes, they were heading toward Smugglers, Max's jaw set firm, Jock enjoying the ride. As they pulled into the harbor, they noticed Woody had plenty of company. A couple of sailboats and several little speed boats had found safe keeping at Smugglers, in more than one respect. Woody came out of the club to greet them.

"Hey, how ya doing, guys?" he yelled. "Max! What you so scowly about? Haven't seen you smile in months. Jock! Thought I saw you fly in before. Come in. We have a good crew here."

He took the lines and tied up the little boat.

"I don't really want to ask, but how's the red boat coming?"

326

said Woody.

"Jock just brought in more parts," said Max. "We should have it now. Have other news, though. Bloody constable arrived at Sandy Cay today, shook Jock down, got some big bucks, and said they were on their way here. They're looking for a boat to bring them."

"They aren't too pleasant today," added Jock. "I'm sure we bought a little consideration with the cash they found in my plane, but the heat's on."

"That's almost funny coming from you," said Woody. "From what I hear you're used to the heat."

"Yeah, but we better take a look around so they don't find anything."

"Shit. We're as clean as a baby's ass in bathwater today. Let 'em come," he said. "What do they drink? I'll have plenty of it. Wish we had some of Lucky's broads about now. That would clinch a clean shakedown for sure."

"Don't count on it," said Max dryly. "For some reason they're serious this time. They're not down here joy riding. Something's up."

"Well, I'll consider where the feelings are coming from," said Woody. "You're the doomsday pessimist, Max. Did anyone ever tell you how depressing you can be? Come on in. You need a cool rum punch to bring you around. Don't let the bastards scare you, man. All they can do is hassle. They've got about as much authority as my little finger here." He raised it up and waved it in the air, limping into the club. Some rather rough characters were sitting around the bar.

"Hey, boys, we've got a welcoming committee on the way. The local police have decided to party it up here for awhile, so just keep it cool and watch 'em get drunk and pass out," said Woody. A few looked around at each other and started to leave.

"Come on, guys. Stay. You take off now and it'll look like you're guilty."

He heard a boat approaching and looked out.

"Jesus, Jock, you weren't kidding. And look who's bringing the bastards. Thought he had more sense."

Woody could see Jackson coming into the harbor with a

Sandy Cay Club boat loaded with officials. "Well, guess we gotta welcome them aboard this little rock. Anyone care to join me?"

The entire place emptied out, with about a dozen people watching as Woody helped tie up the boat. He shook Jackson's hand, then extended it to all the authorities. The head constable looked at all the faces and noticed Jock and Max.

"You boys runs fas' when we's onto yo' game," he said, looking straight at Jock. "Tought I told yo' to stick 'round."

"I don't call a couple of miles running away from the scene," said Jock, shrugging it off. "Where can we go in that little thing?" He pointed to Max's thirteen-foot boat. "We just knew where the cold beer was and where the rum punch socks it to you. Be our guest. What can we get you?"

"We'll take yo' up on some cold beers, but don' you tinks fo' one minit I forgets who and what you is. Who's dis Woodrow Cameron guy. He around?"

"Woodrow! Woodrow! That's your name?" asked one of the sailboat bums still hanging around the dock. Woody laughed.

"That's my name, mon. What can I do for you? Have you ever been to Smugglers before? Take a look around. We've spent a lot of bucks here, improving this little piece of real estate for the islands," said Woody, talking faster than usual. "Hey, Jackson, remember the first day you brought me here? Looks different, huh?"

"It sure do, Woody. It sure do. You must gots lots o' money ta gits all dis done," he said, purposely alluding to the subject of finances.

The constable finished one beer and reached for another.

"That's right," said Woody. "Just help yourself. Anything you want, you just take."

The constable looked at the patronizing man with a twinge of disgust but didn't say anything for a couple of minutes.

"Den yo' no mind iffen we walks 'round de place?" he asked Woody.

"No. Go right ahead. I'll even escort you so you don't miss anything," he said.

"I goes by meself soes I don' miss nuttin'," said the

constable. The younger man laughed. The pilot shook his head, reached for another beer, and the third gendarme sat silent. He was the quiet one, the one to record in his brain everything taking place, the smart one.

"Come on, boys. Let's take a look at dis place. We be back in a bit. You serbe anyting to eats later?"

"Whatever you want," said Woody. "Laura will have a pot of conch chowder ready when you get back. Need anything just let me know. Have a look around."

Inwardly, he was dying. There had been no way for him to move the fuel containers, now empty, to another point on the island. Another boat had also unloaded some bales the other night and no one had swept the place clean. Woody fixed himself a strong rum, then turned to Max and Jock.

"Glad you guys showed up," he said. "There's a lot of shit happening that I can't tell you about now but maybe later. I'm not too happy with that head constable. He's onto something."

"He's the bloke that busted the Sand Dollar operation," said Maxwell, straight-faced and with a bit of snarl to his voice. "We don't stand a chance."

"You want some coke or pot or anything, Max?" asked Woody. "You're in bad shape, man. I got some stuff in the drawer next to my bed up there. Go help yourself, or you're going to boil over sure as shit. You don't know it, but you're like a rubber band strung from here to eternity. Go get something."

He nodded toward the stairs to his loft bedroom, and Max took his advice. He was back in about ten minutes, in a much better mental and emotional state, the coke having unwound his system. He could cope now, he thought. He could handle it.

* * *

The constable took about two hours carefully going over the island. In that time Woody got fairly drunk, knowing that he was going to be in trouble if they saw anything at all. As the chief gendarme walked in, he headed straight for Woody.

"Mistah Cameron," he said, authoritatively. "I tinks you

betta come wid us tomorrow. We gibs you time to gits yo' tings togeda and ta make arrangements fo' someone to take care dis' island. We also wants to goes aboard dose boats in de harbor. You kin spend de night wid yo' pretty wife, den meet us at Sandy Cay by ten tomorrow mornin'. Iffen you not dere, you be in big trouble. Iffen you come and gib us no hassle, we try to be okay wid you, but as you must know, dere are certain tings goin' on 'round here. I gots my report to make. You mights want to make one yoself too, or at least tinks about it. But you gots tonight. Where's dat pilot? " He looked around and saw Jock.

"As to you I wants you at de airstrip ten tomorrow like de rest o' us. I be giwin' you a receipt."

"Sure thing," said Jock, wondering why nothing was being done immediately, the way it usually worked. Maybe they didn't have as much on them as they thought.

With that the constable and his trio walked out without requesting food, but before leaving Smugglers, the head man boarded every vessel in the harbor. One boat had discreetly left while the authorities were poking around in the warehouse filled with fuel containers. The other vessels were relatively clean.

By the time they were gone, it was late in the day. Woody became silent, fearing what would happen to him. In the meantime, he had work to do, and although a bit under the weather from the rum punch he was absorbing into his system, managed to keep his act together. After a quick dinner, he motioned for Jock and Max to follow him to the radio area.

"Listen, guys. I don't want to alarm you, but no one's heard from Howard since he left here. No one. Not Chubby, not anyone. Not even Marjorie. It's almost like he never existed to begin with, if you know what I mean. The *Sea 'n' Be* is also overdue. It's scary as hell. And now these wormy cops crawling all over the place. If I'd had a little more time we could have cleaned the place up, but shit, who expected them at the END of the season. There's some squirrely customers out in that bar, too. One boat got out of here so they should be all right, but Christ! Couldn't you have come sooner?"

"We came as fast as we could," said Jock. "Hell, they shook me down less than a half-hour before we came. I got problems too, man. Don't tell me about yours. I can't even escape with the plane without problems. The whole nose is stuffed with cocaine. I've got to get it out. They'll nail me for good."

"What you going to do?" asked Woody.

"I'll think of something," said Jock, "but I'm not going to go asking for trouble when I stand a chance to make enough to bail my ass out of anything later on. I'm thinking. I'm also not drinking, if you'll notice. I'll come up with something."

Max was still silent, the chemicals in his system keeping him at the simmering point.

"What you worried about, Max? You got nothing to lose. No house, no plane, no boat, no nothing. Your old lady's already in the States and you're fairly clean on what they can catch you on. You're the luckiest of us all," said Woody.

"Thanks," said Max dryly. "Then why do I feel so guilty?"

"Because you're paranoid as hell, Max. You better watch out. They're gonna lock you up one of these days if you can't ever find something to smile at. I don't think you realize how morose you are. You're going crazy."

Max glared at Woody and walked away, heading to the bar for a drink. He wanted to reply but he had no words in him. He was sick and tired of the whole mess, the red boat, Pete laughing behind his back, Pat screwing around and now Howard disappearing. How dare everyone do all this to him, he thought. The rum began working with the coke and he felt himself mellowing out again. Maybe it wasn't as bad as he thought. He'd get away with whatever they were going to accuse him of doing. He had a work permit, he was legal, and he belonged where he was. The merry-go-round in his mind kept bouncing the ponies up and down, the music reverberating on an invisible wire drawn between his ears. Max was into himself, totally oblivious to everything around him, withdrawn, lonely and drained of any feeling. He sat and stared while being ignored. The enemy within was creeping to the outside, wrapping him in a blanket of fears and frustrations.

Jock looked over to where Max sat and realized he had to get him back to Sandy Cay. He talked with Woody briefly on what he might do under the circumstances and wished Woody

331

luck in getting everything together.

"You think I might not be coming back for awhile?" Woody asked Jock.

"I don't know. The constable seemed to imply you were leaving for some time," he said.

"Don't believe them. I'll be back in a couple of days," he boasted. "The only evidence they've got is empty. They didn't find anything big. Not what they wanted, anyway. I'll wriggle out of it. You know Woody, here. No one's going to sling up my ass unless I'm good and ready for it. No, Jock. I'll be right back here. I'll sweet talk and spread a few bucks around and I'll be back. You watch and see. What are you going to do?"

Jock just smiled.

"I can't tell you, Woody, but you'll know," he said. "Don't worry about me. I'm an old hand at giving the slip."

"You gonna leave?" asked Woody, a little surprised.

"You'll see," said Jock. "Right now I need help in getting Max into the boat. He's in bad shape and it's getting dark. His head's all screwed up."

"No shit," said Woody. "He's not what you'd call the lovable type, either." They laughed.

* * *

Jock docked Max's boat and followed him up the path to the little house on the hill. It was a mess since Pat had left, dirty dishes cluttering the small counter and sink, clothes dropped where they had been shed. A layer of dust was over everything and water had damaged the floor from Max forgetting to close the windows against afternoon thunderstorms.

Jock went to the bathroom and found dirty towels in one corner, bits of soap lying on the shower floor, and mildew on the walls and ceiling. It was not Holiday Inn standards by a long shot. He came back to find Max sitting, staring at the floor.

"Why me?" he asked, looking up at Jock pathetically. "Why am I mixed up in this bloody mess?"

"Hell, man. You're the only one clean, like Woody said. You got nothing to worry about. Listen, Max. I'm going to say goodbye now 'cause I don't think I'll be around in the morning when you get up. You listening, man? Comprendo? Good. If anyone asks about me you don't know anything, you hear? Nothing. Last you saw I was tucking you in bed. Got it?"

Max nodded his head, then lay down on the couch, lumpy from a disarranged blanket and sheet. "I don't know nothing. That's easy. I can't stand talking to the bastards anyhow."

"Good. I'm going to try to find out what happened to Howard. It's really bothering me. This last little deal came via someone else, not him personally. You got any matches in this joint? I need a cigarette."

"You haven't been smoking," said Max.

"I know, but after not drinking today I need something."

"You want a joint?"

"No, just a cigarette. I'm trying to think if there's anything on this island I'll miss."

"It sounds like you're not coming back."

"Oh, I'll be back. Bringing people in next week, plus I've got some connections to make at an island to the south of here that I'm not supposed to talk about to anyone, not even my mother."

"What about the cops being mad about losing you?"

"Shit," said Jock. "Someone's always on my ass for something. Woody will keep them busy for awhile, then someone else will take up their time. As long as I get out of here before tomorrow morning I don't have to worry about the future. They'll forget about me and go looking for a bigger fish in the sea."

"Wish I could have that confidence. I've got other problems, too."

"No shit," said Jock. "Want to talk about them?"

"No," said Max, then he talked anyway. "I might not get my work permit renewed. Manny's mad about the generator and there were a couple of other screw-ups that have come to light with the village people."

"I heard about you borrowing some government property," said Jock.

"You hear a lot for not being here much. No one likes me

anymore. No one. After all I've done for everyone," he said, mournfully.

"Don't get on the pity pot, Max," said Jock. "I'll stick by you, ol' buddy. Don't get down in the dumps. It'll get better. Everything happens for a reason. You're here, Pat's there. Maybe you're supposed to go back."

"Where will you be?" asked Max.

"I'll be around. Don't worry about me. Get some sleep or you'll be a basket case tomorrow. Cops will probably be asking you about me, but you don't know anything, right? Nothing, Max, or it's the end. You understand?"

"Don't worry. I hate their bloody guts, especially that black pig."

"Good. Now lay down and get some rest. I'm going to do the same."

Max passed out almost instantly. Jock sat on the porch, watching the stars bounce on the water, the moon rising in the sky. He'd have to chance leaving. It was an opportunity he couldn't pass up. He set his watch alarm for six in the morning. That would be a good time.

* * *

The air was cool as Jock dressed and grabbed a few personal things he had at Maxwell's house. He didn't want to leave anything behind. He tip-toed past Maxwell, sleeping soundly on the couch curled in a fetal position.

The moon was sinking in the sky, ready to give up its post to the sun waiting for its cue on the other side of the horizon. He leisurely walked the back road to the airstrip, going toward Osprey Nest, then along the runway to the tie down area. He did a quick preflight check, unlocked the plane and climbed into the cockpit. In only minutes, the engine was started and he taxied to the runway, the plane piercing the quiet morning stillness.

Jock smiled as he lifted off, happy that he had given the constable the slip. It was sobering to think what he was going to do as he approached the States. In all the times he had cleared customs, no one had ever looked at the plane very carefully and he thought it best to come in as usual, clearing customs and going on his way. It seemed to be a longer flight than usual by himself in the early morning, and his mind wandered over the events of the past few weeks. It bothered him that Howard had not contacted him personally and that the *Sea 'n' Be* was overdue. According to the projected timetable, everyone in the operation should have been enjoying a tidy sum of cash by now, celebrating its return. But there was nothing he could do about it except hope that all was going as planned.

It was eerie flying in the dawn hours. The horizon mixed the sea and sky into a gray blur, each indistinguishable from the other, like a giant chocolate milk shake with swirls of vanilla not completely mixed in. The sun was rising behind him as he ran before it, letting it slowly overtake him. He didn't want to arrive too early or there would be suspicion on filing a flight plan and a lot of other regulations he avoided whenever possible.

He slowed the plane down a few knots, and calculated his arrival for the opening of customs, putting him legal from the nearest point of the islands to the mainland. The customs inspectors would just be coming alive with cups of coffee. He'd have no problem.

He secretly wished there was an alternative pre-arranged, but the phone number for when a deal went bad concerned Howard's operation. It wouldn't do him any good, now that he had ripped the cocaine from another contractor. He knew that the money the constable had taken was his payment for safe delivery of the coke to its destination. Jock could see no sense delivering the goods and then not getting paid, so as long as the word was out that he was pinched in the islands, he stood a chance of coming out financially by peddling the coke himself in the States.

Jock didn't want to chance landing at an abandoned airstrip because the heat was on for planes coming through radar and not clearing along the coastline. It was just as risky to avoid as to face the customs officers. Jock went through the standard procedures for landing and came in as always. He taxied to customs, noticed an inspector he knew and was relieved. He wouldn't have any problems today.

335

He killed the engine, turned off the master switch and got out of the plane, leaving it open so the man could do his job. He went to file the usual paperwork and didn't declare anything. When all the proper rubber stamps were affixed and he had turned in his personal declaration, he walked back to the plane.

"That your bird?" someone asked. He turned to see an aviation inspector walking toward him.

"Yes sir. Getting an early start on the day," said Jock, continuing to walk toward the plane.

"I'm Inspector Wilson of the FAA. We're doing routine inspections today and I might as well start with you. Can I see your paperwork and licenses?"

Jock froze, then regained composure. It's just routine, he told himself. Keep your cool.

"Sure, no problem," he said, reaching for his wallet. He gave the inspector his pilot's license, then nodded to the outside customs inspector as he climbed into the plane to get the aircraft paperwork.

"How you doing today?" he asked him, giving his standard wide smile.

"Okay. How about yourself? See you've been flying a lot lately. You come back empty?"

"Yessir. Just dropped some friends off in the islands yesterday and came back early to get to work. Didn't want to fly at night, you know."

He looked from one to the other as the aviation inspector made notes of his certificates and the customs man finally started to walk away. As he stood there, waiting for the aviation man to complete a few forms, he saw a special task force customs car pull up to the office. An officer stepped out of the car and Jock could see a beautiful German shepherd dog in the back seat. Beads of perspiration began to form on his forehead and he wished he could leave. Instantly.

"Everything okay?" he asked Inspector Wilson, who was moving a bit too slowly for him. "I've got to get to work."

"Just have to check the serial numbers and make sure all the blanks are filled in," he said, routinely going about his business. "I'll only be a couple more minutes and then you can be on your way. It all looks in order. Found a couple of things, but they're only minor and not worth citing you on."

Jock kept looking from the inspector to the customs agent putting a leash on the dog. He wanted to get on his way, to get the plane safely in the hangar, to be done with all the unexpected hassles. As the FAA inspector was finishing up, he glanced over to the car.

"Harry!" he shouted. "Haven't seen you for awhile. How's the wife and kid?"

"Hey, Wilson, how've you been?" shouted Harry, walking toward the plane with the dog. "They don't spring you from the desk very often. What's up?"

"Routine inspections. With all the illegal aliens coming in they've decided to put us back on the beat for awhile. Don't know if it'll do any good. Those guys sneak in and we've got a lot of pilots hiring out their services without commercial tickets. It's a real mess, and we don't have the manpower. So what do you do? Pick a day and hope something will break. We end up giving people like this man a hassle for no real reason. Keeps everyone on their toes, right?" he asked, turning to Jock.

Jock smiled and said, "No problem, but I really do have to get to work. The boss gets mad, you know. Figures he's paying me and I should be there. All done?"

"Just let me sign this off," he said. "When did you get the dog, Harry? Must be nice to have a companion."

"This is no ordinary dog, Wilson. This fellow can sniff out anything. Just turn him loose and his nose does all the work. It's the easy way. They call it a promotion and I call it easy street. Nothing like having man's best at your side." He patted the dog. "He's trained to sniff out dope, explosives — anything illegal. You name it, Weasel here will find it. Let me show you how he works on a dry run, sniffing around even if there's nothing to be found."

With that he gave the dog a signal, unleashed him and watched dumbfoundedly as he went for the nose section of Jock's plane and began barking. In a split second he had a gun on Jock and ordered him to lie face down. Inspector Wilson stood in shock as Harry frisked Jock and handcuffed his hands

337

behind his back.

"Sorry to do this, chap, but this is procedure. If you're clean there's no problem, but when the dog reacts we have to assume the worst for our own protection."

He turned to Inspector Wilson. "Get an inspector from inside and call the main office for a backup agent," said Harry. "We need to have that nose section opened. Where are your keys, son? It'll make it easier if you cooperate, especially if you've got something," he said to Jock.

"Right pocket," said Jock, rolling over so the agent could reach in. Beads of sweat dotted his face and the smile had turned to an expression void of emotion. Inwardly, his guts were in a knot but he dared not allow it to show. He knew there would no longer be a pot of gold on delivery of his precious cargo. All he could do now was work on the least possible penalty. Keep your ass clean, he thought, as clean as you can under the circumstances.

The agent got the key out of Jock's pocket and waited for the inspector to come to the plane. The same one who had routinely walked around the aircraft now looked at Jock with a questioning glance.

"What's going on, Jock? What'd you get yourself into?"

Jock kept quiet.

The inspector took the keys and opened the nose compartment, letting out a low whistle as he looked inside. The dog jumped wildly up and down. Harry went over to Weasel, leashed him, walked him back to the car and ordered him into the back seat. He patted him on the head before closing the door and walking back to the plane.

The customs inspector nodded at the agent and closed the compartment. Harry helped Jock to his feet and began reading him his rights. Another patrol car arrived, and Jock was locked in the back seat and on his way to the federal building. As they pulled away from the airport parking lot, another customs car arrived. Jock was upset, but didn't let it show. He mused on which was worse, being caught in his own country or bartering for freedom with the island constable.

It didn't matter now. He had made the choice. Jock stared at the early morning traffic and made up his mind not to say anything to anyone no matter how hard they tried to get him to talk. That was the law of the dopers. If you got caught, you took it and you never ratted on your fellow scammer. "Rolling over" on others in the trade could mean worse consequences outside of the law.

* * *

As the patrol car left the airport, the customs agents and FAA inspector opened the compartment to see what the cargo was worth.

"Nice cache," said Harry to the agent who had just arrived. "Tag it and plaster a sticker on the plane. What a coincidence, huh? You better get some boys from maintenance to strip this bird apart. We wouldn't want to miss anything."

Inspector Wilson was still almost speechless.

"Do you realize the balls that guy has to stand here during a ramp inspection and bring in that crap through customs? I'm going to pull the files on this character. Joachim Maynard's his proper name. I don't mind telling you I'm shocked. Seemed like such a nice guy, on his way to work and all. Just for kicks, let me call the office and see what they have on him."

"Good idea," said Harry. "Chances are pretty good this guy's had his feet wet with the law before. No virgin scammer would do what he did. He was pretty confident."

Harry and Inspector Wilson left the special agent handling the cocaine and plane and went into the office. A few minutes later, Wilson came back.

"Just found out he's been on the hot sheet for some time. Got caught three years ago with a load of grass and he's suspected of carrying passengers for hire without the proper licenses and insurance. He's not a very nice person, from what the records show. Some mechanics are on the way."

"If I'm not mistaken, he might be the money man we've been looking for, the one who's been transferring the bucks for big deals. If that checks out we've got a big one," said Harry. "You know, if we had gone after the bastard we wouldn't have

339

gotten him. When it comes down to the bottom line, the only one doing his job right this morning was Weasel."

"You trying to tell me it's a dog's world?" asked Inspector Wilson, chuckling.

"No, but I'll say one thing. If this sort of game continues the whole world will go to the dogs. I better be on my way to the federal building to file the report. This will be a good one. Still can't believe that guy's nerve."

He walked to his car, reached and patted Weasel on the head and left. Inspector Wilson watched the customs agent transfer the illegal cargo to the patrol car, then attach a red ticket to the door indicating impoundment of the plane. A line boy came with a tow bar and following the agent's instructions, moved the plane to the back line.

As the agent finished, he nodded to the FAA inspector.

"Good bust," he said. "Can't figure out why he'd chance coming through customs, though. Must have been doing it for some time. Usually the greenhorns skate through under the radar, then get caught landing in the swamps. This guy had to be a pro. Too cool. He barely flinched."

"I did a complete ramp inspection on him, too," said Wilson. "Nothing was that unusual, so I never thought to open the nose up."

"Don't worry about it. It's not your job, anyway. I have a feeling that boy is off to the pokey for some time. Nice plane. Hope it doesn't sit too long. Well, I'll be off. Good luck with the rest of your inspections today."

Inspector Wilson walked back into the customs office, still marveling at the coincidence of the bust. One way or another, dopers were eventually caught, he thought. One way or another.

* * *

While Jock was being taken to the federal building, the constable at Sandy Cay realized he was gone. Max, more rested than the previous day, walked past Conch Inn while they were eating breakfast, opened his shop and began working on the red boat. Less than five minutes went by when the big burly constable stood over him on the dock.

"Where's yo' friend?" he asked.

"Which one?" asked Max, not looking up.

"Yo' don' hab dat many," he said. "De pilot. Where he be?"

"Thought he was already here. Didn't see him this morning. Assumed he came down early."

"Yo' playin' funny, mon. Dat bastard done left de island afo' we waked up. He gone, mon, and I's a bit upset, iffen ya know what I mean."

"Left, huh? I'll be damned. You bloody well sure?" Max loved playing dumb to anyone in authority, particularly a native.

"I's gots eye, don' I? An' I tink eben me ears heard sumpin' in de early mornin' soundin' likes an engine runnin'. Yo' don' know nuttin', right?"

"That's right," said Max, standing and looking up to the constable, pushing his glasses on his nose. "You need me for anything else?"

"Don' need yo' fo' nuttin'. Hear yo' not too useful to no one 'round here. When you gonna gits to Manny's generator? You keepin' 'im from runnin' a business, yo' know. Dat's not too good, 'specially when he gibs yo' de right to works 'round here."

"I'll get to it as soon as I get this bloody boat running. Can't do everything at once. Everyone thinks his problem is bigger than the next bloke's," said Maxwell, wiping his hands.

"Yo' may be right, but iffen I wanted ta keep up in my usual style I tink I'd please de mon who lets me work in de first place. Jis' a friendly suggestion, dat's all. You tink dat Woody mon try anyting funny like dat pilot?"

Max thought for a minute, then shook his head no. "He'll be here. You didn't arrest him or anything, did you?"

"Naw. Not now anyways. We jis' wants ta talk to de gentlemens."

"But not here," said Maxwell, pointedly.

"Dat's right. Not here. Me boss mon interested in dat one," he said, smiling. "He wants to meet de mon dat hab so many stories 'bout him so soon in de islands."

"Oh?" asked Max. "What kind of stories?"

341

"Now yo' know I don' talks about confidential situations," he said, emphasizing each syllable of "confidential" and putting the accent on the last.

"I know," said Max, dryly, and went back to work.

The constable stood for a few more seconds, then turned and walked back to Conch Inn. Max looked at his watch. Nine-thirty. Woody should be on his way. A few minutes later, he heard the whirr of a motorboat in the distance and as he tightened a bolt and stood up, could see the black boat approaching the dock. Woody arrived smiling.

"Morning, Max! Take a line, would you? Great day, man. Look at that clear sky. Where's Jock?"

Max took the line and almost smiled.

"See that clear sky?" he pointed. Woody's jaw dropped as he looked at Max in disbelief.

"You shittin me?"

"Nope," said Max, and he started to chuckle, the first time in months.

"Goddamn!" said Woody, as he jumped up on the dock. "If you're smiling you must be telling the truth. Why did he do it? He could have bought his way out."

"Guess he didn't think so," said Max. "He had bigger and better things on his mind. You should have seen the bloody constable. He's pissed about losing a honkey, but that won't last long. He got Jock's money."

"How much was it?" asked Woody, toning down his voice.

"Don't know. A lot," said Max. "Think we ought to ask for his receipt? We might be able to get it back."

"Christ, Max. How naive can you be? Kiss the green stuff goodbye. You should know better. Jerk probably couldn't even write a receipt. Let's go in and face the music."

"What do you mean 'us'? He didn't say he wanted me. What did I do?"

"You're a sly little bastard, you know that? You can come for my moral support if nothing else." Woody looked around the almost empty marina. "Who does that belong to?" he asked, pointing to a thirty-foot cruiser. "Haven't seen her before, have you?"

342

"No Didn't notice. Must have come in last night. Well," he said a bit slowly, "I guess I'll come up there with you but don't drag me into anything. I'll be the only one left."

"Yeah. Nothing from Howard, huh?"

"Not a bloody word," said Max. The two walked down the dock, past Max's shop and into Conch Inn. A man in his mid-forties was talking intently with the three policemen and the pilot. As Woody and Max walked in, the head constable smiled.

"Well, look who's here. You smarter den yo' pilot friend, mon. He makes me mad, yo' know."

"I can imagine. Well, I'm here," said Woody smiling. "What's going on this beautiful morning?"

"You hear 'bout de murder down sout o' here?"

"No. What murder? What happened?"

"Dis mon, here, he jis' come up from down islands and he say he saw a boat listin' on its side and dat a young couple been murdered and dere boat smashed up."

Woody glanced at Max, a fearful chill prickling his warm skin.

"What was the name on the boat?" he asked, almost hesitantly.

"De *Sea Be*, or sumpin' like dat," said the constable. "You know who dey be?"

"Saw the vessel in here a while back but I don't know them personally," said Woody. "You saw them too, Max. They were tied at the yacht club for awhile."

"I remember," said Max, also feeling twinges of fear.

"Ain' dat de boat yo' did de exhaust work on?" piped up Manny from behind the bar, looking at Maxwell.

"Maybe," said Max. "Could be. I work on a lot of boats and don't always keep track."

"Shit yo' don'," said Manny. "Yo' could probably tell us ta de penny how much you obercharged 'im. Dat boat anchored up ta Smugglers too. I gots eyes. Ya all know dat boat. Or did. Guess dat pretty young gal and her new husband ain' no more. Shame," he said, shaking his head. "What a shame. She sho' pretty."

"Ohhh," said Woody, playing them along. "Now I know

who you mean. Gal always wore sexy duds. You sure it was them?" He didn't want to let anyone know just how close the relationship had been, or his disappointment in a deal going sour. "Did they get who did it?"

"Think it was a ripoff from that down-island bunch," said the man who had just come in. "I arrived on my boat right after it happened, the one I came in on this morning that's on the dock out there. A real bloody mess. Talk is the boys terrorized the guy's wife before killing her with him watching. Real gory scene. Bullet holes, the whole boat torn apart. Guess they asked for it, though. They're estimating the boys ripped off at least ten million in street value. Nice couple like that shouldn't have gotten mixed up with such scum. Whoever put them onto it doesn't deserve to live either."

He took a sip of warm beer from Manny's non-functioning cooler and shook his head.

"It was really bad. I was telling the constable here that no one even had time to get the authorities. The rip went so fast and so clean that it happened before anyone knew it, in a little cove just out of earshot, or I should say gunshot, of the cruising set. That was a beautiful boat, too."

"Where exactly did it happen?" asked Woody, still trying not to be overly interested. The man walked over to a chart on the wall and pointed to a little cluster of islands about three hundred miles south of Sandy Cay.

"There," he said. "Right there. I came around this island here and saw the boat. People were already on the scene and the bodies removed. I don't know where they took them. Anyway, here was this beautiful boat listing in a shallow area. When everyone cleared out a bit I went over in my dinghy. There were hatchet marks all over the inside and you could see where there was a struggle. Blood was all over the carpeting and even on the overhead. It was really bad. I've had nightmares ever since."

"When did it happen?" asked Maxwell.

"About five days ago. I haven't been sober since," he said. "Just put my boat on autopilot and headed to where there's more people. I'll never go again by myself. As a matter of fact, I'm looking for crew going back to the States. Know of anyone?"

"No," said Max. "I live here and don't plan to go anywhere."

"And I live here with no choice BUT to go somewhere," said Woody. "Right constable?"

"You's right on dat one, Woody mon. We best be gits goin, too, afore we's all partying and Manny here hab de shackles on us wid his warm beer and rum wid no ice. You bring a bag or anyting?"

"No," said Woody. "I figured I'll be back later today. Told the wife we were just going to the main province on routine. You didn't say anything about booking me." He looked at the gendarme questioningly. "I have a change of clothes I always carry with me in the boat. You think I should bring them?"

"I tink dat might be good idea," said the constable, smiling. "Yo' neber know when you need mo' clothes den what ya gots, specially goin' to de big city, right mens?"

The three smiled, and Max knew Woody wasn't being told everything. He would have to play their game and hope for the best.

"I'll get your duds, Woody. Wait here," said Max, walking out. He had to get outside. It was totally stifling hearing about the murder of Terry and Juney and the destruction of their boat. And all that cargo. All that cargo that was going to make him rich. That beautiful woman, he thought. That terrific bloke. Gone. Tears welled up in Maxwell's eyes as he realized how futile all his efforts had been to make a quick buck. He glared at the red boat as he stepped aboard the black one, grabbed Woody's clothes and stomped back down the dock. He felt sad about the death of Terry and Juney, but was furious for the mess up.

As he walked back into Conch Inn, Max caught Woody's stern glance. Outside, he whispered, "You're giving yourself away, Max. That's against the rule. Brace up. Nothing we can do, man. Nothing."

"Yo' goin' ta take us to de airstrip or do we hab to walk?" the constable asked Max.

"I'll drive you," he said, and got into his rusting Jeep. He shoved the vehicle in gear as soon as everyone was aboard and looked straight ahead as he drove the short distance.

"Dat Max, he always look mad," said the young officer. "Why you always mad, Max?" Maxwell looked at him out of the corner of his eye with contempt and continued to drive, stopping near the door of the police plane.

"Well, Max old buddy. Maybe I'll see you tonight and maybe tomorrow. Take care of Laura, okay?"

"Sure, Woody," said Max, sighing. "Don't worry."

"Don't you worry either. I'll be back. You just wait. We'll ALL be back." He smiled and climbed into the plane. A few minutes later the bird was taxiing to the runway, Woody in the company of those he most detested, on his way to an unknown destination.

Max felt exhausted as he watched the plane take off. He was angry, grieved, upset, resentful — almost every negative emotion descended upon him at once, tearing at his insides and playing with his mind. He turned the Jeep around and went back to Conch Inn, where Manny had a beer waiting.

"Sorry I had to refresh yo' memory, but dose fellas knowed you done some work on dat boat and I didn't want ta see yo' say de wrong ting," said Manny. "I sorry fo' yo', Maxwell. I'm upset wid yo' fo' udder tings which I won' talk 'bout now, but I's sorry. Beer's on me." Manny walked out, overwhelmed over what had happened.

Max sat, the merry-go-round whirling before his eyes, in his head, around his body, taking him, grabbing him, pulling him. He slammed his fist on the counter, trying to release some of the inner pain. Then he laid his head down on his arms and silently wept like a baby. He was alone. All alone. And no one understood. No one.

* * *

As the police plane landed on the main province of the island country, Woody began to have inner doubts that naturally come when those in authority know more than the individual about his personal circumstances. Although he managed to keep up a good front, he was concerned as to why he was there. The pilot had radioed for a patrol car and as the plane taxied to the

346

ramp, he could see it waiting outside the gate. He smiled to a couple of people he recognized as he walked past the aviation area for private pilots and followed the direction of the constable, now acting like King Kong with his prize catch. Woody got into the car and didn't say anything but managed to keep a smile on his face. The head constable jabbered on island generalities to pass the time. In about fifteen minutes they pulled up to Government House, a colorful yellow building with white trim on the windows and doors. They walked up the steps and Woody was ushered into a small office. The gendarmes left. He was alone in a room with only two chairs, a table with a two-week old newspaper, a picture of the head minister of the province and a calendar showing the previous month hanging on the wall. The walls were standard walnut paneling and the floor a dull gray asbestos tile, some squares chipped, revealing cement underneath.

Woody sat in one thinly padded chair with green vinyl on the seat and back. He had already read the newspaper when the news was fresh. He glanced at his watch. Twelve-thirty. He was hungry and would have given anything for a drink to help him through what he now suspected would be an ordeal. Woody heard people walking back and forth and talking, but it was impossible to distinguish what was being said. He glanced at the photograph, hanging off-kilter on the wall, and looked at the man's face. The black skin hid any wrinkles or markings that would normally show on an aging white man's face. The teeth and eyes stood out of the smiling expression above a well-decorated official uniform.

It was hot, and he was still hung over from the night before. Woody stretched his short legs out in front of him, hands across his belly, and looked at the ceiling. There were acoustical tiles, glued to whatever surface was underneath, with a few tiles coming loose. As he stared, he felt his body temperature rising, dark patches forming under the arms of his light blue knit shirt. He was glad he wore khaki shorts and old sneakers. At least he was comfortable if not dressed for a meeting with the officials. He hoped that if he looked casual everything would be informal. But he was beginning to doubt his thoughts as the minutes ticked

347

away and no one came for him.

He stood up and limped to the door, turning the knob. It was locked. Great, he thought. Locked in a windowless room. He imagined being forgotten, found by some cleaning person days later. You're going nuts to think that way, he thought, and picked up the newspaper. It was better than nothing. He turned to the editorials, something he rarely read. The first was on how the natives should be more courteous to the tourists, that letting visitors sit for a half-hour before taking their breakfast order was not promoting good feelings in the small island nation. It went on about taking pride in the country, about bettering themselves through education, doing a good job, etc. etc. The next was headed "Marijuana Peddlers Ruining The Young People" and went on to stress the importance of keeping the young folks busy and happy, to encourage reporting of illicit drug trafficking and what to look for in youngsters suspected of being on drugs. While it was informative, Woody looked at it as more propaganda. It was all well and good to talk about the evils created by the smugglers, he thought, but they weren't being honest. Woody knew the money spent in the islands by the scammers in protection far surpassed the tourism dollar. Woody thought about the money the constable had just taken from Jock. It wouldn't show up as a payoff, but that's exactly what it was. That money would buy groceries, a gold bracelet for a wife or girlfriend and other items the three policemen would want. The pilot, too, would take his cut. Woody turned to the personal column in the classifieds, noting how different the ads were compared to big newspapers in the States. It was here that births and deaths were made known to family members, where the island people exchanged messages. The newspaper and the radio. Especially the radio. A husband would be told his wife was all right after an operation. Mothers would be told their children were doing well in school while staying with a distant aunt or cousin on the main province.

After reading about other people's troubles and joys, Woody tossed the paper on the floor. Two o'clock. They must have forgotten him. He tried the door again, then paced back and forth in the small room.

He was perspiring, hot, hungry, thirsty and angry. Calm down, Woody, he told himself. They'll be here shortly. Hurry up and wait. Hurry up and wait. That's what the game is all about. So hurry up and wait. He paced some more, his tolerance level dwindling with each limping step.

A few minutes later he had enough. He walked to the door and pounded with his fists. The muffled voices on the other side became silent and he imagined the stir he was creating among employees of Government House. He continued banging on the door. When his fist began to hurt he heard someone turning the lock. He stopped pounding and waited for the door to open. When it did, he was facing a handgun pointed at his belly by the constable.

"Mistah Cameron," he said, emphasizing every syllable. "We's doin' our job jis' as quick as we can but de noise is upsetting to us. What is yo problem? Dese inwestigations take time."

"I'm hungry and thirsty and you've had me locked up in this fucking room for hours. If you're going to press charges then go ahead, but if you're not, you better let me out of this goddamn room or you're going to have a psycho on your hands, not an easygoing likable guy like I really am," he said, clenching his fists as he talked.

"Lets me see what I kin do," said the gendarme, putting his gun away. "I be back in a minit wid sometin' fo' yo'. Okay?"

"What am I supposed to say?" asked Woody. "Whatever you say has to be okay. I don't have much choice."

"Now yo' gots de idea," he said, and closed the door once more, turning the lock.

Christ, thought Woody. What is happening? He sat down and put his head in his hands, resting his elbows on what were becoming wobbly knees. In a few minutes, he heard the lock turn and the constable opened the door.

"Here's a glass o' water," he said. "I kin send a girl out fo' sometin' to eat, but I needs some money from yo'," he said.

"I thought we paid yesterday," said Woody with a snarl to his voice. Then the constable closed the door, smiling until the opening showed only a sliver of his face. It was again locked and

Woody realized he could forget about any food. He felt the water go down his throat, his esophagus, all the way down to his insides. It was reclaimed water from the sea, and even though it wasn't the best in the world, it was at least wet and salt-free. Woody sat down again, picked up the newspaper, and began tearing it apart in tiny shreds, being careful to make them all as even and as long as possible without breaking them. He began to think of what Howard would say if he saw him here. Howard. Woody wondered what had happened to him, if he was sitting somewhere shredding newspapers or if he was even alive. It was not unusual for Howard to disappear for periods of time, but usually Chubby knew where he was, or his wife. This time no one knew where he had gone. He could be on the other side of the world, or he could be dead for all anyone knew. Like Terry and Juney.

God, thought Woody. He put his head in his hands, then got up and paced again, wondering what was happening to his world. Jock was the only smart one, he concluded. I should have gone with him, he thought. But then Laura would have been stuck putting the pieces together on the island. It wouldn't have been fair to her. No, just ride this one out. They won't keep you, he told himself. You'll be back on the island tomorrow. Then he remembered his clothes, still in the car that had picked him up at the airport. He sat down and continued shredding, letting the long, skinny pieces of paper fall to the floor. There wasn't even an ashtray in the room. He thought if he smoked he'd probably asphyxiate himself. There was only a tiny vent in the room, way up in the far corner, about four-by-six inches, not big enough to be used as an escape hatch. Woody thought jail had to be better than this. Then he told himself he must be going mad. The stories he had heard about native jails could keep a fellow straight for life if he truly believed those who had survived. The room was much better. At least there were still normal, everyday voices outside.

He went to the door and put his ear against it, trying to distinguish conversation, but everything blurred together. Maybe in another country he would have understood, but the native jargon was hard enough to understand face to face. Behind doors it was impossible. It was now almost four o'clock and Woody was anxious to get out of his confinement.

He sat down again and contemplated another tantrum when he heard the lock turn. The door opened and two officers stood, one the constable who was becoming a part of his life, the other an officer he had not seen before.

"Our investigation is complete at dis time, Mistah Cameron," said the constable. "We suggist you gits a lawyer to help straighten out yo' documents concerning the workings o' yo' island. Tings are not in order and we tinks yo' need a barrister to show yo' what to do. Now, you comes wid us. We arranged fo' yo' passage on de fibe o'clock plane to de mainland. When yo' gits tings in order yo' kin come back. Until den, well, dat is our suggestion."

Woody looked at him dumbfounded.

"It sounds to me like I'm being deported. Is that what you're doing with me? Because if it is, I want legal counsel right now. You have no right…"

"Mistah Cameron," he interrupted with authority, a smile creeping across his face. "Let me informs you dat we hab ebery right. As to legal counsel, you kin make arrangements tomorrow, in yo' country. Right now we hab to leabe to gits yo' on dat plane. Where yo' tings?"

"In the car that brought me here," said Woody, disgusted.

"Dat too bad. Dat mon off duties now," he said, motioning for Woody to follow.

In what seemed an eternity, they were at the airport. Tourists came and went and it occurred to Woody that he could probably get lost in the crowd, but the two gendarmes were like glue, escorting him to the ticket counter.

"Dis mon want one way ticket on de fibe o'clock plane," said the constable.

"Yessir," said the agent, looking rather questioningly at Woody. "Is he to be accompanied by anyone?"

"No. He be okay," said the constable. "Yo' wouldn' want troubles at de udder end, would yo'?" he asked Woody, who shook his head. Woody would have to notify Laura on the radio through Chubby.

The ticket was purchased with money from his wallet, and before Woody had a chance to even think about escaping his predicament, they announced boarding for the flight. The constable and his partner walked him to the plane and watched as he climbed the ramp. Then they stood in the waiting section to make sure he took off with the big jet.

For the first time since arriving at Government House, Woody sized up how he was dressed compared to everyone else. He had provoked a few stares and mothers had walked their children away from him. Businessmen looked at him in disgust and stuck their faces in their journals when he looked back. Shit on them, thought Woody. I could buy and sell any one of them. Shit on them. He picked up a newspaper that was sitting in the seat and caught the headline; "Motor Yacht And Crew Meet Smuggler's Fate."

He read the first paragraph and felt like vomiting. The *Sea 'n' Be*. Terry and Juney. Ripoff. Millions of dollars. The words blurred together and he finally felt the impact of the day and what had happened. He began shaking and asked the stewardess for a drink. By the time the plane was in the air, he was numbed by what had happened. He felt alone, so alone he couldn't tell anyone, least of all anyone on the plane. He was shunned like a wanted criminal. Fuck the bastards, he thought, and made up his mind that nothing would stop him from doing what he wanted. He'd play their little game of getting a lawyer, but he'd go about his business and no one would really know what he was up to. Fuck 'em, he thought, and smiled. The stewardess came and he ordered another drink. Fuck 'em.

* * *

Jackson heard about the adventures of the police officers and wondered if Jock and Woody would be taken to the main province. When he woke and found that Jock had left the island, it didn't surprise him. He climbed aboard *Cyclops* and headed for the yacht club. It was a beautiful day. He watched the seagulls dive for fish and bits of food tossed from cruising boats cleaning breakfast dishes. The birds were comical, often lining up along the dock pilings into the wind. At the slightest provocation they would take off, fly in different directions, then methodically return to their posts. When Jackson arrived at the club, one of the young native boys was emptying trash containers left by the yachtsmen, and old Clay was going about his business sweeping out the club and wiping down tables. As Jackson opened the screen door, Pete and Charlie came from the kitchen with their morning coffee.

"Morning, Jackson. What's going on? You hear anything about what the police are doing?" Pete was curious and so was Charlie.

"Yeah, mon. All kinds o' tings happenin'. De gendarmes suppose ta take Jock and Woody to de main prowince today but Jock already gib dem de slip," said Jackson, shaking his head. "Musta left in de night fo' someplace 'cause he's gone."

"I thought I heard something early this morning, but I couldn't wake up enough to figure what it was," said Charlie. "I'll bet it was Jock. I didn't think anyone would fly at that hour of the morning and I rolled over and went back to sleep. I'll be damned. Left the island, huh? I wonder where he was going and why he felt he had to get out of here."

"De constable got a lot o' bucks outa Jock's plane in a briefcase," said Jackson. "I saws it. Had to cuts it open ta gits in." He shook his head, a slight smile on his face. "Dey went to Smugglers too, ya know. Don' know what dey found dere, but Woody sposed ta be goin' wid dem today. Dey not say too much, but dey no takes someone less dey hab good reason. Maybe dey gits 'em, huh?"

"Who knows, Jackson. Maybe our prayers are being answered," said Charlie. "Too bad Jock got away. He's the one I want caught. Son of a bitch is driving me out of business."

Pete hadn't said much, but had a distant gleam to his eyes as he fingered his beard.

"Wonder if they found anything at Smugglers," he said, finally. "From the stories there had to be evidence of something going on."

"We see," said Jackson. "Who dose guys, you know?" He was looking at two men walking down the dock off a small fishing boat that had just come in. They looked around the place, glanced at the bulletin board outside the yacht club door and came in.

"Morning gentlemen," said Pete. "What can we do for you today?"

"First off, a couple of beers," said one, a tall skinny man with blonde hair. Both were wearing jeans and knit golf shirts.

"American or German?" asked Pete, opening the cooler.

"Imported's fine," he said, and laid a five dollar bill on the bar.

"Where you headed for?" asked Pete, keeping the conversation going.

"Trying to get back to the mainland. Heard about a guy named Jock but we understand he left already. Any other way off this rock?" The second man was quiet.

"Charlie here can take you. He's the one who services this place."

Charlie came over, put his hand out and introduced himself.

"When do you want to go?" he asked.

"This afternoon, if possible," he said. "Then we have to make arrangements to get back in about three days."

"No problem," said Charlie. "You name the time and we'll go."

"Call it for one o'clock."

They discussed the charter fee and Charlie asked how much baggage they had.

"Just a couple of bags," he said. "What do you know about that place called Smugglers? Stopped in there this morning and the guy's a little wacko."

Jackson, Pete and Charlie laughed.

"Think he got busted for something yesterday. Constable's waiting for him in the village to take him in. Don't know any more than that," said Pete. The two men looked at each other, raised their eyebrows and drank their beer.

"Well, I better gits ta work," said Jackson. "I let you know I hears anyting else."

"Thanks, Jackson," said Pete. I've got a bunch of things to do myself. It's sure quiet without the family here. You'll come

354

back to the island when these boys return, right?" he asked Charlie.

"Yeah. At least it saves my ass on this trip. Only had two over the other day. Cottage business is slow, but we're trying to drum up more visitors with a special discount for the next couple of months. Hopefully it will pick up."

"I'm not going to count on it," said Pete. "We'll probably update the kitchen in a couple of weeks and redo some things in there. The barge should be in any day to do the dock. Lots of money going out of here."

"That time of year," said Charlie. "You're not alone."

"I know," chuckled Pete. He locked up the cash box and walked toward the kitchen.

Charlie went to the radio room and contacted his office. He was happy to have a trip. He didn't like staying on the island without having his own place. He thought about taking a walk, but it was already too hot. Instead, he sat down on the front porch and watched the few remaining yachtsmen and the endless parade of seagulls.

The tide was going out and the various blues of the water were becoming discernible as the sun rose higher in the sky. He felt lazy and comfortable and propped his legs up on the chair next to him. He lost track of time and almost dozed off in the heat. After a while, he heard a boat coming toward Sandy Cay. He squinted and watched it round one of the tiny islands to the west and realized it was Woody's black boat. Jock may have skipped, but Woody was coming for his penance. He watched the boat go into Conch Inn marina and lost Woody as he walked down the dock with what looked like Maxwell. What a pair, he thought. Max was probably still promising the red boat to Woody. Pete came back, grease on his hands, and asked Charlie to help him with an engine. They walked back to the workshop and Charlie told him about seeing Woody.

"Wonder if he'll be able to talk or buy his way out," said Pete. "When they come this far for you they don't like to lose face and come back with nothing. The police wouldn't have gone to the expense of sending a plane, the constable and his crew if they didn't have a plan already on file. Wouldn't that be

355

something if they told him he couldn't come back?"

"They wouldn't do THAT, would they?" asked Charlie.

"If they don't want him here they'll just put him on a plane and he'll be gone before he knows it. They might not even give him a reason. No. Those boys don't mess around at this stage. If they don't like you, man, you're out."

Charlie helped with the engine and a little later, they heard the police plane leaving. Pete smiled at Charlie.

"What a way to go, huh?" he said.

They walked back into the club. As they sat down, Jackson hurriedly came from behind. He had gone into the village on *Cyclops* and returned rather quickly. His forehead was creased.

"What's the matter, Jackson? What happened?" asked Pete.

"Fella jis' come in to Conch Inn from cruisin' down islands. He tol' de story 'bout American couple aboard de *Sea 'n' Be* bein' murdered and carryin' millions o' dollars o' dope aboard. Gots killed and ripped off. Dey inwestigatin' de incident, but word is de down-island boys may hab done it. Dat young couple come in here, 'member? He used ta work aboard de boat, den de owner sells it to him and he marry dat pretty woman. You 'member?"

"Yeah," said Pete, slowly. "You sure? That nice couple, that real sexy gal of his? Murdered? You sure about that Jackson? What are the details?"

"Boat las' seen listin' in a shallow harbor. Dat man down dere who sees de boat afore comin' here said blood all ober and whole boat hacked apart. I's sick ta hear dis. Jis' sick. Too much o' dis stuff goin' on. An' dose two seemed so nice. Who's ya gonna trust anymo'? I's sick I tell ya." He stood there, jaw firm and eyes filled with compassion.

"I remember them coming in," said Charlie. "God. What's going to happen next? Where did they find them?"

'Bout tree hundred mile from here," said Jackson. "Dat don' make no difference. It bad ting to hab happen. People will read 'bout it and dey no wants ta come ta a country iffen dey tinks dere trouble like dis. Eben if dey axed fo' it carryin' a load o' stuff. People no wants ta hear dese bad tings."

They stood there, no one wanting to interrupt thoughts on

356

the fate of the young couple.

Finally, Pete said, "Well, you never know. Best thing is to mind our own business and stay clean. You never know when you're on the other side of the fence who's going to come from behind, either the authorities — like what happened to Woody and Jock — or the ripoffs. Both can be dangerous to your health. You never know what you're getting into. That whole process is so unnecessary. A good job would have let them enjoy that boat. He could have chartered, done so many other things besides run dope. That's sad news, Jackson."

"You tellin' me? I don' know how ta be ta anyone no more. I no wanta gits mixed up, but ya still hab to go 'bout yo' business an' keep de peoples happy. Still gotta keep 'em comin' here. Well, I be gettin' on. Iffen I hears anyting more I lets you know."

"Thanks, Jackson," said Pete as he went out the door. Pete and Charlie shook their heads, not knowing what to say, then went about their business, Pete to the workshop and Charlie to pack for the States. Pete was right, he thought. The murders were totally unnecessary. But people still would reap what they had sown, and the two adventurers had set themselves up. Charlie wondered if there was any connection between Woody's operation and the *Sea 'n' Be*. Max had worked on the boat and she had lain at Smugglers a few nights. No one would probably ever know the full story. And newspaper reports were never accurate. They probably knew now as much as they would ever know about the incident. It was a damn shame, he thought.

* * *

As Charlie flew into International Airport and taxied to customs, he could hardly believe what he saw. He parked the plane, got out, showed the two men where to put their bags and told them to wait while he walked over to the white plane with blue trim on the back line. There was Jock's plane, decorated with a red impoundment tag. Charlie stood there, looked up, and said "Wow!" He peered into the plane, then turned back toward his own, a big smile across his face. The customs inspector saw

357

his excitement and smiled.

"You know that guy?"

"Know him? He's the one that's been stealing my business for the past six months. What happened?"

"He's the guy? Now it adds up. You wouldn't have believed what happened. We're STILL trying to get over our dumb luck. The pilot's in the pokey for bringing in cocaine. It was a big bust."

"What happened?" asked Charlie, and the inspector gave him a blow by blow description of how the FAA had ramp checked him on routine and the dog had sniffed out the goods just by chance. Charlie stood dumbfounded at his luck, his passengers enjoying eavesdropping on the story.

"Do you think someone upstairs is looking after me?" he asked, a big grin on his face and the sparkle back in his eyes. "His partner in crime, or at least one of them, just got hauled off by the gendarmes to the main province a few hours ago. It'll be interesting to hear the outcome of that one, too. You hear about the couple murdered aboard their boat during a ripoff?"

"Yeah. What's the story?"

"Don't know too much, but this group may have been connected. Jock flew in some parts for the boat and they hung around the area for awhile. We didn't know where they went from there, but it must have been south."

"That's really too bad, isn't it?" said the inspector, shaking his head. "They were just kids, according to reports. Probably thought it would be a fun adventure and now look where it got them. Guess there's justice after all. It just takes time."

"I was beginning to think time was running out with this one," said Charlie, pointing to the impounded plane. "Saved my ass just in time. Maybe I can recoup during next season. Well, I better get my passengers through customs and immigration. Take care and keep up the good work. You guys get a medal from me today. Man, I've never seen a more beautiful sight."

"I couldn't tell by looking at you," said the inspector, and waved him on.

Charlie led his people through the commercial entry system, then gave them his phone number to call for returning to the island.

"You need anything, just give a call. I'm in contact with the club. Just let me know as soon as you can when you want to go in case I'm booking passengers."

They said they'd probably know by that night and would be in touch, that there was a possibility of going back as soon as the next day. With that, they left to get a cab. Charlie walked back outside and over to Jock's plane once more. Cocaine. He knew he was into something. That probably wasn't all. Charlie couldn't wait to tell Pete, but this was no story for the radio. He would deliver this one in person. He hoped he'd be going back tomorrow.

Chapter 15

Mad Max

Maxwell tinkered with the red boat after Woody left, but his heart wasn't in it. He couldn't get rid of the horror of the *Sea 'n' Be* murders, Jock abandoning him in the early morning hours and Woody being taken away. He looked around and saw only negatives. The sun made it too hot. The afternoon rains were oppressive. The sea was too changeable. His house was a mess. His shop needed cleaning. His tools were rusting in the salt air. Manny's beer was warm.

He let a wrench drop from his hand as he stared at Conch Inn. Manny's beer was warm because everyone blamed him, Maxwell, for all the generator problems. He picked up the wrench and put it in his toolbox that contained a mixture of screwdrivers, sockets, odd bolts, washers and screws, vise grips and pliers, most pilfered from boats he had worked on over the years.

It was only eleven in the morning but he felt like the day should be over, as if he should go home, fix himself something to eat and drink and lie down for a long sleep. He thought about the good joints he had carefully hidden, and how a few puffs could bring his mind around again. No one was on the dock, and he decided that since Woody was gone there was no sense trying to fix the red boat today. He'd go home and take it easy. He'd relax and forget everything that was happening. Max closed his toolbox and decided to take Woody's black bomb. It would be faster and he wouldn't have to go past Conch Inn where Manny was tending bar, nor the yacht club, where Pete and Charlie would be getting a good laugh on how Woody had been escorted off the island. He turned the key, started the engines, then untied the lines. He backed down, then sped toward his dock with little care of throwing a wake to the few cruising boats enjoying a peaceful anchorage. He went the long way around Sandy Cay Club so that people wouldn't see him, and if they did, maybe not recognize him.

In a few minutes he was tying up the boat and hiking the hill to the house. The front door was full of dry rot and the cistern leaked. With Pat gone nothing mattered to Max. He planned to exist a little longer here, then try to start a new life in the States. It seemed forever since Pat had been in the house. He looked around at the dirty dishes, the laundry strewn on the floor, the open jar of peanut butter providing a gourmet feast for an army of ants. Fatten them up for the roaches, he thought, heading for the small rusting refrigerator and a can of beer. He'd bypassed the need for electricity by putting in a gas refrigerator, but it was undependable and he never knew if the food would be spoiled, the beer cold or, on the other hand, if everything had frozen. He felt the can of beer. It was cool, the way he liked it. Max knew he was out of bread, so reached for a box of crackers and a fresh jar of peanut butter, leaving the already opened one on the counter.

He went over to the couch that also served as his bed and fixed some crackers, sipping his beer and trying to keep his head clear of any thoughts. It was difficult. He felt cheated out of what should have been his share in the deals, including the load ripped off the *Sea 'n' Be*. He resented Jock being entrusted with money and a stash of cocaine. Jock was probably in the States now becoming a millionaire, peddling it on his own and reaping a fortune, thought Max. He was jealous of Woody's self confidence, his joviality even under strained circumstances with the constable. He felt Howard was being aloof and pompous in not getting back to them. And Pete. There were no words for what he felt toward Pete except that he wanted to "get even," to ruin his life like Maxwell thought his had been ruined. He couldn't accept any kind of rejection, and Pete had rebuked him, brought scorn on him, had proven him incompetent as a mechanic. In his own mind Max felt like a master, a mechanic who could fix anything — generators, outboards, inboards — anything mechanical. But the more he worked, the more futile his efforts became, and each job showed a mental deterioration that even Maxwell was beginning to see.

They're driving me crazy, he told himself. They're all driving me mad so they can rip me off, do me in. He firmly believed everyone WAS out to get him when in reality, his so-called enemies wished only to be left alone. Everyone wanted Maxwell to leave, to go where they wouldn't constantly be subjected to him. Max secretly knew this and that's why he stayed. Leaving the island meant he and Pat could start a new life, but Maxwell wanted revenge. He wanted his enemies to pay for his state of mind, and he conjured up all kinds of ways to hurt them, cunning little ways that wouldn't point to him. Malicious things. Maxwell began thinking about what he could do to Pete. It would be easy to ruin his water system, to screw up the radio communications or to mess with an outboard motor or two in the night when no one would see him. But he had a problem. He knew there were snakes on the island and was petrified of them, a flashback to an incident when he was a child in Australia. At night he always carried a flashlight, making it difficult to play a game of sabotage. His fear foiled any kind of retaliation. The nights kept Maxwell thinking of all the things he COULD do, but in reality, he lacked the courage to do much of anything, except write letters. And this he did.

He thought of his last one, condemning Charlie and praising Jock. That was a beauty, he thought, and mentally patted himself on the back. But there had been no results. He had praised Jock as a pilot concerned about the island people, not monetary gain like Charlie.

Now Jock had left the island with a tarnished reputation. It made him, Maxwell, look bad. He began stewing about how Jock had "done him in" by not complying with his, Maxwell's, plan to "get" Charlie and, thereby, Pete. Maxwell was depressed, and lit up a joint when he finished his beer. It was almost two o'clock and he had not accomplished anything so far this day. But he was his own boss and could work when he wanted to. Or not at all. For anyone. Or no one. At anytime. Anywhere.

Maxwell wanted to be independently wealthy, to have anything in the world that was available to the rich. He had been raised a poor Aussie boy, and when he came to the islands years ago he had seen how the well-to-do lived. He envied them, and appointed himself a Robin Hood of the islands, taking from the rich whatever he could squeeze out for poor Maxwell. He truly felt he deserved every dollar he salted away, that the time would come when he WOULD be rich and people would recognize him. He'd live in a big house, have blacks for servants and never kiss ass again.

He could feel the marijuana taking hold, mingling with the beer. He blew smoke rings and felt himself mellowing. This was good stuff, what Woody had held out. Good stuff. He finished the joint, lay back and felt the room whirling around. In a little while he was asleep, the afternoon merry-go-round in motion.

* * *

It was five o'clock when Max woke with a headache and an empty feeling in his stomach. He sat for a few minutes on the edge of the sofa and slowly ran his fingers through his hair. He was wringing wet from perspiring in the afternoon heat and he was hungry, yet there was nothing worthwhile to eat in the house. He put on his shoes and decided to go to Smugglers. Laura might know by now what had happened to Woody and they could talk to Chubby on the radio. He glanced at the ants in the peanut butter as he went out the door and decided to let them feast. The tide had come up and the black boat was rubbing against the dock, chafing the sides. He got in, started the engines, untied the lines and headed to Smugglers. When he pulled in, Laura was standing on the dock. She had recognized the boat, then expressed disappointment at not seeing Woody. Max would have to do for company while they tried to find out what was happening to the rest of the crew. Max managed a thin smile as he tied up, and Laura tried to smile back.

"Hear anything?" Max asked.

"No. Ah was going to ask you the same thing," she said wistfully. She seemed depressed, not her usual self, even to Max, who lived with constant depression.

"Can we make a radio contact?" he asked.

"Not till later, according to what Woody said. Come in. Fix a drink. Ah'll get some dinner together." One of the island dogs had come to keep her company. Usually, they weren't allowed inside the club but with Woody gone and all the boat people gone, Laura welcomed the companionship.

"This place cleared out as if we had the plague after the constable left yesterday," she said from the kitchen. "What's going to happen, Max? Ah can't figure it out. Why would they take Woody without pressing charges?"

"Same as they do anything in this bloody country without telling you. Woody thought he'd be back tonight or tomorrow, but I never thought so. That bloody constable is a prick. He wouldn't let you know what time it was if it wasn't public knowledge. Have anything for a headache?"

"Sho' thing. Over there," she said, nodding to a kitchen cabinet. "Canned stew all right tonight? Ah don't feel like cooking anything."

"Okay with me. I didn't have a thing in my house and I didn't want to face Manny complaining about his generator," said Max. "Did you know that Jock left before daylight this morning?"

"No," she said, surprised. "You mean Woody went by himself with the police?"

"Yup," said Max. "Jock left before anyone knew he was gone. Abandoned ship, in my estimation, but he was doing it for selfish reasons. He had a bloody load on board his plane. He's probably whooping it up while we're sitting here with nothing. All he thought of was himself."

"Ah guess we all do," said Laura with a sigh. "Can ya open this can for me? Everything gets so rusted over here. Ah think it even rubs off on the people. Ah don't have any energy anymore, Max. This place is draining me. At first it was fun, fixing it up and all the people coming around. But it's making an old lady of me. Woody's off on all his business stuff which also complicates things around here and Ah'm always stuck picking up the pieces. Like now. Ah don't even know IF he'll be back let alone when. It really isn't fair. Ah feel pretty used."

"Woody needs you, though," said Max. "You can't just up and leave him."

"Why not? Pat left you," she said, looking straight at him. "Ah don't mean that in a bad sense, but why not, Max? When life gits so complicated and everything's out of control, why

365

not? Ah wish Ah could be back in the States again, at least for a while until all this blows over. IF it blows over."

"It will," he said. "These things are part of the islands. The dopers are bloody more powerful than you think. Don't worry about Woody. He'll get out of it somehow. That type bloke always does. It's people like me, farther down the pyramid, who end up being cut out of the profits without having anything to say about it. Did you hear about the *Sea 'n' Be*?"

"No. When are they due in?" asked Laura. She liked Juney and would enjoy her company again.

"Never. They were murdered."

"WHAT?" she shrieked. "You aren't serious! What happened?"

Max told her what he had heard, with as much description as he thought she could stand to hear. When he finished, Laura was walking around the club sobbing. There was no one to put up a front for and she felt sick, horrified and empty over the story.

"They were such nice, easygoing people," she said. "Such a nice couple. Juney talked about wanting a baby. God, what is happening?"

Underneath, though, she had the gnawing realization that people got what they asked for. Every scammer knew he was taking the chance when he made the first commitment, but it still hurt her to know that two beautiful young people had been wasted. She sat down and looked out over the water. There was such beauty in the islands, she thought, and such grief. Laura longed to be back in the States with normal people. It had been months and she could feel herself becoming "rock happy."

"When are we going to eat?" asked Max, interrupting her thoughts.

"Aw'll get it now. Get a couple of plates and some silverware. Ah just can't get over what you just told me. Ah sure hope Woody is okay."

"He was in safe company," said Max. "Very safe company."

Laura fixed the stew and sliced a tomato, cutting around some questionable areas. The carrots were a bit soft, but she sliced a few and put some french dressing on the table.

"Fix me one too while you're at it," she said to Max, who

was at the bar.

Neither talked much as they ate. Maxwell had never been one of Laura's favorite people and nothing was changed with the two of them alone on Smugglers. He helped carry the dishes to the sink after they were through eating, but didn't offer to wash dishes or clean up. Instead of saying something, she went ahead and did it herself, comfortable in the martyr role she had created.

"At seven-thirty we can try Chubby," she said, calling out to the dining area.

Max came in and asked if she had any pot. "Woody's always got some next to his bed," she said. "Take whatever ya want if it makes y'all feel any better."

That was what he wanted to hear. Woody had some high grade cocaine as well, and if Laura gave him the okay to take whatever he wanted, that would be his choice. But he'd wait until after the radio contact. Instead of going up the stairs, he walked out on the dock. It was quiet, but the no-see-ums were out in force, chomping at his skin the minute he stepped outside. He swatted a few and then realized how fruitless it was. He imagined that if a no-see-um was examined under a microscope, the only thing visible would be the vice-grip jaws of the little bastards. He went back inside.

"No-see-ums are bad. Got any spray?"

"They've been bad every night. Ah think this island is their breeding ground. Do you have them this bad at Sandy Cay?"

"No. Well, sometimes. I think we're a little higher than you are at Smugglers."

"Maybe so," said Laura. "Anyway, we're all out of spray. There's a bottle of something in that cabinet with the aspirin, but Ah don't know how good it is. Goes back to before we all came."

"I'll just stay inside. As soon as a breeze comes they'll be gone," said Max. "Anyway, it's almost quarter to seven. should we try calling?"

"Good idea," said Laura, from the kitchen. "Just give me a couple more minutes here and then Ah can relax too. Fix me another rum, would you Max?"

By the time he'd fixed a couple of drinks Laura was finished

367

and they went to the radio room.

"Woody gave me all the code frequencies and showed me how to work the system. He must have thought Ah might have to do it sometime, but Ah'm still not comfortable talking on it. Using the VHF locally got rid of some of mah stage fright."

"Just a bunch of idiots on the air," said Maxwell. "And no one will be on our special frequencies. That's why Howard set it up the way he did."

"What do ya think has happened to him?" she asked, letting the radio warm up. She dialed in a frequency and made the initial contact with Chubby. Thank God he was on the air.

"*Naughty Lady* back to Woodpecker. Have someone here. Stand by."

"I'm here, Babes. Switch to the next code." Laura looked at Max with excitement as she turned the dial.

"*Naughty Lady* to Woodpecker. How are you doing, Bunchy?"

"Fine, Woody. How y'all? What happened today?"

"They put me on the five o'clock plane to the States because they claim my paperwork isn't in order, but I'll be contacting a lawyer tomorrow. Have some other news. You copy okay?"

"Roger. Go ahead."

"Jock got pinched when he came in this morning and is in the pokey. Doesn't look good. Also heard that Howard upset some of the bigger boys and also may not be around. Did you hear about Terry and Juney?"

"Roger. Maxwell is here with me looking a little shocked. Is Jock out on bail?"

"Negative. We don't have the bread to get him out and wouldn't anyway since he went behind our backs. We don't know who he was working for. The theory is that he was doing a little ripping off himself so no one is willing to go to bat for him. He'll be in there awhile. How's Max doing?"

"All right. A little upset. Any messages for him?"

"Well, not really, except that Sam's back in the States." Laura wished he hadn't said that with Maxwell standing there listening.

"Roger. He heard you. What am Ah supposed to do?"

"Stay there a few more days and I'll let you know the plan. I should be back as soon as I can get something going with a lawyer. Sorry you got stuck there. If you want, you can hitch a ride back with someone. Maybe Charlie can take you."

"Roger. Should we talk again tomorrow at this time?"

"Roger. Let's try for a noon contact as well. As it stands now, I can't legally go back. I may send Mark."

"Negative on that. We don't need your nephew getting into trouble."

"Roger. Okay, then. I'll assume you'll be all right. Has Max fixed the red boat?"

She looked at Max who was conjuring up a scowl on his face and shaking his head no.

"Negative," she said.

"Tell him to get to work. I may be over here, but I still want my work done. Guess that's all for now, Bunchy. I'll let you know if Jock gets out or if Howard shows up. No further traffic. *Naughty Lady* clear."

"Woodpecker clear."

She turned off the radio and looked at Max, who had almost a gloating look on his face.

"Jocko got caught, huh?" he said. "Judas! Who's left? I told him to be careful. I was mad that he went off by himself and didn't include me in his deal, but shit, in jail? That's a federal offense. They'll put the screws to him good, especially with what he had in the plane."

"What exactly DID he have?" asked Laura.

"Five kilos of very good cocaine," said Max. "I knew about it but couldn't say anything. Now that he's caught it doesn't matter. I was hoping that by being quiet he'd share some of the profits with me."

"Always looking for the dollah, right Max?" asked Laura, a bit pointedly. "You know, if you'd spend more in makin' life easier for yourself it wouldn't be as difficult as it seems to have become."

"Don't lecture me about my savings," he said. "Everyone thinks I should spend my bloody money. But I'll be the one enjoying it in the end. I just need enough that I don't ever have

369

to worry again."

"That day never comes," said Laura. "Y'all be in the grave and your money as cold and useless as you are."

"Thanks. I wonder why Woody and Chubby couldn't bail Jock out?"

"Probably because, as Woody said, he was free-lancing. When Jock isn't loyal, why should y'all go to bat for him?"

"He's been all right," said Maxwell, defending Jock. "He's always been fair with me. Even shares in the charters I get him."

"You two seem to be more fair with each other than with anyone else, and Ah think this is one of the things that bothers Pat. Y'all hardly paid any attention to the poor girl after Jock started coming to the island. Do you realize that?"

"No. I think it's your imagination. The booze talking. You want another drink?" She nodded and he headed for the bar. Laura followed.

"Well, Ah guess there's nothing much to be done around here. Ah may try to get off the island, but Ah know from way back that Woody said never to leave unless a white was here. Y'all are the only white man Ah know who could stay."

"Don't look at me," said Maxwell, emphatically. "I've got my own problems. And I want to get back to the States too, especially since no one will help Jock and that bloody bastard Sam's screwing my wife."

Laura was hoping he wouldn't bring it up, that somehow the statement would have escaped him. But he'd heard it just as she had. She couldn't understand why Woody would say that over the radio, knowing Maxwell was with her, but he must have had a reason, she thought.

"I'm going to dip into Woody's stuff and then be on my way back to Sandy Cay, unless you want me to stay here with you," said Maxwell. "It's kind of creepy by yourself."

"Ah'd prefer you to stay, Max, at least until Ah can get my ideas together on what to do. If you want to, why not fix the little red boat here?"

"No," he said. "I need my shop and all my tools. I'll stay here tonight. As long a you don't mind me getting high. It's the only way I'll survive. What a bloody day. Jock escaped, Woody left, Terry and Juney dead, Howard disappeared. Pat's getting laid. I'm going to get high."

"Go right ahead. Ah'm going to bed after a few drinks. Since Ah've come here Ah think Ah've had more rum than water."

"It's better for you," said Max, heading for Woody's room. He came back a few minutes later feeling more on the level. He fixed himself a drink and walked outside. If the no-see-ums had still been out he would not have known the difference. He was armed with enough drugs to be void of any pain — physical, mental or emotional. As long as he could maintain this level of consciousness he would make it through the night, he thought. Woody had left a pile of goodies to choose from, including some quaaludes and some other pills he didn't recognize. It was Maxwell's consolation prize. He could string himself along at a level of comfort as long as he had a good supply. He let his face relax, lay down on a chaise and watched the evening sky blossom. At least he could enjoy the fresh air, he thought. Jock was probably stuck in a cell somewhere with some tough blokes. A few minutes and Max nodded his head, half a drink still left in his glass. All thought was gone, the merry-go-round in slow gear.

* * *

The next day Maxwell felt awful. He had awakened in the middle of the night, wandered into the club and fallen asleep on the pool table. Laura was in the kitchen scrambling eggs, the last thing in the world he felt like looking at or eating.

"When you decide to do someone in you sure do," said Laura, looking and feeling much better after the bad news of the previous day. "What did you take, anyway?"

Max mumbled, not really able to tell her what or how much he had taken the night before, and headed for the bathroom. His insides ached, his head was pounding, he felt clammy all over and he knew he needed something to calm his nerves. It was never this bad before, he thought, and wondered why he was having a hard time functioning. He finished his business in the

371

bathroom and walked up the stairs to Woody's room. A 'lude would take the pain away, he thought. By the time he came back to the kitchen he was feeling almost human again, and told Laura he'd have eggs after all. It was a meal he wouldn't have to fix or worry about.

"You want to take me back in the black boat so you have some transportation?" he asked.

"There's still the little boat," she said, "but you are probably right. Ah haven't run it much, but Ah know how, and you never know when Ah may need it. Ah'll tell you, Max. Ah don't want to stay on this island very long, especially when you hear about people ripping places off and all. It's frightening. What if the down-island boys decide to come here and raid the place and only find little ol' me and nothing worth ripping off? Ah don't think they'd treat me too well. Why don't you putter around here until Ah talk with Woody at noon? Then Ah can have a good idea of what to do. If you're taking care of Smugglers, Woody will take care of y'all. Ah'm sure of that. In fact, Ah'll even promise y'all get paid if it has to come out of my own pocket. Ah simply don't want to be alone."

"I don't blame you," said Max, his voice seeming to float as he talked. "I'll stay here. Woody probably has an alternate plan and I want to hear what the bloody lawyer says about his papers. What time is it now?"

"Almost eleven. Y'all really slept sound. Ah was almost afraid you weren't going to wake up," she said.

"That would have been too convenient," said Max. "I've thought about that a few times."

"Now y'all stop talking like that. What would it solve?"

"Nothing, but I could escape this crummy life."

"Ah'm not even going to try to touch that one, especially after yesterday. Just hang in there like the rest of us, Max. At least you're not in jail, banned from this country or dead at the hand of scoundrels. Hang in there. It'll be all right."

"That's okay for you to say," he said. "Anything you want me to do around here?"

"Not really. Just sort of go out to the storage area and make sure any evidence is gone. Ah was wondering if we could stash

372

all those empty fuel containers somewhere. They're pretty obvious to anyone coming ashore. What about those old buildings on the other side of the island? If we leave for awhile, that would be a good place for them."

"Any suggestions on how to move them there?"

"No. Woody was going to have a Jeep or something sent over on a barge but never got around to it. Can we take them over in the boat at high tide?"

"That's a good idea," said Max. "I'll get them loaded. We should be able to do it in two trips since they're all empty."

"Are you feeling well enough? she asked, noting how haggard he looked.

"Yeah. I'm okay. Just took something for the jitters and all. I'm okay," he said, and walked out to load the containers in the black boat. Laura tidied up the kitchen, then took all the tablecloths off the dining tables. There was no sense being prepared for guests. If visitors came, she could set what was needed. She stacked the ashtrays and arranged the bottles in the bar. In about twenty minutes, Max was back.

"First load's ready," he said. "Another hour and the tide should be just right."

"We ought to try and call Woody," she said. "Let's at least get the radio turned on and warmed up."

They walked to the radio room, got the system working and waited. About ten minutes went by. They heard the familiar call from the *Naughty Lady*. Laura answered and switched to the pre-arranged frequency.

"Hey, Bunchy. Good afternoon. Looks like I'm going to have some difficulty in coming back for a while so I'm sending a plane for you at three today. I have a young guy, not Mark, coming over to babysit the island so you can come back. He's all clued in over here on how everything works so don't give it a second thought. Just be at Sandy Cay by three. Do you roger?"

"Affirmative," she said. "Sandy Cay at three. Who's the pilot?"

"Chubby. See you later today. No further traffic. *Naughty Lady* clear."

"Woodpecker clear," she said, her voice a little wispy. After

373

turning off the radio, she turned to Max and said, "Ah'm going home, Max. Ah'm going back to the States. New clothes. Makeup. Pretty dresses. Ah can't wait to get my hair done. And Ah can't wait to eat a gallon of ice cream."

Max almost smiled at Laura, who waltzed around the club with excitement, telling herself what to pack, what to remember, what to shut off, what to leave on, what notes to leave. He had never seen her this happy since the first meeting at Smugglers months ago. Laura going home. He thought for a few minutes and decided it was probably time for him to leave as well. Pat would be surprised. He didn't dwell on the thought because he didn't know how she would take his coming to the States. She had gotten comfortable without him and he feared what the reaction would be. But there was nothing left for him here. Nothing.

"Laura!" he shouted up the stairs to her room. "I'm going too. I'll move that load of fuel containers and be back." She looked down from the tiny room and shrugged her shoulders.

"Why not? You can return. Your papers are in order. We can both go and that can be the end of it. Ah'll only be a short time. Woody didn't let me bring much when Ah came and Ah haven't had the opportunity to buy anything here. Ah'm leaving with what Ah came with. Maybe Ah'll be back. Maybe Ah won't. Right now Ah don't care. Fix a drink and enjoy today because we are leaving this beautiful rock." Her voice was muffled as she moved around the small room, emptying drawers and pulling a few things from the closet. She also grabbed some of Woody's things. No sense leaving them here for someone else to wear, she thought.

In less than half an hour Max was back and Laura was ready.

"That was bloody quick," said Maxwell. "Women are supposed to be slow to dress and pack."

"Not this one," she said. "Not when Ah'm going back to the civilized world."

Max helped carry the few bags to the boat, and by two o'clock they were ready to leave, Smugglers Cay in fair condition. As an afterthought, Max said he wanted to get

374

something in Woody's room. He ran through the club, up the stairs, and opened Woody's drawer. He took another 'lude and stuffed some of the pills in his pocket. He'd leave the cocaine in case they shook him down in customs. Woody would get him whatever he needed once he was on the mainland, he thought.

He hurried back down to the boat, and in a few minutes, they sped out of the harbor. Laura watched as the buildings disappeared, the wake of the boat opening its arms to what it left behind. She had the strangest feeling. She was leaving what was supposed to have been Paradise, a quiet idyllic island where they would live happily ever after. In leaving, she felt like she was escaping the dungeons of some strange hell, where God-given beauty was mixed with the evils of man's own will. She loved and hated the place at the same time. She wanted to leave, yet already missed the tranquility she knew could exist. In leaving, she longed to return.

They stopped briefly at Maxwell's house so he could get a few things, then headed to Conch Inn. Max tied up the boat next to Woody's red one, walked down the dock, made sure his shop was locked and motioned for Laura to follow him into the inn.

"Want a beer?" he asked. "It's probably warm, but at least it's wet."

"Why not?" she said, and sat down. Manny served up two beers and looked at them both quizzically.

"I'm leaving for a few days," said Max. "If anyone's looking for me tell them I'll be back. Have some business to take care of."

"I 'magine yo' do," he said. "Hear anyting 'bout Woody?"

"They sent him back to the States. He's got a lawyer working out the details for him."

"Dat so?" said Manny. "How you goin' back?"

"Woody's sending a plane," said Max. "Thought I might as well take advantage of it."

"Sho' ting," said Manny. "You maybe look at de generator and find out what ta gets so's when you come back yo' gots all de parts?"

"Not this time, Manny. It's too complicated. Plane's going to be here by three."

375

Manny shook his head, then went to serve another customer. As they finished their beers, they heard a plane. "Let's get our stuff," said Maxwell. "I don't think Chubby wants to wait."

He backed his Jeep to the edge of the dock, and they loaded it with their belongings. Then they headed for the strip, arriving as Chubby was about to walk into the village.

"Well," he said, extending his hand. "If it isn't Maxwell. Hi, Laura. Good to see you again. This all yours?"

"Some of its mine, too," said Max. "I'm hitching a ride back. Haven't seen Pat and want to tie up some loose ends. Who's that?" He pointed to a man in his late twenties, sandy hair and likeable smile.

"Meet Rob," said Chubby, cocking his head as he picked up bags with both arms. "He's going to babysit Smugglers until Woody comes back. I think he was hoping you'd stay around, but I guess a few days won't hurt. Better tell Rob where the boats are and all."

Max shook hands with Rob and explained the boat situation, and incidentals about his house should a storm come up.

"Well, are we ready?" asked Chubby, clapping his hands together. "Don't want to run into those late afternoon thunderstorms if we can help it."

"Ah'm ready," said Laura. Max gave Rob the keys to the Jeep and got in the plane. In a few minutes the engines were started and they were taxiing to the runway. As the plane lifted off, Laura gazed at the many little islands and cays below. It was a beautiful sight resembling a jig-saw pattern. Satisfied that she would be back before long, Laura laid her head back to sleep. It would undoubtedly be a late night, she thought.

* * *

Woody expressed surprise to see Maxwell on the plane, but told him to enjoy himself while he was in the States. He asked if he wanted any "stuff," and gave Max some cocaine and some pills. Max hailed a taxi and waved goodbye. They would meet again in a few days and would keep in touch by phone. Twenty minutes later he arrived in front of the little house Pat had rented. No one was home. He paid the driver, piled his gear on the front porch and sat down. He dipped into some of the goodies Woody had given him and in a few minutes, was almost dozing, stretched out on the front steps. He vaguely heard cars going by and an occasional horn honking, but was oblivious to everything else. When Pat arrived, she sent Sam on his way without Max ever knowing.

Once Maxwell was awakened and helped into the living room they renewed their relationship with each other. They had a lot to talk about and Pat, trying to be a good wife, hoped that Max could adjust to a new life with her away from the island. Although he planned to go back, she had made up her mind that she would not return. She hoped he was not too wasted to feel the same way, but only time would tell.

She, too, had punished her body and soul. Love, understanding, and compassion were all needed in large doses. She wondered if either of them had it in them to give as much as the marriage would require to survive. She wondered if it was really what she wanted. Time would tell. A long time.

Chapter 16

November Northers

Charlie arrived at Sandy Cay the first day of winter — not the official day, but the day everyone marked as the change of season. Winter always began with the third day of the first norther blowing through the islands, and he had brought in two couples on a pre-Thanksgiving holiday.

Although the breeze was brisk that afternoon, it was still shirt-sleeve weather, especially to the northern visitors who had just left snow flurries. Charlie helped load luggage into *Cyclops* and Jackson chatted with the visitors. Charlie could see a change in attitude in Jackson. To the natives, the first norther signified the start of the tourist season, when visitors once again came to the island to spend their money. Everyone's spirits were high following the slow period, and Charlie was elated. He had plenty of flights booked and was eager to have a regular schedule again. As everything and everyone was loaded, Jackson smiled and headed for the yacht club.

Charlie thought how magical the time of year was for the island. People didn't complain much and everyone pulled together like one big family. The fishing guides had new gear and plenty of backup rods and reels, boats were repainted, engines gone over and extra snorkeling and diving gear ordered. Charlie had brought in cargo for the club gift shop so that everyone could purchase T-shirts and other gifts for the Christmas holidays.

As Jackson pulled up to the club, Charlie saw Pete smiling.

"Hey, Charlie! How are you? And look who's here. The Robinsons. We were expecting you. Welcome back!"

Introductions were renewed and Pete directed the visitors to the first two cottages.

"When you get your things put away, come in for a welcome drink," he said. Jackson helped carry their bags, and Pete and Charlie went into the club.

"I could feel it in the air that today was going to be good," said Pete. "Nothing like some cottage bookings, huh?"

"You can say that again. I've barely been holding things together, but I've got a good feeling too. I also have news from the States."

"Oh yeah?" asked Pete, fixing some pineapple juice. Pete motioned for Charlie to follow him to the front porch.

"The dock looks nice," said Charlie. "I can't believe it's been three weeks since I've been on this rock. Has Woody been back?"

"No," said Pete. "Haven't seen him, and from what I hear, the government doesn't want him back. He's still got that guy by the name of Rob at the island sort of watching things. Our friend Maxwell came back for a few days, then towed the little red boat to Smugglers. But that was weeks ago. Haven't seen him since. The house he was living in is boarded up, like he's gone for some time."

"He might be," said Charlie. "I haven't heard too much, but my news is that Jock was found guilty. He'll be in the pokey for a few years, but if he follows the usual pattern on these convictions he'll probably be out before his time is up. He's also going to appeal it. The plane will end up on the auction block. It's too bad the agencies wait so long. They could command a higher price if things went a little more quickly."

"But on the other hand they want to make damn sure everything goes okay. We sort of expected him to be put away for awhile. How long you going to be around?"

"Only until tomorrow. Have two people going out from one of these boats. They called on the radio — and I'm bringing four more people back the following day. Sure is good to be flying again. Island seems to be in good spirits." Jackson had the guests situated and came over to the porch.

"Hey, Charlie. You bring dat tile fo' me?"

"Yeah, Jackson. That's what's still in *Cyclops*. Thought you got it."

"Dat's good. Finishing up de bat'room. Tings pretty good 'round here now."

"I can see. Is it my imagination, or do we have a different type of crowd than we had last summer?" He looked at a couple in their forties at the pool table and some boat people joking at the bar.

"So far I think the regular types have outnumbered the funny ones," said Pete. "Let's hope it continues."

"I ain' seen too much goin' on lately," said Jackson. "We takes care o' some o' it, you know. We no like all dat stuff go on. Not good fo' de people. Couple o' de young boys up to de main prowince fo' school now. Two also went to college in de States. Dey shapin' up. Dat's a good sign."

"It sure is," said Charlie. "What are they studying?"

"One in 'lectronics, de udder doin' business school," he said, "and de boy who goin' to generator school las' year, he go back fo' nudder year. He be all right when he finishes up. Good generator man needed all ober de islands."

"IF he comes back," said Charlie, skeptically. "The big thing is to make it attractive enough for the young guys to come back. They get to the States, start going with the girls and think it's better in the fast lane."

"Dat's a problem," said Jackson, "but we hope dere's enough fo' dem when dey finish up schools."

The two couples now walked from the cottages to the clubhouse, and Pete followed them in. Charlie sat and chatted for a while longer with Jackson, discussing his house and cottage bookings for the holidays. As a boat approached the docks, Jackson excused himself and went to help with the lines. Charlie went inside to join the tourists. Pete was in rare form, recounting stories on the early days of the club. When he came to the one about the snake, Charlie had to interrupt.

"What about the one on your parrot you were going to tell a while back and didn't get around to?" he asked, getting into the momentum of the group. "What was that silly bird's name?"

"Shultzie. You want to hear about Shultzie? Naw. These people don't want to hear about that crazy critter."

Everyone pleaded, so Pete launched into the story.

"About fifteen years ago, when my bedroom was in what is now the kitchen, I had a parrot. Big son of a bitch. He'd sit on my shoulder and shit while I tended bar. Anyway, see that little alcove over there?" He pointed to where a game table was

381

surrounded with book shelves and conversation pieces scavenged from the beach. "Well, there used to be a door where that glass ball is hanging, and that's where my bedroom was. Anyway, Shultzie was quite a bird. Could say a few things like 'goddamnit' and 'gimme a beer' but other than that he was kinda useless. Hated men. I was the only one he'd have anything to do with. The girls, well, Shultzie liked the girls. But he had a bad habit of pecking at men's ears when he perched on their shoulder. Used to let him fly around in here. Added to the atmosphere.

"One day I heard all this goddamn squawking and couldn't figure the dumb bird out. I couldn't see anything and he kept carrying on like he'd flipped out. We had just thatched the ceiling, mainly to cover up the bullet holes made while shooting rats in the rafters one night, and I couldn't see if anything was up there. As soon as I would come over everything would be all right, but the minute I got more than ten feet away, old Shultzie would carry on something fierce, the big cage swinging back and forth, him trying to keep his balance on the damn perch going in the opposite direction and squawking like a mad hen in a chicken pen.

"For the life of me, every time I went up close, I couldn't see anything. I started swearing at him, because I thought he was just trying to get my attention. This went on for hours. Finally, I sat very quietly on the other side of the room and watched. As soon as I was far enough away and Shultzie had settled down, I saw the cage start going back and forth, just a little bit, and I saw this goddamn rat coming down the chain that attached the cage to the ceiling. Thing was bigger than most tom cats, all gray and furry."

Several of the gals made faces as if they didn't want to hear about rats, particularly since they were sitting right where the story took place. Pete stopped.

"Well, if you don't want to hear, that's okay. Anyone for another drink?" He was told to please finish the story. Pete smiled. He loved to tell stories.

"Anyway, here's this big goddamn rat coming down this skinny little chain holding this big cage with the mad parrot. I could see Shultzie looking up, sneaking glances, not moving until the cage became uncomfortable. Then he let loose, screeching and carrying on. As soon as I looked over, the damn rat climbed back into the rafters. Shit, I couldn't blame the stupid bird for being so upset.

"That rat was humongous. I had to figure out what to do. I talked kinda quietly to Shultzie as I snuck into my bedroom and I think he knew I had something planned. I didn't, really, but I knew that it was going to be either the rat or Shultzie and the bird was a hell of a lot more difficult to replace. So I got out my German luger that I kept near my bed, loaded it, and sat with the door cocked just as wide as the barrel. I got comfortable and aimed the thing at that skinny chain and waited. And waited. After about fifteen minutes I thought for sure the rat had gone, then without any noise at all, the cage started going back and forth like a pendulum on an old grandfather's clock. Shultzie looked up kinda nervous like, cocking his head as if he wasn't really looking at the rat, and trying to see me at the same time through the crack in the door. I think he knew it was best if he was quiet, so he began breathing real hard, like he wanted to squawk but didn't want to ruin his chances for a happy life.

"A few minutes later I could see the rat inching its way down the chain. I aimed very carefully, one eye closed, and held the gun steady. As soon as I could see more than its furry head I let a shot go. You should have heard it. A bomb couldn't have been louder. Goddamn rat got away. Jumped right back up into the rafters, and poor Shultzie hit the deck, cage and all, squawking as the rat escaped. Shultzie wouldn't stop screeching. People came running in, wondering what had happened, and here we were, Shultzie and I consoling each other, his cage a mess, bird seed all over the place, and the chain wobbling back and forth at the ceiling. I think I scared the shit out of the bird that day. He was never the same after that. Took to biting my ear. Mean son of a bitch, so I let him know it."

"What happened to him?" asked one of the women, still staring wide-eyed at Pete.

"Someone let him out of the cage one day and he never came back. Had him three years. What do you do? He sure had a change of personality after that day and I couldn't do anything about it. He probably shipped aboard someone's boat. He was pretty well known in these parts. Probably figured it was a better life. Who knows?

"Anyone for some rum punch? I'll fix one blender full before Wanda comes in. Gee, it's good to have all you people in here. It's been dead these past couple of months."

"We heard so many rumors about all the dopers that I think a lot of people cruised elsewhere this fall," said one man. "We came armed to the teeth. It's too damn beautiful to completely give up so we figured we'd come prepared and stay where the action is. We're delighted to be here."

His wife asked if the gift shop could be opened up and Charlie volunteered to show her what was available. It was like old times, he thought. Old times before the scammers came. Maybe the wind was changing and more people like this would cruise the islands. He hoped so. He waved to Pete as he walked out the door. Jackson was tying up another boat that had come in and another was on the horizon. The season had begun.

* * *

About six o'clock, when Pete had gone home for his usual afternoon nap, Charlie noticed another familiar boat coming toward Sandy Cay. Jackson was coiling the fuel hoses and closing down the dock services for the day. Charlie went out, talked with him, and they both stared as the boat approached.

"Isn't that Tom and Sue's cruiser, the one that supplied Smugglers with water last summer?" asked Charlie.

Jackson stared, and as the boat turned toward the island, he said, "Sure ting. Look at her sides. Dat has to be her. Good to see dem back. Dey nice people, you know."

"Aside from being good buddies with Jock and Woody and that whole gang."

"Yeah, buts before dose people came dey not like dat. I don' tink dey inbolbd o' dey not comes back. De udders not come back."

"True," said Charlie. "Let's hope for old times. Look at that stately yacht. She sure is beautiful, isn't she?"

"Dat one classy boat. He tol' me she 'bout sixty years old. Dat sumpin', eh?"

"Especially for the amount of use they get out of her. Sure a pretty sight, especially with that ball of sun behind her. Looks like a picture post card."

"Sho' do," said Jackson. "You sho' likes nice tings, right?"

"That's for sure," said Charlie, "especially in these islands. They get to you, you know."

"I knows, o' yo' not come back after all dat stuff Jock did to yo'," said Jackson.

"Well, that's over now. Let's give Tom a hand."

The two walked to the end of the dock as the vessel came in. Sue waved from the bow, ready with a line, while Tom maneuvered the stately craft from the wheel house. In about ten minutes she was secured and they were on the dock.

"Welcome back," said Jackson. "You come to de right island, mon. Dis place de best o' dem all." He was laughing, giving them the tour guide's approach.

"Boat's looking great," said Charlie. "She'll weather another season with no problem."

"Speaking of problems, did you hear about Jock?" asked Tom, looking to see that no one was listening. "Got ten years, I understand. I was surprised. Neither of us suspected he was into all that. And Woody. Can you believe he can't come back? Here we were in the middle and didn't even know it. I feel pretty naive."

"We all do," said Charlie. "I knew he was into something. That's why I was so damn concerned. He didn't need my people to make a living. They were just a cover for him."

"And now Maxwell." Tom shook his head and looked quizzically at Charlie, who expressed surprise.

"What about Maxwell?" he asked.

"About a month ago he went crazy or something. No one really knows if he had a nervous breakdown or if he overdosed, but he's in the hospital. I guess he's progressing all right. He was all strung out."

"No shit," said Charlie. "They have him on the flight deck?"

"Yeah. No one but Pat can see him. May be a while before they turn him loose. Let's go have a drink and celebrate coming back. I don't know about you, but I'm sure glad to be here."

"Me too," said Charlie. "Max in the booby hatch. Wait till Pete hears that. At least Max will get the help he needs now," he said, shaking his head. "We all thought he was a pretty sick son of a bitch. Maybe now he'll get his head screwed on straight."

"Let's hope," said Tom, pushing the screen door open. "Wanda!" he said, and walked over to the bar. "Look who's back. You better fix us our favorite rum punch or we'll go somewhere else."

"You no go no place else," said Wanda smiling. "Yous two belongs right here, where you be now. I gits yo' punch pretty quick. You no hab time to run someplace else. De boat sho' lookin' good from right here. You paints it?"

"Sure did. Top, bottom, sides, inside and out," said Tom. Sue smiled and as usual, didn't say much, but anyone looking at her could tell she was happy to be back. Tom recognized a couple off another boat and, after picking up their punches, went over to renew acquaintances. Charlie saw Pete coming on his Jeep and went to meet him, smiling from ear to ear, bursting with what Tom had just told him.

"You look like you just swallowed one of those cats out back," said Pete. "What's up?"

"Tom and Sue came back with the news that Max is in a psycho ward. Has been for a few weeks."

"Jesus, what happened? He finally use too much of that funny stuff or did he just flip over naturally?"

"They don't really know. He and Pat are together, though, with her the only one allowed in."

"Not that he'd have a swarm of visitors," said Pete. He sat for a few seconds digesting the news.

"That has to be the best thing that ever happened to the mean son of a bitch," he said. "I wish him all the best. Maybe they can use some crazy glue on him, huh? What do you think?"

"I think your problems with him are over, at least for awhile, and I also think that you have one of the best seasons ahead you've ever had," said Charlie.

386

"Helen will be delighted to hear about Max, but she'll probably want to send him a get well card," said Pete. "In the funny farm. I'll be damned. If I were still a drinking man I'd be off the deep end in fifteen minutes celebrating. In the booby hatch. Something else."

Pete shook his head, keeping a faint smile on his face, and walked with Charlie to the club. He went over and welcomed Tom and Sue back to the island, then had Wanda fix him a cranberry juice. He couldn't remember feeling so good. Number One Agitator in the nut house. Maybe the island would have some peace. Cocktail hour was enjoyed by all, and when the dinner bell rang, Pete motioned to Charlie to join him.

"We can feast tonight, man, because it's a smooth road ahead. It's like old times again," said Pete. They joined the guests, and Pete relished everyone bugging him to spin his salty yarns of the club and his early days of struggle. He always loved to talk, but tonight was special. Today the albatross was lifted from his neck, a fair wind in the sails.

* * *

The next morning as Charlie was getting ready to fly back to the mainland, a big shrimp-type vessel came in with a crew of five men, all looking like they were diehards of the sea with the owner outlining what he wanted done while they were docked at the club. He gave a fuel order to Jackson and told him they wouldn't be staying long, but that they needed a few things and would let him know anything for the future. Jackson treated the crew as he would anyone else, although he got the feeling the owner wanted preferential consideration. The man walked toward the club, his crew behind on the boat coiling lines, washing down the decks and keeping busy. He was a commanding sort, and Pete and Charlie elbowed each other when they saw him coming close.

"Whose that, a friend of yours?" asked Pete, nudging Charlie.

"No. Never seen him before. He must be a friend of yours."

"Not mine," said Pete. "Wonder who he is."

387

As the man walked through the screen door and looked around, it was obvious he had never been to the Sandy Cay Club before. Pete got up and went over to him.

"Nice yacht you have there," he said, extending his hand. "I'm Pete Mathews, the owner and whatever. Need anything special?"

"No, not now. Name's Red Cronby. Just bought Smugglers Cay from a guy who had to get out of the place pretty quick."

The man's hand remained extended as Pete and Charlie looked at each other and put their hands to their heads as if they couldn't take it.

"No shit?" said Pete, his cigarette hanging out the side of his mouth and looking in disbelief at the man with the white yachting shirt, dark blue jeans, new deck shoes and heavy gold wrist watch. "You bought Smugglers from Woody?"

"That's right. Something wrong?" He looked from Pete to Charlie and back. "He highly recommended your place for getting anything we need. Said you had air service, fuel, a mechanic, anything I need. Am I in the right place?"

"You got it," said Pete. "You might as well run a tab. You want to start by picking up Woody's bad debts? What are you drinking? Wanda, give him one on the house. After that charge him double."

Red looked at Pete not quite knowing how to take him.

"Double? Why?"

"Just kidding," said Pete. "We do a lot of that around here. As a matter of fact, I thought you were kidding about buying Smugglers. You got the papers and all to prove it?"

"Not with me, but the deal's been closed. Take possession tomorrow. Sight unseen I bought it. Told me it's a real Paradise. Have the wife coming down shortly after I check it out."

"Here's my card in case you want to fly her in," said Charlie. "Woody say anything?"

"Just that he wanted to say goodbye in person. Said I should do it for him, so here's goodbye from Woody." He raised his glass of rum punch as if toasting the bar.

"And a goodbye to Woody," said Pete, holding up his cranberry juice. "And hello to...what did you say your name

388

was?"

"Red Cronby."

"Red Cronby. Say hello to Red Cronby, folks, the proud owner of Smugglers Cay." He took a sip and put down the glass. "You going to change the name or live up to its reputation?" asked Pete.

"What is that?" asked Red, rather naively. "What reputation?"

Pete and Charlie looked at each other and smiled.

"Nothing in particular," said Pete. "Nothing in particular. Welcome to a crazy corner of the world. And good luck. I think you're going to need it. Have you met Jackson?"

"The dock man? Not formally," said Red.

Jackson walked in, and Pete made the introduction.

"This is Red Cronby, Jackson. He just bought Smugglers Cay."

The look on Jackson's face was unbelievable. He didn't know what to do or say. Pete and Charlie burst out laughing and so did he. Red Cronby couldn't figure it out, but he laughed, too. A laid back place he thought. Laid back and a little looney. It would be perfect.

About the Author

Martha (Marty) Crikelair Wohlford is a professional writer who brings a wealth of knowledge and experience to her work. She has sailed all her life, is a private pilot, diver, photographer, musician, and graphic artist.

She is a graduate of St. Mary's College, Notre Dame, Ind., where she majored in English Literature and Creative Writing. Her career began as a feature writer/editor for several newspapers and magazines. She established her own public relations firm in the early 1970s, and her combination of photography, writing and graphics skills have resulted in numerous brochures, catalogs, ads, websites and image pieces for a variety of clients.

Drumbeat No Lie is the realization of a dream she has had since the 1960s—a dream to write delayed by career and raising a family. She has also written If I Can't Be Dead, How Can I Live, a non-fiction self-help book for women battling alcoholism and addiction, and two children's books: Little Star's Big Day, a Christmas story, and Splash, the Staniel Cay Cat.

Marty spends most of her time at her home in Staniel Cay, Exumas, Bahamas, where she continues to write , enjoy life, and nourish her spirit.

Internet: www.mwpr.com • email: marty@mwpr.com

LaVergne, TN USA
24 July 2010
190641LV00002BA/1/P